SURRENDER TO HEAVEN

Maurice Frisell

 www.trafford.com

North America & international
toll-free: 1 888 232 4444 (USA & Canada)
fax: 812 355 4082

Dedication

To those whose hearts and hands have touched mine

My gratitude

To Marie—Mizie—Olivier Licciardi
For her invaluable assistance with Surrender to Heaven

And Christina Stine
And Ronnie Barrera, RN, NFA

Sincerely
Here and here after

Maurice Louis Frisell

PART ONE

. . . the road to heaven is filled with briars and thorns

1

The night was bleak; intensely cold. The Connecticut River was a mute frozen ribbon of ice. Great drifts of swirling snow were steeped high on either side of its banks . . . Vermont was literally a glacier. The county of Fairlee had not seen nor felt the conciliatory rays of the benevolent sun for many days, and the small town lay grasped in a fist of hushed white snow—witnessing a sickly glare by day and a cold blackness by night. Fairlee ceased to function. Schools, shops, offices and work establishments were all abandoned. Domestic pets were kept indoors at all times, and in the rural districts vigilant fires were kept in barns and stables to prevent the perishing of livestock from the embittered hand of winter. The piazza-roof of St. Ann's Priory was spotted with the corpses of frozen pigeons.

It was long past dusk, and the greyness that had filled the day now dissolved into a dismal sheet of frigid night. From the east there was ushered a blast of icy wind . . . and with this gust of nature's rebellion against mankind, there appeared out of the night, against a dead white background of snow, the cold silhouette of a boy. He tracked over the frozen road, bewildered, lost and confused, and now like an empty soul, he walked through the wind and night numb and bereft of thought, for remembrance had long squandered itself in exchange for hunger and cold.

Above him, the sky appeared like an endless black canopy stretching ever onward until it draped behind the snow shrouded mountains; the stars seemed but a handful of scattered ice-crystals flung against the angry night . . . shimmering in remarkable beauty! The boy pushed onward. A blast of icy wind whipped across the wasteland moaningly—twisting the snow drifts into unspeakable white phantoms. The bitter wind lashed at his body, it bit and stung, it cut him down sending him sprawling into the snow. The unfortunate boy managed to stagger to his youthful limbs endeavoring to plod forward, lifting one weary foot before the other and sinking ankle deep in wet icy matter. Fatigued and numbed with cold, he was almost willing to fall upon the snow and surrender to his enemy: *sleep*. In the distance he spied a solitary light. He halted his progress; startled and overjoyed, it carried new life, and hope, and freshness to his heart!

He burst upon the snow laden path thinking of warmth and shelter; he scrambled downhill, staggering, stumbling, endeavoring to balance his weight on benumbed legs. However, to his disappointment, the illumination was more distantly removed than it had seemed, and yet with ebbing heart and frozen feet, he did not relent; but held fast to his gleaming goal in the distance.

At length, he found himself before the towering black gate of St. Ann's Priory. It must have been the hand of fate that left the gates so unbarred, for never had they been so neglected after dark. His tired body fell against them and they turned slowly inwardly, then once more he fell upon the snow, and once more he found the life to climb to his feet; but only to falter a few steps further and fall ponderously against the massive oak door of the priory.

Fortunately the heavy thud which fell against the door was heard. Momentarily there was a turning of a key and the snap of a latch; a cloistered hand was on the knob. The Reverend Mother Eugenia had opened the door with an air of doubt for she was not quite certain that she did hear the sound. The frigid blackness of the night exhaled an icy breath upon her cheeks and the wind sailed past the door in a hushed strangulation of a roar.

"Of course, it was only imagination," she told herself. "There's nothing here." Then as she moved back to shut the door she realized that whatever lay at the foot of the door was not a heap of snow;

although to a careless eye it certainly would have appeared so. She breathed the name of *Mary*, and before another moment had past she dragged the half frozen creature within, closing the door behind. A second later Mother Eugenia seized the little silver bell which rested on a nearby table and gave it a vigorous ring. It was just a matter of moments before a curious wide eyed Sister Theresa responded to the alarm.

"Quickly!" demanded an aroused Reverend Mother, "Help me get him into the parlor—we can put him on the sofa." When the little nun didn't immediately spring into action, the excited superior snapped her off. "Well don't stand there gaping, Sister! The Lord has seen fit to lay a lost soul at St. Ann's door. Do as I tell you," she reproved once more, for even the good Sisters occasionally grow short of temper when tension sits high.

Sister Theresa executed the request without a why or wherefore. Mother Eugenia lifted the body by the shoulders and her assistant carried his feet, and together they succeeded in laying the boy on the great leather sofa. "Why he's only a lad," observed Sister Theresa catching her breath in little puffs as she straightened up, and turning to the good mother. "But what on earth brought him forth on a night such as this? He's near death!"

"Help me slide the sofa before the open fire, Sister; we must see that he gets warm," murmured the prioress, now concerned only with the boy's health. She gripped the sofa by its overstuffed arm and proceeded to slide it over the floor. Little Sister Theresa pushed and pulled vigorously before she could manage her end of the sofa to budge. Then, when she finally succeeded in getting the sofa to move, the sofa's foot slipped over the boards in the personification of the cricket chirp. Again Sister Theresa paused to replenish her breath, but before another moment passed Mother Eugenia had commenced to discharge a string of orders.

"I'll feed the fire," she said heaping a scuttle of coal upon the enfeebled embers, then ordered the little nun to hurry to the dispensary for some quinine. She put her hand to the boy's forehead and observed that he was flushed with fever, and as the nun went hurrying out of the door, the Reverend Mother called out to her to bring along some hot water bottles and blankets.

Soon Sister Theresa returned with the articles which were requested. A crackling fire with great licking flames were leaping up the flue, and the big leather sofa with its half frozen occupant lay before the roaring blaze. It wasn't too long afterwards before an aged Sister Sabina appeared in the room juggling the hot water bottles which were heavily swathed in gleaming white towels. She came toward the sofa in a huff of alertness; her nimble feet peeping to and fro beneath her somber black habit. "I came as soon as possible," she remarked giving the water bottles to the Reverend Mother. "Believe me when I say, "I literally heated liquid ice'—I thought the kettle would never boil."

The Revered Mother quickly slipped the bottles beneath the blankets while the two nuns remained motionlessly by her side looking down upon the boy's pallid face. She then tucked the covering more tightly about his legs, adjusted the pillows at his head, then prepared to take his temperature. Some moments later she removed the thermometer from his fevered lips and stepped across the floor into the better light. The pale gas flame caused her cheeks to glow.

Sister Sabina parted her lips to speak but forced no breath between them. She read the thoughts on the woman's face and deemed it wise to remain silent; Moreover the knitted brows and the grave expression which was shadowed upon the Reverend Mother's face drove all thought from her mind. "I believe we'd better telephone for Dr. Mill, Sister Theresa," spoke the Reverend Mother in a quiet clear tone; yet somehow her voice conveyed an atmosphere of alarm.

Sister Theresa obeyed the command; she imparted a little curtsy, turned on her heels and sped from the room. The Prioress relapsed into her former state of meditation; her eyes resting on the youth who lay before her. His face was as white as the pillow he slept upon. She noted his broad forehead and the warm dark hair brushed back from his throbbing temples; his rugged eyebrows and the sensitive bridge of his nose; the masculine square of his chin was already obvious beneath his boyish mouth.

Sister Sabina came nearer to view him; she turned to face Mother Eugenia. "Who is the lad . . . do you know, Mother?" The Prioress swayed her head in the negative, silent and consumed with her own thoughts. "Surely there must be some identification on his person?" persisted the aged nun.

"I have already made a thorough search of his clothing, Sister," she replied somewhat offended at her subordinate for not giving her due esteem for such an elementary curiosity. "There's not a thread of evidence as to whom the boy might be," she completed, then frowned in an air of impatience, "What's delaying Sister with that call?"

Sister Theresa's high young voice was almost smothered under the clatter of her running footsteps as she called from the dark vaulted hallway in response to the Reverend Mother. Soon she appeared in the arch way to inform her that the doctor could not be located, explaining that he departed hours before on a previous call.

Mother Eugenia slapped her forearm as a gesture to display her disappointment of the matter, then half murmured something to herself about it always being the case when one was really in need of a physician. "Well, we'll just have to care for him without professional advice," she said determinedly, then lifter her eyes toward Sister Theresa, who still lingered in the doorway wringing her hands and waiting expectantly for further orders. "Ring the caretaker's house," she was told, "and inquire if there's any brandy; also ask Mrs. Tergauer if she would be so kind as to send her husband to the priory. Tell her it's urgent." Before the last syllable had rolled from Mother Eugenia's lips, Sister Theresa had quite wheeled herself from the room.

Sister Sabina, feeling quite awkward by her idle spectating, inquired of the Reverend Mother if there was anything she could do to help, and, if merely to give the old nun some task to get her out of the way, she sent her off for more blankets and hot water bottles. Once more she took the boy's temperature and was quite certain now that he had developed pneumonia! She understood that her work was already cut out for her; she must sweat the fever out of him.

Then when Mr. Tergauer, the caretaker, came over to the priory, the Reverend Mother had him set up a cot in the dark oak panel room. The boy could rest much better on that she thought.

All through the night she remained vigilant at the youth's side, and refused to be relieved by the other nuns when they came in from time to time to bring her the things she requested. All through her watch she never failed to administer the proper doses of quinine, and altered the hot water bottles whenever necessary; also she applied mustard plasters and hot flannel cloths to his chest. There were intervals when he would tussle and turn on his bed throwing the covering from his body; then sometimes he would have great fits of coughing, and there was a course grating sound in his voice; he'd gasp for breath in great wheezing sighs.

When dawn came, filling the windows with its grey still light, the youthful stranger, who found his way to St. Ann's, was sleeping peacefully. "St. Ann's will take care of you," the Prioress murmured sponging the tiny beads of perspiration from his brow. Then once again she took his temperature; the fever was still high, but he was greatly improved. The crisis had passed, and as she crossed the floor moving to the window she smiled: "Youth can weather almost anything." Then she paused to glance through the frosty window pane . . . All was white and still without.

It was late morning when Dr. Mills finally arrived at the priory, and he and the Reverend Mother gathered in the little study just off the main hall for conversation. "I think you have handled the situation admirably well," the doctor told her. "I couldn't have done any more for the boy. Just continue to give him that medicine; he has a fine constitution and will pull through without much fuss. The worst is over now." Then he looked over to her, and in a voice that seemed full of discretion he made an attempt to wheedle information from her, "And you say there was absolutely no identification on his person?" He lifted his brows anticipatingly.

She replied that there was none so far as her knowledge went, and leaned back in her desk chair feeling very tired hoping perhaps the doctor might leave soon; moreover she felt that this seemed not the time to discuss the boy in general, but rather a time when the condition of his health should be more important to the doctor. She concluded by telling him that the boy's origin was obscure, just as his coming seemed mysterious.

"Then, we know nothing of him?"

"Nothing—"

"But what on earth will you do with him at the priory? I realize that he must remain until he is well enough to be moved; yet, it's most irregular to house a boy in a nunnery. I think we should make some arrangements for placing him in the foundling home. He's still quite young," he remarked then somewhat astonished, he added: "Why, we don't even know his age nor faith."

Mother Eugenia warned as she watched him knot a grey and red muffler about his throat.

"Have no fear, that I'll do," he remarked with a laugh, and he grunted with a chill when she opened the door. His breath literally hung before his face, frozen like a little puff of white cloud. "You know, I do believe the lad might prove a blessing," he cried tilting his chin toward the pallid sky; "The sun is trying to peep through." Then he dropped his voice in a quiet confidential tone, and touching his hand to her forearm said to her: "You know, if I didn't know you so well, I would think that you hadn't a thought planned for the boy." Then with a wink he added: "But I know you, don't I?" And with that he departed passing through the black iron gates which still rested in the haphazard way that the youth left them when his half frozen body pushed them open.

The Reverend Mother closed the door behind her, listening to the bells of Dr. Mill's sleigh, which were fading fast in the distance. The expression of his face lingered in her mind. The twinkling of his black eyes, and the tight drawn lines about his mouth. She stood there for a time thinking how wrong the doctor was. Imagine Dr. Mill assuming that she had made plans for the boy? When was there time to plan? How absurd the medics can be at times, she thought. They assume that they are God, understanding all the intricate entanglements of life and death. That's it; they witness so much of living and dying, that they really learn nothing. When doctors cease to be philosophers and learn to concentrate more on medicine, the world will have fewer ills and more remedies.

Just before noon, Sister Theresa came to Mother Eugenia's study informing her that the boy was awake. Upon arriving at the parlor, now a make-shift sick room, she paused in the open doorway. A lively fire loomed in the open recess of the chimney, crackling and sputtering in cheery alliteration and a tongue of orange flame went leaping up the fire shaft. The boy reclined placidly on the bed and two pillows supported his dark head, his arms resting above the counterpane, and though he was awake his eyes were closed.

The Reverend Mother went over to him and took his wrist; his pulse throbbed beneath her cool white fingers. To her it seemed a trifle weak, but keeping time in perfect rhythm. All appeared well and his fever went down. In a moment he opened his hazy blue eyes and looked at her, then shut them tightly; his head rolled to one side and he was asleep. Sister Theresa came into the room then, inquiring of the boy's health. The Prioress crossed a finger over her mouth gesturing for quiet. "He's sleeping now," she said. "We mustn't disturb him."

"Mrs. Tergauer sent over some hot broth," commented the little nun. "She inquired if there was anything that she could do. Of course I said no, but if we needed her services, I was certain that you'd send for her."

"You did right. The broth can be saved for later." Mother Eugenia touched her hand to the boy's head, "I'm sure he's going to be alright," she murmured worriedly. "I'm glad he's sleeping, he needed the rest."

"And so do you," balked Sister Theresa assuming a voice of authority. "You've been up all night, I do wish you'd try to get some rest. I can stay with him."

The Reverend Mother looked over to the young nun, and felt grateful that she had someone such as she to rely upon. She told Sister Theresa that she was tired and would be glad to get a little rest, and later walked from the room reproving herself for being sometimes a little cross with the lively little nun, but of course, Sister Theresa understood the good Mother and really didn't mind at all.

I've got a fine beef brisket, Amy, and I want you to fix me up a nice vegetable bunch." Mrs. Tergauer said to Mrs. Schwartz, who managed the vegetable stand in the Fairlee town-market. "A good soup warms you up these cold days," she added then started to handle some of the vegetables in the bins, feeling first this one and then that, "My, these tomatoes are soft," she put it down. "Why do you know that the cold killed all my fine house plants!" she commented as a matter for conversation.

"I declare," muttered Mrs. Schwartz pretending interest. "Ah, there you are, Em; I fixed you the best bunch in the place. I'm lettin' you know, that I don't fix all my customers with a bunch as fine as this," she remarked calling Mrs. Tergauer's attention to her generosity. "There I'll just stuff it right in your market bag, Em." Amy Schwartz proceeded to place the vegetables into Mrs. Tergauer's market sack, when she was close enough to whisper into her friend's ear, she lowered her voice in a confidential tone. "Tell me, Em, what goes on these days at St. Ann's? I understand that a tramp ups and takes sick right on the priory steps, and the good sisters takes him in just like that."

Mrs. Tergauer took in an astonished breath. "*A tramp*! Why Amy Schwartz! I ain't never heard of such malicious gossip. Gussie—that is, Mr. Tergauer tells me he ain't nothing but a boy."

The woman lifted her brows on hearing this information; "Oho! so you haven't seen him either?" she cried, then went on to say: "Seems like the sisters ain't lettin' nobody know what goes on there."

Again Mrs. Tergauer was forced to take in her breath; her chin fell to her chest. "Really Amy! where do you get your twisted news? Like I said, he ain't nothing but a boy."

"Well don't be gittin' mad with me, Em," Amy Schwartz slapped her forearm and pursed her thick lips. "I'm just repeatin' what my customers tell me. Some say he—" she checked her words and thought it better not to say too much out of the way on account of her friend being so close to the nuns. "Well, Gawd only knows where the boy popped up from. Him comin' out of the cold on a night such as that. It would be different if he was one of our boys, but no one seen his face before. He might be a criminal for all we know."

"It's supprisin' how some know more than me who lives right on the priory grounds, Amy Schwartz," she said snapping her off in a dry brittle tone. "What's more I'm sure he ain't no criminal."

"Then why did Dr. Mill stop in at the constable's office asking all kinds of questions? Tell me 'bout that, Em dear?" she asked in triumph and mockery, enjoying her little victory.

"Oh, Dr. Mill ought to mind his own business. His nose is too long for his own good! Why, the idea, spreadin' gossip like that 'bout the good sisters that way. He should be ashamed of himself . . . Anyway he ain't never 'round when a body really needs him." Mrs. Tergauer forcefully picked up her basket and put it on her arm; she could feel her anger rising and she thought it best to leave. "Good day, Amy," she muttered rather coldly." see you tomorrow," and with that she departed on quick and wrathful heels. When she reached the door, she pulled her shawl more tightly about her shoulders and walked out of the market place. She being a good Christian woman wasn't the sort to spread gossip about the nuns at St. Ann's, moreover she didn't like the way Amy spoke of them. "Amy means well," she said to herself, and shrugged her shoulders regretting that she lost her temper. Then as if to make excuses for herself she added: "Yes, Amy means well, but sometimes her tongue is too dern long and loose."

Before giving the medicine to the boy she decided to place a drop of honey on the tip of the spoon, knowing that the bitter pursuer would be high treason to his pallet.

The boy shrugged his shoulders and emitted a choking cough; his features twisted in a grim mask. He thought nothing could be more vile than the ominous brown liquid which was conveyed to his fever parched lips. For the first time since the boy had been at the priory, Sister Sabina observed that he was sitting up and perceiving his surroundings. His fingers fumbled at the loosely fitting nightgown that he was wearing. The old nun smiled in spite of herself; the flannel gown belonged to her. She watched him for a time and a vague expression loomed in his eyes as though he were in a lost world. He glanced at the crackling fire which was dancing on the marble hearth, and when he glanced toward the window and saw the snow, he shrunk within himself at though a sharp pain flashed across his mind. His eyes returned to the sharp black figure of the nun, and viewed her for a time as if she were something strange and new; then reclining on the pillows he closed his eyes on everything listening to the singing voice of the golden fire. He felt secure and presently fell asleep.

At length, when he again opened his eyes he discovered Mother Eugenia seated at his side. He almost smiled as if in recognition of her handsome face, and surely he did recognize her for of all those who attended him, Mother Eugenia was most familiar to his memory.

"I found this in your pocket," she told him, showing the boy a little silver medal of *St. Christopher.* "The chain was broken, so I placed it on a nice new one for you. May I put it about you?" He did not reply, but his eyes said enough to satisfy her, then he stirred from the pillows so the chain could be placed about his throat. "Aren't you going to thank me for the chain?" the Reverend Mother murmured endeavoring to prompt the boy into speaking. "Dr. Mill says you're going to be all better," she lifted her eyes motioning to the lean figure of the doctor who stood on the opposite side of the bed.

"Speak up, boy," said the doctor; he intended to sound amicably, but his words lacked expression. "Tell Mother Eugenia your name boy."

The Reverend Mother frowned on the doctor's approach; however, since the doctor had hoisted the banner, she thought it best to continue the questioning and not dismay his mind by augmenting another. She touched the boy's hand and softly said: "Yes, son, what's your name; we are greatly concerned and are anxious to know what prompted you to venture forth on such a night?"

Figuratively, beneath their curious eyes the boy was a picture of stillness. Mute and tallow faced, he lay listlessly upon the pillows wide eyed and staring. Patiently they waited for him to speak; the boy grew tense with so many eyes watching him and waiting so anticipatingly upon him that he suddenly turned his face into the pillows to escape them. Both the Reverend mother and Sister Sabina opened their lips to speak, but Dr. Mill quickly commanded a gesture for silence. He bent over the boy to examine the expression of his eyes. Then after long tense moments of waiting, the doctor motioned Mother Eugenia toward the fireplace and spoke to her about the boy's condition in grave subdued tones.

Then old Sister Sabina, who could no longer restrain the curiosity within her, demanded to know what was the matter with the boy, for she thought that he behaved as though he had completely lost his memory. Dr. Hill completely astonished her when he informed her that she had surmised correctly. That was precisely the trouble with the boy. He was suffering from loss of memory . . . amnesia; physically he seemed to be on the mend, but the doctor stated that he believed that shock and exposure to the cold had driven all past memory from his mind.

"But of course, he will recover soon," the Prioress was quick to assume.

"Perhaps, and perhaps not," reflected the doctor. "It all depends on the boy himself. In some cases recovery is usually rapid and in others, the memory is never restored." he opened his satchel: "I want you to give him this sedative about a quarter of an hour from now. It's important that he rests." He shrugged his shoulders," who can really say, perhaps when he awakes, he'll probably behave as though nothing what so ever has occurred. "Well," retorted Dr. Mill in his usual brisk off-handed manner, "a doctor's time is not his own and I must be getting along. Don't bother to see me to the door; I know my way out. Good day."

"Oh, not at all, doctor, Sister Sabina will see you out . . . Good day to you."

At last when she was quite alone, Mother Eugenia fell upon the prie-dieu and lifting her voice she cried: "Oh, Mary, Mother of God, please help the boy! Please!" Then she knelt there for a long while and prayed. The silent youth watched her from the corner of his eye. At length when she seemed quite through at prayers, she came over to the boy's side, and looking deeply into his eyes and placing her hand on his she said: "Tell me, my son can you not remember who you are?"

Not contemplating a reply, she was quite astonished when he spoke. He told her that he was really trying to recall the past ever since he awoke, but it was so dark and early then and he felt really too tired to do anything but rest.

The Prioress silently wept and thanked God. This was far more than she expected. If he could speak intelligently, then perhaps all was not lost. "My son, why didn't you speak in such a way to the doctor just then?"

"I couldn't . . . Really I couldn't; not just then," he said modestly.

Again she patted his hand, "Of course, I understand," she comforted him and he appeared to be very relaxed in her presence. "But do you know your name?" she asked, "Can you remember?"

He swayed his head: "No, ma'am, I can't even remember how I came here; all I really remember is the snow," and when he spoke the word he shrank within himself.

Mother Eugenia grew much afraid that such an impression might permanently sear his memory; she felt she must change the subject. "You haven't yet thanked me for the chain which I gave you," she said smilingly. "Don't you like it?"

"But I do," he replied toying with the silver chain about his throat. "I shall always wear it; I'll never take it off."

"I'm pleased that you like it," she said looking down at him, and suddenly she smiled: "We must see about getting you some proper clothes." Then she adjusted the safety-pin which held the loosely fitting gown from slipping from his shoulders. For a time she studied the handsome lines of his frank boyish face and the brightness of his sparkling eyes. The Prioress thought that the bright clear light of his soul was shining through his eyes. The boy parted his lips to speak, and it occurred to her that he was searching for some way to address her. She told him her name, and he asked of her why was he in bed?

The Reverend Mother was quite astonished by the question; if it had not been so honest and innocently expressed, she might have found cause to laugh. Apparently the boy felt no after-effects of his illness. "Why boy—" she stopped rather abruptly regretting that she had addressed him in such a manner as though he were an inanimate object . . . even objects have names, she thought, if he could but just remember his. "Son, you have been ill," she told him.

He confessed to her that he didn't feel ill, and was very tired of lying in bed. Then looking into her face, he requested if he might sit by the fire for a while. The Reverend Mother remembered the sedative that the doctor had left. At first she had intended to decline the boy's wish, but seeing the energy and life sparkling in his eye, she thought well of it. "Of course, you may," she replied. "If you feel well enough, I can't see what harm it will do." She threw a blanket over the leather chair, and it called for little or no help from her to get him from the bed and into the leather chair. She placed one arm about his waist and with a few wobbly steps, he succeeded into the chair. Then she put another blanket over his lap, bringing it over his knees she tucked it about his legs and the remaining folds she heaped under his feet.

A timid knock rattled at the door, and when Mother Eugenia gave the command to enter, Mrs. Tergauer curved her head and shoulders around the edge of the door.

"My! will you look at that now, he's sittin' up already!" cried the woman entering and closing the door behind her. She crossed the floor moving nearer to the boy; she had one hand clasped over the other and a small cane basket dangled on her forearm. "Now, no need to warn me Abbess Eugenia," she cried laying one finger at the side of her nose, "I won't be staying long." The Reverend Mother smiled at the woman's wholesome behavior.

"Ain't he a fine lad," observed the woman. "He's a bit peakish yet, but good food and sunshine will fix that up, eh?" For some reason Mrs. Tergauer amused the lad and his nose wrinkled as a joyous grin swept over his face. He watched the woman as she wrangled a small bottle from her basket; she brought the bottle fort h and held it high for the Prioress to see. "Look here, Mother," she said, "I brought the lad a fine bottle of onion syrup. It's just the thing he needs. I always give it to Gussie when he comes down with the croup. I make it myself," she admitted proudly.

"Thank you, Mrs. Tergauer, you've been quite generous," smiled the Reverend Mother accepting the homemade remedy.

"Ah, think nothin' of it—What's a body for if they can't be of some good now and again." Mrs. Tergauer turned her attentions to the boy and taking his hand she gave it a gentle pat. "Ah, that's a good boy, what do they call you, son?"

He suddenly went tense and stiff, and Mother Eugenia was quick to catch the startled expression in his eyes; the blood came into his pallid cheeks while his confused mind groped aimlessly for an avenue of escape. To avoid Mrs. Tergauer's eyes, he turned his face sharply to the fire. "Mrs. Tergauer!" intercepted the Reverend Mother, her voice came from her throat sharp and loud; she soon regretted her tone, but was pleased that she managed to divert the woman's attention from the boy. She paused and in the briefness of it all, the cunning sharpness of her subconscious supplied her lips with the proper words. "Why it's quite easy to guess," she told the woman in a clipped broken voice," the medal about his throat plainly tells you . . . His name is *Christopher*."

"And so I should have guessed," laughed the woman quite cheerfully. "Why I don't even know how to use the eyes in my head." the boy's clear eyes came to a level with the Reverend Mother's eyes in a moment of overwhelming gratitude. She nodded her head and smiled in recognition of his thankfulness. Soon they were all three laughing happily. No one noticed the tear that the Prioress brushed from her eye.

2

Victoria Fransworth, a slim handsome woman in her late fifties, gazed steadily through the French windows of her Charleston mansion. Her back was turned to a stout greying man who was dressed in a neat business suit. For a time never a word passed between the solemn pair, and the only sound in the plushed gold and crystal library was a small fire whispering on the marble hearth.

Soon the woman turned from the window, her black flowing taffeta gown crackled with a soft somber swish as she crossed the heavy carpeted floor. Her aristocratic face seemed tired and spent; she even appeared much older than she actually was, deep pain and much anxiety dimmed her dark blue eyes . . . eyes very much like Christopher's, if not exactly the same. She paused at the great mahogany reading table, and fumbled abstractedly with a few of the great number of cards and letters which rested there. There was hardly a corner of the English speaking world that had not been touched by the untimely death of the beloved John and Paula Fransworth, their fame had spread far over land and sea, and both critic and public agreed that they were the greatest exponents of histrionic art.

For many days now the many, many kind letters of grief and sympathy found their way to Victoria Fransworth's door; but regardless how harmoniously their feelings might have coincided with her emotional state, none had any effect as to tranquilize her laden heart. At length she spoke to the gentleman who had remained quiet all this while fearing that a careless word might add further grief to the woman's great dilemma.

"Freddie," she said locking the fingers of her trembling hands," I have known you a long time, ever since I was a girl, and as a friend and the attorney of my late husband, who was also your boyhood chum; I ask you this one favor . . . Find my grandson, Johnny for me. I can't believe that he perished with his parents in that terrible fire! Oh, God!" she sighed abysmally, "is it not enough that I am deprived of my son and his lovely wife! Must I lose my grandson as well?"

"Please, Victoria you're only succeeding in making yourself ill with grief," said the attorney mustering to her side. "I have done everything humanly possible to locate the boy but he has just seemed to disappeared completely. Have faith. I'm certain that any day now, they'll discover some trace of the boy," he told her endeavoring to encourage the woman. "Be grateful that you at least have Hank to fall back on . . . at this rate you'll put yourself in an early grave." She suddenly began to quake in tears and he put his arm about her shoulder pleading with her, "Victoria, my dear, please don't weep!"

"Oh, what good is Hank and his wife, Freddie," the woman wailed in despair, "answer me that? What good are they to an old woman? All the more for them they say—Oh! I hear them whispering like thieves behind my back; they are glad that John and Paula are in their graves—Glad I tell you! No, Freddie, they are of no comfort to me . . . All I had in my declining years was my little Johnny, and he too seems to have been snatched away from me! Was anyone so ill-fated as I?"

"Victoria," he cried her name endeavoring to be firm; "You are imagining these things about Hank. It's no good for you to go on this way . . . You must promise me that you'll pluck up in spirits." He dropped his hands to his sides; "If it'll do any good, I myself will go to Piermont in search of him, but God knows that I have done my best to trace Johnny. I promise you," he said noticing the change of expression and spirits. "I'll not leave a stone unturned until I learn something of the boy, believe me."

"Oh, thank you, Freddie! You don't know how relieved I am, now that you've told me that." Then she seized his hands in gratitude and told him once more of the dreadful occurrence that threw its black cloak over her happy little world: "It was their final performance of the season, Freddie and after that they were to come home to me so that we could be altogether for the Christmas holidays . . . Oh, how I planned and waited for them!" Her shoulders sagged and she continued to talk as though there was no one in the room but she and her mournful memories. "But I guess I really knew of the tragedy before the black news reached me . . . That preceding night, I dreamed that the entire forest was on fire. I tried to put it out but there was no one around to help me do it. Then early the following morning I heard Hank below stairs shouting to the servants when they carried him the morning paper. I heard them telling in excited voices and in one black second I understood all . . . At first I tried to tell myself that I was still dreaming and that nothing in the world happened to my children. But alas! the awful news was brought up to me, and I read for myself the bitter account of how the theatre they were performing in caught on fire, and of them dying in the blaze! Oh, Freddie!" Then she fell into weeping again: "How glad I am that you going to do this thing for me. I know in my heart that I could rely on you . . . you're all the friend I've got left in this world, Freddie thank you again! How good it is of you to desert your practice and go in pursuit of an old woman's desire . . . Good of you Freddie," and with that she clutched his hand in a profound strength of gratitude. "As my attorney, I grant you full liberty to use whatever amount of money you might need, but don't fail me Fredrick Lang, promise you won't!"

Victoria Fransworth slumped into a faded blue velvet chair; she was tired and worried as she thought of so many vile predicaments which might be confronting her grandson, but how was she to guess that he was now in excellent care at St. Ann's Priory.

"You look tired Victoria," said the attorney, "I'll leave now, and come to see you tomorrow. I'll tell you then about my plan for finding the boy," and with that he kissed her hand and departed from the room.

So thus Fredrick Lang departed from the Fransworth library, to plan his search and anticipate some way of satisfying the longings of the rich Victoria Fransworth; to bring her grandson home for her to love and cherish; and to help lay a vast fortune at his command, but how and where should begin? Surely a theatre of charred timber and ashes would be of little help in aiding him to find the Fransworth heir, he thought worriedly. And though the boy's mortal remains were not discovered in the debris, this could not be construed as a definite indication that he hadn't perished in the conflagration with his famed parents. "Oh, why did I suggest sucha thing?" he demanded of himself as a colored manservant closed the mansion door after him. "How hopeless the situation seems. Where so many have failed to discover the boy, how can I hope to succeed? Never-the-less, a promise is a promise and I'll not disappoint Victoria, now. Not if I can help it by God!" He looked back on the tall white mansion and its vast surroundings of evergreen trees. The winter winds grabbed at his hat and he held it firmly on his head. Again he glanced over his shoulder toward the house and he thought of the woman in her grief. At least he would try, he thought. If only for the sake of comforting her, and he quickened his steps with zeal and determination.

In the days that followed the snow and winds still hushed at the windows, and the swirling drifts pilled ever higher. Within the cloistered wall of St. Ann's, life continued, but somehow different from its usual pattern. The innocent nuns found the boy's coming an odd attraction to their free moments: some read to him, while others entertained him with long hours at games; those who were musically inclined played hymns of the piano for him. All played a part in helping him to while away the endless hours of recuperation. They addressed him by his new name, and he himself repeated it over and over until it was familiar to him as one's name should be.

Christopher, Christopher, echoed the nuns, why it speaks of Christ! A fine name for a boy . . . boy the promise of man, and man the image of God! Of all the sea of faces that came to Christopher, none was so familiar to him as the Prioress herself; courteous and submissive, yielding to the demands of her vocation, her regal carriage and the sensitive bridge of her nose boasted of an aristocratic quality. She and Christopher became good friends.

Now that he was quite well enough to dress himself and walk about, he busied himself by visiting the chapel and praying with the nuns. He spent long hours in the library reading the pen dipped adventures of Dumas and Stevenson, of cavaliers and kings, mystery and terror, swashingbuckling pirates, treasures and ships, and windy days at sea. Many a morning he could be found idly reclining in the sun drenched solarium, dreaming the dreams that only a boy can fashion. The memory of his past seemed to be lost to oblivion. At times the Reverend Mother could detect a frown shadowing his features, as his thoughts fell into one black mental abyss after another, stumbling and clutching at fleeting wisps of memory that drifted across his mind. Often he would sit and brood questioning his origin to great lengths.

One morning the Prioress was informed that a couple had come to the priory to see the boy, with the belief in mind that Christopher might be their lost son. Waiting for Sister Sabina to usher the people in, Mother Eugenia sat before her desk. A lurid glare filtered through the wet panes of the north windows, drenching her study in a murky depression of grey illumination. A smoldering fire struggled for existence upon the hearth, while without a lashing wind caused a sluggish mist to sigh against the windows. As she sat there pondering in her solitude, Sister Sabina's words came ringing back to her . . . "They're here, Mother; the boy's parents have come to take him away." At least that was the quick conclusion the old nun derived, when she was told they were here to see the boy.

How strange are life's circumstance, the Reverend Mother thought: a boy materializes from the frozen night and takes my heart . . . Why I loath to see him go. In some respects it's really the snow who is to blame. In milder weather, he would have completely passed on, making his way to the village and our paths would not have crossed. How strange is winter? It comes and the snow banks high at the door; those without are locked in its grip; those within are cut away from the world . . . It seems that each dwelling becomes a kingdom. However, the snows melt and the kingdom dissolves, and is restored to a fragment of a small community and the world invades the threshold—How small is life!

Shuffling footsteps followed by a rude clatter of the door lock aroused her from her musing. The door rolled inward on its hinges. Mother Eugenia's eyes met with Sister Sabina's, and the old nun appeared lost and timid as she stood framed in the heavy oak facing. She stepped aside, turned to the threesome behind her and with a clip nod of her head she motioned for them to enter. A rigidly, extravagantly attired couple of middle age swept into the study, followed by a thinish grey haired woman, who was swathed in a plain black coat. The Reverend Mother rose to her feet to greet them; she smiled then beckoned to some chairs. The thinish grey haired woman was the first to speak.

"Good morning, Prioress Eugenia," she stated coldly. "I am Miss Wilson, of the welfare and this is Mr. and Mrs. Delvin of Post Mills. They believe the boy you have here might be their son."

"Oh," exclaimed the Reverend Mother rather surprised," then you are not sure the boy is their son?"

"Well, from all indications . . . That is," the thinish woman fumbled her words as she spoke: "From the description Dr. Mill relayed—well the description seems to fit the boy."

"Oh, I just know he must be our Peter!" broke down Mrs. Delvin, her voice cracked in emotion and she choked between sobs. "I just know he is!" Mr. Delvin endeavored to comfort his wife, and in time she managed to resume her former self.

Mother Eugenia folded her hand and waited for silence before she spoke. "I'll permit you to see the boy, but I must be assured that there will be no emotional out bursts, or comments of the like. The boy had been ill—pneumonia, in fact. Not only that, but he seems to be suffering from lapse of memory. The slightest disturbance might prove injurious to his condition." She paused in order to place more emphasis on her next words, "I do not wish the boy to feel that he is being watched in any way . . . I'll bring him in here on some pretense. Please try to pretend that you are not deliberately looking his way; if you are his parents, I am sure that his memory will return when he sees you. However, if he is your son and does not recognize you, again I plead for no emotional out bursts." Again she paused, this time lifting her eyes toward the man who stood by the door, "Sister, please ask Christopher to help you carry a fresh skuttle of coal into the room."

The nun imparted a bow of her head, taking her leave quickly and silently. When the nun left on her errand, the thinish grey haired woman, Miss Wilson, uttered some comment about the Reverend Mother referring to the boy as, 'Christopher'. Mother Eugenia quickly surmised Miss Wilson, as a trouble maker, and later her suspicions were proved. She gave the woman a curt and plausible reason, and silenced her.

Just then the door opened with a clatter and in stepped Sister Theresa and Christopher with a coal skuttle swinging between them; seeing the faces of three strangers, Christopher halted at the door and the smile faded from his face. To avoid their glances, he drew within himself; he wanted to turn from the door but the tugging force of Sister Theresa on the other side of the handle pulled him across the room to the hearth.

Christopher did not recognize the Delvins, and the down-trodden expression on Mrs. Delvin's face seemed quite obvious that the boy was a stranger to her. Together Christopher and Sister Theresa eased the skuttle to its place on the hearth. The room reflected an awful silence.

"That's a good boy," spoke the Reverend Mother. "Christopher really is strong you know," she said feeling that she must compliment him and booster his moral. The youth squared his shoulders and smiled; his spirits soared. To Christopher, Mother Eugenia's voice fell over him like a protecting shield. "That's all, Chris," she told him, "you may leave now."

He smiled again, took up the empty skuttle and left the room, unaware that those strange faces had come to look him over, and return him to a world he lost. Mother Eugenia wished that she could find some words to comfort the Delvins, she felt pain and remorse for the despondent mother.

"You mustn't give up hope, Mrs. Delvin," she said. "I'm certain that if you will pray to Our Father and hold on to your courage, the Almighty will find some way to return your son to you."

"I'll try," whimpered Mrs. Delvin, "I'll try. I'm sorry to have taken up so much of your time," she went on to say. "You've been quite generous . . . and now, if you will excuse Mr. Delvin and I, we will be on our way—"

The Reverend Mother began some reply about it being no bother at all but broke off her words in a middle of a sentence, for Mrs. Delvin suddenly distracted her by suddenly springing to her feet and rushing from the study on the verge of tears. Her husband made some hasty excuse for his wife's behavior and followed after her. The thinish grey haired woman remained; together she and the Prioress paused to listen to the rushing footsteps and the noisy bang of the front door open and then slam close, once by Mrs. Delvin and then again by her husband. Mother Eugenia felt she must pray for the safe return of the woman's son.

"I had no idea that she would take it this way," murmured Miss Wilson, "I had stressed beforehand that the boy might not be their son. I trust she hasn't disturbed you," she said rather off handishly; "I experience such incidents quite often."

The Reverend Mother explained that she was not disturbed in the least, then wondered why Miss Wilson still remained. She thought since, Christopher was quite obviously not the boy they were seeking, it occurred to her that the woman should make some polite pretense at leaving. But in time Miss Wilson soon cleared up matters by stating that she was also a representative of the Kramer Foundling Home and wanted very much to discuss Christopher with the Prioress. At first Mother Eugenia did not answer the woman, but thought how correct her guess had been when she recognized the woman as a trouble maker. At first when that vicious thought crept into her pious mind she regretted it bitterly and silently reproved herself for imagining such a thing. The muscles tightened about her mouth and her pulse quickened as she waited for Miss Wilson to speak.

"I realize that it is quite irregular to house the boy within the priory, Mother Eugenia," said Miss Wilson in a voice that seem to drip with cryptic politeness, "and if you will only give the word we shall be only too happy to take the boy off your hands."

The Reverend Mother was overwhelmed: "My dear Miss Wilson," she responded in a clip breath endeavoring to curb the rising anger in her breast. "You speak as though he were a parcel, and all one needs to be rid of him, is to stamp him and post him away."

"I imply no such thing, Madam; surely you must know that all waifs must be turned over to the proper authorities? I only prompt you to your duties."

"I think that I am aware of my duties in this world," she told Miss Wilson quietly. "I thought I made it clear to you, my dear Miss Wilson, that Christopher is in no way suited for a change of environment. As I have informed you, the slightest emotional disturbance might prove injurious to his mental health. You understand, I do not wish to be troublesome, but the boy found his way to this establishment and I believe it my duty to see to his full recovery."

"From what I understand," said the woman moistening her lips, Dr. Mill lead me to believe that the boy had recovered. It was he who advised me to look in on the matter."

"It would seem that Dr. Mill is in charge of this nunnery," murmured the Prioress quite annoyed. "However, no matter what he or you may say, Miss Wilson, I will not have the boy moved from St. Ann's . . . No, not until he is well enough for a change, and on this I remain firm." Then as a threat she added: "If necessary I will write to the bishop and have him look in on this affair;" as a final gesture the Reverend Mother clasped her hands together. "Now, good day Miss Wilson, I believe the Delvins are waiting for you."

The woman departed then with a very angry expression staining her face, and after a while when Mother Eugenia leered through the frosty glass of the casement windows, she could see Miss Wilson stepping up into the rear seat of the Chandler. She appeared to be talking high and fast as she tucked the lap blanket about her legs. Mrs. Delvin in her white duster and yards of superfluous veiling wound about her hat and throat, seemed to be far away and musing; her expression was not that of a gay woman of means. Mr. Delvin glanced over his shoulder to see if the Wilson woman was ready and then he lowered his goggles to his eyes. The motor turned over and the entire machine seemed to quake and tremble; the gears grinded into place and with an abundance of noise they curved the drive and sped away.

She returned to her desk. The fire livened up now; it popped and sputtered, a coal crumbled and a new tongue of blue and orange flamed flowed into being. The mist had ceased to fall and a low sighing wind rounded the corners of the building. "Of course, Miss Wilson was right, she thought. The authorities should have been notified . . . it's the law. However, why so much dispute? Dr. Mill had seen to that commendably well. If Christopher was to recover, the foundling home would be the last place on earth to retrieve his past; surely Dr. Mill must be aware of that? 'I realize that it is quite irregular to house a boy within the priory—' That's what Miss Wilson had said. Dr. Mill had said something of the same . . . *quite irregular.* There was no need to remind her of the inconformancy of it all. True, it did stray from the pattern of everyday lives of the convent, but what else could she have done? The situation speaks for itself. St. Ann's would have been damaged in reputation if the boy was refused admittance on that bleak night; the slanderous gossip would have never died. Yet, the ensuing chaos which threatens the boy's mental state is equally significant as the fever which burned his person, but this is unforeseeable to those who would will him away to less congenial surroundings. If there were someplace where she could house him, she thought; someplace and someone who would see that he received the care which was needed so that he may recover in memory. Then perhaps, there would be no reason to place him in the foundling home. Tomorrow she would speak to Mrs. Moore of Kramer House, but today she must think and plan.

3

During the night a new snow had fallen, and once more they were snowbound. The morning seemed cluttered with a multitude of petty obstacles; Mr. Tergauer had come down with a heavy chest cold and would not venture out of doors, which of course, left no one to drive the Reverend Mother into Fairlee. And even if he could have done the task, it would have been of no value, for during the night the horses strayed from the stables, and now their hooves were frost bitten and they couldn't have been hitched to the sleigh.

She was out of sorts with the day, yet she was determined to carry out her plans. Just before noon she telephoned the Kramer Foundling Home. "Undoubtedly, Miss Wilson had informed you of yesterday's occurrence, Mrs. Moore; "Mother Eugenia said through the mouthpiece. "I gather, also, that Dr. Mill has explained to you about the boy?"

Mrs. Moore's voice came through the wire clear and compassionately: "All Dr. Mill told me, Reverend Mother, was that the lad seemed to be suffering from lapse of memory and there is a fair possibility that he might recover. However, I want you to understand that I didn't authorize Miss Wilson to behave as she did. She merely was to accompany Mr. and Mrs. Delvin." Again Mrs. Moore's voice filled with solicitude, "I must say, that I feel very sorry for them . . . . poor Mrs. Delvin, she felt quite certain that the boy might be their son."

"Then, Mrs. Moore I am pleased that you understand about the talk I had with Miss Wilson, and I realize that I should apologize for my rudeness . . . You know that I would be the last one on earth to interfere with your work. It's just that I feel a personal responsibility for the boy."

"You needn't explain to me, Reverend Mother, I can understand your feelings; I have an attachment for every one of our children at Kramer, as it is now I am fretting because our coal supply is low."

"Mrs. Moore," began the Prioress, "I know quite well that eventually the boy must be turned over to Kramer House; but I was thinking that owing to the boy's illness, don't you agree that it would be better if he could be placed with some family that would care for him and give him this extra attention he needs?"

"My dear Reverend Mother, when you come into contact with so many homeless children as I, you will learn that they are rarely claimed by anyone, and to place him with some reputable family . . . well, if I could place all or even some of my children with some loving people, would be my greatest joy! It appears that the townspeople of Fairlee have enough to support. God knows, that we're crowded to full capacity now, to say nothing of our hospital room . . . Still if you have a family in mind—"

"No, no, not at present; but if I should—"

"If you should, that would be perfectly agreeable with Kramer House and the County of Fairlee. Now I would like to say, that if it is not too disrupting, I would appreciate your housing the boy until there comes a break in the weather. If he were to have a relapse by exposing him to this cold, I'd never forgive myself; besides as of yet, I have to secure a bed and make room for him. The county seat seems to think that we can manage for everything on the meager support they give us. Believe me, Reverend Mother, if it weren't for private donations here and now we'd have to close our doors."

"Well, Mrs. Moore permit me to thank you for your kindness and if every—Didn't you mention something about your coal supply?"

"Reverend Mother," Mrs. Moore sputtered with embarrassment; "I didn't mean to imply that you—"

"Nonsense, we have an abundance of coal at St. Ann's, just send around your handy man, and I'll give you whatever amount you might need to tide you over . . . Good day Mrs. Moore," and with that she rang off. The matter was practically settled, she thought. All she needed to do now was to find a suitable home for Christopher—but who? She stirred from her desk; despite the crackling heap of flames that were dancing on the hearth, her study seemed damp and chilled. She lifted her eyes to the heavy framed painting of the 'Last Supper', which hung above the mantle; she paused and viewed it a long while, and then stepped over to the frosted casement windows. The snow lay thick and white under the brooding grey sky. She trembled as she visioned Christopher trudging his path through the snow and wind on that frozen bleak night not so long ago, bewildered and lost with only the cold trembling stars, his silent companions, wheeling in their own frigid orbits.

The Reverend Mother winced: God! how severe a night to be a castaway on that white frozen waste; enough calamity had befallen Christopher, and she would not permit more to pursue him. She would find a suitable place to house him until he would be claimed by his own, that is, if there were any to claim him. It was far more than fever and exposure to cold that usurped his memory; some day she would learn what did black out his past. He must have experienced something fierce, his mind was to sharp and keen to falter on the diminutive.

At length, after turning the matter over in her mind, she knew that the only possible solution was to board the boy. Mrs. Moore was right, no one wanted to support any more children than they already had, at least not in Fairlee. She would speak to the Tergauers, and ask them if they would be willing to board Christopher. They had no children of their own, and felt that they might be glad to have a youngster about the house. She would arrange for everything, and the boy would present no problem to their budget; she herself would reckon for his support. True she was vowed to poverty, but she knew of a way to obtain the money which was needed. The Reverend Mother Eugenia was extracted from a distinguished family of property, and there still remained her share of an estate which she had never claimed. For once the money could be put to good use, and there would be no need for one penny of it to pass through her hands . . . She sat down and started a letter to her family's attorney.

Within a matter of days, all the arrangements were completed. There came a prompt reply from the attorney in Richmond and on the following Monday the Reverend Mother held council with the Tergauers and the one and only notary public and attorney that Fairlee had, a Mr. Loyd Daunce. Mr. and Mrs. Tergauer were quite willing to accept Christopher on those terms.

Mrs. Tergauer was joyously overwhelmed; the sheer delight of having Christopher under her roof was in itself enough to please her; but the high note that sealed the agreement was the opportunity of having easy money come into Mr. Tergauer's hand. It was the duty of Mr. Daunce to see that the money was properly allotted to the Tergauers semi-monthly for Christopher's board and keep. So thus it came about that Christopher took up lodgings in the little caretaker's cottage on the priory grounds. At first he found his new surroundings small and strange compared to the vast square room at St. Ann's, but so was everything strange to a mind, that was scarce three weeks distance on the winding causeway of remembrance. However, all that is green and novel must mellow, and the new will effectuate itself into casual familiarity, as so did the polished pine floor of his room with its heavy oak bed and highboy with its oval mirror, the writing table and the mantel shelf which held the many books he carried from the priory library, The many volumes, which Christopher thought stood like sentries on the bridge of adventure crossing into the palace of dreams. From his window and through the barren branches, he could see the walls of St. Ann's, looming high above the desolate trees, climbing above the snow thatched roof of the house and stable. What a surprise would be in store for him when the thaw breaks and the snow melts . . . when green returns to the warm black earth, and spring puts forth the first chaste foliage of the season. How abhorrent not to recall the gausy wings of the dragon fly, or the balmy blue of a summer sky as the silver, capped waves break over the sunlit sands of the rocky shore.

When Emily Tergauer first brought Christopher into Fairlee to purchase the necessary clothing he needed, the townspeople, who were gathered on the pavement would cease their conversation and look upon her and the lad. Their curious glances caused Christopher to flush and feel ill at ease, for they eyed him from his crown to the sole of his shoes without the decency to appear casual; but this was quite the opposite for Mrs. Tergauer, for she figuratively glowed in their reflection. As she walked beside the boy she seemed high spirited and there was a touch of vanity in her gait as she endeavored to keep space with his strides.

With those whom she had acquaintance, Mrs. Tergauer would pause and make him known to them, and though he was but a boy he was as tall, if not taller than the men and women she introduced him to. The firm grasp of his hand and the mellow husk quality of his voice won him the admiration of the men, but it was his handsome head and the warmth of his smile that charmed the women.

It required fully a week to equip Christopher with the things he needed; true the matter could have been over with in less time, but Mrs. Tergauer had purposely arranged it so that something would always bring them into the village. She knew that the unnecessary staring of the townspeople caused Christopher pain, but it was only their curiosity which caused them to do so—it was only a matter of their getting used to his presence, and he to theirs. So in time it was no longer a novelty to see him on the streets; he ceased to be a stranger and his presence mellowed into every day familiarity. Everyone seemed to like him, and all who saw him were quick to bid him the hour of the day. Even Mill Wilson, whom everybody said, was as cold as the snow on the ground, could not resist to nod and smile upon him.

Time did not lay idle and heavy upon Christopher, in the mornings he would rise early, long before the sun would brow the hill, and assist Mr. Tergauer in refilling the empty coal skuttles and putting them in their proper places in the priory. After breakfast he'd track across the frozen ground to the priory, and wait for the Reverend Mother in her study. Soon she would enter, her manner clip and scholarly, she would bid him good morning, then give him the books and matter he needed for the day and begin to instruct him in the fundamentals of Latin and English grammar, mathematics history and geography. She tutored Christopher long and well; his mind was agile and he was quick to learn, but occasionally she was forced to reprove him, for like all scholars he had a tendency to dream and drift at the height of an important, but tiresome lecture. However, the evenings until dusk were his, and in time he discovered Lake Morey, and he made friendships with the boys and girls who played there, and very soon he learned to ice skate. Moreover, all appeared to go well with him; Christopher had taken root to his new surroundings and no longer did he seem like a lost thing. True, his past had been hewed away like some curtailed pine, but now the future seemed bright and certain.

One of the calamities of life is, that the world will not let us be what we will, and no man may circle in a secluded orb retired from public view; ugly confabulation will encroach on any and every domain . . . And so thus it was when one late Saturday evening that Gus Tergauer stepped into the town saloon to slake his thirst after a hard days work. He scarce was at the long mahogany bar long enough to take a draught from his schooner of beer, when some slobbery and unkempt looking wastrels started to hurl some indirect and abusive insinuations toward him. Gus knitted his eyebrows for he was not certain that the drunkard had directed the remarks to him. He paused the beer glass at his lips and viewed the man from the corner of his eye.

The slobbery wastrel seeing that his accusations were too vague nudged his drunken companion in the ribs, and mentioning Tergauer in his conversation passed some low remark about him taking Christopher under his roof. His companion responded agreeingly, then heaved a jigger of whisky down his throat, and in a vile manner they laughed scornfully.

Without a seconds hesitation Tergauer pushed his open hand against the man's shoulder and he fell back against the sharp edge of the bar. The man winced when he saw a black hairy fist flying toward his face. Like a battering ram the fist drew back and forth, each time coming in direct contact with the slobbery man's mouth.

Soon the blood came flowing from the man's mouth like a small river; then suddenly the drunkard hoisted a muddy boot from the sawdust floor and pushed it with full might into the pit of Tergauer's stomach, which set him over backwards! The impact caused him to slide across the floor and his body collided with the table and chairs; the table turned over and the chairs clattered noisily to the floor.

High language filled the saloon! The men, who were engaged in small talk and strong refreshments, had now divided themselves on either side of the room, jeering and swearing, while others placed wages on which man would be the victor. Meanwhile the man, whom Tergauer had struck had to grip the edge of the bar for support, and between his panting and swearing he used the back of his hand to wipe away the black oozing blood from his mouth. Then his surly companion walked up to him, and giving him an encouraging pat on the back shoved him into the center of the room. He called his friend by his name, then later cursing Tergauer, rallied him on to whip the life out of the man on the floor. But by this time Gus Tergauer had climbed to his feet, and when he lifted his eyes, he saw the man rushing toward him with a knife in his hand! Instantly he sped upon the man and kicked his clenched fist; the knife flew to the ceiling. Then he threw his entire person upon his enemy and in the next moment they were rolling upon the floor. Somehow the man got possession of the knife, and Gus Tergauer in his efforts to get his hands on the weapon, knocked it once more from the man's grip; the knife went sliding across the floor until it disappeared between the legs of the men who stood by.

Soon Tergauer had his assailant flat on his back, and with his knee against the man's chest, he pressed his rough fingers upon the man's throat. Beside them lay a broken beer schooner; its jagged edge was dangerously sharp! Gus Tergauer seized the glass by its stem, and pointed the sharp edge toward the man's unshaven throat. Fortunately from behind him appeared two cool headed men, they caught hold of Tergauer and pulled him off the prostrated man, saving both from an unnecessary fate.

"Git out of my damn place, Tergauer," cried the proprietor, "before I throw you both in jail!"

Mr. Tergauer was quick to explain that it was the other man who assaulted first, but it appeared that the proprietor had understood both sides of the quarrel that's why he urged him to leave, for he intended handing the trouble makers over to the constable. With some tactful words he persuaded Mr. Tergauer to the door, explaining that the man had been drinking and knew not what he was doing. He also added that he thought highly of him for taking the boy under his roof, and some of the other men echoed the proprietor's sentiments; most of them being family men understood quite well how Gus Tergauer felt.

When he departed from the saloon, he felt justified in having defended Christopher's honor, but still he couldn't forget the man's unjust accusations, and that evening before going to his cottage he went directly to the priory to see the Reverend Mother; for he was determined to have the doubt in his mind settled for once and always. Standing before the Prioress, he stammered and stuttered, very much embarrassed at not being capable of expressing himself. Finally red faced and not knowing what to do with his hands, he clumsily said: "Well, I just got to know something' about the boy's life; his family name or somethin' of the kind."

The man's words startled her, not because of what he said or implied, but because she knew not the boy's surname, or Christian one for that matter. The name he now carried was one she improvised on the spur of the moment. She cast a quick glance at the man; he appeared to be waiting anxiously for her reply. Mother Eugenia knew that she could not turn him away without some satisfactory explanation. What was she to do? She couldn't allow the boy to be branded, above all not in a small town like Fairlee . . . Then at last, she struck upon the conclusion; she smiled and thought of her own family name. However, the smile soon changed into a frown, because it occurred to her that she was about to tell a lie.

Nevertheless she composed her mind and felt that in some way the Savior would forgive her this once, and since she was apt to tell one falsehood, she might as well tell another and put an end to all further interrogations which might arise in the future. She turned to the man and said: "You're quite right in wanting to learn the boy's name, Mr. Tergauer. I should have told you so in the beginning . . . and while I think of it, I may as well tell you the boy's age." She paused for she had already thought of giving her family name to the boy, and now she would bestow on him the date of her own birth anniversary. "He'll be fourteen, this coming June 16th.," she told him quietly, "and as for his family or past life—Well, there's no reason to go into that now . . . True his memory and past are lost, and no one has come to claim him as of now, but I want you to understand, that clearly woven on the inside pocket of his coat was the name, Christopher Wensdy."

4

"It seems news travels rapidly in Fairlee, Dr. Mill," said the Reverend Mother in a tone that was slightly apart from her usual gentle voice. She was standing at the casement watching the steady drizzle of the morning weather. Dr. Mill, with his back toward her, sat in the big leather chair before the fire. He appeared to be remote as though his thoughts had wandered and slipped into one of the golden chasms of the crackling fire before him. "Surely I thought you above all would be the last to be taken in by the townspeople's idle gossip," she went on to say. "I'm inclined to believe that they loiter about one another's doorsteps, saying: 'Won't go in just yet, who knows what startling news may fly from St. Ann's walls' . . . I told you, doctor that I did not know what the boy's name is."

The sharpness of her final words caused the doctor to turn around. "But how was I to know that you merely told Tergauer such a thing to protect the boy from slander," he replied in defense. "Naturally, when Constable Davis informed me that you learned—" he stopped sharply, then added, "*Christopher*, I believe you call him . . . Well, I felt that I should speak with you, but if you find my visit disturbing."

"Nonsense," she retorted, "of course, your visit does not disturb, Dr. Mill. It's just this idle prattle—Well, I had no idea that people talked so much about things that didn't concern them."

"I'm afraid it's the way of the world."

"So it would seem."

The doctor rose from the chair he sat in; he fumbled with some object on the mantle then crossed the floor and paused momentarily at the window. "Another bad day," he said commenting about the weather. "Oh, isn't that the boy—Christopher, coming across the grounds?"

The Prioress raised her eyes, then went over to her desk. "Yes," she answered, "he comes every morning at this time; I've been tutoring him," and with some amount of glee in her voice she added: "He really is a quick lad in his studies."

"Good," murmured the doctor returning to the hearth and stirring up the fire, "then I shall have an opportunity of seeing him again." He returned the fire tongs to its rack, and straightening up from his position he turned to face the Reverend Mother. "Has he improved much since last I saw him?"

"Physically, his health couldn't be better, and as for his memory . . . Well, there has been no indication of the slightest degree that his past is returning to him. Of course, there are times when vague shadows seem to cross his mind as though something might be coming back—but then he shrugs his shoulders and resumes whatever he was doing, and I realize that all is gone again . . . Do you think he shall ever recover his memory, doctor?"

Dr. Mill pursed his lips; "One can never tell for certain. In most cases of amnesia, recovery is rapid; sometimes the patient recovers from the malady in six or seven days, sometimes sooner. We mustn't try to rush an extreme condition such as his. I'm sure his memory will return . . . Besides, someone might turn up any day to identify him."

The door opened with a clatter then, and Christopher, tall straight and slim, stepped into the study. He did not see the doctor sitting before the fire. The Reverend Mother standing with her back toward the window greeted him; and he echoed her cheery good morning in his husk boyish tones, and sweeping off his cap revealed a shaggy head of warm dark hair. It wasn't until he began to unbutton his bright blue plaid jacket that he noticed Dr. Mill. His features relaxed into something of a disappointed frown; Christopher lowered his dark blue eyes, and said: "Excuse me, Reverend Mother, I didn't know you had a visitor; excuse," he reiterated then started to turn from the room.

"It's alright, Christopher, come on. It's only Dr. Mill, you remember the doctor, don't you?"

Christopher nodded his head, and wiped the palm of his hand against his trouser leg. "Y-yes, ma'am," he stuttered.

The doctor called him over, and when Christopher came to his side they shook hands. "Let me look at you boy," said Dr. Mill tightening his fingers about Christopher's hand when he felt him pulling away from his grip. "Don't be afraid," he balked, "I shan't eat you."

Mother Eugenia frowned upon the doctor's attitude, but then all doctors possess that lofty, disdainful opinion of themselves as though they viewed everyone like lowly germs in a test-tube, holding everyone in contempt as if one's physical presence annoyed their astute M.D . . . . that little weapon they use to probe into the soul of the inferior breed.

"I'm not afraid, sir," replied Christopher in a quiet sober tone, and this time he freed his hand from the doctor's grip.

"My," bleated the doctor, and from force of habit he touched his fingers to his brow; "I do believe I have failed to make friends with the boy, eh Reverend Mother? Ah, no matter," he grunted using the arms of the chair to push his weight up, "I don't believe I liked doctors either when I was a boy . . . . And now, if you will excuse me, I think I'll be looking after my practice." When he reached the study door, he stopped and turned to nod his head to the Reverend Mother. "Perhaps I'm a bit too premature," he said, "but in the event that I do not see you in the coming fortnight, I wish to extend my greetings for a Merry Christmas! Good day Mother Eugenia, Master Wensdy," then with a laconical smile on his thin lips, he turned out of the room closing the door after him.

"Master Wensdy?" echoed Christopher, "What did he mean by that Reverend Mother?

Mother Eugenia sat down in the great leather chair by the fire. It was just typical of Mr. Tergauer to inform the whole town, and yet not speak a word to Christopher, she thought complainingly to herself. She lifted her brows, "Come here by the fire, Christopher, I want to speak with you. The matter is important," she told him, and when he came over to her side she took his small hands in hers. "Now, Christopher," she murmured struggling to find the right words, "there are some things that must be faced openly—to hide them in the shadows will only make matters worse. We both know that you cannot remember who you are, or where you came from; also you understand that Christopher is not your true name—"

"You don't have to worry about me, Mother Eugenia," he told her in an air of honest comprehension. "I know that I have no memory," and this he told without a wince as his young eyes met with hers. "It doesn't frighten me anymore and I'm not afraid . . . Besides, I like my new name; it kind of seems like it always was Christopher. Anyhow, I remember all the other things, and maybe who I was is not so important."

A tear came into the Prioress' eye and she smiled in order to conceal it; no wonder they say youth is golden, she thought. "Perhaps you're right," she told him. "The important thing is that you are well, and shall grow up to lead a good clean life. Dr. Mill says your memory may return at any time; but until then, we must have a name for you . . . that's what the doctor meant when he called you Master Wensdy."

"Then, that is to be my name for always?" he sheepishly inquired.

"Well, perhaps not for always . . . Only until your memory of your own name comes back to you, or until your parents come to claim you."

"But how will I know they are my parents?"

"I think you will know somehow," she said giving his hand a little pat of encouragement; "but you needn't trouble yourself about that just now."

Christopher repeated his new name orally, and then turning to the Reverend Mother he said: "I like that name; I'll always like it. I know I will."

"I am pleased that you do . . . It was my family name, Christopher," she said lightly and her thoughts turned back to the days of her girlhood and her departed father.

"Then I shall like it all the more," he said, and there came a tremble of gratitude in his voice, which potentially moved them both to tears.

"Now young man," said the Reverend Mother sharping the edge of her words in an endeavor to throw off the cloak of melancholy. "Suppose we get down to our lessons . . ."

Christmas came . . . by far the first and merriest that Christopher had ever known. He told himself, that if the past was lost it mattered not, for in his boyish way he knew that the future lay golden and untouched before him, and he was happy! Christmas Eve was spent in Fairlee, at Amy Schwartz' little cottage. Christopher hadn't been there very long when he was left to shift for himself. Mr. Tergauer slipped off to join the men, who were in the kitchen drinking toasts to the season; and his wife sat amid the little huddle of women who sat before fire in the parlor talking fast and merrily.

Christopher felt very lonely despite the fact that he had to move from place to place in the crowded parlor to avoid obstructing the path of the different people who wanted to cross the room. Once when he lifted his eyes toward the hall he saw Dr. Mill enter. He winced when he saw the doctor and thought it strange that one man could cause him to feel so uncomfortable. "I suppose the doctor is alright," he told himself, "but I just don't like him . . . I guess it's his eyes, they look at me so funny."

To avoid the doctor he left the parlor and went into the dining room; there he saw a rather tall brownish haired girl who greeted with a cheery, "Hello."

"Hullo," responded Christopher in a quick tone, glad that at long last someone had taken notice of his presence. The girl offered him some punch and before he had time to reply, she presented him with a crystal cup of the ruby colored liquid. Christopher nodded his head as a token of salutation and then thanked her for the drink.

"My name's Abigale Trent," said the girl introducing herself and taking a sip of the drink in the same moment. "What's yours?"

"Christopher Wensdy," he replied and there was a slight lift in his voice. He repeated the name once more, not because the girl didn't hear him, but because he wanted the pleasure of hearing it for himself. Moreover, he had not known the pleasure of presenting himself to anyone before, as he could remember, and he found himself smiling happily. When he brought the cup to his lips, he thought, what joy it is to have a good name. He felt secure.

"Quick! return your cup to the buffet," Abigale cried in alarm, then she touched her hand to his forearm, bringing hand and cup downward with a certain amount of strength that was surprising to Christopher.

"Why?" he asked obeying the command, not because he wanted to, for he thought the drink very different and delightful, but because the girl seemed genuinely alarmed and there was a touch of panic in her voice; but again he questioned: "Why?"

"We're not supposed to touch this," she whispered. "It's not for the children; it has high spirits in it," but this time she wasn't really speaking in her own voice, but rather in some strange way she used the voice of her Aunt Amy, for it was her Aunt's words that she was echoing. "But don't worry," she went on to explain, "we'll drink later—Right now, my sister, Louise is coming this way."

Christopher had scarce released the cup when a slim dark haired young lady came up to speak with Abigale.

"Abby?" Louise Trent questioned her sister in a high sophisticated and reproving tone. "Aunt Amy would like to know why are you down stairs, and not with the other children in the playroom above?"

The girl standing at Christopher's side wined, very much troubled with her sister's unwelcomed presence and in a harassed breath she cried: "Louise!" then turned her back and folded her arms.

"You haven't been at the punch, have you Abigale?" murmured Louise with her fingers interlaced over her stomach.

"Really Louise! I'm not a derrick, you know."

"The word is derelict; besides such a term is not proper for little girls to use.

Abigale couldn't have been more bored with her sister, especially since she referred to her as a little girl. She displayed her contempt by making a face at Louise, then suddenly recovered herself, regretting her actions, but this wasn't because she was rude to her sister, but for the reason that Christopher was so near. She forgot he was there. "Louise," Abigale said in a more propitious and agreeable tone," have you seen Larry Mall? I saw him come in a few minutes ago . . . he seemed to be looking for you."

"Was he really, dear?" spoke Louise rather sweetly, forgetting her scolding and scrutinizing her reflection in the mounted mirror above the buffet. "Remember what Lou has told you, heart—about the punch I mean." She patted Abigales cheek, then saunted away humming.

"I guess we may finish our punch now," said the girl trying to decide which cups were theirs; for there were so many half-filled ones on the sideboard.

"These are ours," said Christopher lifting two cups and giving one to Abigale. "I remember ours were nearest the bowl."

"What are you going to be when you grow up, Christopher?"

"I don't know, I guess I haven't given it much thought, have you?"

"Oh, yes," she cried eagerly, "I think of it all the time. "I am going to be an actress," she said over emphatically," a great one like, Sarah Bernhart! Of course, my Aunt Amy, doesn't think much of the idea, she says only sporty women rouge up and become actresses— But any way, I think it's better than being like Louise, she wants to get married and have five children—three boys and two girls. My cousin Kit says, Louise is boy crazy . . . Aunt Amy says, Kit ought to know, because she is, and it takes one to know one. Anyway that's how I always get rid of Lou, by telling her Larry's around. I guess it ain't—isn't nice, but it works."

Both Abigale and Christopher laughed.

"You talk plenty," he said, "don't you?"

"I guess I do," she admitted frankly, "but an actress must be a good conversationalist both on and off the boards—that's stage talk, you know," she explained with some amount of pride in her speech. "One must improve their vo-cab-u-lary; of course, I make a few mistakes once in a while, but I'll learn not to when I'm ripe

43

enough to do the things I want to do. Don't you think I've chosen an exciting career?"

"Do you think you'll like people pointing at you, saying there goes Abigale Trent?" said Christopher feeling that there is a certain blessing in being obscure.

"Oh! yes," beamed Abigale, "that's the great reward for the emotion and heart break that an actress must endure before she can be great. Truly great . . . But my name won't be that, I'll call myself, Tren Sarah!"

Christopher had no desire to be rude, but he thought the name devilishly funny. Possibility it was the manner in which she spoke the name, or perhaps it was the ridiculous, flamboyant way she threw back her head to tilt her chin skyward, but whatever it was, it called for great discipline to suppress the laugh within himself. Fortunately Abigail did not notice the restrained grin and twisted expression on Christopher's face, but this was because at long last, she discovered the opportunity she had been waiting for. Most of the adults had left the dining room, and the few that still remained were too deep in conversation to absorb the actions of any adolescent.

Long before Christopher had entered the room, Abigail had been busy at pouring cup fulls of punch into a quart size mason jar, and she had completed filling the jar when Christopher first entered the room, but could not carry it away herself without being noticed; however, now the path was open for escape.

Dropping her voice in a confidential tone, she urged Christopher to conceal the jar inside his coat and follow her. Before Christopher's mind could conjure up the motive Abigail might have had for her cabalistic play at piracy, he found himself accepting the jar and concealing it under the fold of his coat. To prevent the bottle from slipping, he had to press his arm against his stomach, then he followed Abigail out of the room and together they mounted the steps to the playroom above.

When they entered the room, the boys and girls who had been waiting anxiously for Abigail's return, greeted them with jeers and laughter for they didn't believe that she would return with the drink, then observing that she was empty handed, they laughed all the louder.

"Ah! Miss Actress," cried Charley Lock to Abigail, "did you get the stuff? You're the last to come back." They had been playing the game scavenger, and each had to secure a required something; it was Charly who first suggested the game.

"Behold! My Lord," she replied playing the dramatic again; then she turned to Christopher, "Open your coat and give me the bottle." She placed the jar of punch on the table beside the other articles; there was: a broomstick handle, a man's black derby, a saucer full of melted snow, a turkey feather and a handful of gravel.

"We didn't think you had the nerve to swipe the punch," grinned Charly pushing his fingers through his stringy black hair, he was a lean raw-boned boy with crude, handsome square features, and a large wide mouth.

"Who's your friend, Abby," interrogated Ruth Celine, a rather mature girl for her thirteen years with full bosom and wide hips; she sat down to the piano and struck the first chords of Adeste Pidelis. She gave Christopher a long sheepish glance, then continued with her abstract plucking of the keys.

"Oh!" cried Abigail demurely remembering her etiquette, "this is Christopher Wensdy . . . and this is: Mary Fay, Charly Lock."

Christopher nodded and acknowledged them very cordially, and in the following moment Charly Lock was patting him on the back. Later, Oscar inquired of Charlie, since it was he who suggested the game, who was to get the prize?

"What is the prize anyway? "Mary's wide saucer blue eyes wanted to know.

"The winner gets to suggest the next game."

"Aw to heck with the winner," protested Oscar. "I'm tired of the game. Let's drink the punch before somebody comes snoopin' around."

"Alright by me," agreed Charly and he began to ration out the drink.

"Then I guess there's no question about it," said Abigail, "I'll suggest the next game. The punch was the hardest to get . . . I am the victory!"

"*Victor*," somebody was quick to correct her.

45

"Of course, that is exactly what I said," remarked Abigail; she was quite accustomed to being dressed down in her use of words, so she simply ignored her hecklers and sipped her drink.

"I suppose Abby did get the hardest task and I do think that she should be the winner," commented Mary, who always played the role of the good puritan. "Besides I am too tired after chasing after the turkey feather to dispute—Anyway, I already know what the next game will be—"

"Theatre!" The small groups exclaimed in the same breath; although there was a note of protest in their voices, they really didn't mind.

"Well, who in the heck are you going to be tonight?" said Oscar, plaguing her.

Abigail batted her eye lids, "We can do without the *profanity*, Oscar," she told him; but Oscar seemed too amused to correct her and he dropped his arms to his side in a vainless gesture. Abigail placed her hand to her heart and continued: "Tonight, I shall be the great Paula Fransworth!"

"Aw girl, she's dead."

"Yes, I know and my heart is mourning for the beautiful Paula, that's why I must pay tribute to her tonight." Abigail's somber tones and over dramatic actions caused her companions to laugh, and if Christopher had not been so completely absorbed in the merry making, the name of his departed mother might have awakened his sleeping memory; he bordered so near his true identity, and yet, the breach between he and his past was too steep a chasm to be forged by the fall of a name from the lips of a stage fevered adolescent.

The holidays ended, and Christopher resumed his accustomed routine. The morning that he was to report to the Reverend Mother for his lessons, he went across the grounds from the Tergauer's cottage to the priory. He leered through the chilled window panes; the Revered Mother was seated at her desk and she appeared to be writing. Christopher tapped on the glass to gain her attention, and when she lifted her eyes, he wrote on the frosted glass . . . HAPPY NEW YEAR 1910.

5

Christopher packed his suitcase with great concern. He knew that any moment now, Mrs. Tergauer would be up to see if he laid in his clothes correctly, and though he packed with great care, his thoughts were still on the conversation he had with the Reverend Mother earlier that morning.

"New things come with the New Year," she had told him, "therefore it will not be I who will teach you in the future."

Christopher recalled how his heart skipped a beat when she told him that. His first thoughts were that he believed someone had come to take him away, and an ordeal like that seemed too much for him to bear. He had no wish to take up a new life with people he didn't know. "You mean I'm never to see you anymore?" he said, at last finding his voice and a deep tinge of orange flushed into his cheeks. He turned his back on her saying: "No matter who it is, "I'll not go with them. I won't!"

"Christopher," she called endeavoring to hide the pain in her heart, for she felt the agony and insecurity that haunted the boy. She placed her hands on his firm broad shoulders, and he turned around to look at her. "Of course, you'll see me . . . As often as you like, Chris," she never called him that, but somehow this time it seemed right.

"Then what did you mean . . . you'll not teach me anymore?"

The Reverend Mother chucked him under the chin: "My silly little friend," she said smiling, "why don't you let me finish what I have to say before you fret yourself to death. I was keeping it as a surprise. I simply mean that you will be a permanent boarder at St. Thomas'."

The boy's face brightened: "You mean that I'm to go to St. Thomas', the school on the other side of Lake Morey!"

"Yes, I spoke with Father Mitchell just before the holidays. Your grades here met with his approval and he'll place you with the boys in the junior year—and I just know you are going to like your housemaster, Brother Angus, a fine man, all the boys speak well of him." She looked into his eyes, "I hope you'll like your new quarters, Christopher . . . I think you'll be happy there."

Suddenly he threw his arms around her which seemed to startle the Reverend Mother, "Thank you!" he cried. They both choked and swallowed hard; Christopher fought to restrain the tears of gratitude welling in his eyes.

Mrs. Tergauer knocked at the door. "Already Christopher?"

"Yes, ma'am, come in. I guess I've just about packed everything 'cept this coat. I will have to carry it on my arm, it just won't fit."

"My! that ain't a bad job for a boy," she said inspecting the bag and trying to avoid his eyes. Mrs. Tergauer felt that at any moment her spirits would crumble and she would break down and weep. "If you will help me press down on the lid," she murmured just to have words to fill in the emptiness, "we kin snap the lock shut."

"There, that's got it! Did Mr. Tergauer take down by box of books?"

"Oh! Chris," her voice trembled with a lump of restrained tears. "You'll look like a walkin' library with all them books. Oh, Chris! how I'm goin' to miss not dustin' them for you," and with that she buried her face in her apron and wept.

He put his arm around Mrs. Tergauer and she turned to sob on his shoulder. "Please, Miss Emmy, I won't forget you and Mr. Gus, believe me I won't. I'll come to see you lots . . . Why St. Thomas' is just right 'cross the lake."

Emily Tergauer straighten up and stifled her tears. "Oh, I'm actin' like an ole wet hen, and just makin' you feel bad. Pshaw! You'll be back before I can even miss you. Besides, the schoolin' and the boys will do you good." She managed to control her emotions, taking on a more positive air about herself. "Now, we better get started, or I'll have you late on your first morning."

Outside in front of the cottage door, Mr. Tergauer waited for Christopher in the buckboard. He had only pulled up when the door of the cottage opened. A pair of fine spirited chestnut studs champed at their bits, their sleek brown hides fairly glistened under the winter sun; the restless animals clapped their hooves in the dust snorting and puffing little clouds of frozen breath. Christopher was rather nervous as to what lay ahead of him; he came out, then excitedly turned to Mrs. Tergauer; he kissed her goodbye then strode quickly to the buckboard. He tossed his suitcase onto the trailer and climbed aboard taking his place on the bench next to Mr. Tergauer. He caused a clicking noise by tighting his lips to one side of his face, he pulled at the reins and the horses lunged forward. Christopher waved his final farewell to Emily Tergauer, who was standing in the cottage door waving, and weeping into her small blue handkerchief. The horses pulled forward and they rode off in silence, but he didn't look back to see if Miss Emmy was still waving, and as they curved the drive Christopher could feel her eyes on his back; already he felt sick with melancholy. Then as they were about to pass the priory windows Christopher bit his lip to keep from crying, he simply couldn't bear to go past the Reverend Mother's study, and he prayed that she wouldn't be looking out when they rolled past; but in the same moment, he thought it would be worse not to see her once more. Suddenly he was swept with a feeling of gladness and forgot all pain when he saw the sunlight flash on the glass panel as it swung outward and Mother Eugenia waiting for him to pass.

"Good luck Christopher!" He heard her cry as he pulled off his cap and waved it at her; a burning tear came into his eye.

Now they rolled through the heavy iron gates, turning down the road to St. Thomas'. It wasn't until Mr. Tergauer tugged at the reins and turned the team at Fork Road that Christopher looked back over his shoulder; through the bare and sleeping branches he sighted the steepled roof of the priory and the cross on top, for a while it towered high in the distance then seemed to drop suddenly out of view behind a giant clump of evergreens.

Neither Mr. Tergauer nor Christopher had spoken a word to the other since the boy tossed his suit case onto the trailer and climbed aboard. The crude but kindly man eyed Christopher fondly from the corner of his eye. He felt he could advise the boy on certain matters, and many a kind and fatherly passion stirred in his being, but somehow he couldn't fuse his emotions into words. The circumstances seemed terse and awkward. On they rode with the only sound between them being the steady clopping of the suit case and the wooden box containing Christopher's small library.

Once more they turned the road and it wasn't very long before the massive clock-tower of St. Thomas' began to rise above the dark purple haze of the forest. "Look through them trees, boy! You kin see the school from here . . . won't be long now before we're there, eh?"

Christopher murmured something, replying in the affirmative; he wished that he could be more cheerful to the man, but somehow he didn't feel very receptive. At length, after driving through a small patch of woods, they drew up to the school. Before the gates a somewhat tall and stockly built blond haired youth of Christopher's age, was standing in the road to greet them.

"Hey!" cried the boy looking up to a rather surprised Christopher, "your name Wensdy?"

"Yes," replied Christopher astonished but glad to have lighted on someone who seemed to know him.

"Brother Angus sent me to look after you," explained the boy. "Just dump your stuff to the ground, Black Luck will be along with the pick-up any minute now. Wait, I'll haul aboard and give you a hand." The words were no sooner out of his mouth when he had already gripped the little iron rail beside the seat. He secured a footing in one of the spokes, then threw a leg over the side, in the next second he was standing in the buckboard.

Christopher faced Mr. Tergauer to say good bye and shake hands.

"Blast it, Wensdy! What the tar you've got in this box? I'm having a devil of a time to budge it . . . come give a fellow a hand, will you?"

"In a minute," retorted Christopher over his shoulder in a clip distracted voice. He slipped his hand out of Mr. Tergauer's hand, then swung his legs over the seat into the trailer.

With all the grace of a tornado, the boy tossed Christopher's bag over the side. The smooth finesse was enough to startle Christopher to pain and he felt the punishment his brand new bag received when it bounced to the ground, rolling into the snow. Christopher was relieved that this mad Hercules could not do the same with his box of books, and with some amount of lengthy directions on his part, together they eased the box to the ground.

Mr. Tergauer uttered his final farewells to the boy, then pulling on the reins he rolled off. As for Christopher, he bent over, picked up his suitcase and scrutinized it for possible bruises.

"What the blessed freckles is keepin' Black Luck? I told him to be down at the gate for two—the blackguard! Oh, well . . ." he shrugged his shoulders, thrust his hands into his pockets and cocked one foot on top the box of books. "I guess I better introduce myself, I'm Hans Ellgate."

The boys shook hands.

"Christopher Wensdy is mine . . . I hope we'll be friends."

"And here the same—I hope you don't find me too hard to swallow, and I'm afraid that you're going to have to excuse my swearing. I forget sometimes, especially about the dorm, Angus is always boxing my ears for it . . . but you'll get use to me." Then with a leer he added: "You'd better—we're going to be roommates."

Christopher smiled despite the fact that he wasn't quite certain whether or not he was going to like this garrulous wind tunnel. However, he had to admit to himself that the yellow haired rogue did possess a good smile and winning ways, even though Ellgate was now ramming the toe of his boot into the side of Christopher's box a bit too vigorously. Christopher didn't say anything, but simply watched and listened while Ellgate swore furiously at the colored man's tardiness. His back was turned toward the school, therefore he couldn't see the belated darkie coming up the path, but still he continued to swear, yet, not once did he turn around to see if the man was approaching.

"Look," said Christopher putting a hand to Ellgate's shoulder, "isn't that Black Luck coming now?"

Ellgate wheeled around. The slow, sluggish rate in which the darkie traveled caused him to eject a new and highly potent stress of language which fairly burned out Christopher's ears. Not to imply that Christopher's ears were too delicate for such subtle dexterity, but one must bear in mind that he was new in memory, to say nothing of his chaste relations at the priory and the God fearing Tergauers. But if it can be said that a mortal usually reflects his environment, then it is to be assumed that there came moments in the future when Christopher could pronounce such choiceness with an art that even moved the learned Ellgate.

Ellgate passed through the gates and Christopher trotted after him, and they approached the darkie who pulled a small hand cart behind him. "What speed, Luck; I must praise you on your punctuality . . . I've only been waiting long enough to freeze my head off."

Black Luck smiled revealing a mouthful of shining white teeth. He ignored Ellgate's sharp tongue, knowing that it was only a manner staged by the boy for effect; he knew that none of the students would overstep their bounds with him for fear he'd turn their names in to the dean for non-respect. Moreover, all the boys regarded him with reverence, looking upon him as a personal servant and valet . . . always being under paid for his services and most time pursuing the boys for his fees.

"Take Master Wensdy's things to Warwyck Dormitory, Luck, and put them in my quarters—room 205."

"Y'suh, Masta El," he answered touching his battered hat and smiling at the boys, then he proceeded to load the baggage onto the hand cart.

"—And, Luck it must be up in ten minutes or no more jobs from me," he said in order to display some authority before Christopher, then turning to him he said with little or no ceremony: "Pay him a dime, Wensdy."

Ellgate's sheer audacity amused Christopher, and he paid the darkie the amount requested with a little over for good measure and friendship. Again the darkie smiled, out this time with more self-indulgence. He doffed his hat to Christopher then sauntered away in happy spirits.

"Another thing, Luck," cried Ellgate, "if Brother Angus asks you for me, tell him I'm where he sent me—in the library reading Virgil. That will keep his wig on for a while. Come along Wensdy," then he swaggered away with his hands in his pockets and Christopher at his side.

"Ellgate, are we really going to the library now? I thought I'd like to see the grounds first," said Christopher eyeing the many buildings, particularly the great tower inset with a clock on all four sides.

"Not on your life, Wensdy," came the happy rejoinder, "although that's where we're supposed to be. Brother Angus thought I should take you there to keep out of trouble. He's been on my heels all day . . . Like a loon, I returned this morning, thinking that the other fellows would do the same, but now I understand that the Christmas vacation won't be over until another day yet. Imagine how I felt, when I returned to find Warwyck Dorm dead as a grave. I guess most of the fellows will pour in tomorrow night," he added. "Say, Wensdy must you carry that coat with you? If any of the upper-classmen see you they'll take you for a greenie and beat the hide off you."

Christopher silently winced, he regretted that strange, new, intangible something which seemed to scent the very air he breathed; but most of all he loathed being just a new boy, unfamiliar with the customs at St. Thomas'. He was joyed that he already achieved Ellgate for a friend, and worried if the other boys would accept him so readily.

"Say, you are a lanky cuss, aren't you?" observed Ellgate putting a slight strain in his gait to stay with Christopher's strides. "Rattin'

smart of you to come in blue serge too, and 'specially good idea
to put your legs in long breeches. Nobody wears knickers at St.
Thomas', 'cept the greenies and they're quick to change. Hey! here's
the chapel. Let's cut over and stick that hellish coat of yours under
one of the pews, then we can be on our way."

They boys paused in front of the school's chapel and Ellgate
hurriedly crossed himself, then gripped the coat off of Christopher's
arm; he darted up the stone steps, disappearing within the open
door of the church, then returned almost instantly upon the scene;
short of breath, but not in energy. "Don't worry ol' fellow," he said
observing the perturbed look in Christopher's eye. "Your coat will
be perfectly safe in the chapel. No one ever goes there—I mean at
this time of the day," he corrected with a mocking laugh.

They started off and Christopher looked over his shoulder trying
to study the grounds and the position of the chapel so he could find
it again when the time came to retrieve his coat. Later he inquired
of Ellgate as to how they could spend their time until curfew.

"Not much," Ellgate rejoined. "The gym is closed and there is
absolutely nothing doing down at the ball field. We could go skating
on the lake, but that'll mean we'll have to go to the dorm for our
skates, and that's out of the question . . . We might run into Angus,
and bible reading is not the thing I want to do just now."

"Then why not show me the grounds?"

"If you'd like," he whined, "but we could go over to Lilly's Sweet
House, but I'm as broke as the *ten*."

"Is it very far Ellgate? I have some money—"

"Bless your hide Wensdy!" he cried tossing his hat into the air
and catching it again. He patted Christopher on the back, "I plum
forgot that you're fresh from the apron strings, and are loaded with
wampum. Heck no," he retorted, "Lilly's ain't far. We can take
Robin's Path. It's a short cut through the woods and as we go I'll
point out the sights to you."

As the boys drew across the grounds and nearer the woods,
Ellgate, like the boastful swagger he pretended to be, flaunted all
the knowledge he possessed concerning the great school. First he
showed Christopher the rambling college, the huge stone building

with the clock tower, that was to play an important moment in his future life, but now he was inclined to be disappointed that this was not the building where he was to take up his classes. Since the boys were tracking their way north, this offered no opportunity for him to see the junior school. However, they did pass beneath the high wall of the seminary, and with little persuasion and great curiosity, they scaled the wall. Once atop their stony perch they achieved an excellent view of the grounds and the quietly shrubbed buildings.

In time the boys forged their way to Robin's Path, but to Christopher's dismay there wasn't a robin to be seen, nor did any build their nest there. Ellgate related the legend of how some ten years before, the Robin brothers and a party of students cut a path through the woods to Fairlee. The woods weren't the property of the school, and St. Thomas' was in dire need of funds, which was one of the incidents that helped to make the path famous. The county became highly indignant at the prank and took legal action against the impoverished school, claiming the students had destroyed public property, and the legislator insisted that every foot of the timber had to be paid for. The results: The school paid the cost of damage and the students were expelled. In order to clear the family name, and reinstate the prankish boys, the Robin family purchased the grounds and donated it to St. Thomas' School.

Then at length, when Ellgate completed the story, they arrived at a little cottage; they crossed the road and entered. When they opened the door a little brass bell tingled merrily above their heads. A bright scene flashed before Christopher's eyes; the little cottage seemed swarmed with boys and young men all garbed in the conventional blue serge.

Perhaps, one more pair of pants and another patch of blue serge would have passed unnoticed, but at that moment the jolly pink cheeked and plumb Lilly, chanced to glance up from whatever she was doing and caught sight of Christopher. She sketched a mental picture of him and resumed her business. Lilly always made it a practice to greet each new boy personally and give him a free sample of her wares, (as the business men say: *a get acquainted offer*), and most of the boys looked upon her sweet shop as their second home.

The cottage buzzed and hummed with a multitude of voices and activity. Some of the boys were seated at little tables drinking hot chocolate; moms were talking, and others were singing merrily. Occasionally a ball of paper would sail across the room and hit some unsuspecting fellow behind the ear. Christopher noticed a clump of boys standing before an oblong window which separated the dining room from the kitchen. He could see Lilly disappear, then return with a long tray of steaming pies fresh from the oven, all of which were cut in sizable pieces. The boys swarmed around her, to say nothing of the mad few, who were in the kitchen feasting on whatever delight suited their fancy. No sooner had the poor woman set the tray of pies on the counter when they were gone. The boys slapped their coins on the counter and snatched the desired cuts of pie. Then occasionally there would be a cry of: 'Put me down for a nickel's worth, Lilly. I'm short of the rest.' It seemed like a small miracle how the woman kept all the figures in her head until she could set them down in what the boys referred to as her 'short change book', and never did she falter in setting the proper amount beside each boy's name. However, the big miracle was how she managed to collect every time allowance week rolled around, which seemed more than Black Luck could manage to do.

"Come along Wensdy," urged Ellgate digging the bony end of his hand into Christopher's back to get him to move on. "Push through the mob, I see a table at the corner window." Just at that moment a wad of paper sailed across the room and caught Ellgate on the bridge of his nose. "Why the dirty loggerheads!" he muttered under his breath, "I'll fix 'em!" He stooped to the floor and came up with two sizeable balls of paper which he joined together with an elastic band; then he selected a suitable victim whose head was turned in a desired direction. He set his arm.

"No!" cried Christopher stopping Ellgate's hand. "Let me send it off!"

"Why, you loveable blackguard!" exclaimed Ellgate. "here, go right ahead . . . Get that skinny lout at the far end."

Ellgate laughed loud; then Christopher discharged the missile, his companion imparted a wild dash for the table and Christopher followed close to his friends heels. "I didn't think you had it in you," Ellgate sang out as Christopher slid his legs under the table. "I bet he didn't know what hit him. I saw it all; it was a direct hit. He jumped a mile in the air!"

"I guess it was poor sport to do it," Christopher managed to announce between chokes of laughter, "especially when I don't think it was he who hit you." And with a snicker he added: "But it was fun though!"

"Pshaw!" Ellgate ejected waving a hand to pass the incident off. "But it was darn good that it got him . . . I thought for sure the thing was headin' for Lilly's window. It would have been our tails, then. Lilly's strict on window breakin'."

"You bet I'm strict on window breaking or anything else that breaks around here, Master Ellgate," Lilly said stepping out of the crowd, and as if out of nowhere appeared at their table and startled Ellgate.

"Oh, Lil! where'd you come from . . . thought I just saw you in the kitchen?"

"Can't a body come out of her slave house," she chimed placing her little fat hands on her hips.

"This is a new boy, Lilly, Chris Wensdy."

Lilly nodded her head; "Please to make your acquaintance, Master Wensdy, but it's a sin you have to get mixed up with this black hearted devil," she said with a wink of her blue eye, then she gave Ellgate a love tap on the head with the handle of her wooden spoon. "That's a good arm you got there Master Wensdy. Oh! yes, I saw you hurl that wad of paper . . . Perhaps you'll go out for the nine come spring, eh?"

Christopher smiled. "Maybe, ma'am."

"Ah! he's a handsome shy devil," rejoined Lilly shaking her hand through Christopher's dark hair, "isn't he Master Ellgate?"

"I suppose if you say so."

"Well, what are you boys goin' to feast on? You know I always give every new boy that comes to my sweet house a free helpin' of sweets for a whole week. "She waved her head toward Ellgate,

"Maybe that's why this devil was so quick in bringin' you in here, eh?"

"Aw Lilly!" cried Ellgate blushing to the very roots of his yellow hair, "you oughtn't said that."

"Now quick, lads make up your minds what you want. You know I ain't got time servin' you fellows. Just popped out to meet the new boy here."

Presently they told Lilly what they wanted, and while the boys waited for their refreshments they chattered merrily. Then suddenly from behind a set of closed double doors, there was issued a torrent of shouts! jeers and wild laughter which was soon followed by the sound of over turned table and chairs crashing to the floor! Then came a screaming avalanche of crumbling china and glass ware.

"Hey! what's the rumpus?" cried Ellgate to Christopher. "It seems to be coming from the other dining room; jump atop the table, Wen, we'll see the whole show!"

The racket, which fled from behind the closed doors, was so great that it over shadowed the din in the section that now housed the boys, and even the noise around them had already reached full pitch. Fight! Fight! Echoed and re-echoed above the clangor. Immediately Lilly ceased whatever she was engaged in and stormed out of the kitchen. Her over stuffed form weaved in and out of the boys and of those who didn't get out of her path fast enough she'd give them a few licks of her wooden spoon. She had just arrived within a yard or so of the closed doors when suddenly they flung open before her face. Two robust fellows held a rather heavily set youth between them. His coat was practically torn to shreds and he was kicking and cursing furiously. They gave their victim a thrust and sent him sprawling to the floor; his head struck with some force against the toe of Lilly's shoe.

Lilly, plump and great in strength, bent over and pulled the fellow by his collar and up to his feet. While she dragged the woebegone student to a standing position, she released a stream of hot angry words at the innocent fellows who were standing in the open recess and puffing for breath; for it was they who put an end to the commotion. "Now, Martin explain yourself and explain fast!

You know I don't allow fightin' in my place." As Lilly spoke Martin's eyes were trained on the wooden spoon flying beneath his nose.

"It wasn't, it wasn't us Lilly," faltered the young man Martin, a college student and one in good standing with Lilly. "You know yourself, Lilly that it was you who spoke to Father Mitchell and made us obey your rules that the other student cannot dine with the college men on account of the homebrew."

"Yes, yes, but that don't explain the trouble—go on, or I'll clop you with m'spoon! Speak up."

"Well, ask Masky," came the clip reply, "he started it!"

Lilly still had a grip on the boy's collar and she gave him a vigorous shake at the said point, almost choking the breath out of him. "Well, lad? Speak." Masky remained tight lipped, but he soon cried aloud in pain when the spoon came down on his shoulder.

From behind one of the younger students, who was standing on top of the table cupped his hands and shouted: "That's the girl Lilly, give him the works!"

Lilly swung around. Her grave expression literally petrified the boys and not one would dare to antagonize her when she was truly angry. "Git off m'tables!" she cried, "the lot of you, and right now!" The boys pretended to carry out her command, but no sooner had she turned her back when they returned to their former perch atop the tables, witnessing the dispute with gusto. "Well, Martin?" demanded Lilly with some amount of anticipation in her tone.

"We had nothing to do with it, Lilly," he replied, then motioned to another young man. "It was Richards and I, who put an end to the fight. Get Masky to talk, he'll tell you what you want to learn."

"I'll tell you the whole story, Lilly," came the heated voice of another student, who possessed a bloody nose and being shackled between two young men, who appeared more disrumpled than Martin and Richards. "I'll tell you what you want to know," he reiterated in termination, "and I don't care if you report me to Father Mitchell for it, either!"

"Here! here! unhand that lad," she cried releasing Masky, and approaching the student. "Someone run to the kitchen and bring back a bit of ice in a rag so's I kin put it on this poor lad's nose." Lilly was deeply moved at the sight of the boy's bloody nose and her anger grew all the more to think that any of her boys, as she affectionately called them, should be so injured under her roof. "If I told you once," she went on to say, "I told you a hundred times—No fightin' in my place! Keep your fights at St. Thomas'. Next time I'll report the whole lot to Father Mitchell." It was always the *next time* with Lilly. "And don't think I won't," she added as a threat. "Remember, I know every one of you by face and name." Just at that moment a boy came running up to her with some ice wrapped in a napkin. "Ah! that was quick Williams, thank you. Give me the ice. Now go help yourself to some puddin'. Now you," she told the bloody nose chap, "sit down in this here chair, and lean back your head. Hold this ice rag to your nose, and tell Lilly just what happened. No, hold it this way," she corrected, "so as to stop the flow."

"Well, you see Lilly, you know that Masky won't pass onto the college until after the half, so he's not allowed in our dining room on account of Father Mitchell doesn't want the high school drinking the brew—"

"Yes, O'Niell—hold the ice on your nose in the right way, or I'll hit you myself."

"It's cold . . . Well, I was drinking my brew, minding my own business—it's kinda hard to talk with my head back . . ."

"O'Niell!"

"Alright," whimpered the boy. "Well, he starts with me for no reason at all. He always sneaks into our dining room so he can drink the brew. First he told me he didn't have any money, and would I lend him some to buy brew. I told him, I was flat; why doesn't he ask you to put it on the 'short change', but he replied: 'Lilly wouldn't do that', you know on account of him belonging to the high. Anyhow, I gave him mine, and asked you to put another bottle on the 'change' for me. I really didn't want to do this, because he had been drinking on the other fellows and already had enough. After a time he wanted more and I refused him. It was then that he started to get mean, and make all sorts of remarks. Finally I said: 'I think you had enough Masky, you know that you're out of bounds. Lilly will get into trouble if the dean finds out you are here' . . . And then he answered: 'I don't care if she does.' Then the first thing you know, he sends a flying fist to my face! I wasn't going to take that, not from a bully such as Masky—so we fought! Believe me, Lilly, that's the truth. I swear it."

"I believe you O'Niell. I think this is the first time I had trouble with you in my place . . . Why, I knew you since a little thing. But I'll deal with this Mister Masky, this ain't the first time I had trouble with that one." She raised her voice, "Somebody bring Masky to me!

The boys looked around, then someone nearby answered: "Why, he's gone Lilly. I guess he sneaked out!"

6

A sick greyish glare filtered through the windows and a slow monotonous rain was sliding down the glass when Christopher awoke from a heavy night's sleep; directly across the way Ellgate was sleeping on his stomach and his head was under the pillow. Christopher leaned back on his bed and rested his eyes on the ceiling, then his eyes began to inspect the room. There was a double locker which towered from floor to ceiling; before the window rested a large writing table and in the corner of the room were some bookshelves, except for one religious picture, the walls were bare.

Before Christopher slipped out of bed, he crossed himself and said his morning prayers, then glancing at the small clock which rested on the night table between the beds, he saw that he had yet fully an hour before the morning bell, so he decided to uncrate his precious books and line them upon the shelf. He moved about the room very cautiously as not to disturb his sleeping roommate; when he had completed arranging his books and hanging his clothes in his side of the locker, he went out of the room and walked down the hall to the wash room.

The lavatory was completely deserted, except for one small boy who was much younger than Christopher; evidently he startled the boy when he came through the door for the lad fairly shrunk within himself when he saw Christopher. Endeavoring to be propitious in his approach he bad the little fellow good morning, for he was eager to make friendship with all the boys. True he usually possessed a somewhat husky voice, but now being fresh from sleep his tones were amplified and the youth fairly quaked in his boots. Seeing the boy's perturbed behavior, he inquired what was troubling him.

"Nothing sir," the boy lightly replied avoiding Christopher's eyes. "I hope you'll understand, sir, that it isn't quite eight o'clock yet and I really didn't mean to linger in the wash room so long."

"What are you talking about?" inquired a baffled Christopher, "and why do you address me as *sir*?"

"Aren't you Masky?"

"No. Why do you ask?"

"My roommate and I have just moved in at Warwyck Dorm," the boy went on to explain, "so you see I've never seen Masky, that's why I thought you were he."

"Is that any reason to look like a scared rabbit?" said Christopher splashing cold water on his face.

"Oh, yes; you see, Masky is the senior in charge of this floor and he has made it a rule that no greenies are to be in the wash room after eight o'clock. He wants the wash free for himself. Why just before we left for the holidays he caught my roommate here and for not obeying his rules he twisted his arm severely. Even at that he didn't allow him to leave until he fell on his knees and say a prayer before him. Oh!" the boy cried sucking in his breath and turning almost white.

"What now?"

"I guess I babbled too freely—you might be his friend. I'll catch it now!"

Christopher laughed as he reached for his towel and his thoughts returned to last evenings episode at Lilly's. "No, I am not his friend and you needn't fear that I'll betray you." The boy seemed relieved. "If Masky insists on bullying you younger fellows, why don't you turn him in to Brother Angus, I'm sure he'd put a stop to it."

"I couldn't do that," admitted the boy, "it would be tattling."

"I guess you're right," spoke Christopher and he felt sorry for the boy wishing that he could help him. "But if I were you," he continued, "I'd have it out with him. Perhaps this isn't good advice, but since you won't report him, and I admire you for it—well, I'm sure he can't lick the both of you together. Have it out with him." he repeated.

"Would you really do that?"

"Sure, if he continued to bully me, I would. Show him you're not afraid and he'll leave you alone."

Soon the boy departed feeling that he had a friend in Christopher.

"Ah, here you are Wensdy!" cried Ellgate ambling into the wash room, his slippers clopping over the tile. His yellow hair seemed like a windblown haystack and his pajamas seemed more off his person than on. "Didn't expect to see you up before me. I see they're beginning to stick the greenies in our dorm. One of the little cusses almost knocked me down."

"A little fellow with red hair?"

"Yeah, he looked like a scared jack."

"No doubt he thought you were Masky too; I was just speaking with him."

"Has Masky been bullying the greenies? I told you he was nothing but a prig. The dirty dog once tried to give me trouble, but I got him told good and proper. If he's not trying to cause trouble for somebody, he's whispering dirty jokes in your ear. Last spring Father threatened to suspend him. He and his crowd used to sit on the seminary wall and sing lewd songs that were of great offense to the seminarist. I tell you Wen, he's a trouble maker, stay clear of him. Oh, blast it! there goes the last bell, we better get a move on, or we'll be late for breakfast."

The boys returned to their room and started to dress when a knock came at the door. A student curved his head and shoulders about the edge of the door and delivered a message that Brother Angus wanted to see Christopher in his study.

"No need to look so alarmed ol' friend," said Ellgate noticing Christopher's distress. "Perhaps he only wants to welcome you; I'm sure you haven't broken any rules so far. It's probably nothing," he said. "Go along and I'll wait for you by the dining hall."

Christopher applied a light knock to the study door. No one answered. He waited awhile, then entered stiff and tense. He glanced about before sitting down to wait, and soon fell into comparing the study with that of the Reverend Mother's. At first he could notice very little difference between them; a similar oak desk, leather furniture and a religious picture or two. "Yes, much was the same," he told himself, "and yet, there was something strangely different, but what?" Presently the thought came to him that there wasn't any Mother Eugenia to greet him this morning, and he wondered, could it only have been yesterday that he spoke with her for the last time . . . How long ago it all seemed now. He observed the window of Brother Angus' study, it afforded no view of the grounds—that was what he missed; all he could see from this window were the ugly branches of some sleeping oak. No, he thought, this study is not at all like the one he knew . . . Angus' study was nothing but a square box. Suddenly he had a fit of nostalgia for the priory grounds, then in another wild moment he wished that he could remember who he truly was, feeling that somewhere in the world he might have brothers and sisters, and this was the first time that he felt truly lost. He wanted to cry, but dared not grow so weak!

A photograph of a group of young men rested on the mantle shelf. The picture caught the boy's fancy and for the moment he escaped himself by examining the photograph, and thought that one of the men must be Brother Angus, and assumed that the stout chap near the center must be the house master, but presently when the man entered the study, Christopher learned that his assumptions were quite wrong. Brother Angus turned out to be a tall gentleman in his prime, comparatively handsome, with his dark hair streaked with slender wisps of grey.

"Good morning, Master Wensdy."

Christopher rose to attention: "Morning sir."

"So you're Mother Eugenia's prodigé," crooned Brother Angus in a friendly mellow tone.

It was a strange and pleasant experience for both Christopher and Brother Angus to look upon each other for it seemed as though life itself was holding a mirror to the pair, and though there hadn't been a thread of kinsmanship between them, their strong resemblance was uncanny. Except for Brother Angus' friendly dark eyes, Christopher was strangely enough viewing a reflection of himself twenty years hence, and in the obverse the man saw himself once more a boy.

Brother Angus shook Christopher's hand and immediately there was a quick admiration between them. "Let me welcome you to St. Thomas'," said the house master. "I hope you will feel at home here and that you will look upon me as your counselor, for as house master it is my duty to look after your needs and help you to adjust your problems, and I want you to feel free to come to me at all times. Is that understandable, Christopher?"

Christopher nodded his head.

"I trust you fully appreciate what the Reverend Mother is doing for you, son, and will use your time wisely and well while you are here. Remember she expects you to be a conscientious student."

The house master soon noticed that the boy appeared to be spent and a look of torment crept into his blue eyes. Christopher sat on the edge of his chair, his lower lip was quivering. My secret is out! he thought. The house master knows I have no memory.

"Christopher, look at me son," said Brother Angus firmly, and yet with enough compassion in his voice as not to alarm the boy further. "Yes," he murmured as if he had read Christopher's thoughts; "I know about your memory. Mother Eugenia deemed it wise that I should know, and this she did in order for me to understand you to the fullest. Hiding the malady within your heart will not help make you well, Christopher . . . But you needn't fear," he said softly, "your secret is safe with me and no one shall learn it from my lips. This I promise you. Not even Father Mitchell knows—as far as he's concerned, you're just another student at St. Thomas'." He laid a hand on the boy's shoulder and squeezed it firmly. "Trust me Christopher Wensdy," he told him, "I want to be your friend."

Christopher looked up into the man's face, a deep flow of something spirit like seemed to well from his being. Perhaps my father might be something like him, he thought. Unknowingly he prayed; profoundly wishing that he could remember. He turned his eyes from the house master, and for a time gazed fixedly on the little blue and orange flames dancing gaily over the coals in the grate. Christopher felt strongly indebted to Brother Angus and he desired to express his appreciations to the man who befriended him.

After a time the brother approached him, saying: "I trust you are getting on well with your room mate?"

"Yes, sir," Christopher rejoined and he made an attempt to smile.

"Now that's what I like," the man answered with that bit of music in his voice which always won him the admiration of the boys. "Smile . . . You'll find it remedies all ills. Man is the only animal that laughs, my dear Christopher; remember that as you get on in years." Brother Angus brushed a finger beneath his nose to try and cover his grin when he said: "I hope you did not put in too much time at the library last evening . . . Virgil is overwhelmingly interesting, but it's not good for growing boys to spend too much time indoors—especially on books."

Christopher found something he could laugh at. "No, sir we didn't."

"Oh, I'm very glad to hear it . . . Master Ellgate is such a book worm that sometimes I fret for him. He might impair his vision. and one more thing," said Brother Angus feeling in a mood for humor, "I wish to warn you and hope you do not take offense in what I say; but I must implore you not to use any harsh language in the boy's presence. He's rather sensitive to that sort of thing, do you understand me?"

"Yes, sir, quite well," replied Christopher and he permitted himself to laugh.

"Good! and now that we have an understanding between ourselves . . . and Master Ellgate, I shan't keep you from breakfast any longer. Good morning, Christopher."

"Good morning, sir."

"Oh, incidentally," the house master cried as Christopher reached for the door knob. "Is this yours?" he asked fetching the boy's coat from the closet. "It has your name in it."

Christopher saw his coat and grew stiff. This was actually the first thought he gave to the garment since Ellgate told him he placed it beneath the pew in the chapel.

"It's quite fortunate for you that I chanced to stop at chapel last evening. If Father Mitchell had discovered it there, you might be on the carpet this morning."

"I'm sorry sir, but I just forgot that it was there. I really did mean to pick it up later, but it was really quite late when we came back from Lil—"

"*Lilly's*," said he completing the name. "I know, I saw you and Ellgate there when I visited the sweet shop earlier. Well, I'll excuse it this once, but mind that it doesn't happen again. And since we are discussing Lilly's place, do you know anything of the disturbance which occurred there last evening?"

"Nothing 'cept that there was a fight."

"Well, no matter," the house master shrugged his shoulders. "I just thought I'd inquire . . . Now run along to breakfast and take good care of that arm. Oh, yes, when I departed by the side entrance, I saw you hurl that paper ball. Maybe you'll try for the team this spring?"

The rain had ceased, and the sun endeavored to move out of the path of a grey cloud as Christopher started for the dining hall.

"Well, what the blazing fires kept you so long?" inquired Ellgate, who seemed very impatient at having to wait for Christopher so long. He urged a friend, who had been waiting for him, to tag along with them. "No doubt the old man had to preach the scripture 'fore he let you off. What did he want anyway?"

"Nothing much, but if you'll remember we never did go back to get my coat from the chapel."

"Blast the luck! I hope I didn't get you into any trouble, Wen?"

"No, he was very decent about it."

"I'm glad. *Mother Angus* usually is a good sport. Oh, say," he cried remembering his friend, "this is Charly Lock."

"Yes, I know him. Hi! Charly. Why do you call him *Mother Angus*?"

"I don't. Just made it up right then. Where do you know Lock, from?"

"We met at a Christmas party . . . Abigail Trent's house."

"Oh, I see."

"Watch out! look who I see coming up the walk," retorted Charly Lock with considerable distaste in his speech. "Quick let's scoot on the other side of this shrub. He's sure to ask a million questions 'bout why we're late for breakfast."

"Who is it?" inquired Christopher taking his place behind the shrubby.

"None other than the meanest blackguard in school," rejoined Ellgate peeping through the branches and sneering. "It's Brother Francis."

"What's he done?"

"Everything. Why, just before the holidays, when Schneider couldn't recite *Antony's speech*, he called him to the front of the whole class and took down his breeches to switch his neckid arse in view of everybody. He'd do that to any boy who won't jump through his hoop."

"Oh!" moaned Christopher as he sensed the full impact of the man's harsh character as he brushed past the hedge. "I hope we don't go to his class for anything."

"Don't worry, we do," spoke Charly and then he laughed at Christopher's distress. "Let's go to breakfast."

Some one hour or so later the boys were loitering in the streets of the town. They paused in front of the Fairlee Opera House, and read the billboard: STARRING TONIGHT—MISS ETHYL BARRYMOORE—IN MID CHANNEL—HER GREATEST TRIUMPH! Soon Abigail Trent passed before the opera house and she was quite surprised to see the boys. She had also read the bulletin, and went into all sorts of theatrical exaltations, and she was certain to impress on the boys, that she too had hoped to be a great lady of the theatre. The boys spoke to her for a little while, but they soon contrived an excuse to depart, for they could no longer endure the girls dramatic fever, and they left her standing before the play house to muse on her future career.

Once when they had ambled down a side street near the far end of the town, Charly Lock snickered, and digging his elbow into Ellgate's ribs whispered: "Didn't know we were in this neighborhood . . ." There was a devilish leer in his eyes as he motioned his head toward the opposite side of the street. "But I reckon you did. I guess you just wanted to pass the place, well, me too for that matter." He laughed, "Say you'd better let Wensdy in on it, he looks kinda puzzled."

Christopher lent an ear to Ellgate's whispering lips; it required only a few select words, and no more—He was quick to comprehend. "And that pair leaving the place now," said Christopher, "isn't that Martin and Richards, the college men I saw at Lilly's last evening?"

"Sure is, and it looks like the devils want to get away without being seen—picture that will you, ha! ha! I guess that's one thing Lilly ain't got for sale. I suppose we'll be going there when we're a little older.

The boys began to laugh quite loud and carefree, and the young men who had just departed from the place in question turned to each other somewhat red faced and embarrassed. They did not brave to turn around and reprove the students for fear that the heckling would grow worse. Instead, they quickened their pace and walked briskly away; but how were they to know that the boys were amused by something of their own making. The guilty . . . are so guilty.

7

The bleakness from January to March dwindled away and in April the eternal blush of spring returned to the frozen earth in all its green magnificence! It seemed rather strange for Christopher to imagine that he had been enrolled at St. Thomas' for so long. Each day earned him new friends and adventure; moreover, he always managed to be the first in his studies and at play. By June he had learned to box and take active part in all sports; at baseball, he was always voted a must at every game. He was hailed champion of the school!

Although Christopher had won the admiration of all his school mates, he had little success in acquiring Masky's friendship. Not because he didn't try, but mainly because Masky was headstrong, adhering to no one's opinion or purpose, preferring to fraternize with a select, wild crew of his own choosing. He deeply resented Christopher for crowding him out of the limelight, so to speak, and once or twice during the semester the boys arrived at bitter opposition toward the other.

The day before St. Thomas' was to close its door for the summer, word fled through the school like wild fire that there was going to be a fight between Masky and Wensdy! Many of the boys who were on their way toward Lilly's suddenly turned back and sought the rear of the chapel, a most secure and out of the way place where the fights usually took place.

"What!" screamed Ellgate when the news reached him; "I must get there immediately. If only to back up my old friend. Hey you there!" he called to a grade student, "Just run over to Warwyck Dorm and tell the fellows there if they want to see Wensdy beat the *you know what* out of Masky, then tell 'em to head for the chapel. Besides, we may need them if Masky's crowd wants to start anything—and hurry or you might have me to answer to!" He then spat on the ground and cried at the height of his lungs: "*Hallelujah!*" With that he raced across the grounds like the speeding winds. In another minute he came tearing through the quadrangle, and arrived at the scene of action just as the combatants were beginning to strip away their shirts. Two of Masky's burly companions were on either side of him whispering directions in his ear.

Ellgate pushed his way through the crowd of boys and stepped into the ring. "Why don't you send a fellow a word" he said softly, stepping behind Christopher and helping him to pull his arms out of the shirt sleeves. "I was clear on the other side of the grounds when the news came."

"Ellgate!"

Both of the boys faces brightened in a warm grin. No words were necessary to express Christopher's gratitude and each sensed the mutual recognition of comradeship that crossed between them. Ellgate tied a clean white handkerchief around Christopher's fists, making certain that the knuckles were fairly well padded. "Don't worry about a thing, Wen," he told him assuredly. "I've already sent word to the fellows of our dorm in case Masky's crowd wants to get rough. And listen, don't open your mouth to say a word, or try to help yourself a bit . . . I'll direct you, remember, that's what I am here for. Just try to save all your strength and breath for Masky!"

Soon one of Masky's companions decided to elect himself as referee and stepped into the ring with Masky all stripped and thirsty for battle. Ellgate did the same, walking boldly up to the boy. "Are you the one who's going to referee this match?" he asked of the boy in distrustful tones while his eyes expressed his contempt for Masky as he took him in from the little roll of flesh about his middle to the plumpness of his shoulder.

The boy replied that he would wish contrary to Ellgate's wishes; he wanted Black Buck to handle the affair, but at the moment he was nowhere to be seen.

"Alright," continued Ellgate in his loveable boastful air; he jerked his blond head in a devil may care gesture, "What's the beginning signal—handkerchief or whistle?"

"I'll drop a handkerchief," the boy scowled in reply.

Ellgate shrugged his shoulders impishly, and before he stepped out of the ring, he whispered one more bit of precious advice into Christopher's ear.

Loud shouts arose from Masky's side of the ring for the bout to commence; by now both sides were fairly overwrought, agitated, impatient and eager for action. A hush prevailed over the thickening crowd of boys that was increasing by the moments. The rays of the hot June sun seemed to provoke their excitement; either side seemed vicious, ready to pick a quarrel anywhere. The boy dropped a dirty white handkerchief to the ground! The hot voices of the students leaped into the air with a shout of: HURRAH!

Christopher, pale and handsome, danced into the ring on a pair of long legs; his broad shoulders and small waist seemed to roll in perfect rhythm on slim hips. Although he was inches taller and more muscular than his opponent, compared to Masky's robust, stocky body, his slim lithe form seemed too light for the stoutly and strongly made arms and shoulders of a battering ram such as Masky.

The opponents came together, sparing for a moment or two without either setting in any positive blow. Then before Christopher could realize what struck him, Masky sent a hot fat fist to his loins; Christopher's head rolled back almost disjointedly; again Masky seized the opportunity and hurled another fist to Christopher's mouth! He lost his balance. The weight of his body set his feet into a backward shuffle and he fell back onto the crowd of boys. Just then Charly Lock, who had only arrived at the scene of commencement but moments before had by this time worked his way into the front of the crowd in time to break Christopher's fall with his own body. Somehow he managed to steady him and with a healthy thrust pushed him forward into the ring.

"Good work Charly!" shouted Ellgate making his way around to him. "Keep your head down Wen! Watch out! Now, now, clip him with your left!"

Christopher followed Ellgate's advice. He succeeded in getting in a blow but it wasn't a very good one, seeming to have no effect on Masky.

"What seems to be the matter with Wen, Ellgate?" whined Charly in disheartened tones. "He can't seem to get into the play. If only he had a little more weight; he seems so light against Masky."

"Don't worry, he'll pluck up!" He growled almost angrily at Charly. "Masky will tire soon, I know him. Besides he's soft and sports too much weight." He turned his eyes from Charly onto Christopher, precisely in time to shout his directions. "Keep to the right Wen—to the right! Now, duck!" he shouted and jigged about quite excitedly in his own little spot in front of the crowd. "Compare the bodies for yourself, Charly. Though Wen isn't so strong in the arms, he's good all over. Hard, straight and lively from neck to ankle, with a lot of spring in those legs of his. I tell you he's sure to walk away a champion! Besides, you can see the clear white of his eyes and the fresh look of his skin; while Masky is quite the opposite. Too much food and brew and no exercise. Yes, Masky is powerful, but that's all in looks. Keep away from him Wen," he implored. "Take it easy, take it easy! Now! come in for the blow . . . Ah! good boy." Ellgate laughed loud and easy like a mad man gloating over gold when he noticed Masky quake under Christopher's last powerful cuff to the jaw.

The sun was shining down furiously upon them; the bodies of either boy was glistening, all wet and shiny with sweat. Christopher's perspiring back reflected like polished bronze in the sunlight. His head was down with his chin to his chest, while his backbone seemed as an arrow bent for action!

Christopher moved closer to his opponent; his fists hammered against Masky's body in sudden violent striking. His arms trembled from the excitement, and for a time he grew tense; fearing that his strength might ebb away. However, when a thick cloud drank up the sun, it shaded him and a cooling breeze managed to drop into the midst of action, fanning and refreshing his hot thirsty body. The breeze also performed a refreshing job on Masky, for he returned to life fresh and full of fight. Christopher's hands were up now, trying to ward off any recurring motion that might chance to come in contact with his bloody mouth.

Masky, observing that his opponents body was free for attack, saw the opportunity to end the battle in his favor; then as fast as lightening he set in one, and then two fat fists into Christopher's loins! This time it appeared that the burly Masky would really be the victor; for the wind was truly out of Christopher and there was no Charly Lock in back to steady his staggering body.

"Finish him off!" screamed the boys of Masky's party.

Quick as the wind Ellgate jumped in back of Christopher. "Open your mouth! Suck in some air! Wake up!" he bellowed, quite furious at Masky's foul tactics.

Christopher forced the lids of his blue eyes upward; his friend's voice was ringing in his ears; his innards were burning hot, and his head seemed to be spinning sickly. Eager voices, with Ellgate's in the lead, encouraged and rallied him on to new fight; somehow his breath and strength sped back to him, and he returned to the center of the ring fighting mad.

He now fought more cautiously, getting more distance between them and parring his enemy's blows. Now he saw his opening and lead his opponent about the ring; striking him with minor blows, but mostly tiring Masky, for he appeared to be growing short of breath. Then the moment came; Masky dropped his guard, and with direct lunging blows he caught him one, two, then three strikes on the chin! Masky's knees buckled beneath him, then with another stiff, sharp right hander Christopher deposited Masky quite neatly on the grass. With panting breath he hovered over the sweating fellow sleeping at his feet.

For a time Christopher remained there too winded to move a muscle, and at any moment he himself was apt to collapse to the cooling green for rest. But then at that moment Ellgate came to his side, wrapped an arm about Christopher's waist, and threw one limp arm over his own shoulder, then walked him away.

Great cheers intermingled with resentment seemed to radiate from the crowds; some praising and others decrying the triumph of the victor! But at the time it all mattered naught to Christopher and the happy din simply drummed musically on his sleepy, tired ears . . .

8

"Would you mind telling a fellow just how it all started?" probed Ellgate in long draggly tones as he administered a fresh applicator to the swollen lips of the victor.

Sprawled on his back, Christopher gazed steadily at the pattern of black shadows stretching diagonally across the ceiling. He was reluctant to answer and closed his eyes on the question, relaxing his muscles and sinking deeper into the springy comfort of the bed.

"You sure put up a good fight, Wen," continued Ellgate lighting on the more amiable side of the past; for although Christopher had been victorious in his plight, he appeared to be low in spirits. "I was proud of you," he remarked searching for a change of expression in his friends' face. "I guess you really did everyone a good turn. I know it did my heart good to see Masky get what he deserved." Then he laughed in his free generous way, "Why, I bet old Masky is still snoozing it off there on the quadrangle green."

Christopher jerked the application from his lips and squirmed on the bed in a convulsion of hearty laughter. He laughed so hard that tears sprang into his eyes; however, no matter how easily he laughed, the expression on his face wasn't one of mirth. Each uproarious peal brought pain to his battered lips. "It isn't very sporting of you to do this to me, Ellgate," moaned Christopher, finally suppressing his laughter. "It hurts me to move my mouth . . . Tell me, has any of the swelling gone down?"

"No—well, not so much as you can notice. I'm glad you're feeling better otherwise . . . I should think you'd want to celebrate after lickin' Masky that way. Maybe if you'd tell a fellow what's on your mind he might be able to help you cheer up."

"Aw, it's really nothing," he groaned. "I suppose I'm behaving like a dunderhead . . . perhaps it's what Masky said—anyway that's what started it if you want to know. I had been looking all over for you and couldn't discover your whereabouts, then I happened to meet little Lenny, the greenie from our dorm; he told me he overheard you mention that you might be going over to Lilly's. Well, at the time I was crossing the grounds for Robin's Path. I saw Masky and his friends lying on the green. At first, I started to circle the college building to avoid him, but that way was too long and I wasn't looking for trouble so I could see no harm in going past them. When I did, Masky turned to one of the Carlton twins and said loud enough for me to hear: 'where the hell does this mindless idiot thinks he's going!'; then he laughed in a kinda dirty way, cursing me and my character with the lowest words I have ever heard! I couldn't take that from Masky, Ellgate." He flushed and lowered his eyes, saying: "You know why."

Ellgate realized that Christopher was referring to his memory and it caused him some amount of worry because he believed Christopher had forgotten about his trouble; for they had not spoken of it ever since that night long ago in early winter when Christopher awoke from a frightening dream. There in the dark of their room he poured out the troubles of his heart to his friend, and felt all the better for doing so. All the pain had seemed to pass away ever since then, but now he fretted for fear the old storm would brew snow.

"Aw! Wen, you're a blockhead!" bleated Ellgate. "That slimy blackguard, Masky doesn't know a thing about you. He was only showing off before his rowdy friends. Anyway, I thought you were all through with that business—besides, this is no way to spend our last day. Tomorrow I start for home and I'll not see you until September. I've got a good idea!" he beamed. "Let's celebrate after that beating we gave Masky—Let's go over to Lilly's and order the works!"

"Dear, dear," muttered Brother Angus in plaguing tones as he halted the boys at the foot of the stairs. "where can these two handsome bucks be going at this devil may care speed? I trust the building is not on fire!"

"No sir. No," Ellgate tensely rejoined, feeling quite certain that Brother Angus had gotten wind of the fight by now. "We're just stepping out for a bit of fresh air."

"My, my, Ellgate . . . clean shirt, scrubbed face, combed hair— you also, Master Wensdy? This must be a special occasion?"

"N-no, sir" said Christopher trembling in his boots; he could almost hear Brother Angus saying: 'Return to your room and start copying the Constitution of the United States.' "*What Luck*!", he murmured beneath his breath.

"Christopher Wensdy, what on earth's the matter with your lip?"

"Fever blisters, sir," intercepted Ellgate in a shaky voice.

"Is it your lip?"

"No, sir."

"Then thank you and shut up." He turned to Christopher, and amused himself at the boy's expense. "Is it really fever blisters?"

Christopher swallowed hard. "Yes, sir."

The house master lifted his shoulders pretending to take the boys at their word. "Oh, well," he yawned. "I'll not delay you further, but if I were you gentlemen, I wouldn't dare step outdoors . . . They tell me it's devilishly hot without and that most any one is apt to drop out owing to this intense heat." Brother Angus endeavored to quell the laughter boiling within him. His hand screened a grin as he said: "I myself had planned to stroll over to Lilly's for some refreshments—I understand that's she's made some delicious ice-cream for this very warm day. But now that I see those fever blisters tormenting your poor lip, no count brought on by this intense heat, I don't dare venture out of this building. Don't you agree?"

"Yes, sir!" the boys expelled in one voice, not realizing what they were agreeing to.

Again the house master had trouble in hiding his laughter. "Why, only some half hour ago, Black Luck stormed into my study requesting me to fetch a bottle of smelling salts from the dispensary. He told me John Masky fainted right on the green from this intense weather . . . Can you imagine a robust fellow such as he fainting?" He pursed his lips. "Imagine fainting!" he repeated in a tone of pretended awe. "And minus his shirt at that!"

Possibly if Ellgate and Christopher hadn't worn such woebegone expression, Brother Angus might have mastered his emotions, but as the situation remained, he grew too weak and gave vent to his desires. He had all he could manage to control his quaking frame, otherwise he would have doubled up in laughter.

In the early morning Christopher saw Ellgate off on the train; he stood in the grey drizzle and waved farewell to his friend with a laden heart. The light monotonous misty rain sprayed upon his face as he lingered beside the tracks waving to Ellgate on the rear platform until he seemed nothing but a small speck in the grey wet distance. It seemed to Christopher as if his first day from St. Thomas' would be as boring as the summer weather. Even when he returned to the caretaker's cottage he found disappointment; Mrs. Tergauer had departed for West Fairlee that same morning to visit her sister who was readying herself for the birth of her first child. And even on this of all days, he didn't get chance to see the Reverend Mother for she was busy at task and could not see him.

He whiled away the day by trying to read but this too seemed to offer little escape. He knew now what it was to have a memory and it was causing him pain. He was lonely. The following morning, after breakfast he saddled one of the horses and went for an easy gallop around Lake Morey, and as he came around the shore close to the picnic grounds he sighted Abigail seated in the grass by the water's edge. The thunder of the horse's hooves startled her from her muse and she sprang to her feet. Christopher halted and slid out of the saddle; after a time they fell into conversation.

"What are you doing so far out alone?" probed Christopher permitting the thirsty animal to drink.

"I felt so lost this morning that I just started to walk and didn't stop until I discovered myself here."

"Where are the girls?"

"They've taken up summer classes this year."

"Yes," he told her feeling his own loneliness, "it is a sad feeling to be without friends."

"We'll always be friends won't we, Chris!"

"Always . . ." he leaned against the side of the horse and thrust his fists into the pockets of his jeans; "Remember once you asked me what I was going to be when I grew up?"

"Yes."

"Well, I've decided. I am going to be a priest."

"Chris!"

"What's the matter with that?"

"Nothing. I think it's wonderful, at least it's a career, and that's what I want most out of life, is a career. I just couldn't bear to be just another everyday human being. I want something great!" Abigail turned her eyes away from him. "But I guess now that you're going to be a priest, you'll probably hate me because I've told a lie. I really didn't mean to do so, but it all happened so quick."

Christopher was puzzled. "What are you talking about?"

The girl turned crimson and began to stammer her explanation. "The other day, John Masky was in town, and I was on my way to read the bill board in front of the opera house. When I reached there, I discovered him in the arcade. I ignored him, because I know what sort of boy he is—Well, before I know it, he crept behind me and whispered some ugly words in my ear; "Abigail's soft features suddenly turned grim. "I turned around and slapped his ugly face! He got mean then and told me worse things . . . that's when I told a lie, Chris! I told him if he didn't stop it, I was going to tell my boyfriend. Then, when I said that—he wanted to know who—the only name I could think of at the time was yours."

Suddenly Christopher broke out into a fit of wild happy laughter. "So that's why the dirty pig picked on me!"

"What do you mean?"

"Don't worry Abby, I don't think he'll bother you again. I licked him!" he admitted in a proud laugh. "Can't you see my lip?"

The girl's face brightened into a broad smile. "Then, you really don't mind?" She saw his laughing eyes and understood the answer.

"But understand that I don't want a boyfriend," she continued. "I have to have my career first."

Christopher climbed up into the saddle and when he glanced down on Abigail's face he observed that there were tears in her eyes. He questioned the trouble.

"I'm glad you licked him!" she rejoined with a sob. "He said some awful things to me . . . It's hard for a girl to grow up."

Christopher wasn't quite certain just how to interpret the meaning. He was flooded with a warm tense feeling of life! He reached out his hand for her and pulled her up into the saddle beside him; he saw her small undeveloped breast spring beneath her dress. Christopher had offered to ride her into Fairlee, but in one vibrant moment she agreed to ride off into the woods with him.

The following morning Emily Tergauer returned from her little journey; she announced at the breakfast table that her sister, Marie had given birth to a five pound baby girl, she babbled to her husband for some length of time about the event, then made some pampering excuse to Christopher about not being at home to welcome back her boy. Latter she promised him that she would make a strawberry short cake with the berries she had brought back from the country. Christopher thanked her in a light off handed tone, but his mind was not on eating cake. He missed school and Ellgate more than ever this morning; moreover, he hadn't seen the Reverend Mother yet.

"Oh, Gussie," Mrs. Tergauer continued between mouthfuls of coffee, "there's somethin' I ain't told you. Amy Schwartz's niece, Louise is going to marry that Mall boy." She turned to Christopher, "You remember Abigail Trent and her sister Louise, don't you, Chris?" Then without waiting for a reply from the boy she continued to mumble to herself, uttering in absent tones, "I guess I'll be fixin' that blue dress of mine over . . ."

"Isn't Larry Mall the handsomest thing you ever saw?" murmured Ruth Celine turning her eyes upon the newlyweds who stood amid a crowd of middle aged people who were endeavoring to offer their congratulations simultaneously. "I think he's an adorable green— Louise must be the happiest girl in the world."

"Oh, Ruth, look at Abby; you're making her blush," Mary said plaguing the girl who stood between them. "Why, I don't believe Abby's still proud at having Larry for a brother."

"Oh! stop your nonsense," scoffed the girl in defense. "I am proud of Larry. I think he's quite good looking."

"Do you think he's as good looking as Christopher?"

Abigail stomped an indignant foot and turned her back on her companions. "Some girls wish only to grow up and marry," she spurned in a lofty stage voice," but that's because they have no artistic fire in their souls. I turn my back on such and dream of the day when I'll be famous, while you Mary and Ruth will remain in Fairlee to marry some dull boy. But not me! I shall go on to a greater life; marriage is not for great women, it dulls their sheen. You'll regret the things you do to me . . . someday I'll return to Fairlee a great actress, like Paula Fransworth, you'll see!"

Mary and Ruth exchanged astonished glances and then burst into a loud hollow laugh.

Christopher, who was standing at the far corner of the room, assumed that the girls were laughing at Abigail for another one of her word slanders and was moved that they should taunt her so. He looked at Abigail and thought she seemed quite comely in her yellow gown and the little bouquet of pink roses which she carried in her small hands. They matched admirably with the opulent blush of her cheeks. Once, when their eyes met Christopher colored to the roots of his dark hair, he grew so embarrassed for he didn't want Abigail to know he was watching her way.

"Hey, Wen!" a summoning voice called from behind. Christopher whirled about in a quick little spin; the voice possessed a casual spark in it very much like Ellgate's, but it was only wishful thinking on his part for when he turned about it was Charly Lock. "Come on," he urged. "Let's walk around and see what's going on."

Moments later the boys discovered themselves at the rear of the house. They were squatted on a little patch of lawn, fraternizing with a group of boys who were two to three years their senior. The boys were strangers to Christopher and even Charly admitted that he had never laid eyes on them until now, but supposed that they must have arrived from West Fairlee with some of the wedding guests. One of the boys, who was rather thin possessed a shock of blazing red hair and a great abundance of golden freckles, opened the front of his shirt and cozed forth a small brown flask of whisky, while another of his companions displayed a fistful of hand rolled cigarettes.

"Hey Slim, who's this clodpole?" asked the one with fire hair to one of his associates and the tone of his voice reminded one of Ellgate, but there was utterly no comparison between the two. "Do you think it's safe to bring the stuff out before them?" he muttered in quiet tones.

"Aw! it can't do no harm, and besides it's too late now," he replied then laughed in a somewhat foolish lilt. "I reckon we'll have our own li'le party." He opened the flask, "You take the first swig quick like and pass it 'round. I'm animous for my share."

Christopher and Charley exchanged troubled glances; neither of the boys had ever tasted raw whisky before, at least not directly from the flask, and it appeared that smoking would be in the balance. It didn't take them long to realize that they had sat in with a tough lot; what's more the flask was rapidly rolling their way. However, they were quick to comprehend that a withdrawal at this time would prove fatal and decided to sit there and take their medicine without a whimper. Again Charly looked at Christopher and hoped that he would give some sign of departure, but he gave Charly an eye to indicate that he knew what was best for them. He wouldn't move even if he might chance to scent the aroma on his breath, to say nothing of the tobacco that was to follow.

Finally it was Christopher's turn to take the flask. He brought it to his lips; when he did, the boy who sat beside him gave it a higher tilt and more than Christopher had intended to consume spilt down his throat. The liquid didn't stop burning until it scorched his lungs, smoldering ever downward until it suddenly reused another little fire in the pit of his belly. Never in his entire life could he recall tasting anything more vile! His eyes were burned and running water when he passed the thing over to Charly.

Suddenly there came a burst of cheers from the front of the house. One of the boys was startled by the outcry and questioned the one named Red, who appeared to be the leader of the group. "Be calm you stupid rabbit!" he answered with a tongue which seemed to be growing heavy. "It's only the bride throwing her flowers away. They do it at all weddings."

"And that ain't all," put in another fellow laughing in a low uncouth voice.

"Ah, catch what you mean," rejoined Slim in a voice that had now become sensual with too much drink. Then he inhaled deeply on a wet cigarette and whispered into his friend's ear.

Red laughed loud and coarse taking another mouthful of the whisky. As for Christopher he had become too sick to take any part in the wile discussion. The flask had come his way for a third time and now someone was urging him to take a long draw on a cigarette.

"Get a wink of this little one!" bellowed Red, nudging Slim in the ribs with his elbow. He swayed his red head to the left of him toward a pale face boy who was considerably their junior. The boy was too startled to move. No one noticed him sit in with them and it seemed as though his ears were burning at such gathered information.

"He looks as though he didn't know they did it," Slim giggled tormenting the little fellow. "well, I would do it," he snickered again. "But I'm scared my paw'll take a strap to my tail if he found out." He nudged Red and together they laughed. "We sure would, eh!"

Just then an old man appeared on the scene looking more like a derelict than a wedding guest. He passed by the boys with a step that seemed more like a stagger than a walk; by the glassy appearance of his eye it was quite obvious that the man was drunk. The boys sprang to their feet when they observed him; however, he quelled the startled group by saying "Don't mind me boys it ain't none of my business." Then he walked away disappearing behind a clump of shrubbery; he returned in a few seconds buttoning the fly of his pants. He approached them again and laughed in a high cracked voice: "You youngsters are sure wearing hot breeches alright. I guess there's no doubt 'bout it, you're sure ready to walk the road of life. I know 'cause I've been listin' to you all the while" Then he slapped his skinny thigh. "Now if you boys want to hear some real good jokes, gather 'round me."

Eagerly the boys crept nearer the old man; but as for Christopher he climbed to his feet and departed in a hurry. Something in his stomach wanted to be released and right now! Before he could reach his destination something told him he would be very sick.

PART TWO

1

It was a bright Spring Sunday in May as Christopher walked along the road to St. Ann's priory.

The happy years of school life have sped away, and Christopher, the man of twenty looked back upon them as a treasure. But his days at St. Thomas' were far from over because now he resumed a new life amid the very walls that fostered his boyhood. Possibly it was his past association with the Reverend Mother or Brother Angus, which directed his path to a devout life, but no matter what, he was contented with his vocation at St. Thomas' Seminary. The humble reverent living, and the robes of a seminarian ratified his way of life. He would soon be ordained. It seemed he was destined for an appointed life as a clergyman . . . Faith herself had preserved his life in order to bring him to the gates of the cloistered.

Christopher passed through the towering black gates and stepped briskly up to the massive oak door of the priory; he pulled vigorously at the bell knob, released it, and it immediately snapped into position. While he waited for the door to open he turned his eyes skyward . . . Bright blue were the heavens and hither and yon puffed pillowy white clouds. In the distant west a sweep of pink heavens dropped behind the cool shadowy dark of the forest. To the left of him a blue throated house wren flitted from branch to branch in a small yew tree, the gay winged creature chirped merrily in little clip staccato tones.

Christopher silently reproved himself for not having called on the Reverend Mother these many weeks; he felt a deep gratitude to the kindly woman and wished that there was some way in which he could repay her. After all, the money for his clothing and education derived from her family estate; she even endowed him with his very name. He almost forgot that. He trembled with emotion when he thought of what might have befallen him if it wasn't for the kindness of this chaste woman.

Presently the door rolled open on its huge, oiled hinges; Sister Theresa shyly curved her head and shoulders around its facing. Her small face flushed with surprise and she bade him to enter; her merry eyes twinkled with hospitality. "The Revered Mother will be overjoyed to see you," she told him. She imparted a curtsy and darted a few steps before him. "One moment," she whispered as they paused without the study door. She wrinkled her nose, "I'll just say, a gentleman is here to see you." Then she tapped slightly on the door, opened it and stepped in. The Reverend Mother was seated by her desk. "Beg pardon, Mother, but a gentleman is calling on you."

"A gentleman?" she frowned, then glanced at her appointment pad. No, she hadn't expected any callers this day. "Did he state his business, Sister?"

"No, he just wishes to see you."

"Very well, show him in—*Christopher*!" she cried when he entered and a joyous smile broke upon her lips. "Oh! what nonsense," she laughed. "Are you and Sister Theresa conspiring against me?" She rose from her desk and crossed the floor to greet him, "This is a pleasant surprise!"

They clasped hands, then settled down for conversation. Soon someone brought in a pot of tea. "Ah, this is truly like old home week to be in your study once more, Reverend Mother."

"A pleasure! I assure you; but tell me, how are you getting on at the seminary?"

"Very well indeed. I believe I have discovered what I've been searching for."

"Then your mind is made up?" she questioned in order to smoke out his emotions. "You're quite prepared to devote your life to God?"

"*Quite.*"

"Do you have no regrets . . . you don't feel as though you might wish to pursue another life?"

"No . . . why do you ask?"

"Because Christopher I want you to be absolutely sure that this is the life for you. Far be it from me to dissuade you from such a vocation . . . I feel it is the happiest for me! But I want you to be absolutely positive!" she stressed upon him once more. "My boy, this is the greatest decision of your life and once you take your vows, there is no turning back. It is not like just any profession where one may change their mind at will. Your mind, body and soul are to be consecrated to the service of God. I can think of no finer tribute for a man to make to his creator than to hallow his life to his maker"

"You needn't fear, Revered Mother, I know my mind. I have discovered peace, and peace is the most important thing of this earth."

"I have no fear for you, Christopher. I sensed your deep mood of responsibility the moment I laid eyes on you." Then she looked into his honest open face, she placed her hand on his, thinking that the maturing man possed a more sincere vibrant quality than the noble boy she knew. "No, Eugenia," she murmured happily to herself, "you have made no mistake in taking this boy under your wing—he's proven his worth!" There followed an awkward silence in the conversation, and for a long while they sipped their tea saying a word to the other. "You look rather peekish," she said, uttering the words to fill in the breach. "I don't think you got outdoors enough these days. Our spring afternoons were not meant to be spent indoors, you tell that fussy monsignor of yours, I sent word that you should take the day off and go fishing."

"I'm afraid that he would bite off both of our heads if I were to carry back such a message."

They laughed merrily together.

"Seriously Christopher, you are looking pale; I'm afraid that you have been studying too hard." She noticed that his face seemed flushed, and he lightly changed the subject because he couldn't bear to have any one pay too close attention to him. "By-the-by, what ever became of that friend of yours . . . what's his name—"

"Ellgate."

"Yes. As of yet you haven't mentioned his name; at one time that's all you spoke about. Doesn't he keep in touch with you?"

"We correspond. He's away at law school just now."

They chatted for a little while about Ellgate and then the conversation returned to Christopher's life as a clergyman. This they spoke of for a great length of time until he announced that it was time for him to leave as he didn't want to be late for vespers. The Reverend Mother saw him to the door. Once outside Christopher paused on the stone steps. In the Western sky the setting sun stretched golden horizontal of a crimson, pale blue heaven, a cool gentle breeze came whispering down the road, blowing upon his cheeks and ruffling his dark hair. Christopher turned an uplifted face to the Reverend mother and taking her hand in his he spoke to her in a richly shaded voice. "One more thing before I leave," he told her compassionately, pausing for a time to measure his words. "I would like to thank you from the very depths of my heart for the many kind things you have done for me . . . and I ask God to show me some way in which I might repay you, if only to show my gratitude." Blood flooded into the Reverend Mother's cheeks. "But I realize that no matter what I should ever do, I can never return the service or make adequate requital for everything you have done for me. Believe me, God! I will always be grateful."

"You embarrass me Christopher Wensdy, I never want you to speak of such things ever again." Her lip quivered as she spoke his name; it seemed to tremble and ring in both their ears. *For your name shall be my name, spake Isaiah, and we shall all be one flesh—children under one Father.* "I am vowed to poverty," she told him humbly, "and so will you be one day. The money I used was from an estate I never truly claimed. I keep it in the hands of my attorney, as some relative of mine will spend it foolishly. It is there for me to do good with, and since I am passing this way once I am trying to do all the good I can. I have done no more for you than any other," she said solemnly, "and what I did was done because I wanted to. You are not in my debt Christopher, never feel that. God has laid our work before us; we can only obey. I feel that is why we must never question the deeds of others . . . the good or the sinner. But what we can do is to try and bring the misguided back onto the path of righteousness."

Once again Christopher thanked her; he nodded a farewell, then turned on his heels to depart. "Good bye, Chris," she called after him in a light voice. "May God speed you; come back to see me soon . . ." he looked back over his shoulder and smiled. It was the last time he was to lay eyes upon her again.

Twilight was descending when Christopher reached the seminary. The great clock in the university tower was striking six and already it had grown quite dark; as he crossed the grounds he could hear the crickets in the tall tender grass by the lake tuning up for the evening symphony. The long walk from the priory, fatigued him, and he felt quite drowsy. If it had not been for the fact that he was quickening his steps to reach the chapel in time for vespers, he would have willingly rested on the cool grass beneath the willow and meditate on the still quiet beauty of twilight.

One Sunday morning as Christopher kneeled in church, listening to the Mass, he seemed greatly aware of the full importance of his life as a clergyman. The spirit of God kindled a vevid flame in his heart! He felt he couldn't wait until his ordination; time was not fleeting as quickly as he would wish it. He longed for the day when as a priest he could teach the wisdom of God. He wanted to shout to the world that he was fashioned in the image of his Creator who died for the sins of the world.

A surprise awaited Christopher as he walked from the cool dark of the church into the bright sunlight. Standing beneath the arbor of a tall white birch was Ellgate. They saw each other and livened their strides to meet. "Get ready to pack," he beamed in a bright laugh, "I've spoken to the prefect and he's granted you a long vacation. You're to spend the summer at my family's place."

2

Christopher felt perturbed when he stepped off the train, for he hadn't been in any public crowd for so long, and he sensed his awkwardness with burning cheeks when people chanced to glance his way. He was completely embarrassed when the old lady mistook him for a priest. "Good afternoon Father," she greeted cordially and retrieved the salutation rather crudely when she noticed that he wasn't wearing a clergy collar.

He walked up and down the depot platform impatiently waiting for Ellgate to return from the baggage room; hoping that he wouldn't be too long at the task. No one ever felt more dislodged from their orbit than he on that sunny afternoon in late July. However, he endeavored to behave as casual as he could under the circumstances for he had no wish to cause his friend any regret by inviting him for the summer. Christopher appreciated Ellgate's generosity, but wished that he might have spoken to him first about leaving the seminary for a little while. He thought Ellgate rather presumptuous to go above his head and speak to his Superior about granting him a vacation without consulting him first. When at last he found something he could smile at; he could imagine Ellgate calling on his superior and saying: "Look here old fellow, I think Wendy is in need of a little rest. How about it? . . . A little place on the New England Coast, you understand. He'll be in perfectly goods hands with my family—"

When Christopher frowned upon himself for not being more friendly toward Ellgate on the trip up, he decided to atone for his careless behavior. God had bestowed a friend on him and he was abusing the gift.

Mrs. Ellgate welcomed the chug of the family car as it skirted the sun baked road and turned up the drive; the nickel plate and bulk of the radiator with its winged cap flashed in the sunlight. She stood on the sprawling veranda waving a delicate lace handkerchief to the young men in the rear of the automobile. What an elegant age, she thought. The chauffeur sitting behind the controls was the personification of the coachmen of grandmother's day.

The machine rolled up to the house; a typical summer residence on an extensive scale, very long and rectangular in form. The great veranda was of a red brick tile, and the marble entry opened into a hall on the either side of which, separated only by a row of pillars, was a living room. Then came the drawing room, and at the back was the billiard room; the entire first floor seemed to consist of arches and columns. The effect was cool and spacious, while the hard polished floors reflected the many vistas of French windows.

Before Ellgate and Christopher had time to get out of the automobile, Mrs. Ellgate had darted into the entry to summon the household of their arrival and in another second she flitted back out. By this time the young men were upon the veranda and the chauffeur put their baggage into the hall. Mrs. Ellgate threw her arms about her son's neck and kissed him fondly; there after she turned to Christopher: "Well, at long last we meet," she said in her mild voice, reaching up to kiss Christopher's cheek. "I've been telling this boy of mine through the years, that I wanted to know you."

"Mother!" protested; her bright skin was flushed a rose red as she put a sheepish hand out to Christopher. At first meeting Elaine was a little confused for she wasn't quite certain that she knew how to talk to a seminarian, but then, Christopher smiled to her in his carefree way and she knew that everything would be alright. "It's good to meet you Christopher. Hans has said so much about you, that I just know we're going to be good friends . . . Welcome to our house."

Christopher released her hand, smiling at her once more. "Thank you, Elaine." his shy voice came from his throat in a warm husk quality, "How sweet . . . how very sweet to welcome me. "Yes, we are going to be good friends."

Elaine backed up a little and put her arm around the waist of the young woman who had just come down the steps to join the little group. "And now, I want Hans and Christopher to know my newest and dearest friend, Mrs. Paul Hastings . . . but please call her by her given name *Rue*! She detests formality."

Rue nodded her beautiful head in acknowledgement to Ellgate and he took her hand in something of a gruff boyish manner. He squeezed her hand, then released it with the quickness of a casual introduction. But it was an altogether different beginning when Christopher clasped hands with Rue. The whiteness of her slender hand seemed to lose itself in the lock of Christopher's strong brown fingers; the tight grasp of his virile strength almost carried a pain to her arm, but she did not squirm but tried to tear her fingers away from his grip. Rue thought that his were hands that held fast to life causing her to grow aware of some profound sense of security. From his great height Christopher looked down upon her, clumsily sputtering forth a word or two of concedment; her nearness awakened his senses to both a fire and cold that he had not known before. Their eyes met for a second and Christopher thought that he could not turn his glance away until she was ready to give him permission to do such.

Then quite suddenly, to Christopher's relief, Elaine gave a little joyous squeal: "They're here, Mother! a hack has rolled up to the door."

"Who's here?" demanded Ellgate of his sister. "Elaine what are you talking about?"

"Charly, you clown! Don't you recall inviting him"

"Yes, but Charly doesn't make a *they*."

"I'm afraid that Elaine isn't capable of expressing herself," said Mrs. Ellgate. "At first Charly wrote in reply that he didn't think he was able to come up. Of course, naturally I had Elaine to write him our regrets, telling him if he found it possible to visit us after all, he was quite welcome to bring a friend. That's all there is to it, Hans, darling. Now run out and meet your guest." Then she started to stay away about something about having the servants prepare refreshment for the young people.

Presently the two of them were standing on the veranda. Christopher was somewhat surprised to see Abigail Trent step down from the hack. Elaine sped down the steps to greet her, and Ellgate and Christopher followed close behind her heels. Rue leaned against one of the columns which flanked the veranda and watched the proceedings with folded arms. She saw Ellgate, Christopher and Charly exchange handshakes and pat each other on the back. Elaine and Abigail introduced themselves because for the time being, the three comrades had forgotten the women, they even forgot about the driver of the hack who waited bored, but patiently for his fare. They were so engaged in their loud idle babbling that the driver was forced to ask Abigail for his wages. She gave an easy laugh when he did, then started to open her purse to pay him willingly, but just at the moment Charly woke up to the proceedings, and interceded in time. Gradually they moved indoors where flood of introductions commenced once more.

Elaine sat before her dressing table touching a fluffy powder puff over her prim face, then stopped to admire the results. She nodded her head approvingly, then smiled. A young lady knows when she's charming and really doesn't need to be informed of such, but likes to be reminded of the fact if only to hear what her mirror has already said. Her hair was of a golden hue like her brothers but she was pleased that her eyes were brown and not blue as his were. Everyone said she had her father's eyes and of this she was proud, for she loved her father deeply.

Presently Elaine's door opened and closed rather carelessly; she glanced into the mirror above her dressing table and caught a glimpse of Rue's dazzling reflection. Her silken dark hair was dressed in the most flattering coiffure and her gown was a very exquisite fabric. Rue stepped over the carpet to the full length mirror pausing rather nonchalantly to admire her figure; she glided her tapering white fingers over her round smooth hips then walked over to Elaine's dressing table. Everything about Rue seemed to enchant a sheltered young woman of Elaine's breeding. Rue's beauty, her extravagant clothes and her great hoard of jewels. Although Rue was too clever as not to drop a word as to how she came about her wealth, she didn't mind displaying the fact that she was rich. Elaine was curious to learn, but was too discrete to ask . . . Perhaps in time she would discover what she desired to know. Yet, Elaine couldn't help but wondering. There was a strange air of mystery about her newly acquired friend that puzzled her. She was even secretive about her husband, but did tell Elaine once that he was somewhere in Peru on some great engineering project, and at one time he had a great deal to do with the Panama Canal. Then too, there were those awful tales concerning Rue's past. How mean of people to talk so vilely about a person they had scarcely known, thought Elaine. She wouldn't believe those tales . . . she couldn't! That's why she invited Rue to visit her for a while. She had to know more about Rue for she had liked her from the first moment they had met.

"Well, Elaine, he did live up to your description," murmured Rue in reference to Christopher. She touched a little perfume behind her pink ears; her black eyes were snapping in merriment and her voice came like music from her lovely white throat. "But what a shy thing he appeared to be," she continued, then cooed devilishly: "he needs to be mothered, Elaine, don't you think?"

Elaine was astonished at Rue's implicating tone. "Rue, really! you shouldn't say such things. He's studying for the priesthood. Of course, to me, he might have appeared shy. But that's his way of life. They teach them to be humble. His way of living is so completely different from ours that I fear that he might think we are heathens. From what Hans tells me, I know that Christopher is broad minded enough, but still I hope no one is careless enough to offend his way of thinking." Elaine wrinkled her nose then grinned. "Still I must agree with you, Rue. He is exceptionally handsome." Elaine pulled open the center draw of her dressing table. "this is a photograph of he and Hans when they were college chums."

Rue accepted the picture and examined it thoroughly. "I once read a story about the Great God Pan," she said. "I'd like to think of him as being pan."

"No, Rue, he couldn't look like Pan, he had dark eyes, I think, and Christopher's are blue. Besides, Pan was half goat and possessed horns."

'How disillusioning," Rue rejoined sardonically. "horns . . . half goat! Undoubtedly I must have some other god in mind. But dark eyes or blue, what's the difference? It's the man inside that counts."

Someone knocked on the door just then and Elaine gave the command to enter. The knob turned, the door rolled inward and Abigail swept into the room somewhat distressed at the faulty clasp of her dress.

"What is your Charly like, Abigail?" she plagued her, then settled herself in a blue velvet boudoir chair.

"He's not my Charly," returned Abigail still as content in her wish to be unattached in her young life. "I have plans of my own," she went on to explain. Besides I have no idea what you're talking about." She walked past Rue and gave her attentions to Elaine. "The darn clasp of this dress popped off, have you a needle I can borrow?"

Elaine obligingly searched the top of her dressing table for a needle and after some moments of futile efforts she said that she'd go down the hall and borrow one from the maid. Abigail and Rue watched the door close after Elaine, then Abigail sat on the bed to wait for her return.

"Now what's this business about Pan?" inquired Abigiail. Her head was down and she was rummaging in her purse for something. At length she came up with a packet of cigarettes and matches.

"We were just comparing men to Greek Gods," said Rue and she stretched out her hands to examine her well cared for nails.

"Oh" was Abigail's light unconcerned reply and didn't give any more attention to the thought. "Do you mind if I smoke?" she said to Rue. "Most people think it scandalous for women to smoke, therefore, you see, I must keep it a secret."

"I think it a scandal for most people to think," rejoined Rue in bright mocking tones. "Of course, I don't mind if you smoke. After all, this is a free country and everyone is entitled to their own way of living."

"Will you have one with me?"

"Thank you, no. I really don't care for the habit, but you're obliged to burn the house down if you like. Your smoky secret is safe with me. I know Elaine won't mind if you do." She laughed; "Smoke, I mean. She's quite understanding about a lot of things, even though she still has a great deal to learn about life. I think her family keeps her down too much, but I suppose one day she'll try out her wings." Rue changed the subject. "Have you known Charly very long?"

Abigail exhaled a puff of cloudy blue smoke. "About as long as I've known anyone else. the four of us were always good friends. Charly, Chris, and Elaine's brother . . . the boys attended the school near my town and there were occasions when we saw each other. Of course, Charly always did live in Fairlee and still does. So do I for that matter. Yes, we've had our good times together, but I don't like to reminisce. It's the sign of impending age. Besides the old times can never come back."

"You say that as though you have truly lost something in your life," said Rue observing the clear honest expression on Abigail's face.

"I guess I have," Abigail rejoined. "But it's something I can't seem to explain . . . It's like being stifled in one's own back yard and no one can help me but myself, but the truth of the comedy is, that I just don't know how to help myself. I reach out for the things I want but can't seem to grasp them. I don't know," she sighed. "I guess it's me." She reached over and crumpled her cigarette in one of the pin dishes on the dressing table. "Maybe it is my Aunt Amy. She's getting on in age and wants to tie me down to her side. It must be wonderful to be free like you, Rue. I suppose you can do anything you want. But Oh! there I go babbling again. But that's your fault, Rue, you seem so easy to talk to."

"Thank you, Abigail, but on the contrary it's you who are so easy to talk with. But what ever gave you the idea that I was so disgustingly free . . . I have a husband if you will remember."

"Yes, I forgot. But you seem so young to be tied down."

"Well one day we'll have a long talk about him together. I have a feeling that we are going to be friends. Somehow, you seem different from the rest of the people I've met around here."

"I truly wish that I was," sighed Abigail. "I'm really not though. The only contrast is that I just want different things than they do. That's all." Then with an air of impatience she cried: "where in the thunder did Elaine go for that needle?"

In the room next to Elaine's, Ellgate was sputtering out his apologies to Christopher. It was an embarrassing moment for both men for it seemed that Ellgate had quite unintentionally intruded on his friend while he was chanting his evening prayers. "No need for apologies," said Christopher trying to lessen his friends distress. "I suppose you've come to fetch me for dinner?"

"Yes," he admitted, then continued to murmur his excuses. "I guess I'm ignorant of such things. I should have known, or at least knocked."

"Let's not hear any more about it," he replied waving his hand as if to brush the incident aside. "On the contrary it is I who am ignorant of social behavior. I'm afraid that I've forgotten how to conduct myself even with my closest friend . . . we learn one life only to forget another."

"I'm glad to hear you say we're still old friends, Wen—let's always keep that. But one thing," he added with a grin, "I'm sure God won't mind if your heathen friend makes a suggestion."

"Please suggest."

"Mightn't I loan you some brighter clothes—after all, colors haven't hurt anyone yet." Then he uttered with a more serious tone. "I hope I haven't been offensive, Chris?"

Christopher smiled.

"—And if you do . . ." Ellgate grinned discovering that old spark of comradeship in Christopher's glance. "Well, if only for old time's sake, I'll just have to whip the bark off your hide."

They both laughed.

"As for now," continued Ellgate, "I'm going to fetch Charly out of the bathtub before we will all be detained for dinner. Charly seems to think that he can soak out all of Vermont's green mountain dirt in our tub." He patted his friend on the back, "Go to my room and help yourself to whatever you need. I'll join you in a minute."

After dinner the small party settled down in the huge vaulted sitting room. The scene was a very quiet and domestic one; some were settled here and there engaged in simple informal talk and sometimes discussing everything in general. The evening was incredibly warm and the French doors were thrown open to the summer night. After a time, the maid wheeled in a refreshment wagon and served ice-tea for the ladies and something more pungent for the men.

"I think when a man has found God, he has found himself," Mrs. Ellgate said to Christopher as they sat side by side on the sofa. She was a refined woman possessing aristocratic features and in her day she was regarded by many as a beauty. Christopher found it easy to talk with her. She possessed most of her son's free easy manner and he most of his mother's good looks.

At first the conversation between them consisted of Christopher's duties at the seminary and his future life as a clergyman; it concluded by Mrs. Ellgate insisting that she would be present at his ordination, for she was a devout woman and most of her life had been dedicated to church and social work. Moreover she impressed on Christopher of how proud she was that he had taken up such a life. In fact she repeated her sentiments more than a score of times during the entire course of their little chat. When the conversation was brought around to her son, Hans, she lamented Ellgate's lack of interest in God and feared for his welfare and reclamation. She urged Christopher to try and bring her son back to God for she herself could not do anything with him on that account. It was here that Christopher managed to inquire of her as to what great dilemma caused Ellgate to stalk out of the house like a madman, for he deserted his friends to go for a walk and sulk by himself. She explained to him that his sudden outburst of rudeness was due to Sarah Morrison, Hans' fiancée; she telephoned after dinner to express her regrets because she could not come up to visit with them this summer owing to the demands of her career.

"Sarah is in nurse's training school, you know," she told Christopher, "and Hans is as furious as ten thousand demons because she cannot get away. But it's not the child's fault, you understand. It's just that Hans is too hot headed for his own good. I saw him deliberately hang up in the girl's ear when she told him she couldn't come. Oh, I tell you I fear the outcome. Sarah is not the sort of girl to take his temperamental outburst too lightly."

Although Christopher endeavored to train his ears on the words Mrs. Ellgate was uttering to him, he found it very difficult to keep his thoughts with her. It was not because the woman's conversation bored him or that he was being purposely rude, but because he could not keep Rue's presence from breaking in on his thoughts, and even now he found it hard to keep his eyes off her face.

Rue was seated with Elaine and Abigail before a small mahogany table looking at pictures through a stereoscope; they would take turns at looking through the optical instrument, mumble comments to each other, then giggle in subdued tones. Christopher wondered what great secret Mr. Ellgate Sr. and another gentleman by the name of Mr. Lang could be plotting that it should keep them hovering beneath the arch of the open French door for so long a time. Then later, Christopher turned his eyes toward the far corner of the room where Charly Lock was seated. Not long ago he was sitting erect in his chair thumbing through an art book, but now he was slumped down with the book open in his lap and sleeping lightly with his chin on his chest.

Presently Mrs. Ellgate got up from her chair and rang for more refreshments. Christopher's eyes followed after her and as he did so, his glance chanced to lock with Rue's. He quickly turned his eyes away recalling the first moment they met. He remembered that even then her dark eyes held him fast in her spell . . . eyes that were virgin like and yet worldly mysterious. No woman had caused him to feel awkward in her presence before, and yet without uttering a word, Rue caused him to be aware of his clumsiness. Why was this so? He could glance at Elaine or Abigail without alarm. What was this witchcraft that was wrapped in this woman's being? Her very presence dominated the room he sat in and that night when he was to fall asleep he dreamed of her. A dream that aroused desires in him which were not in accord to his chosen life.

It was a little past eleven that night when Ellgate returned from the Greenwood Country Club. Evidently his angered tramp into the summer night had carried him there for his clothes were scented of tobacco smoke and his breath boasted of several rounds of whisky. He was in a chipper mood for he greeted everyone loud and lively. "Damn you fellows and lets get some spirit into the game!" He sang in a bright lively voice then staggered over to Christopher, and in the next moment he suggested to Charly and Christopher that they have a game of cards. Elaine boasted that the girls should join them, but her brother turned around and gave his mother a ridiculous wink of the eye. Then he looked over his shoulder to the girls: "Sorry ladies, but the game is strip!" He put his arms about his friends shoulders and hurried them off into the rear of the house, slamming the billiard room door noisily behind them.

The following morning on the cool shaded, tiled terrace, immediately before everyone was to settle down for breakfast, Mr. Ellgate Sr. announced that he and Mr. Land would merge their law firms. So the occasion was commemorated by toasting the partnership with champagne! This was a new and extravagant way of opening the morning, or so Christopher thought; to say nothing of the outrageous hour of eleven A.M., particularly when he was accustomed to beginning his day at sunrise. But on this particular morning he had put aside his robes, and a change of clothes sometimes means a change of unvarying routine, and although this swift social life was contrary to his way of living he made the most of it and endeavored to enjoy himself. Moreover, these were the things one might do on a vacation; soon the holiday would be over and he would be back in his cell at St. Thomas', devoting his life to God.

Christopher viewed the man, Fredrick Lang, and lifted his glass to honor the partnership, but how was he or the grey haired man to know that each was stumbling over the other's path and neither knowing the other's identity? If Mr. Lang had still been on the alert for the lost heir of the *Fransworth* fortune, he might have recognized the young man who stood only a few feet distance from him. But that search had been long abandoned and *Victoria Fransworth* was now many years dead; her fortune divided among greedy relatives and a good portion was willed to the devoted Mr. Lang.

Possibly it was Abigail who carried the conversation around to discussing the theatre, and the Fransworth name always did manage to create a stir whenever it was mentioned and there were many who still cherished the memory of Christopher's mother. Abigail talked incessantly for more than twenty minutes on the Fransworth name and profession, because no one else could get a word in on the subject. That is, not until Mrs. Ellgate possessed a knowledge of the topic that was quite interesting to her. She ceased her babbling immediately and let the woman have her say. And if Christopher had possessed the slightest recollection of his past life, an entirely new world would have opened up to him.

"*Paula Fransworth!*" Mrs. Ellgate exclaimed at the breakfast table. "why I'll never, never forget that gown she wore in: *A NEW WOMAN*... My, that was a play you should have adored, Elaine!" the woman said to her daughter with some amount of pleasure in her voice as she reflected on the glory of her youth. "... Those closing lines at the final curtain—*Oh, God! Not since Mother Eve, was there a new woman more woebegone and wretched as I ... And if death calls into his arms I'd fly*—And John Fransworth!" she went on to explain to the bright attentive faces about her; "I'm confessing to you, Elaine, that if I had been a year or so younger, and not married to your father, I would have thrown myself at his feet. Never was there a man more handsome than he!" Then she began to laugh and flushed at her antics, "How foolish we are when we're young," and then with a ring of astonishment in her voice she said: "why, come to think of it, Elaine, he resembled your brother Hans' friend very much!" Mrs. Ellgate lifted her eyes searching for Christopher, but he was no longer seated at the table. Apparently he had slipped quietly away without being seen.

3

A breeze blew off the ocean. Short and clean but it was a lazying sort of refreshment, and the morning air was touched with a tang of salt sea fragrance that could only belong to the summer warmth of a gypsy life. Beyond the white chain of the bed lay the lonely line of the horizon and here and there drifted the willowy puff of a low sleeping cloud, and the sands of the beach stretched golden and silent under the burnish rays of the sun. Christopher could feel the heat of its light upon his back as he walked along the beach alone and sullen. His hands were thrust into the pockets of his trousers, and as he walked the tip of his shoes kicked up little explosions of sand. But presently he had to sit upon a rock and empty the sands from his shoes; when he completed the task he just remained there for a time watching a fleet of crying gulls wing their way seaward with the blown wind and running tide. It was here some moments later that Rue discovered him, deep in thought with his eyes resting on the hazy grey of the distant horizon. He climbed to his feet with a start. "You hasten to a running position?" Rue murmured permitting the words to roll musically from her moist red lips. The sun was on her face and her dark eyes caught the sunlight.

Christopher emitted a halfway laugh in reply. "No," he admitted modestly. "It's just that my thoughts were out with the tide and I was surprised to discover that I had an audience." he sensed a strange feeling with Rue standing before him. Her eyes seemed to penetrate him, and he flushed to the roots of his dark hair when he recalled dreaming of her the preceding night. To avoid her glance he turned to face the stretch of the water before him.

The wind blew freely and the spray of the salt sea air was faintly scented with the delicate richness of Rue's perfume. The combination of which was strangely intoxicating to the young man, who knew he must hold himself off, but still the fragrance of sea and perfume tumbled about him; blowing upon his cheeks and into his nostrils until he was almost dizzy from the want of life that was in Rue. Finally she said: "You look like a little boy standing there alone and lost not knowing which way to run." A throaty laugh moved through her frame, then she sat down by his feet and folding her legs under her; she muttered beneath her breath: "Your troubles are that you are afraid of life."

Christopher overheard her words and flashed her a glance that was as stern and sharp as flint. He squared his shoulders preparing to release a blast of angry thoughts upon her, but suddenly he remembered the station in life and the subservience joined to it, and after all, she was but a woman who knew not what she spoke. He bit his lip and inserted his fists into his pockets in an effort to compose himself. Rue trembled when she caught the flash of anger spark like blue balls of fire in his eyes, and something within her being awakened to the virile strength slumbering within that tall muscular frame which hovered above her. Then a moment or so later when Christopher withdrew his hands from his pockets he accidently pulled out with them his rosaries, and they fell silently upon the sand. It was a tense moment for them with the symbol of God between he and her; for a time each stared upon the round black beads laying but a fraction beyond the tip of Christopher's shoe. Rue felt an uneasiness tremble within her heart that seemed a strange intangible fixture of pity, fear and love. How quickly the thought had escaped her, that this mild mannered man before her was actually a seminarian persuing his God!

Once more she turned her eyes to the rosaries with its crucifix lying half buried in the sand. Then in the blinding moment, like the fire, thunder and rain, Rue knew that this was the man she wanted for her own! To live with and cherish . . . But how was she to win? Between them laid a thousand years of crusades; tabernacles and incense burning on the candle lit altar of piety; the image of Jerusalem's shepherds and prophets speaking with the tongues of men and angels, reaching up in fiery passion on the broad sweep of heaven! Rue reached out her hand and picked up the sacred beads while Christopher looked on her actions with tense, observing eyes; Rue brought the silver crucifix to her lips and kissed it . . . Her war with heaven had begun! She knew that she must be the victor; moreover, she noticed the gleam of satisfaction in Christopher's eye when she took the cross from her lips and placed the beads into his hands. Their hands touched and for the moment he held hers fast in his grasp. Then he did a thing that came as a surprise to Rue; he bent his head forward and kissed the back of her hand as though she were some *Modern Madonna*! Rue trembled at his act of humility; she freed her hand from his and sped briskly away leaving him alone on the silent wind swept beach.

The summer stretched forward—golden, listless and carefree with bluer skies and long warm days. The healthy outdoor living, with long hours of beach lounging tanned Christopher until he was as brown as bark. Most of the buoyancy of his boyhood seemed to return in him, and the same joyous feeling seemed to rekindle in Ellgate, for each found their boyhood in the other, a memory that was dear to both.

One Saturday someone suggested a riding party on horseback for a bit of exercise and perhaps to explore the country side. At first everyone thought it a grand pastime, but then Mrs. Ellgate was forced to back out because the *Botanical Society* telephoned to say they wanted to inspect her Rhododendron beds, she explained to everyone in gleeful tones that her hot-house Delphiniums were definitely Blue Ribbon Specimens! So naturally she had to excuse herself from the party, and before they were ready to depart Abigail pleaded a sick headache and wouldn't be able to go along, and Charly did the expected thing and stayed behind until she would be feeling better. By now the party that would have included seven people had dwindled down to four. Ellgate and his sister; Rue and

Christopher. Possibly it was Rue who suggested the outing if only to display her fashionable riding habit, or if not to flaunt her skill as an equestrian. And there was no doubt about it, she sat her horse like a champion. But in the course of events it was Elaine who boasted of the suggestion and claimed all rewards. She sat her little mare like a timid girl and eyed her brother and Christopher with deep admiration preferring to think of them as two strapping gallants who straddled their steeds with long sinewy legs like knights in the tournament wrapped in gleaming armor and poised for the lists.

The little party rode at an even pace. They had not been long on the woodsy bridal path when a chipmunk, quite unexpectedly, darted in the path of Elaine's mare. The little animal tangled with the horse's forehooves, frighting it out of control and the nervous beast reared on its haunches! Suddenly Elaine was panic stricken, she lost control of the reins and the terrified animal lunged a little to the left, throwing her violently to the ground! All too quickly the horse which Rue rode was startled beyond submission at the calamity and uproar of the men's voices. The animal bolted, charging wild and freely down the open bridal path!

"You care for Elaine—I'll go after Rue!" Christopher shouted to Ellgate in sharp excited tones. He endeavored to restrain the neighing animal beneath him; reining his steed, the noble beast reared on its hinderparts, showing his teeth, champing at the bit, and kicking up a cloud of dust. In time he mastered the animal, clapped his thighs to the horse, and galloped away—the wind in his face and his vision sharply ringing in his ears.

Swiftly as the driving wind, flying mane and a set of thundering hooves pounded tumultuously upon the narrow, dusty causeway. Soon Christopher was gaining on the chase. He sighted Rue's upturned derby lying in the middle of the dusty path; he thundered past it, and demanded more speed by grinding his spurs into the horse.

Sharply in the distance he caught a fleeting glimpse of Rue and the runaway horse as they curved the path. Her dark hair was flying unruly in the wind and he could see that she was straining every muscle she possessed to hold fast to the beast. Her lithe body seemed to bounce like a rag doll that was tied fast to the saddle, and Christopher feared that any moment she would be thrown beneath the beating hooves! At length, Rue sensed the pounding hooves in back of her, then felt Christopher race beside her. His boot scraped her boot and as they raced side by side, Christopher leaned over and seized the dangling reins, bringing the agitated beast to an abrupt halt! The animal snapped into gentle submission, obeying the power in his strong arm and brown fingers.

Christopher was short of breath. Quickly he dismounted and lifted Rue from the saddle; for a time he held her in his arms, face to face with her beating heart crushed against his chest. They spoke no word, and the last thing Rue noticed before she closed her eyes was the little nerve throbbing at his temple She yielded her lips and Christopher moved his head forward to kiss her—but suddenly he stopped and eased her to the ground. "we must get back," he told her. "Elaine may be seriously mayhemed." The words sounded to his own ears as if they had been spoken by a stranger; he felt awkward, and no longer comprehended his own actions. There was something magic-like in Rue which he could not understand. His power was all spent and he felt himself tangled in her web.

Elaine was severely bruised, but that was all; the doctor explained that an alcohol rub and a few days in bed and she would be as well as ever.

In the days that followed Christopher avoided Rue as best he could, but each day he found it more difficult to escape her. The more he endeavored to drive her out of his mind, the more she took possession of his thoughts; her hauntingly beautiful face and dark eyes seemed to be everywhere he turned. Christopher knew that he must escape his surroundings. Her very nearness and the shallow cut of her gowns filled him with a weakness that was alarming. There were times when her eyes spoke to him with a power that captured his desire. He was flooded with thoughts of holding her in his embrace, and sometimes blamed her for tempting him, but then he would turn sharply about and reprove himself for thinking ill of her; for as one who had embraced the clergy, it was his duty not to think ill of anyone. As for Rue, she was determined to win

Christopher for her own. She admitted to herself that she had fallen deeply in love with Christopher. Moreover, she had never forgiven him for that day on the road, especially when the fault was his for arousing desire in her; she was too frightened and lacking in breath that day to think of love or passion.

In August, the Greenwood Country Club held its annual charity dance. Mrs. Ellgate headed the committee, in fact she had the privilege of managing the affair ever since Elaine and her brother could remember themselves. Except for the time the family journeyed abroad one summer, but that was too long ago for either of them to recall in detail. Naturally, Mrs. Ellgate was excited over the event as though it were really her first big social endeavor. She insisted that the young people cancel any previous engagement they might have had planned, for she refused to excuse anyone. "The *Charity* has to be an overwhelming success!" she said jubilantly. "Everybody has to attend." And that was final which afforded no amount of mental anguish for Christopher. He knew that there would be dancing, and feared that such a past time would be too frivolous for one of his station. But still with a reluctant heart he agreed to go along, and eagerly he wished for his holiday to draw to a close. The life he had cut out for himself was rapidly being consumed by a trifling social life which he didn't understand, and most of the time he felt lost and confessed, like one who had strayed too far from the shepherd's flock.

The promised evening was a gala one. A small orchestra supplied the music; the ballroom and terrace was decorated from one end to the other with strings of Japanese lanterns. The refreshment room and grounds were thickly peopled with young men and women in evening dress. Elaine and Ellgate seemed to be thoroughly acquainted with the majority, for every now and then someone called out to either.

Christopher appeared strikingly handsome in Ellgate's dinner jacket and he admitted to his friends in a jovial and honest tone that it was the first one he had ever donned. But of all the lovely young people at the gathering, there was none more beautiful than Rue; she was the rapt beauty of the night looking more like a goddess than a woman, and many a masculine head turned when she glided past.

Mrs. Ellgate had the oblong table near the bandstand reserved for her young people, as she lovingly called them, and from time to time, when she was not dancing with Elaine's father or inspecting the proceedings of the evening, she would stop by and see how they were getting along. She came from behind and kissed her son on the cheek; her graceful diamond hands resting on his shoulders. "Tut, you naughty boy! It's shocking for a mother to find her boy this way," she said lightly. "Hans, you smell of a distillery, mamma should box your loving ears."

Ellgate reached up and took one of his mother's hands. "Is your *Charity* the success you hoped it would be?" he kissed her palm.

"Tremendously so, and I'm glad that my young people are enjoying themselves." She glanced over to Christopher who sat between Rue and Abigail. His fingers clutched a cocktail glass and he appeared to be musing in deep thought. Sometimes his serious face worried her. 'Oh! oh! there goes your sister Elaine. She's taken the Warren boy for another spin on the dance floor." She winked at her son, "You know, Hans, I do believe Elaine's setting her cap for that boy."

A round of laughter circled the table.

"Then, Mamma," Ellgate murmured, "suppose I set my cap for you. I may just as well have my fling while Sarah's not around to stop me."

His mother tapped him on his cheek: "Hans, I'll slap you if you brood. After all, dear, it's not the child's fault. She simply couldn't get away. Now stop that nonsense and take your mother for a turn on the dance floor. This is my favorite waltz." He got up from the table and together they started toward the dance floor, but before they left Mrs. Ellgate telegraphed a stern gesture for Christopher to get up and dance.

". . . . And that's a good idea," bleated Charly, intercepting the message. He took Abigail by her wrist and brought her to a standing position. "First thing you know," he said, "old age will be upon us before we can find out what life's all about." he pecked Abigail on the cheek and led her away by the hand.

Rue and Christopher sat at the table alone. She drained the contents of her glass then set it down again on the linen cloth. Christopher felt rather foolish and the situation seemed unbearably awkward. He looked at Rue from the corner of his eye. Neither spoke a word, and yet there was so much that could have been said and as many things he wanted to say into the delicate quality of those beautifully shaped ears of hers. But he was a man who stood aloft in a world that confused him. A stranger before a host of society. He drummed his fingers upon the table, then in a moment of frustration he took up his glass and drained it dry; later he took up another glass and repeated the action. The orchestra stopped playing then immediately started up another tune. Christopher hoped that somebody would return to the table and relieve the tension he felt, but evidently they too must have taken another dance for no one returned. By this time everyone had left their tables and it appeared that he and Rue were the only pair who remained seated. Little beads of perspiration stood out on his upper lip and he wished that Rue might start up a conversation and relieve him. He drank another whiskey. It belonged to Ellgate so he simply reached out and took it. Finally he reached and took Rue's hand. She stood up and they started for the floor. The orchestra started to play another waltz and he was grateful, for that much he could manage the steps with little trouble, he thought, and perhaps he wouldn't have to hold her so close; although in his heart of hearts he wanted to.

On first movement the steps were greatly difficult for him to catch onto, but after a few stiff glides and turns, he seemed to manage fairly well. He brought her in a little closer to him.

"You're in love with me, Chris, aren't you?" Rue said in a voice that was so hushed and soft that Christopher wasn't certain that it was Rue who spoke to him, or the echoes of his own desire. His mind seemed to spin and he was in doubt whether or not he gave a reply for the will to answer was so strong in him. He felt her in his arms. It was the first time she had been there since that day on the road when he helped her dismount from the runaway horse. He felt her warmth and magic; it gave him an overwhelming feeling of youth and life. He feared that if he didn't keep himself strong he would be compelled to surrender to her charm.

Rue, can't you understand what pain it is for me to deny you, he thought, and buried his nose in the warm blackness of her perfumed hair. Unknowingly he brought her closer to him. Rue rested her head on his shoulder. She was content. She seemed to be winning her little war and her heart was purring like a kitten; she closed her eyes and followed his steps to the dance music. They both were young and she was in love. It was a perfect evening after all, she thought. She would not think of her troubles tonight . . . tonight was her victory and everything would have to wait until tomorrow. Rue knew that Christopher would belong to her—perhaps not now but it wouldn't be long until it was so. She felt his strong arms about her. The music had stopped and started up once more and they were still dancing . . .

Flimsy quality of her flowing robes; her dainty feet were incased in silver sandal slippers, and the beauty of her dark silken hair tumbled carefree about her shoulders. The mere thought of her loveliness consumed Christopher with a fire he had never known before. Suddenly with an overpowering determination he swept Rue up into his arms and carried her within the room. The door silently closed and the little ribbon of shimmering light beneath it was immediately dissolved by sudden darkness.

4

Christopher relinquished the life he had, and returned to the security within the walls of the seminary, but in all the weeks since his return to St. Thomas' he found it incredibly hard to take Rue from his thoughts. To tear himself away from her arms and beauty proved an overwhelming battle with his heart and soul. He was promised to God, but lost himself with a goddess and the conflict was enough to destroy him. He sought escape by filling every second of his day with work study and prayers, and though he was ever constant at the altars and tabernacles, he grew conspicuously absent from both confession and communion. It had not been an easy task to frequent the crowds and keep virture as chaste as the white robes of the cloistered. But he blamed no one for his weakness. It was his fault alone and he prayed to God for strength. *I will lift up mine eyes unto the hills from whence cometh my help . . . my help cometh from the Lord.*

The weeks wore on wearily, slow and brooding, and it was only with the courage of a giant that Christopher found the heart to continue. His mind wanted to follow God but his heart was with Rue. Then, one dark and dreary Sunday afternoon when the lightning flashed and rain fell in torrents from heaven, Christopher knelt in the candle lit chapel chanting his rosaries when he was summoned to the prefect's office where he was informed that he had a visitor. Later when he opened the door of the visitor's hall he was startled and thoroughly surprised to see Rue.

"Chris, Darling," she cried stirring from the leather divan and crossing the room; she dropped her parasol on the heavy mahogany table and hastened to his side.

He quickly closed the door after him. "Rue! Rue, what are you doing here?" His voice conveyed a quality that was neither cross nor pleased; he only knew that that one person he wanted near, but dared not hoped to see again, was standing by his side.

Rue stretched her hands out to him, but he made no effort to receive them, "You are angry, Christopher . . . Aren't you pleased to see me?"

Christopher pleaded with her to go away. He told Rue that they were not meant for each other; he hoped that his words might offend her and silently prayed for her to leave. He gave her his back and turned to look out of the window to the wet rolling ground. "How can you say such a thing is true, Christopher," she stood behind him and placed her gloved hands on his shoulders. "Have you forgotten what we mean to each other? This is me, Chris. Rue," and there was a pleading tear of torment in her voice.

He pulled away from her and pounded his fist into his open palm. "I've forgotten everything!" he told her.

"You could not have forgotten everything, darling . . . no one can forget the words, *I love you!*"

Rue's words touched his heart and he could no longer pretend that he was strong, nor indifferent to her. He took her hands and kissed the backs and palms of them and even her finger tips; then swept her in his embrace, holding her close to him, kissing her mouth and brushing his lips against her glossy hair. For a moment the pain and confusion that he had known in his heart seemed to grow quiet and die away. "Rue! Rue! Dearest, I can't explain this feeling of joy! Just this once let me fill my arms with you; to kiss your lips once more, then I must erase your image from my heart." He kissed her lips, then released her from his embrace. "Please, Rue, now you must leave me forever. Our lives together can not be! May

God forgive us both for it is blasphemous to speak of love within these sacred walls."

"No, Chris, I could never!" she sobbed. "How could I possibly leave you in the grey of these silent walls. I can feel its cold air about my heart. No, my beloved. I could never leave you . . . You must come away with me and live the life that was intended for men and women to have. If you ask me to go away, then you can not really love me!"

He bowed his shoulders and kissed her hand. "Love you? . . . Rue, I adore you! But it is too late for us; perhaps if we had met sooner or in another circumstance it might have been, but . . ." Christopher's voice almost cracked; his hands started to tremble then he fell to his knees and buried his face in his hands. "Oh, God!" he cried, "sustain me *my Father* and give me strength!" Rue came to him as he kneeled upon the hard floor; she put her arms around him and even when he was in such a humble position his height caused him to stand just a little above her waist. His arms went around her and he put his face against her dress. "No, Rue, you must go away! I promised my life to God; what's more, I'm to be ordained in the not too distant future."

"Please, Chris, hear me before you say another word," she murmured beseechingly and then she turned to face one of the holy pictures which hung on the plain high oak wall. "Holy Father who looks upon me from heaven. Forgive me! My voice calls out to you, I beg only for the heart of the man I love, and if he blames me and thinks that I am truly bad, then I am totally lost! Have mercy, for ours was only a natural sin of life . . . I hope it will be understood by him that I love!"

Christopher listened to her words with kneeness; her behavior troubled him. He rose from his knees and taking her hands in his he bade her to sit upon the leather divan. "What are you trying to tell me?" he said solemnly. "I fear that there is something you want to tell but don't know how."

Rue squeezed his hands until her nails bit into his flesh, then turning her face away from his searching eyes she said in a light trembling voice: "I'm pregnant, Chris . . . I'm going to have your baby." Suddenly she began to weep in a choked subdued cry. He wrapped his arms around her, and Rue smothered her face upon his shoulder. Christopher was thunderstruck! For a long while he remained alarmingly pale. His troubled mind clashed with confusion and like a crushed metallic thing he held the beautiful, sobbing and trembling woman in his arms. His life had always seemed to him nothing but a contorted bundle of tragedies since he first woke up to memory in the somber walls of the nunnery, and now once more he had the audacity to bring impurity into the seminary. He felt like the damned. The arch sinner of the moment. Could he fall to his knees now and beg his Creator for clemency? No. Like a weakling he yielded to passionate caprice when he had been piously schooled against temptation. Through the closed door of the reception hall came the thin piping music of organ music and the shuffing feet of the seminarists, chanting their rosaries their way to vespers.

"It is a wonder you don't revile me," said Rue with tear swollen eyes. "But if you could look through all this and remember our love, I will be like your devoted dog. Come away with me, Chris. I beg you. We could live a life that everyone will envy. Give me your heart, Chris! I want to travel but most of all I want you with me."

"I have no choice in the matter," he rejoined despondedly. "At the moment I am at your command . . . And leave this place, I must do at all cost, or surely they will disrobe me and force me out . . . But where are we to go on such short notice?" He smiled at her sardonically, "I am a pauper in every sense of the word."

Almost immediately Rue seemed to spark into an energy that was more like her old self. "Money is the least of our worries, Darling. I am rich enough for both! Come away with me, that is the only important thing, and I promise you it will never be regreted."

"But what of your husband?" Christopher asked in shame. He had almost forgotten that she was wedded and from her actions it appeared that she managed everything in her power to keep it a quiet thing.

"All the more my shame!" she sobbed.

Christopher's cheeks turned a flaming red; he couldn't bare to look her in the face; he felt like a degraded mongrel and wished that his Creator would strike him dead on the spot. "I would at least like to have the honor of paying for my own child," he murmured woundedly. "I'm not the sort of man to take money from a woman." Then his mind turned to Ellgate; he smiled with a feeling of relief, "I must tell Ellgate of my problem. I can trust him and I am certain that he will loan me enough to see us through until I can earn enough to repay him." Christopher winced at the thought of money. Once he thought his life was to be vowed to poverty, but now all that was to be put behind him. How fickle are the stars that govern our lives. Christopher hoped that his friend would not look upon him with scorn; he felt the only one he could unburden his shame to was Ellgate.

"No," said Rue; the nostrils of her beautiful nose were dilated. "We'll not tell anyone that we are going away together. If we breathe a word to one jabbering idiot the entire universe will learn of our elopement."

"This is such a cowardly way to depart in the night like thieves. I think I ought to confide in my closest friend, Rue."

"Believe me, Chris," she rejoined imploringly, her hand tugged at the black sleeve of his elbow. "I know better in such matters. It's best that we depart without assistance of outsiders."

"He shrugged his shoulders in despair: "If you think best."

"It's the only way." She reached up and kissed his cheek; Faith gambled in her favor and she seemed to be winning her little victory with heaven. "Can you operate a gasoline engine?"

"No, I've never tampered with automobiles; they are an entirely new invention as far as I'm concerned. Besides, we could never depart in a contrivance of that sort—the noise would wake the dead."

"Perhaps it's just as well," she said excitedly. "I can buy a carriage and a pair of horses in Fairlee. At what hour are you prepared to leave the seminary?"

"I've already missed vespers," he answered still doting on his duties. "I think to avoid suspicion, I should at least put in an appearance at the supper hall . . . Curfew rings at 8:30, and everyone should be asleep by 9: o'clock." He looked into her dark eyes and kissed her cheek. "If everything goes well, my dearest you will find me standing on the road in front of the university tower one hour past curfew." Christopher glanced toward the window; the rain beat against the glass in a furious pound. "I loath to send you out in this weather, but it's best that you leave now." He kissed her hand.

"It doesn't matter. I told my cab to wait until I came out. Adieu until tonight," and for reassurance she added: "On the road in front of the university." He helped her don her hood and cape, then she swept from the room. Both their hearts skipped a beat.

The supper hour dragged on. Christopher occupied his usual place at the long melancholy table and tried to behave according to form, but he possessed little or no appetite. Prayers were said before and after the meal. At long last when the curfew bell finally sounded, he mustered all possible haste and retired to his cell. Once there he proceeded to gather his meager possessions into a bundle, although there was not much to keep him busy at the task: a few changes of linen, four white shirts, two black cravats and perhaps a book or two that he treasured. In less then three fourths of an hour he prepared himself to depart. He kneeled beside his narrow bed and murmured his last prayers within the walls of the seminary. Soon it was time to turn out the light for the night and when he crawled beneath the bed covers he was fully clothed. Therein the darkened gloom of his cell he waited nervously until the proper moment would present itself to depart. The lightning flashed illuminating his humble quarters while the rain beat hellishly against the walls of the somber building.

Some forty minutes later Christopher shook himself free from a crazy tormenting dream. Startled from his unintended lapse into sleep, he sat bolt up in bed, seized the small clock beside him, then returned it haphazardly to its shelf. It was time for him to leave. He strapped his bundle onto his pack in pack fashion, and sped forth into the wild, wind lashed night, stealing from the building across the wet ground to the university tower. By the time he reached his destination to await Rue's arrival he was wet to the skin. The brooding black clouds rumbled themselves into a furry and the rain lashed down on the anticipating Christopher in an avalanche of course swelling drops of water.`

He stood beneath the dripping eaves of the tower, straining his eyes up and down the inundated road, tensely listening for hoof beats or grinding carriage wheels. Finally, after some disappointing moments, when a crash of lightning lit up the roadway, he sighted in the wet distance a carriage and a pair of poorly driven horses which indicated that only a woman could be controlling the reins. His heart rapped against his chest; he saw the horses galloping through the downpour, their nimble hooves wildly splashing through the puddles of water. Again the lightning flashed and this time it played about Christopher's feet in a lively saraband. He ran out onto the road. The horses were slowing down. Christopher sprang forward seizing the reins and brought beast and carriage to a sudden halt! Then Rue called out to him; her jeweled fingers handed him the reins. Immediately he jumped into the carriage beside her.

"Good heavens, you're drenched!" he heard Rue cry as his lifted arm brought the whip down upon the horse's hinds. The animals whinnied, reared, then bolted forward speeding the lovers into the gaping blackness of the chilled wet night.

They rode onward and onward through the wet dismal night until presently they came to a fork road. Christopher pulled at the reins; the carriage jolted to a halt and he turned to look at Rue inquiringly. In his haste and excitement of his decision it never occurred to Christopher as to where they might journey. The first road was little more than a path that would eventually lead them back to Fairlee. The other was a wide road that Christopher had never traveled before. In that hesitating moment of deciding roads, the heavens opened and a bolt of fiery lightning struck a huge fir tree, hurling it down directly in the path of the first road. Rue sought Christopher's hand, it was wet with rain. "It's destiny pointing the way for us, Chris," she said tightening her fingers about his hand. "That way is closed to us forever. There's no returning . . . What is the nearest town on this road?"

"Thetford, I believe," and he released the reins in that direction.

"Is it very far?"

"No, not very. Why do you ask?"

"I'm anxious to stop somewhere so you can get out of those wet clothes, *silly*." Rue threw the lap robe about his shoulders, then she fastened the ends of the robe with her diamond dress pin so it wouldn't slip off. Christopher grumbled at her because she pinned it too high to his chin. "I don't want you catching pneumonia on me," she scolded. Rue's concern for him moved Christopher's heart, and for the moment he postponed the numerous questions that were running through his mind. Moreover, he was cold and wet and he turned eager thoughts toward the moment when they were to settle someplace and talk over their problems. He was tired and sick with worry at the prospects of fatherhood, and the dreary ovation of rainy weather had not helped to make things easy to bear. Christopher cracked the whip over the horses demanding more speed; a tiring journey lay ahead of them and the rain indicated no sign of relentment.

At length, they reached Thetford, cold, wet and tired. At 3 A.M. they boarded a southbound train. Rue explained that they should go to her beach house on Long Island. She wired the servants to put the house in order and when they arrived there, Rue dismissed all the help. "We can be alone for a change," she told Christopher, "we don't want prying eyes around to trouble us. We're both tired and need some seclusion."

It was early September. The weather was very warm and the sighing winds blew off the oceans to the sunlit sands of the shore with a whispering promise of Indian Summer. Rue's house was a large and beautiful place. A small sail boat bobbed lazily at its mooring and there were acres of private beach which gave one a sort of beguiling fancy as if being tucked away on some south sea's island, safe and free from a care worn world. The house had been an anniversary present from Rue's husband, Paul, and he spared his wife no amount of luxury, but as Rue had often quoted him: 'He was rich enough and could afford her little extravagant caprices.' Just to think of Paul caused Rue enough unhappiness to make her cross for hours. How could she possibly be happy with an old man such as Paul now that she had won Christopher.

She had found happiness with Christopher and that made her world of luxury complete, but ever since they had settled together, Christopher insistently pursued her with the matter of getting a divorce, and the problem of divorce caused Rue a great deal of torment. Not for the fact that she loved Paul Hastings, but for the simple reason that her marriage to him meant security and untold wealth. So far she had been successful in delaying Christopher's demands that she break off with Paul and marry him.

Rue wondered what would happen when she could no longer put Christopher off with lame excuses. She was almost beside herself with the thought, and feared the moment. True Christopher was strong and without doubt capable of supporting her and their expectant baby, but how could she possibly accustom herself to live on some meager income that he might earn. The thought of such a middle class life sickened her! Never could she return to the dreadful poverty she had known as a girl. The thought was madding to her imagination, so she put the entire problem away until some other day. This was a time to live! For now she must contrive some alibi to satisfy these foolish middle class notions of Christopher. It would be a long while until the baby came, and in the meantime she would think of something until then. Rue told Christopher that she had written to her husband and asked him for a settlement and that he was not to trouble himself with unnecessary worry. Everything would come out alright in the future. The important thing was to make the most of the moment. As for Rue, she could see nothing for her to fret over; it would be at least another year before Paul Hasting's return from South America.

The days were beautiful and too inviting to remain within the house; most of their time was spent upon the beach. With the aid of two pieces of slender drift wood and the use of some blankets, Christopher fashioned a lean-to for them to lie under when the sun became too hot to bear. Rue plagued Christopher about his selections of colors in making their funny little tent like pavilion. He chose a brilliant orange blanket for their sloping ceiling and a somber green one for the carpet, but all in all it seemed a cozy little dwelling, serene and sunny. To them it was like a place that was protected by balmy winds—completely lost from the world. A seclusion of complete happiness.

Christopher wore only a large blue handkerchief of Rue's about his loins as he lay asleep in the sunlight with his head in Rue's lap; she protected the delicate nakedness of her skin by wrapping her body in the flimsy covering of a silk sheet. Her dark wavy hair tumbled loosely about her shoulders. Her back was turned toward their pavilion and it protected her from the sun; she bent down to kiss his lips and he awakened quietly. "Did you dream?" she softly inquired.

"I did, and yet it was not so much a dream as it was a promise," he said reaching up for her hand and holding it fast. "I was conscious of my head in your lap and the sun on my body. I dreamed that we were in the sun just as we are now, and together we talked of our baby to come. I remember saying to you that I wanted the child to be a girl, and hoped that it would look more like you than me, because I was born without hands and didn't want her to look like me. That part of the dream was bad and you wept for my sorrow. I told you not to cry, and then I wanted to kiss you and drive away your tears, but when I went to reach out for you a cloud drank up the sun and I couldn't find you anywhere because there was no light on the earth. It seemed that we were to be parted forever. But suddenly somewhere in the dark I heard your laughter and you called out to me. It was then that I awoke . . . . It was a foolish, lonely dream."

"But why did you imagine yourself without hands?" she said sympathetically as she indolently stroked his hair back of his sunburned temples. The sun had tanned his handsome face to a healthy glow. So different from the pallid expression he wore the day she visited him at the seminary. Had happiness with her borne back the health to his long muscular body that now stretched before her on the sands. How she loved him! Rue kissed the fingers of the hands that he dreamed he no longer possessed.

"Rue," he murmured her name languidly, "perhaps I had such a dream because I am not using my hands to earn money to bring my child into the world. I feel so small living here in Paul's house. I must go out and earn a living and prepare for you and our baby.

Rue, supposing something should happen to you! We should prepare for the day when your time comes."

Rue put her hand over his mouth. "Silence Darling," she said to him, "you promised that you wouldn't think of such things. At least not for a while. Remember this is our honeymoon. Let's worry about today, tomorrow will soon take care of itself. Promise me, Dear." Then she gave forth a little laugh. "How like a man," she snickered. "You worry for nothing." My time is far off, and I'll remain slim for a long while, so you needn't fear that you'll have to sleep with a swollen consort."

"Don't say that, Dearest . . . I have no fear for that. It's only for you that I worry." He pulled her down beside him and kissed her. "Maybe I should grow a beard or perhaps a mustache to look more on the fatherly side," he said and kissed her once more. "Would you like me with a beard?"

"I'd adore you anyway," she replied feeling his arms around her and rubbing her cheek against his face. "But please Darling no beard or mustache. I much rather you the way you are." Then a look of consternation crept into her eyes. She pressed closer to him, making him promise that he would not question the future until the proper time. "Love me, Chris," she whispered, "and hold me tight. Happiness lasts for so short a while. Say that ours will endure forever!"

Christopher kissed her mouth and tightened his arms about her until she seemed to be crushed against his chest. "Frightened little goose," he said, "now tell me just who it is that's afraid of the future? If God wants our happiness to last . . . it will. It's in His hands, so why should we worry? I'll always be here, Rue . . . You know I will."

"You're a fatalist, Chris. You believe too much in destiny. But I know somethings," she said in a hushed voice; "that what we treasure today most can be lost, and things do change. I fear change . . . it usually breaks up the good." Rue rested her head upon his chest; she could hear the beat of his heart and her thoughts went back to his words about God. Was their happiness o last? She was struck with a dread read . . . Had he forgiven her for inducing him to come away from the seminary? Would the Creator punish her for that sin? Rue bit her lip to keep from crying. She must never lose Christopher. Her happiness depended too much on him. Things will be different when the baby comes, she thought. My little baby whose heart is within me is the better part of Chris. The baby is the great bond between us. He would always cling to her as long as there was the baby. How glad she was of that!

"You're so still, Rue; I can hardly hear you breath." Christopher's voice breaking in on her thoughts so suddenly almost startled her. Then in a tender tone, he asked her to tell him her thoughts.

"I was thinking that this little beach with its absurd little tent is our Eden," she murmured rolling onto her back and resting her eye on a distant cloud. "What do you suppose Eden was really like, Chris?"

"Like nothing we could imagine or have the tongue to describe." Christopher turned to rest on his side and supported his weight on his elbow with his hand against his face. He smiled and looked down upon her. Rue seemed exceptionally beautiful with her golden face smiling against the dark careless spread of her silken hair. "Why do you ask? Is it because you feel like Mother Eve with the life of our child within you?" He bent his head and kissed the hollow at the base of her throat.

"If I feel like Eve, my dearest, it is only because I am made fruitful by Adam's son. Our lives beat with one heart and one purpose . . . for each other!" Rue looked at him with her searching eyes: "You are not sorry about us, are you, Chris?"

"If I were, Rue, I would not only be ungrateful, but insane. I can't believe that I had a life before you. The gloom of the unhappy past is swallowed up in my rapture and prophetic inspiration of you." Once more they kissed and he laid down beside her.

For a long while there was silence between them. Then Rue said:

"Chris, I could never understand that part about the serpent tempting them. Somewhere along the line when they were copying and recopying the scriptures, somebody got careless and omitted something."

He lifted his head from the gentle curveness of her shoulder and shot her a quizzical glance: "What in the thunder are you talking about?" A wry grin played on his lips, "You don't make sense."

"Adam and Eve, of course. Don't you think God knew what would occur if two physically perfect humans were placed nude in a garden of such paradise and bliss?"

"Of course, he knew. The important thing was that they gave their word and later broke it."

"But—"

He cut her dead. "But it is entirely too infinite for us to venture into detail over just now. You must have been a poor bible student, my dearest Rue." Christopher suddenly crouched upon his haunches and in the next moment he swept Rue up into his arms and carried her down to the mooring. She yelled in a surprised glee, kicking up her legs and at the same moment tried to steady the sheet about her body. "It's time to go for a sail!" he demanded in a short laugh and at the same moment trying to juggle her wiggling body in his arms.

"But, Chris let me go into the house and put on some clothes. I can't go out to sea swaddled only in this flimsy sheet! Please, Darling put me down! Chris!"

He laughed again, and with nimble caution his long legs stepped over the glimmering abyss of water, alighting from the rough wooden mooring onto the deck of the little sail boat. "Chris," she cried once more, "I really should go back and get dressed. It isn't decent to go out to sea like this. Supposing we're seen! Let me go back and I can bring back your shirt and pants."

He silenced her lips with a kiss. "It will serve you right," Christopher laughed freely. "No one should be so Bohemian under the broad sky of day."

"What about you with only a handkerchief for protection, smart Alec!" He gave her buttocks a slap and then kissed her cheek for that remark. "But one moment, Darling," she said composing her features in serious grimace. He paused and listened intently, and she asked: "Wasn't it hard for them to keep their promise?" Christopher rolled his eyes back into his head as a gesture of exhaustment and in the next moment he lowered her to the deck and rolled her over as though she were a barrel. "Chris!" Rue had all she could master to keep her improvised toga from slipping off her body. "Really, Chris," she pleaded with him. "I can't go out this way. Let me go back to the house, please Darling?"

He stood before her tall and bronzed in the sunlight and looked at her with a sheepish glance of surrender. "Very well, if you must," he said in a grumpy tone. "But make all possible speed. If you're not back in time for castaway, I'll hoist sail without you." She was trembling with emotions and thoughts when Christopher put his arm around her shoulders and steered the crimson sailing craft over the breeze ruffled waters into a golden ray of setting sun.

5

Christopher murmured to Rue, warning her to beware of her footing as they walked down the slippery gangway, disembarking in the raw wet afternoon to set foot in Liverpool. Rue's gloved hand griped Christopher's arm and she turned her face into the rough cloth of his shoulder to avoid the icy mist that was blowing into their faces. The weather giving forth with a dreary ovation, they remained side by side beneath a dripping pier shelter while a customs inspector rummaged through their luggage and personal paraphernalia, and more than once Rue was forced to scold the inspector for handling her jewels too roughly.

Christopher watched on unconcernedly while his eyes met with those of so many uncomfortable men and woman who were bundled in great coats and galoshes while they hustled to and fro to retrieve their personals. There seemed to be a multitude of people greeting each other on that day, they threw their arms about their loved ones and smothered them with kisses. And all about them, spotted here and there were care worn weary men in khaki. Grubby newsboys were bursting through the noisy crowds shouting the ever lingering bulletins concerning the Archduke Francis and the Sarjevo incident. Black headlines streamed of Austria's pretended outrage and alliance with the Kaiser. No one seemed truly happy, and the green breath of war hurled her infectious mist about the globe as hell seemed to thunder from everywhere.

Finally the ordeal with the customs inspector was over with. Despite the inclement weather, Christopher found no difficulty in securing a carriage. Rue steadied her hood and drew her ankle length fur cape more tightly about her; she grumbled something about splashing her slippers in a rain puddle but Christopher gave no heed to her complaints. He helped her into the coach and followed in after her, slamming the carriage door behind. Soon they were sped away in a driving rain to a downtown hotel.

It was still raining the following morning when Rue carried breakfast to Christopher's bed. She placed the tray on the night table then started to wake him. "Wake up, Darling it's late," Rue cooed in his ear, then she kissed the side of his face a number of times until her lips met with his. "Wake up," she urged once more. He opened his eyes and rolled over on his back. Rue proceeded to pick the pillows from the floor and place them behind his head. Still very much asleep, he spoke and inquired of the time.

"Past eleven. I've brought you breakfast."

"Rue, you shouldn't—"

"Shouldn't bring you breakfast?"

"No," he answered apologetically. "I mean let me sleep so late."

"You were tired and needed the rest. Drink your orange juice." She handed him the glass and placed the tray on his lap.

"I really should get out of bed, Rue—it's very late. I'm not used to sleeping so late."

"Nonsense, now eat your breakfast. I took great care to get the right things for you. Besides you didn't sleep well last night, you were restless and I had to see that you kept the covers on—I think you had bad dreams."

She looked at him with her sharp blinking eyes and he felt like a sleepy hairy lion and she was his mate, the lioness who braved the cutting bleeding rocks of the mountain carrying food in her mouth to his den. He was cross with himself. "I don't remember dreaming," he answered. "Did I say anything?"

"No, but you perspired a great deal," she said, then suddenly she began to laugh, mocking his expression and tantalizing him. However, she quickly curtailed her merriment; she didn't like the growing doubt in his eyes and she had no desire to anger him. No man appreciates a woman's laughter when he is in doubt as to what she's amused by. "Don't look at me that way, Darling," she continued in a coy voice, endeavoring to quell his skepticism. She fumbled with a loose button on his pajamas, "I was only poking fun at you. When a man asks if he talked in his sleep, he usually means did he speak the name of another woman." She bent over and kissed his forehead. "Forgive my little jest, love." Rue started to change the subject and then suddenly the button came off of his pajamas. "I must buy you some new things," she said lightly. "These are too worn . . . I don't like you in these monastery rags."

He suddenly stopped eating and brought his knife down to the silver tray in a loud indignant bang. "Rue, please, I wish you wouldn't speak that way! Anyhow, they are not *monastery rags*, as you call them. With a little mending they will be perfectly good enough for me. Besides, you'll not buy me anything—I'm not a *gigolo*! God made me healthy, I can work."

Rue pulled a handkerchief from her breast and dabbed it to her eyes. She pretended to cry. "I offended you, Christopher, we always quarrel when I mention that place. It is not my fault if I wasn't born like you—You hate me because I'm not of your faith. Soon I'll be all swollen, and you'll hate me all the more!"

"That's not true, Rue and you know it. There is only one God, and every man must revere *Him* in their own way—How else can we be free and happy?" He took her hands in his saying: "Listen, Rue, we must straighten out our lives." He spoke to her in a very compassionate way. "No one is to blame for what has happened, what's done is done." He lowered his eyes, "Things cannot go on this way, something must be done, I—I don't want my son to be born . . ." He couldn't resign himself to the vile word of illegitimacy; he closed his eyes and his own obscure past and confused life came flying back at him. It brought him pain not to know his true self.

Rue felt Christopher's fingers slip away from her hands; she looked at his face, he seemed spent and worn, there was pain in his eyes intermingled with an expression of disregard. His lack of spirit startled her and for the moment Rue felt that he had escaped her; moreover, she feared that when her figure would lose its form she would no longer be attractive to him. She must win him back, she thought. Her beauty was her only weapon. It would be bitter medicine to lose him. She knew that this was the only man she had really loved. She won him with her cunningness, then she must hold him by the same method. She would promise anything to keep him and she would begin by pretending that she was weak, appealing to his strength for her great support. Suddenly she put her head on his chest, her voice cracking in little heart-breaking sobs. What was she to do? Christopher could offer her no support, at least he could not keep her in the pomp and splendor in which she had grown accustomed. Christopher, she loved with all her being, but if she were to get a divorce—and, surely that's what he implied when he told her: '*We must straighten our lives*'—and this she must promise to do. But to divorce Paul Hastings, would mean divorcing her wealth. She could never mend clothes and scrub floors like any ordinary woman . . . As her mother and grandmother had done. The mere thought of it was mean and sick to her imagination. How could she return to the poverty she knew in her childhood? No! she could not do that—it would be unbearable! Rue sobbed more bitterly when she brought to mind the vile things she was forced to do before she married Paul Hastings. What days of utter hunger, rags and pitiful squalor!

No! Rue made up her mind. Her life would not be one of poverty, she would have Paul Hastings' money and the man she loved also. But Rue must be clever, she thought, and as she lay there with her head on his chest, she knew what she would do. Between her subduing sobs and tears her agile mind developed the plan. She wrought it from a rough scheme into what she thought was a practicable delineation, she would merely tell Christopher that her attorneys were having difficulty in securing the divorce since she and her husband were both living on foreign soil. This would be her stratagem, her great little game of subterfuge and she would repeat that story whenever necessary until he would believe it. And when that plan would become ineffectual—Well? . . . well that would be another day, and she would think of something . . . something.

Christopher smoothed down the back of her hair stroking her head sympathetically; he couldn't bear to have Rue cry that way and he was angry with himself for having started their little quarrel. "Please, Rue Dearest . . . don't cry. Your hurt is my wound and when you are melancholy so am I. Rue sit up and look at me." She lifted her beautiful face and put her cheek against his. Her lovely dark eyes were red and tear swollen. "Darling, what's happened to us . . . I don't want to make you unhappy. I only want what is best for us. We must put our affairs in order, Rue. If not for the sake of decency, then for the sake of our baby . . . don't you understand?" Their eyes met and Rue sniffled a halfway reply; he took her face into his hands and with his thumbs he stretched her rose red lips into a smile. He made up his mind not to question her anymore that day about the affair. She promised him that her attorneys were taking care of the matter and that seemed good enough for him.

Rue went over to her dressing table and applied some powder to her face and near the corners of her wet eyes. She came back to him and sat down upon the bed. "I am going to order you some fresh breakfast," she said with all the air of a long married wife. "This is too cold for my darling to eat."

"No, Rue. Don't bother, I'm not really hungry." He threw off the bed clothing and pushed his feet into his slippers then looked about for his robe. Rue picked it up from the floor and helped him donn it. Christopher tied it about him then settled himself in the large wing-chair beside the fireplace. The rain had ceased to fall but the morning was still grey and cold which caused Christopher to feel more so and out of sort with life. He took up the morning paper which rested on the table beside him. The black headlines screamed of nothing but the war—Kaiser Wilhelm and Belgium's struggle for survival. In one corner of the paper a small article told the story of American nurses volunteering for war services on the Belgium frontier. It gave a small list of their names and among them was Sarah Morrison. Christopher sat up and read the article with interest. He called Rue to his side. "Look, Rue," he cried excitedly. "Ellgate's fiancée has volunteered for war duty. Did you know her?"

"Only slightly. We met once at the Ellgate's town house, I remember she seemed a lovely girl with a lot of ambition for her career." Rue sat in his lap. "If she and Hans were engaged, I think he will have his hands full in holding her down. She was too inspired with the fire of Florence Nightingale and the white gauze of surgery to devote herself to any one person, she told me. She'll be in her glory at some soldier's hospital." Rue's thoughts wandered back to the wide-eyed and tawny haired Abigail. "In some respects, Sarah puts me in mind of that Trent girl . . . She too was full of ambition, but for an entirely different cause, you understand."

Christopher smiled: "Yes, you mean Abby. She seemed like a crazy little thing—always wanted to go on the stage." He sighed, "I guess someday she will. I hope so for her sake."

"Chris, you don't think America will be sucked into this horrible war!"

"I hope not. Anyway, Germany and the Kaiser ought to know better than to trifle with us." Christopher filled his lungs with air, and in a feeling of pride he said: "I guess we showed the world what we can do back in the *Spanish American. Remember the Maine!* as I use to hear Mr. Tergauer say whenever he grew angry at the world." Christopher reflected on the past and his thoughts went out to his friend. "Poor Ellgate, he must be mad as thunder and damned broken up about Sarah. I pray that nothing happens to her. He loves her deeply, you know." He put his arms about Rue, "But if America should go to war, and I pray that she doesn't . . . I should want to fight, Rue. I want you to understand that."

Rue trembled and put her face against his chest. "Of course, Chris, I understand," she said but her tone conveyed only a promise of the moment with the make-believe quality of lines in a play. Rue left him and strode over to the window and looked down at the busy wind swept street below. The grey ugliness of the tall, rigid commercial buildings filled her spirit with gloom. "Chris, are you happy here in Liverpool?" Her back was toward him and she spoke with all the coyness of a spoiled child. "What I mean is, do you like the city."

"I don't know. We've only arrived; how can I tell until we get accustomed to the place," he spoke to her over his shoulder and his eye caught the blush of her cheek. "Rue," his tone was demanding, "come over to me." She hesitated for a moment then with some reluctance she sauntered over to his chair. Christopher reached out his hand to her and she sat down in his lap. "Before this game of cat and mouse begins, supposing you end it right now and tell me what's really on your mind?"

"Well . . . it's that," she curled the ends of his hair around her fingers until the proper words could frame themselves in her mind. "It's only that I would like to go away to some small winter resort until the baby comes. It is too crowded in this big hotel and soon I will be too swollen to go about in public. Would you mind so terribly if we were to go away once more?"

"No, not if you really want. But where would we go, have you a place in mind? It would be good to get away someplace all to ourselves and wait for *little Rue*." His mind went back to Rue's divorce but made no mention of it. If only the affair was settled he could be a much happier man. With the birth of the baby they would have to show some sort of certificate of marriage in order to christen it properly. He turned his thoughts to the lighter side. Why should he worry: Everything between them was certain to come out right."

Rue got up from his lap and went over to the mantel-shelf. She picked up some travel folders then came back and sat on the hassock before him. "I asked the bellman to bring these up when I rang for breakfast this morning." She shuffled through the pack until she located the one she desired. "This is the place, Chris. I'd like to go there; it sounds so romantic. Lake Crystal located high in the mountains and it's not too far away. No more than a day's journey by train. Can't we go there, Darling!" She threw her arms around his neck, "Besides, I want to show you how well I can ski."

"I'm afraid that there will be no skiing for you. You want to kill yourself? Remember you're to be a mother!" he laughed then kissed her.

"Oh! Chris, what do you say?"

He leered at her with his bright blue eyes as if she were really a spoiled child: "When do we leave, Darling?"

A light snow fell the afternoon they came to the resort. It was an out of the way place which seemed to be encompassed on all sides by a mountain chain of high jagged snow peaks that spiraled in white brilliance against a blue winter sky. It seemed accessible by only one path, and that ran parallel with the railroad. They were both glad that they had left the harsh cry of the city behind them, for the little township conveyed a promise of peace; moreover, it appeared to be free from the thick winter crowds who sought nothing but slothful pastime. Rue locked her arm with Christopher's as they walked from the drowsy depot and past the shops and post office toward a rambling log building that boasted of the name *Queen Ann Hotel & Tavern*. A lilt of joy and excitement seemed to fill the atmosphere around them; it seemed to be in the air and upon the smiling faces of the people who walked past them. At the Queen Ann, Christopher held audience with the renting agent and rented a cabin. Thereafter he joined Rue in the refreshment lounge. He came up to the small table she sat by and drawing up a chair sat down and proudly presented Rue with the key to their future home. Christopher caught the eye of a waiter and ordered the meal. Then just before they were readying to depart a dreamy eyed young girl came over to their table.

"I trust you'll not think me rude," she said to Rue in a very sheepish tone. "But it seems that your husband has hired the only available sleigh in town. The others are on the road and we can't see any possible way to get to our cabin. I was wondering if you would be so good as to give us a lift?"

Rue exchanged glances with Christopher; the girl appeared to be so terribly distressed. "Of course we shall be pleased to do you the favor," Christopher told her. "What is your cabin number?"

"29; I know that's asking a great deal, I understand that it's quite a little ways from the village."

"Did you say 29!" Christopher beamed with surprise. "Rue, these people are going to be our new neighbors. What a happy coincidence!"

"What a happy surprise!" Rue recited taking the girl's hand, "I hope we grow to be friends."

"Thank you so much," the girl cried with appreciation. "But now if you will be so kind as to excuse me, I'll wait for you on the gallery. Robert was so angry with the driver when I left him, that I fear he might strike the poor man down." With that she sped from the refreshment room, leaving Christopher and Rue confused but so thoroughly amused. He paid the bill, and they went out to join the couple on the gallery. They came out into the fresh snow and air to be immediately confronted with the harassed couple.

The young man extended a hand to Christopher. "I know you must think the deuce of me for being forward, but you see we're in a hellish predicament." He seemed flushed with embarrassment when he introduced himself. "I'm Captain Robert Scott of His Majesty's Cavalry, and this is my wife, Isobel."

They shook hands and exchanged greetings.

"It's an honor to know you, captain," remarked Christopher. "I am Mr. Wensdy and this is Mrs. Wensdy," he felt Rue's eyes burn on his face. "I had just mentioned to Rue how fortunate for us to have such a pleasant person as your wife as a neighbor, even though we are a whole long mile apart." He nodded his head toward the sleigh and the impatient driver. "We better climb aboard, twilight will be descending upon us within the hour."

Rue and Isobel occupied the front bench and Mr. Scott and Christopher sat in the rear seat. After they had been upon the snow streaked road for a time Mrs. Scott turned around to face her husband, and informed him she suspected that Rue and Christopher were newlyweds the same as they. Mr. Scott put the question to Christopher if there was any truth in his wife's prophecy. Naturally Christopher confessed it to be true and later threw in the surprise climax of his approaching fatherhood. The couple squealed with delight and hoped someday for the same blessing. By the time they deposited the Scotts before the door of their cottage they explained, that the captain was on army leave and had eagerly accepted this opportunity to wed. Finally they departed in gay spirits and each was addressing the other by their given names.

It snowed the first night they spent in their cabin, and before Christopher turned out the lights and crawled in bed with her he banked the chimney with enough logs so the fire would burn all night.

They were happy in their little cabin with its polished pine floor and the white bear skin rug sprawled like a friendly thing before the roaring flames on the hearth; and to make their coziness complete, Rue dressed the windows with heavy green curtains: "Green for youth," she told him," with just enough color for the promise of spring. The snows came thick and swirled high against the door. Snowbound and happy . . . each contented with the other. Christopher had never known Rue to look so beautiful. Sometimes she would read to Christopher as he lay upon his back before the trembling glow of the fire, and when she grew weary of the proceedings he would take up the volume and read to her. When they no longer found pleasure within the books, they would enjoy their favorite past time of conversation—idle talk between lovers, and then more chatter concerning this, that and really nothing in general, but it was good just to be near each other and listen.

Friday afternoons were the days Isobel Scott usually came over to accompany Rue on her visits to the doctor. Often, when Isobel came to visit with them, she would jest with Christopher and delight in his dilemmas. The blood flushed into his cheeks when Rue mentioned on numerous occasions how Christopher would stir out of a perfectly sound sleep, tense and startled, to inquire if she felt well as he dreamed that her time had come. Once Rue told him laughingly that she feared he might have to visit the hospital before she did. It was a grand joke between them. As the days sped past their friendship with Robert and Isobel Scott grew increasingly. Isobel possessed a crafty hand with needle and yarn and one day she presented Rue with a knitted baby ensemble.

Christopher soon came to the door. "What! No kiss for me?" He gave Isobel a bear hug.

"Hey! That's my wife," Robert laughed. He approached Rue and wrapped his arm about her shoulder, "How's the little mother on such a frosty morning, eh?"

"Delightfully well, thank you," she told him. A shine was on her smooth round face, "Now, Mr. Scott would you be so good as to escort me into the cabin? I am freezing out here."

They went into the warmth of the cabin. Rue and Isobel went into the kitchen and prepared lunch for the men to take with them on their outing; later the four of them gathered about the fireplace laughing and talking. Robert sat beside the gramophone and kept changing the records at fitful intervals and playing music that seemed entirely out of rhythm with the chatter. Christopher stood before the roar of the chimney place with his back turned against the crackling flames. Soon he began to refill the cups that Isobel and Robert dangled on their index fingers. "Stop juggling my wife's chinaware," he smiled in a jocund way; he could feel Rue's eyes upon his face when he referred to her in that manner. "Hold your cup still Isobel before I spill coffee in your lap."

"Heaven forbid!" Isobel chimed gaily. "My mood is too languid to disturb. Be careful, Chris, you runneth my cup over" Isobel laughed at her remark and she succeeded in spilling a drop on her skirt. "Oh!"

"You own fault, Mrs. Scott, your pun was phlegmatic." Isobel put out her tongue to him. She was sitting on the sofa next to Rue who held out her half empty glass of milk, giving Christopher a wordless plea to pour coffee into her glass. "No lady . . . cannot do . . . doctor's orders remember," he told her with the wink of his blue eye and then passed her by to fill Robert's cup."

"Chris—" Rue called his name in a long extended tone. "Isobel can't you plead my case? I'm certain that just a taste of that Brazilian brew can't hurt me nor the baby. It's an established fact, a woman in my state should have the things she craves, everyone know that."

Isobel glanced toward Christopher sheepishly. He exhaled a heavy sigh of surrender. "If you must have it . . ." he proceeded to pour out some coffee into the glass but only enough to give the milk a somewhat brownish tint. "Infant!" he called her as in defense of his defeat. Rue's jaw fell, then she framed her lips to protest and he bent down to kiss her. "Be a good girl," he said. "Daddy knows what's best for Mamma."

Rue purred in contentment. "Very well, Darling. I'll do what Papa thinks best." Then she turned to Isobel, her round face smiling and full with the anticipation of motherhood. "You see Isobel what a fortunate girl I am. I always have someone watching over me. You should train Robert to be so attentive. Right now he's behaving like a spoiled boy, and the racket of that gramophone is driving me to distraction."

Robert was playing the *March Milataire*, whistling in accompaniment while simultaneously his hands and foot beats kept in time with the lively rhythm. "My dear, Rue," rejoined Isobel, "All men are but boys; hair grows on their face and chest, and they call themselves *man*. It's a complex that their fathers gave them when he presented them with long pants and told them about life. We must accept the fact." Isobel sought her husband's eyes: "Robert!" she cried: "Robert cease that damn noise!" Robert made grimaces at his wife, then opened the doors of the gramophone so the music could pour forth louder. Isobel shrugged her shoulder and exchanged an exasperated glance with Rue.

"It's best that you let him be," said Rue. "The child's enjoying himself."

"I'll fix him," reflected Isobel, an impish grin shadowed her thin lips. "I'll let him have his way for now, but tonight I'll make him sleep with that musical contrivance. See how he likes that!"

"That's marital gratitude," Robert bleated to Christopher in a voice that seemed choked with laughter. He stopped the machine, then went over to put his arms about his wife. "What a wretch you are," he told her. "If you continue your wanton ways and give me just another piece of your subordination, I am going to throw our marriage license into the fire and spread the disgraceful rumor that you're nothing but my mistress!" He wrapped her in his embrace and together they laughed happily, unaware of the dreadful wound they caused their friends.

Christopher could feel his face burn with embarrassment and Rue's heart skipped a beat. She looked at Christopher's face and thought: Oh! No . . . no . . . Darling! It's not that way with us . . . Our love isn't a cheap one . . . No, Chris, don't be hurt by such a thoughtless remark . . . God married us, Dearest. you said that much yourself . . . Remember we stood under the white moonlight on the deck of our little sailboat . . . Oh! Why didn't we take our little boat and escape to the south seas . . . how easy it would have been to escape forever! . . . Chris, I love you! Christopher came over to Rue and squeezed her hand in his. She was grateful for the strength and understanding his grip conveyed to her frightened heart. How tight his fingers burn over mine, Rue thought. Clinging to me forever like the little life within me! . . . Thank you. Thank you for everything, God!

Christopher bent over and rubbed his whiskered cheek against Rue's smooth face. "Newlyweds," he told her. "How green they are. They believe a piece of paper makes a marriage."

Suddenly Rue burst into a joyous laugh. "yes, Darling, newlyweds."

"You see Isobel," Robert told his wife, "when I am a long married man like Papa Wensdy, I'll be able to philosophize." He got up and stretched. "Well, let's get started papa, if we're ever to get any place. I'm anxious to get out into the snow. Are you ready?"

Rue and Isobel saw to it that they had the things they needed and then saw them to the door. Christopher kissed Rue goodbye for the day. "You're sure you will be alright while I'm gone? I mean you're alright and everything?"

"I've never felt better in my life. You—" She suddenly stopped dead and was forced to catch her breath by inhaling through her mouth. Rue fell against him.

"Rue!"

"Now please, Dear. Don't fuss about me like a mother hen. I just felt a little dizzy and had to catch my breath, that's all. It happens all the time."

"But—"

"But nothing." She put her hand to his face, "Don't worry, I'm alright. It was only our baby giving his father consent to leave."

He kissed her. "Oh, Rue, Rue you're beautiful."

"That's an exaggerated lie! And you know it. I look like a swollen balloon." She looked into his eyes, "But thank you anyway. It was a sweet lie and I adored it. You'll see how beautiful I can be after the baby comes. I'll be a slim new woman for you once more, and set you wild with passion. Then I'll show you how beautiful I can be. We'll go places and have a marvelous life together!"

"I think it's a marvelous life now." He put his fingers through her hair, "As soon as spring comes, I'm going out into the forest and gather the first wild blossoms of the season so you can wear them here. In that little knot of hair above your left brow."

Robert called after Christopher, urging him not to delay any longer. He had the skis lined up and he seemed ready to depart. "What can be so interesting as to keep you clinging to each other in that manner?"

"I'm only inquiring of my husband if he had donned his longies. I never knew a man that disliked wearing underwear so much. I don't want him catching cold in this snow. After all, it's a wife's duty to look after such things. Doesn't Isobel do the same for you, Bob?"

"She already looked after that task before we left home."

"Well, there. You see."

"Yes, but you can't tell me all that billing and cooing had anything to do with drawers!"

"Oh, get the dickens out of here! And you too, Chris. Isobel and I have some woman's talk to hash over."

The morning was bright and sunny when Christopher and Robert said farewell to their wives. The day promised to be beautiful and calm, but toward the end of the noon hour the sun disappeared behind the mountain chain and it began to snow. In a matter of minutes the fine pelting snow began to drive hard; the wind puffed bitterly and the men found themselves in a blizzard. Robert indicated a small shelter house in the distance. They started to ski toward it but in order to reach there they had to risk the ordeal of crossing an ice-bridge, which welded the bluffs of two snow shrouded mountains. The distance between them was but some nine foot breach. Gambling whether or not the ice-bridge would sustain their weight was left to the decision of risking their lives in crossing the bridge, or perishing in the cold of the howling cry of the blizzard. It began to grow dark. Robert exchanged glances with Christopher. In another four minutes they would not be able to see two feet before them, and to gamble on the possibility of skiing back in the storm would be foolhardy. Christopher moistened his chapped hands, then in another moment he kicked off his skis and threw them over his shoulders. "I'll go first," he quietly determined, then turned to walk over the thin bridge. The wind blew strong through the deep white chasm almost setting him over into the throat of the frozen walls below him.

"Don't be a fool," demanded Robert catching Christopher by the arm. "I'd be a coward to let you risk your life first. Think of Rue and the baby, if not yourself. I don't have so much to risk." For a moment they looked at each other. Their brows fringed with white, and their faces raw in the cold wild furry of snowflakes. The wind beat wildly about them; each felt a mutual respect for the other.

Christopher pulled away and went out onto the bridge. "When I reach the other side, I'll throw you a rope," he called over his shoulders.

Robert watched helplessly after him admiring his spirit and courage. He saw the wind pull at Christopher's trouser leg, and snatch his knitted cap aloft with the gale and flying flakes. When he seemed no more than a yard or two on the bridge, the ice nearest the other side started to crack and the bridge dropped with a sudden jolt, causing him to fall to his knees and sprawl flat on his stomach! Robert turned sick and pallid, while Christopher lay tense and breathless with his face against the cold wet ice. Robert looked at Christopher. He felt fear gripping at his throat; he lamented his earthly station because he was unable to aid his prostrated friend on the ice who hovered before his eyes with the breath of death and frigid air above and below him! Robert had all he could govern to restrain himself from crawling out upon the bridge, but he realized too well that the slightest amount of added weight upon the slippery suspension of ice would mean sudden death for Christopher.

After a moment's delay, Christopher's breath returned to him and he began to slide forward on his stomach to the other side. The crawling journey was slow, tedious and dangerous, but at length his frozen fingers felt the scrape of crunchy snow and he pulled himself onto the land. It was almost simultaneous that Christopher on one side and Robert on the other heaved a sigh of relief.

Christopher lifted an arm and waved across to Robert whose person seemed white with pelting snow looked the personification of an animated snow-man, leaping into the air and beating half frozen arms against his body. In another moment a slack hemp tied to a black stone missled across the abyss. Robert jumped into the air and caught it with his gloved hand; he tied it securely about his waist and later crawled out onto the ice. When he was barely in reach of the other bluff, the ice gave completely away beneath him crumbling below the precipice and ever downward into the steep decent! Robert wailed a cry of terror. He dangled in mid-air like a broken marionette and the balance of his life was tied to the rope which Christopher clutched in his raw wind burned hands! Terrified with the awful realization that Robert's life laid in his courage, Christopher could feel the sweat sliding along the small of his back, fear charged his muscles with a strength he had never known was in his being, for within a matter of a few seconds he succeeded in hauling Robert to the top and was pulling the breathless man to his feet, and the security of the firm snow under foot.

Back at the cabin Isobel stirred about the room almost frantic, her nerves acutely strained to the breaking point. The storm had blown itself into a complete fury; the winds sighed cryingly about the cabin and the snow piled high against the door. Twilight turned into black night without a sign of the men, and though that gave her cause for alarm, it wasn't by far her main worry. Rue had been complaining with fierce labor pains for more than an hour, and to make her adversity full of perplexity the storm had torn down the telephone wires and she could get no word to the village doctor. The baby really wasn't due until early spring which was a fair three weeks in the future, but the agony and gaunt impression of suffering in Rue's black sunken eyes gave every indication of premature birth! Poor Isobel so inexperienced in such an ordeal chewed her nails; prancing from kitchen to bedroom preparing for the task she was forced to undertake. Her heart trembled in her body and she prayed for the return of Christopher or Robert—Anybody! Isobel set four great pots of water to boil, then she banked the fire with enough wood and coal until the room was moist and warm. She racked her brain for what was needed in such emergencies! She gave a quick glance toward the satin lined cradle that seemed to wait expectantly for its little occupant. The thought of it made her feel faint! "What are the things I need to do it!" she cried aloud. "Ah! . . . a knife . . . ointment . . . soft white cloth. Yes! plenty of it! Plenty! . . . Some blankets you idiot! . . . Oh God! Knowledge and courage!" She went over to Rue and began to cut away her clothes. "Poor dear! I know! I know! It's quicker this way." Rue twisted and squirmed on the bed and at times she'd lay still as if dead. Her beautiful dark hair lay flung about her head in a rumpled mass. At times it seemed the only thing that was alive about her. In a voice that was high, thin and flat, no more than a whispering cry, she'd repeat Christopher's name over and over. His child was to be born and he was stranded aloft within the crude walls of a frozen shelter station on an empty wind-blown mountain!

At the shelter station Christopher paced back and forth over the rough wooden floor agitated with the wind and snow that imprisoned him. He feared the blizzard might hold him there for days; he was beside himself with worry for fear that something might happen to Rue in his absence, and on more than one occasion Robert was almost forced to knock him down in order to restrain him from breaking out into the raging cold. For he had taken up with but one aim, and that was to be near Rue in her hour of delivery.

Robert rummaged through his knapsack and brought forth a small flask of brandy. He uncapped it and passed it over to Christopher. "Here," he told him, "take a mouthful of this. You look as though you could stand the whole flask. Your face is as white as the snow." He paused and watched Christopher gulp the liquor. "Besides, I can't see that your being there is going to help her any."

"I've always had the dread suspicion that it would be this way. Just when I couldn't be near her, I knew her time would come." Christopher pounded his fist against his palm. "Bob", he said tensely, "supposing she should die while—" he broke off and turned his face to the wall. He felt like dropping to his knees to pray for Rue's safety, but he was embarrassed with Robert standing so close. A few words of the Lord's prayer raced through his mind, but he was so distracted that he couldn't seem to construct the prayer in its proper order. Silently he cursed the snow and wished that it would stop and it would be day so that he could run and see if Rue was well. But he heard the howl of the wind and the monotonous snow pelting against the shelter, then he remembered the breech between the cliffs and the path that now lay lost under the drifting white. He compared his life with the moment and thought how so much alike they seemed. His life went wandering into the lost black path of night, consisting of nothing but a few broken cliffs and ravines that would never form anything sound or logic that he could term right. He turned to Robert. "Have you got any more of that Brandy?" He took the flask and drank greedily, then wiping his mouth on the back of his hand, he asked Robert what was the soonest hour to leave.

"Surely not until daybreak," Robert replied, observing the wild look of pain and anticipation in Christopher's eye. "It will probably stop snowing by then and we can leave in the first light of dawn. We have quite a little journey ahead of us as far as I can judge it. Now that we're on this side of the breech we'll have to circle around the lake before we even enter the village." He squeezed his hand upon Christopher's shoulder. "Spirits up ole man. Rue's a strong girl; I'm sure she'll come out of it alright . . . You're only causing yourself a lot of grief. Nothing gained by worrying, you know. For now what do you say if we try to get some sleep. I want to get a fresh start so I can be off to see that baby of yours if it's arrived."

"Perhaps you're right," he murmured, then slumped down against the wall with his knees to his chin. He pulled his jacket over him to try and escape the chill of the room. Was it yesterday, he thought, he laid upon the warm sands under the moonlight with Rue by his side, her figure slim and her skin firm and cool under his touch? The blue ocean shining in the warm sun seemed like another age entirely compared with the harsh music of wind howling without the thin walls of the shelter. He wanted to think of Rue and what would the baby be like, but he was fatigued with the cold and cares of the day.

Soon he was forced to surrender to a deep drowning sleep and the world became lost in the infinite soft black of slumber.

In a little while Christopher felt Robert's hand upon his shoulder, shaking him roughly and telling him the day light had come at last. He rubbed his eyes wondering how time had fled so quickly for it seemed to him as though he had just shut his eyes for a moment's rest. He climbed to his feet and his legs felt stiff and cramped with a damp chill in his bones. Robert waved the flask under his nose and he took a swallow of the brandy. It was a vile taste so early in the morning, and a poor substitute for breakfast. The flavor of it caused him to shudder and he could feel its smoldering effects in the pit of his stomach, but at least he could find some good in its remedy, for it drove off his chill. They bundled themselves warmly and started on their way. The snow had ceased to fall but the wind out across the drifts in a bitter fury sighed over the endless stretch of white ground before them. By moon-time they finally skirted the edge of the lake and they knew the journey was at long last coming to an end. By the time they entered the village the sun made a fittish attempt to shine and when they were no more than five minutes in the street they were hailed by a group of men who greeted them joyously. While the men were explaining to Christopher and Robert that they were members of a searching crew who were preparing to go out and rescue them, Isobel rode up in a sleigh. The village doctor was seated by her side. Robert sprang to her side.

"Bob!" she cried, throwing her arms around his neck. "OH, Darling, I was near frantic with worry. We were getting up a searching party! Thank God you're alright!"

"Isobel!" Christopher interrupted nervously. "What about Rue? I had a feeling she—" The doctor approached him, and the strained look in both his and Isobel's face conveyed a horrible message that set him wild with alarm! "Rue isn't—"

"Your wife's going to be alright," the doctor told Christopher, "A village woman is up at the cabin with her now." He lowered his eyes and eased his tone. "It was a premature birth," he said solemnly. "It was no one's fault, the baby was—"

"*Born dead!*" Isobel sobbed and flung herself against Robert's chest and wept heartbrokenly.

Christopher was paralyzed with the news and he heard nothing said to him in way of comfort, nor did he seem to see the curious little crowd that huddled about him. His eyes were blank of all expression and a swollen tear ran down his cheek. It was the only tear that he could shed for he was really too stunned with grief to cry. His throat was too frozen with pain to utter any sound of remorse. He was only a stiff mechanized tissue of bone and flesh that presented a figure of man, that was all, and no one disturbed him when he started to walk away, for it was better to leave him be in his hour of torment. At length he stumbled into the cabin and went over to Rue's bed, where she lay waiting for him. They simply looked at each other and knew the pain that each was feeling. Rue patted the covers for him to come by her side, and when he did, he fell on his knees and rested his head on her breast, and through dim, sick waves of melancholy, he swallowed the hard tears that he could not weep.

6

On a wet brooding afternoon, the relatives, friends, close neighbors and curious townspeople of the recently departed Amy Schwartz, crowded into the churchyard at Fairlee. They stood in the swirling wind blown mist, beneath dripping umbrellas swaddled in raincoats and wet galoshes to pay their final homage to the woman they had known so intimately. Charlie Lock held his umbrella over Abigail Trent, the niece of the deceased woman; he placed his arm about the quaking shoulders of the grief stricken girl. Abigail turned her face into the rough cloth of his shoulder and wept silently while the requiem droned in her ears.

On the opposite side of the open grave stood Mrs. Tergauer and Mother Eugenia; the flower smothered casket was practically resting before their feet. The Reverend Mother bit her lip and silently chanted her rosary, while the unrestrained woman at her side wept openly.

"Poor Amy," she sobbed bitterly in a pitifully subdued voice that seemed barely audible. "I knew her, girl and woman, Poor Amy!" Her words came from a frozen throat and they seemed to break through her lips without her knowledge. She covered her face with her hands, weeping. Slowly the coffin was lowered into the gaping wet earth, and the mournful gathering of sullen people had begun to disband. They seemed to move in a sluggishly inert pattern, plodding in somber motion to the forlorn rhythm of the wet mud drumming on the casket lid.

Mother Eugenia took Mrs. Tergauer's arm and started to move away. When they had gone a little of the way she paused looking over her shoulder to view the beautiful blue eyed young woman who wept before the freshly turned earth of her aunt's grave. She felt deeply concerned and was stricken with a remorseful pain for her. She will be alone in the world now, pondered the Reverend Mother. If only she could help . . . However, she deemed it wise not to approach Abigail now; beside, the young man with her was urging her to come away.

The Prioress could see his face now, she recognized him and was a little startled. Of course, the face was slightly changed with maturity, but she knew it after all the years.

This was one of Christopher's friends—on her desk was a photograph of the three of them: Charly, Christopher and Ellgate. She thought of Hans Ellgate and wondered why he had not written to her as he had promised when she had last seen him in her study on that afternoon so long ago. He had told her that if ever he should learn anything of Christopher's sudden plight into nowhere, she would be the first to learn of it. He was determined to uncover the mystery which veiled his friend's past. How distant in the past that all seemed now . . . and what of Christopher? she thought. How strange that he should disappear so completely? Christopher—she almost murmured his name aloud, then she remembered that Mrs. Tergauer had known Christopher also. She almost forgot that. The wind was tearing at her habit; she managed to catch hold of the end of it, drawing it more tightly about her person. She quickened her steps and walked out of the Churchyard with Mrs. Tergauer on her arm.

The doorbell rang, resounding merrily and musically, tingling throughout the empty furnish less rooms and bounding up the angular stairs until it's sound reached Abigail in a bare, but much ransacked pillaged room. She sat on the floor encompassed on all sides by a small canyon of cardboard boxes and wooded crates. The bell sang on while she still continued to pack the box before her, hoping that whoever it might be coming to console her in her grief, might go away and leave her alone.

All these past nine days, ever since her aunt's death, sympathizers had been dropping in unexpectedly to refresh her spirits; they only succeeded in aggravating matters. Moreover, Abigail knew what she wanted to do now, her mind was made up and what was more, she refused to listen to any home spun advice, at least not anymore from the people of Fairlee. The bell rang again and again and this time she surrendered; she shuffled to her feet. Abigail groaned, her young bones ached from stooping for so long a time. She inhaled on a cigarette she was smoking, and then suddenly stamped it out. Her hands waved away the veil of evidence which lingered about her. it wouldn't do her any good to have someone inquire about the odor of smoke which clung to her breath, so she hurriedly slipped a licorice drop into her mouth before she left the room. Abigail frowned upon the thought of having to keep her smoking a secret. True, she had only taken up with it of late, but after all this was 1915; but Fairlee was such a small place and so far behind the time, which was bad enough, but the people in it were so shallow minded.

As fast as her legs could carry her, she clamored down the steps. "O! damn!" she cried lightly when the hem of her dress caught beneath her heel." One day woman will learn to wear shorter skirts."

Finally her hand was on the brass door knob; she saw through the faded lace panel that it was Charly Lock who had come to call on her. She murmured his name under her breath. How was she going to break the news to Charly, she thought? Charly, who had been so good to her these days . . . Charly, who loved her, but his simple ideas of domestic bliss and five hundred dollars in the bank did not conform with Abigail's philosophy. She just couldn't live in Fairlee for the rest of her life; she had to make something of herself before she could really and truly be happy. She opened the door remembering that she must be kind to him. She would never deliberately hurt Charly, he was too god and kind for that.

"Good afternoon, Charly—had no idea it was you ringing." Well, those words were said solicitously enough she mused and hoped that she could maintain as much grace throughout their entire conversation. She stepped aside to admit him, then closed the door. "I gathered as much, "Charly said. "That's why I was so persistent—I knew that you were home." He looked at her and smiled; there was a smudge of dust on her face, but he decided not to tell her about it just now.

"Charly, what amuses you so?" Abigail murmured, with the back of her hand she brushed a wisp of her tousled hair from her forehead. She turned then, and caught a reflection of her face in the mirror. It was the only article which adorned the long and bare hall they stood in.

They exchanged glances and laughed. Charly supplied her with a handkerchief from his breast pocket and he attempted to wipe the smudge away; he also contrived an effort to kiss her, but she quickly turned her face away and swept from his embrace. A clumsy silence separated the foolish and awkward gap between them; Abigail left him standing there and walked into the empty parlor. He followed her. Their footsteps thundered sharply over the carpet less floor, and the booming din clattered to the ceiling; then dying away to the dark corners of the room.

"What have you done here, Abby?" She turned around and looked at him; her eyes carried an expression of a satisfied achievement. "I sold it all, just this morning," she admitted gleefully. "I sold it to the second hand merchant," she reiterated. "I think he gave me a rather fair price. Of course, I'm keeping the valuable things and sending them to my sister, Louise . . . things I know she'll want to keep—you remember Louise, don't you Charly?"

He had drifted away on her and his thoughts carried him to a little bridge of trouble; he couldn't understand why she had sold all the furniture. He wondered, what could her new plans be now? He returned with a start when she repeated his name. "I should hope I do remember Louise," he said in a quick voice. "Chris Wensdy and I got drunk at her wedding," he mirthfully said. "Dad whipped the devil out of me for doing so—to say nothing of the predicament poor Wensdy got in."

"O! I remember that . . . next day, we girls were to have a picnic and you and Chris weren't permitted to join us." She laughed, "O, we were so angry! I don't believe we spoke to you boys for weeks after." "Much has happened since those days," pondered Charly. "Wasn't there a scandal concerning Wensdy sometime back?" "No scandal, Charly, undoubtedly he just made up his mind to leave."

"But that's just it, he left without a word to anyone. I remember there was talk." "There's always talk in Fairlee, Charly," was Abigail's sharp reply; a light spark of anger seemed to curl the very ends of her words. "People just wait for something to talk about in this town. I suppose that they'll talk about me when I leave."

"When you leave?" Charly's voice had suddenly gone flat; "What do you mean?" Abigail saw his face and she was touched with a pain of melancholy for him. This was certainly no way to inform him; this way was so crude and careless, there was something beggarly and utterly despicable about the whole affair, but the words had just seemed to slip out without her knowledge. She suddenly changed the subject, turning to the packing and her sister Louise for escape, hoping that this sudden refuge would suffice, if only for the moment until the time was ripe.

"Please help me with the crating Charly? I want to get these things off to Louise. Poor dear, she was so upset! She wanted to come down for the funeral but it was simply impossible with the children and all, and now, one more on the way—"

She stopped; Abigail could not go on this way, not with that startled look in Charly's eyes. *Good grief,* she thought, he looks as if he would like to strike me! Charly lowered his head and sank down to sit on top of the packing cases. He felt as empty as the room he sat in. There was no need for Abigail to say more; he already knew what she was about to say. He was hurt beyond measure, but most of all, he felt utterly stupid with that blue-white diamond ring burning in his vest pocket. Just because he knew that Abigail would be alone in the world and would need someone to care for her he jumped to conclusions like a foolish jack-in-the box. Now, Abigail was stuffing him back into the box without mentioning a word. Women possess a strange gift and can subdue a man without much effort—it's a magic fiber in their beings.

"Please, Abby . . . I'm not blaming you for anything." He lifted his face and forced a smile, "Remember, I always said, I would keep trying until you finally made me believe that you were not for me." "O, Charly, I feel like a wretched mongrel for causing you this pain. You know there's no one I like better than you—" "But I'm just not the one, is that it?" "Don't say that Charly, it's not that." She waved her hands in a gesture of despair, what could she do to patch up his wounds? She broke down and sobbed: "O, Charly, I want to do things with my life—be someone. I want a career!"

Charly was silent. There was nothing that he could say or felt like saying; all the talk was out of him. He had wooed and lost . . . what more could he do now. He tightened his fingers about her hands and kissed her lightly on the cheek.

"Listen," he said to her in positive tones. "So you want a career? I have a friend in the theatrical business in New York, I'm sure he'll do anything I ask him. I'm going to be the first to help you in this career of yours, Abigail Trent, and damn you! You'll not stop me at that." She looked up at him breathless and startled. "Charly!" An affectionate, melancholy smile shadowed his lips.

7

In the spring Rue and Christopher took a suite of rooms at the Queen Ann Hotel. The cabin reminded them too much of their loss and Rue was still not well enough to travel. Rue yearned for the gaiety of city life; she grew restless with life at Lake Crystal for most of the winter crowds had long departed to seek enjoyment in other capitols, and her days of recuperation seemed so dull. As for Christopher, his heart was still clouded over the loss of the baby, and as far as Rue was concerned she seemed to have forgotten all about the matter behaving as though the ugly affair had happened to someone else who belonged to another world that was far removed from her. She was too taken up with the fashions of the day and extravagant living to brood over things that happened yesterday. She thought of visiting Paris and shopping for new clothes, but she suddenly remembered that France was at war and frowned upon it like it was a thing that brought her an irksome and personal inconvenience. South America loomed up to her as a place that seemed untouched by the world's cares but she could not risk the awful possibility of running into Paul. She flushed when she thought of her husband. She would have to get a letter off to him soon. It seemed a tedious strain to Rue the way she had to dispatch mail to Paul in secrecy, and such lies she was forced to write him! Pretending that she was always visiting with friends of distant relatives. If only she were rich enough to let Paul go his way, then perhaps things would be different. The thought of Paul made her sick and uneasy. Why did she have to remind herself of him? Christopher was troubling her once more with the matter of her divorce. She was glad they slept in different rooms now, it would be much easier to delay the matter now that they weren't so close. Poor Christopher, she thought, why couldn't he understand? Always brooding and troubling himself about things that really didn't matter. She hated the mean little job he had taken in the village. Coloring picture-cards for a travel agency. Oh, how indignified! she thought. He told her he had to do something in order to respect himself. How middle class! They had had a quarrel over that and now she waited for him to return from a walk around the square. He always did that whenever they had their little disputes. When he comes back, I must give him a kiss, she thought. That will make everything alright between us. But right now, she must concentrate on her costume. There was to be a ball in the hotel tonight and she must look her loveliest. She laid down for a nap leaving a note on the table for Christopher to wake her when he returned.

It was late when he came back. Rue had already taken her bath and was in costume when he was just preparing to shave. Rue swept him a quick glance, and to her he seemed tired and worn; she frowned upon the paint stains on his fingers. Perhaps he will feel and look better after a hot bath, she thought. At least she prayed for that much and hoped that the evening wouldn't end in a quarrel, for she heard him grumble something about cutting himself and later curse when he turned on the bath water.

Rue sighed as if to forget the matter, then called in her maid to assist her in putting on her blond wig. The golden blond hair instantly transformed Rue into another woman of eighteen century Paris! Her low cut gown and voluminous skirt was fashioned in a brilliant white, edged in gold lace and strayed with shimmering diamonds. She wore earrings of emeralds which was traditional of the beautiful gay woman she portrayed. The maid fastened a necklace of emeralds about Rue's soft white throat and she waltzed up to the full length mirror to admire the results. She was breath-takingly beautiful! A queen; a perfect Venus in her own sphere! Rue laughed merrily at her dazzling reflection. "Ah! Flora," she said to her maid, "do I not look like La Dame Aux Camelias?" Then Rue threw up her arms excitedly: "Flora, where are my camellias? my costume is lost without them!"

"I have them right here Mrs. Wensdy. White ones as you ordered," murmured the maid. "Shall I help Madam to pin them on her dress?"

"No! no! Flora. Not on my gown but in my hair! The way *Violetta Valery* wore them!" Rue took one final glance of herself and she was pleased. The gold hair was in direct contrast with her lovely dark eyes. She smiled; then with a lift of her gown she turned from the glass and swept toward Christopher's room, humming the gay strains of *Sempre Libera*. The mere title of the melody caused her to tremble with a little inward laugh. Christopher was combing his hair when she came into the room. He was wearing only his black tights; his back was toward Rue and it amused her to see him so clad. His long muscular legs thrust into leggings and the snug fitness about the hips and hard buttocks accentuated the broadness above his waist. His torso was no longer brown as she knew it when they first met but white. She thought of their glorious days under the warm sun and the loss of it made her feel sad. "My poor, Chris," she said to herself, "now the melancholy Hamlet. How appropriate for him." He put on his dark blue doublet and she came over to him and pinned a sapphire to his chest. "There my darling," she told him. "Wear this jewel," and with a little laugh she added: "No one will think it real." He made no conversation with her but continued his dressing. Rue felt his eye on the cleft of her breast and she put her hand there to cover it. She knew too well that he disapproved of her daringly low cut gowns. She thought of explaining to him that it was merely the fashion of the costume and really not her fault, but instead, she remained silent and contrived some attempt at pulling it up a little higher. Rue sat down on the bed and cooed to herself. She could tell in her heart of hearts that he was pleased with her beauty, but also knew that he wouldn't compliment her for it, because for some reason he was cross with her. Like a spoiled child Rue racked her brain for anything she might have done within the last hour to bring about this situation, but she couldn't. She shrugged her beautifully curved shoulders and forgot the matter entirely. Tonight she would only think of being gay. After all, she was masqueraded as a great lady. She must act the part.

The orchestra was playing a lively polonaise when Rue and Christopher entered the ballroom. Rue walked proudly over the dance floor with her jeweled hand resting on Christopher's arm, and many a head turned in observance of Rue's beauty as she passed by. Presently Isobel went over to meet them and they joined a party of people at a near-by table. Isobel, who was costumed as the Maid of Orleans, performed the introductions; endeavoring to maintain a smiling face in spite of her melancholy mood, for her husband had departed early that morning to rejoin his regiment, and the incident had left her quite broken in spirits. She talked loud and fast pushing herself into the merrymaking as an endeavor to forget. The orchestra started up another fast rhythm and Christopher invited Rue to dance.

"Who is that engaging woman?" Asked one matron to another when the handsome couple danced by them.

"Can't you tell?" rejoined the second matron. "That is *Violetta* in her truest form. I've heard talk of her and I must say, I admire her honesty for coming as the *Erring One*, for she is truly that," and the woman laughed at that remark.

"No, no," protested the first. "I mean who is she really?"

"A Mrs. Wensdy, I understand, although we have never been introduced properly."

"And that handsome gentleman, her husband?"

"Who can truly say, my dear. You know the sort of age we live in. But I say he is too attentive to be her husband, but the registar tells me they are man and wife, and I must take the registar's word for that. Look! look!" the woman cried excitedly. "Did you see the way he kissed her throat? Does that look like marriage to you?"

"Truly I am loath to say because my husband hasn't kissed my neck in twenty five years . . . Perhaps they are newlyweds."

"Indeed not. I know better. Don't you recall, she's the one who lost her baby last winter."

"Poor dear, what a tragedy! Then that accounts for it. For I understand that when married people lose a child they make up for the loss by falling more deeply in love. A minister told me that once."

"What do ministers know about such things?"

"I'm sure I can't tell you, dear." Then the woman murmured in an abstract tone: "Remind me to make it a point to have Mrs. Wensdy to tea. I must learn more about her."

The dance soon ended and Rue and Christopher returned to their table, but Rue did not remain seated for very long. One gentleman requested her to dance and after him came another and another. The evening was to come to an end with Christopher having danced but only one dance with her. Later he danced with Isobel and each made an attempt to console the other.

"What are your plans, Isobel, now that Robert has returned to his regiment?" Christopher asked of her. Not that he was so curious to learn, but it was an awkward moment of silence and he wanted to make conversation.

"I've already made plans to visit with my parents in Coventry, and wait. Just wait until this horrible affair of war is over." She muttered with a despondent shrug of her shoulders. "What else can I do except pray. Pray that nothing happens to Bob. I fear he'll be going over soon," she told him rather sullenly, then quickly changed the conversation. "Rue tells me you will be going away soon. Have you any definite place in mind as to where she and you will travel?" The news came as somewhat of a surprise to Christopher. He didn't recall discussing anything about going away with Rue, although he was greatly aware of her restlessness. He made some evasive remark about it and got away from all talk of traveling.

In the days that followed the breech between Rue and Christopher seemed to widen. He was busy with his job and she was consumed with the small social life about her. Isobel was no longer with them and that left Rue idle of companion and she fell into company with a rather wild sort of crowd that recently moved into the tavern. She was never home when Christopher arrived from work and when he left in the mornings she was usually asleep. One Saturday afternoon

Christopher proceeded to the desk in the lobby and inquired of the clerk if any mail from America was received in his name. Without further ceremony the clerk turned about and searched the box in routing fashion, then passed a professional looking envelope with a New York post mark into Christopher's out stretched hand. He had waited many weeks in secrecy for a reply to his inquiry, but when the clerk handed him the envelope he accepted the ominous letter with reluctance and a feeling of guilt; like a vile fellow who committed a harsh deed in the night. He turned from the desk bitterly reproving himself for his up-braiding; moreover he felt that he had not the prerogative to correspond with Rue's attorney—especially without her knowledge of the deed. But he had to quench the brooding doubt which cloaked his thoughts whenever he interrogated Rue about her divorce. As of late, he no longer put the question to her for Rue displayed much ebullition when he did, and most times the results would conclude in a bitter quarrel. And Rue's temper could be fierce, while he rarely emerged as victor. What man can truly say he has had the last burning word when disputing with a woman.

Now in his hand he held the answer to his doubt. But suddenly he was possessed with a strange feeling, and he no longer wanted to learn the contents of the letter. True, the deed was done and nothing could sponge away that, but he could destroy the sort and never trouble himself with the thought again. He would resign himself here and now; he would make his life with Rue. Why should he try to alter his destiny? No man could truly do that. He wanted to run to Rue and patch up all their little difficulties. To take her in his arms and love her. After all, what is life but man and woman in a civilized jungle conforming with the prudish whims of the public. Christopher squared his shoulders and held his head high; his eyes, clear and blue, sparkled with glee; he was light of foot and took long strides of the heavy carpeted lobby until he reached the stairs. He started to mount them, but soon halted in his tracks when his eyes fell upon the great mirror which was flushed against the wall. It stretched from floor to ceiling and took in the complete breath of the panel it clung to, but it was not the object of decoration that impressed him so much as was the scene it reflected. The mirror was so arranged that it showed a clear picture of the refreshment lounge. He could see Rue seated at a table drinking and talking with a gentleman companion; the sight of which caused him pain. Why did this mean thing have to happen when he had composed himself for a new life with Rue?

"I don't blame you for starin' so, Gov'na," the surly voice of the bellman broke in on his thoughts. "Ah been givin' 'er the eye myself . . . a nice looker, eh?" Christopher was thunderstruck! He was too astonished to answer the man, and the fellow rambled out his opinions, never once associating the man he spoke to, with the person he spoke of. "That there bloke with 'er is Mister Flemming, our instructor 'ere. 'e 'as takin' a shine to the lady, I'll say . . . Of course she's 'igh class, but the word goes about—" Before the man could utter another word, Christopher, red with rage, clenched his powerful fist and struck him in the face with such a devastating blow that it sent him sprawling to the carpet. Christopher stood over him for a moment but the man just lay there, apparently knocked out. The commotion drew people from the lobby and refreshment room, and among the crowd was Rue and her gentleman companion. She flushed crimson when her eyes met Christopher's. She could see the anger burning in a brilliant red upon his face. She put her hand to her throat not knowing what to expect, and wondered if Christopher would cause a scene, but instead he turned on his heels and sped up the stairs.

Christopher did not sleep at home that night and when he did return it wasn't until late Sunday afternoon. Rue heard him enter and go quietly to his room. She reclined on a satin Chaise Lounge and waited, thinking that he would be in to see her presently. She was wearing a flamingo colored bed-jacket which was trimmed in expensive white fur. Two silken pillows sustained her back while to the left of her lay a novel and a box of bon-bons. She took up her silver hand mirror and subjected her beautiful face to a minute inspection. She wanted to look her prettiest for Christopher today and perhaps that might please him, she thought. She turned her face to the left, then to the right and was pleased with the reflection therein and carelessly laid the mirror down. Then she glanced around her luxurious room; it's richness delighted her. Her eyes took in the large basket of white and yellow roses at her side and something completely impish giggled within her breast and a thrill went through her to the very end of her toes. She wiggled them inside her silken slippers. She recalled the little card that accompanied the roses. *From an Admirer* the card and it were initialed in a bold hand. Rue giggled again. Perhaps this admirer, whoever he might be, could possibly be of the nobility. She was thrilled, but suddenly a serious expression darkened her lovely features. It would be of no value to have Christopher discover this card, she thought. Especially when he already seemed so displeased with her. "It isn't fair," she murmured aloud. "Not when I have been so sick." Nevertheless she would call him to her side and they would make up. She wondered why women must pamper men and then quickly assumed that the trait was owing to maternal instincts. Rue thought of her own brief span of motherhood. "I must make Christopher forget our lost child," she said. "I will ask *my boy* to sleep with me, and then he will be his old self again." She pursed her moist red lips and murmured: "Ah, my poor Chris—"

She called to him in the next room; she heard him stir from his chair and waited for him to enter her boudoir. Rue glanced at him. His hair was rumpled and he wore a plain white shirt which was open at the collar; she looked upon the blue serge trousers he wore with a frown of displeasure. Why must he cling to those wretched monastery rags? she thought. He possessed others. Rue patted the lounge with her soft white hand, her jewels caught the light which burst into little flames of sapphire, white, and crimson. He was rather reticent when he came over and sat on the lounge beside her. Rue reached out her hand and smoothed down his hair. She offered her lips to his; they kissed but in the next instant he was back on his feet walking nervously back and forth.

Christopher thrust his hands into his pockets and swung around to look at her. "Rue," he said in a choppy tone, "I, I must speak with you."

"About what Christopher, Darling?" she murmured demurely, affectedly coy and modest to the letter. She raised her eyebrows and reiterated: "About what, dear . . . about what?" Rue looked at his face and suddenly caught the flame of exasperation burning in his eyes. She realized that her little game of cat and mouse was pushed too far; she put her hand to her forehead and pondered on the disturbed look about him.

"Your divorce from Paul Hastings, Rue. That's what I want to talk to you about!" She flashed him and insipid glance as though he were speaking to her in a foreign tongue. "Damn this nonsense, Rue! Stop behaving like a child and try to take on an intelligent air."

"But I told you Chris, my attorneys wrote that it will take a great deal of time to put it through the proper channels. Oh, why must we always talk about the darn divorce! Divorce!" she cried. "That's all I hear from you." Again she looked at him, but he appeared to be very much unmoved. She decided to play on his sympathy. "How can you trouble me with this awful thing?" she whimpered. "Especially when I have been so sick."

His patience seemed at the breaking point and he flashed on her in anger." How easily you lie, Rue! God knows you never had any intention of getting a divorce!"

Rue suddenly went cold, in spite of the rouge she wore, she seemed pale and breathless, but at least she had control of her voice, perhaps she could out talk him. "How can you reproach me this way?" She choked. "You know I've filed suit. I've told you so. Is not my word my bond? Oh! Why must we quarrel?"

She left Christopher with no alternative. He had reached the end of all her lying and took the letter from his pocket and gave it to her wondering what she would tell him now. Rue unfolded the letter very clumsily. "It's from your New York attorneys, Rue," he said watching the confused expression on her beautiful face. "They say they have no knowledge of the Hastings' divorce suit. The case never was filed with them."

"And so now you know!" she cried after a bewildering moment. She was indignant and completely outraged. Rue choked from loss of breath, but when her voice came back to her she lashed at him in bitter tones. "Yes, it's true! I did not breathe a word to my lawyers." Her voice was wild and grating," But what would you have me do?"

she cried. "Divorce my rich husband and live in a hut with you and poverty. What a fool I would be! Do you think you could keep me in this apartment—buy jewels like these?" She displayed her tapering fingers," and to say nothing of my clothes. Can you afford it?" Rue all but screamed at him, "whose money did you think kept the roof over our heads and put the food in our bellies? Yes! yes!" she cried in heated tones, "Paul Hastings' money. HIS! HIS! And never once did he question me like a foolish and suspicious thing as you. I spent his money as I so desired and spent it with freedom!" Once more she looked upon him in a vile side-long glance. Her temper had completely unleashed in a furious element. She spat in his path. "*You stupid ass in monastery rags!* What right have you to question me?" She beat upon her breast and in the next instant she flung her hand mirror to his head. The little silver mirror hurled past Christopher's temple, struck the wall in a thunderous peal, then crashed to the floor in pieces. For a moment there was silence between them. Christopher squared his shoulders, looking Rue directly in the eyes. The composed and gentle manner in which he viewed her, filled Rue with a vague and phantomless terror. What would he do? she wondered. Would he strike her back?

He nodded his handsome head to her and for the first time in many weeks he seemed positive of his actions. "Goodbye, Rue," he said in a voice that was almost abstract and phlegmatic. "It all seems to be a laughing little tragedy that we should come to such ends. But you have just told me in no uncertain words what sort of role I play in your little act and I'm sorry. Not sorry for our moments together, but sorry for being such a weak and sputtering idiot. I see that I was only sculptor's clay in your delicate white hands. Your beauty is your power, my Rue. Guard it wisely, for heaven made you too beautiful and there is where the danger lies. I was caught in your web of beauty, but now I feel free, because your temper has made you ugly to me. In all briefness, I feel indifferent . . . I guess that the tragedy of love, my dearest Rue—it's not death nor separation, but *indifference.* Perhaps that is why the real Venus is in cold marble so that she is senseless to all passion and admiration. The creator was wise to make her a myth." His lower lip quivered and a cold perspiration stood out on his brow, for he made up his mind to drink in her beauty for the last time. "Goodbye, my Dearest," he said softly, "have no fear that I, or anyone will take your wealth from you . . . And as for me, I'll simply leave in the monastery rags you first saw me in—" And with that he departed from the room almost broken in spirit. Rue pretended a very pitiful and heart rendering cry. He looked casually over his shoulder to the closed door in back of him. Rue's sobbing voice came through the heavy wooden panel and inside she was thinking: *He'll come back. He'll only go for a walk around the square like he always does . . . But he'll come back. I know he will.*

PART THREE

1

Christopher walked the streets of London. His entire appearance was one of a completely abandoned wretch; he was hungry, weary, unshaven and unkempt. Here in this metropolis of towering stone and fog, a place where time had fashioned pink marble and monumental alabaster in palace form, came an intruder; a stranger in a strange place without so much as a halfcrown to weigh in his palm or to shut his fingers on so that it might support his ebbing spirit.

Onward he plodded, mingling with the vile and noble creatures who walked abroad in the black spring night, drifting through a maze of narrow twisted streets which led him everywhere, and yet nowhere. He traveled from fashionable squares in Mayfair, clubs in Pall Mall, Buckingham Palace, the Admiralty and Westminster Abbey, from the strand with its theatres and hotels, and from Picadilly, down to the Limehouse . . . Limehouse, with its lust and treachery; it's hushed opium dens that seemed to lurk like precarious shadows, slumbering in the blackness and which were forced to quake like evil things before the breath of dawn.

Worn and feeble he no longer had the strength to put one foot before the other; he sank into the gaping blackness of a doorway and slept. When he awoke, a damp chill in his bones and the fog in his throat, he looked out to the dimly lit street and saw men and women pass before his eyes as though they were phantoms in a dream. Sea faring men of low morals were sounding high language through their grubby beards, jostling through the street in merry groups, laughing and talking until they turned into a café where each time the door opened and closed lively music poured forth into the street.

Christopher climbed to his feet and started down the poorly illuminated street; in his heart he hoped to find some suitable place where he might lay his head for the remainder of the night. He had not gone very far when two cheaply dressed young women, scarcely in their twenties, approached him. One of them was so bold as to cling to his arm while the other paused under the street lamp and touched a bit of rough to her already over painted mouth. "Come with me," said the first one who had taken hold of his arm, and being much enamored of his manly grace. "I know of a place where we can escape this wretched fog."

"Oh, push 'im aside," murmured the second, who appeared well schooled in the profession and could tell at first glance how much coinage a prospect carried in his pocket. "Away with the bloke," she continued, addressing her companion by name. "Can't you see 'e ain't no better than a tramp?" and with that the solicitors went their way, disappearing out of the wan yellow light into the hushed still blackness of the brooding fog.

Once again he started on his way but fate would not have him be free of the villainy which sped abroad in the vitiated night. Further along the way he was hailed by two or three young men in khaki who inquired of him where they might satisfy their desires for a price; however, before Christopher could find time to answer them, they were immediately distracted by a cry which came from across the narrow street. They lifted their eyes toward the direction of the sound, and recognized a fellow recruit who hovered in the recess of a second story window. His army tunic lay open in a slothful manner and his yellow hair blew in the wind; he waved to them, calling out in a hoarse drunken voice to come over. The invitation was snatched up without a moment's hesitation, and they went across the way laughing in a rough manner and dragging Christopher with them.

They stepped out of the fog and through the door into the dimly lit establishment. The place seemed filled with tobacco smoke and soft weird music came from an automatic coin piano. Christopher could see drowsy looking men and women sitting in booths behind a spray of beaded curtains. The sweet sickening scent of paregoric fumed in his nostrils—he knew at once they were drinking warm laudanum. Not only was he housed in a place of sensual sloth, but the very walls around cried: "Opium den!" Presently they were greeted by a thin hollow cheek women with cheap dyed hair. Soon they were crowded into a booth and a tallow faced slant eyed Chinese boy brought on a tray of drinks. Christopher scented his glass with caution. It was only whiskey, so he drank without fear. The woman who chose him for a companion sat beside him, thigh to thigh; she rubbed her face against his whiskered cheek and with her arms about his neck she kissed him freely. She possessed natural red hair and might have been a raving beauty some fifteen years past, but now she seemed nothing more than an overly rouged, haggard and depraved women approaching her matron years. Christopher drank the whiskey before him, and then another and another; then because he had eaten little or nothing that day, he had gotten quite drunk within a quarter of an hour. He seemed to lose all control of his emotions and cared nothing for his actions, for he exchanged kisses and embraces with the woman without care or decency. All during the evening the woman referred to Christopher as her *little boy* running her fingers through his hair and patting his head in an affectionate manner. Then at long last when they looked about, they discovered themselves seated alone in a deserted booth. The woman looked at him and laughed: "Ah, my little boy. Your friends have slipped away with their girls to find romance." Later when they were walking across the floor toward the stairway, he with his arm about her waist and his head on her shoulder for support, for he was too drunk to walk alone; he asked of her, in a thick tongue, as to where they were bound. She smiled and put a kiss upon his lips. "Where else," she whispered. "To take my darling boy to bed."

The harsh light of morning crashed through the thinly curtained window. Christopher was rudely awakened by a hand that tugged roughly at the blanket he had wrapped about him; he felt it slide off his bare shoulder and down to the small of his back before he had time to snatch it around him again. He rolled over on his side pushing himself up on his elbow to see a fat oily-skinned oriental woman glaring down upon him with her black beady eyes. A ridiculous smirk shadowed her thin lips as she babbled on in her high chiming, rhyming language, and as far as he could understand it appeared that she wanted him to get out of bed in order that she could make it up. Once more she started to sing song at him, then, began to pull on the sheet under him. He got out of bed and threw the blanket about his body in toga fashion. He began to look for his clothes but the only article he could locate were his shoes and socks. He inquired of the Chinese woman to tell him where his personals might be found. It was a vain gesture. She couldn't speak a word of English and her absurd babbling started to drone in his ears. Her small black eyes took him in from sole to crown, and for no sane reason she began to laugh at him.

At that moment, the red headed woman came into the room. The Chinese woman ceased her mocking laughter and disappeared from view. Christopher asked once more for his belongings. The sight of her red hair, disheveled and tangled, looked to him like flames of hell; the lines about her slant green eyes were caked with powder appearing like crevices in wet pallid sand. By daylight she seemed a perfect horror and he wondered whatever he saw in her the preceding night. He must have been insane or drunk! Undoubtedly drunk because now he could taste the bitter aftermath of that cheap rotten whisky. The woman stepped over to a curtained corner and drew back the gaudy flowered material, revealing an improvised locker. She brought forth his clothes and gave them to him. He waited for her to leave or at least turn her back so he could dress, but she did neither. Christopher decided that if she didn't possess some small humility, he'd display no pride. He dropped the covering from his body and stepped quickly into his trousers; in another moment he pulled on his shirt, but when he went to look for his coat it was nowhere to be found. She told him: "The other bloke took it by mistake, I guess." Her words turned his stomach and he wondered if she was actually that low to bed with another after he had fallen asleep. He was ashamed and disgusted with himself. He wanted to get out of the place as fast as possible. She offered him a seaman's coat and cap; he took it quickly and made for the door, but she caught him by the sleeve. He turned to face her; she dug into the bosom of her flimsy kimono and came up with a five pound note. He appreciated her kindness but was outrageously insulted! He turned out of the room slamming the door after him. Christopher put on the seaman's coat and cap and walked down the lurid, dark, dusty hall; the place seemed filthy and he sensed the dust choke his nostrils. Suddenly he began to itch and hoped he hadn't caught lice; he was sick with nausea and felt contempt for everything in general.

All that day he walked the corrupt narrow slick streets of the Limehouse, and once during the afternoon he sighted a carrot heaped on top a garbage pail and he picked it up and ate it ravenously. He was glad when at long last the night and the black brooding fog settled down upon him for it seemed to wrap about him protectingly, hiding his face and shame from the world. But with the call of the dark and night the vile creatures stole from their sinister hiding places and crept into the shadowy lamp lit streets. The tarnished laughter of fallen men and women filled the dark and questionable persons lured him into the dark to sell him unspeakable things.

In the early light of morning, Christopher awoke with a start, and after a time, when his brain was freed from sleep, he remembered stealing into the church and stretching himself on a pew so that he might sleep. The hard smooth oak caused his strong young bones to ache from so long and stiff repose. He sat up; his stomach burned owing from so long an absence of food. He felt dizzy. At the altar an old woman knelt in early morning worship. Christopher felt profane and berated himself for appropriating God's house as a place for repose. He stooped down and reached beneath the pew for his shoes, and when he did a little mouse leaped out of one of them and scurried into a crack for sanctuary. Although the church was not of his denomination, he knelt on the floor and prayed. In humiliation he chanted: "*Marie semper Virgine, teriam pro fidelibus defunctis dicite, et ominpotentem Deum etiam pro me orate.*" Then he crossed himself and departed from the church, thinking that not even the murmuring Thames could cleanse him of his iniquities.

The sky was clear and a bright sun flashed in an azure heavens; its rays dried the pavement and vanished the fog. Suddenly Christopher spied a sparkling disc lying on the sidewalk. His pulse throbbed and his blood ran joyously through his veins . . . it was but a mere shilling, but who can deny that the mere discovery of a lost coin has not brought them joy sometime or other? He concealed the coin beneath the sole of his boot looking cautious about him, and waited for some length of time until there was a distance of space between himself and the passer-by, for he feared that one of them might claim the treasure for their own. Soon he gingerly snatched the object from the pavement and slipped it into his pocket. This at least could put a crust of bread and a mouthful of coffee inside his shrunken belly. Immediately he sought an eating place and breakfasted on whatever the small coin could afford. Later, he once more walked the streets; his spirits somewhat elevated. Moreover, he now possessed a couple of two-pences to jingle in his pocket.

By noon, good fortune seemed to beckon in his path for at the very end of Portugal Street, he came across a little printing shop that advertised for hired help. The sign in the window boasted that it would pay: 17 shillings & sixpence per week for such services. Christopher turned into the shop. In the far corner, a matronly woman was operating one of the presses. "Good 'noon ma'am," spoke Christopher, drawing up to his full height endeavoring to appear respectable despite his rumpled clothes and grubby whiskers, but with the seaman's coat and cap he wore, he seemed no better than the villains who stalked Limehouse. "I am applying for the position advertised. Could you direct me to the proprietor, please?"

"The proprietor is long deceased," said the woman suddenly stopping the press and scrutinizing Christopher from head to toe." 'E up and died twenty year ago with the cholera in the summer of '56; I'm in charge 'ere." She put her hands on her bulging hips, "So, it's a job you want? Well them's the wages I pay. If you want the job, take the sign from the winda and iffen you don', git along wi' you. I had a good boy and I give 'im less than that—But 'e was the kind that's got spirit in his veins, so 'e ups and joins Sir General 'Aig's army."

"Thank you," rejoined Christopher. "I'm very grateful for the job." He started to the window to remove the sign.

"I'll tell you your duties in a bit from now," murmured the woman. "As 'tis, right now's quits fer me . . . Time fer me noon day meal." Again she looked at Christopher with concerning eyes. "I 'ope you're an 'onest lad?" she said thinking that perhaps she might have been too prompt in accepting him. But at a second glance, she knew that no one could doubt the handsome square cut of his jaw and the clear set of his dark blue eyes. Moreover, he had approached her in a very gentlemanly manner. She thought it was foolish for her to think otherwise. Besides there was gentleness in his manly frame that pleased her. She looked upon his face again; he seemed pale and she wondered when last he sat down to a solid meal. "'Ave you 'ad your dinner as of yet, lad?"

"I've had breakfast," Christopher admitted proudly.

"I didn't ask you that," she replied. "I suppose you ain't got a tuppence to your name, nor a place to lay your head?"

"I'm not stony broke ma'am," he said opening a clenched fist and displaying the coins he possessed. "And as for lodging—Well, I'm newly arrived and haven't found suitable rooms as of now . . . But I hope to look about as soon as I'm free from work."

"Bah! Don't be lying to me," she told him endeavoring to be stern with him. "A couple of tuppences and no place to board—to say nothing of the fact that your body could do with a good meal." She blinked her eyes concerningly. "Well, the good Lord can't say Charlotte Wessly ain't never been kind to a soul in want. There's a place I have to let beneath the stairs. 'Taint much, but it's a place to sleep and wash. At least it's a roof over you 'ead. You can 'ave that." She waved a hand at him, "Now, git along and wash up. You can't sit at me table with them dirty mitts." Then she started to walk away saying: "I'll bring you down a razor," and with that she began to climb the steps which lead to her living quarters.

Christopher thanked her from the bottom of his heart and watched after her as her plump little figure climbed the stairs until she was out of sight. In the next moment she reappeared at the head of the stairs and leaning over the railing, she called out to him. "'Ere lad! . . . Catch this." Christopher looked up and the old woman dropped a straight razor, a brush and some soap and towels into his outstretched hands. "By the way," she cried. "I can't be screaming like this—I'm sure your good mother gave you a name?"

"I'm called, *Christopher*, ma'am."

"Eh, just that and no more?"

"Christopher Wensdy," he replied grinning up at her but actually he was alarmed for at any moment he feared that she might topple over the balustrade for she leaned so far over.

"Well, Christopher, you may come up as soon as you can and git your dinner." She went away but returned in a minute. "I almost forgot," she cried. "Don't forget to bolt the door, and I want that you should 'ang out me *Out To Lunch* sign."

Christopher went to his small room beneath the stair case. He was very pleased with his quarters despite the fact that he knocked his head once or twice on the slanting ceiling; his little room contained a small chest, a single bed, and in the far corner was a wash basin with a chipped mirror mounted above it. He pulled off his shirt and prepared to shave, then later he filled a round tin tub with water and sat down. The water was warm and the soap was white and foamy. "What luxury!" he laughed," to sit in a rough bottom tin tub with my knees up to my chin. I could soak here for days!"

2

The days moved rapidly for Christopher; he busied himself with work from the time he opened the shop in the morning, until closing time, and as the weeks slipped past he began to think less and less about Rue; eventually a day would pass without him once breathing her name.

Now that Mrs. Wessly had acquired help, the shop caught up with the volume of work which was assigned to her charge for print. She and Christopher grew to be close friends and the day arrived when she trusted him implicitly. She permitted the business to fall more and more into his charge with every new day. Moreover, she found more time for herself and could even enjoy the luxury of setting aside one day a week when she wouldn't set foot into the little printing shop.

One quiet afternoon while Christopher crouched within the shop window to wash the large square plate glass, he was distracted from his work by the sight of a lovely blond haired woman who window shopped on the other side of the street. He saw her pause before the aquarium shop to talk with Mr. Peres, the proprietor, and then she walked away smiling. Christopher watched after her until she disappeared from view. He took up his sponge and resumed his job of window washing, then soon forgot all about her. Some time later, when he had completed the task, and was returning from the rear of the shop after putting away the sponge and bucket, he was thoroughly surprised to see the very young lady he admired come into the shop. Christopher admired her light golden hair combed so neatly in place. She was so exceedingly lovely and wholesome in appearance that Christopher had much difficulty in averting his eyes from her fair countenance. He was enamored of her at first sight. Their eyes met and the young lady was suddenly forced to turn her glance in another direction.

"Good afternoon," Christopher greeted cordially, and like an experienced clerk he stepped behind the stationary counter. "May I assist you?" he asked. She returned the greeting and told him that she wished to purchase some writing materials. Christopher displayed the articles on the worn oak counter, inquiring of her if she wished to purchase any of the materials she viewed by the gross. He assumed that she had been employed by one of the business firms in the neighborhood.

"Good heavens, no," she cried, quite astonished at the question. "Only a small packet will do," she explained, "and some writing fluid."

"Beg pardon," said Christopher. "I only thought you were shopping for some office. So many women are employed in man's work nowadays with the war going so badly. I meant no offense. Mrs. Wessly would never forgive me, if she thought I was deliberately rude to one of her customers." The lady assured him that she took no offense in his inquiry. She completed her purchase and he began to wrap the materials, but he performed the task with such an amount of fumbling and inertness, which was all part of his plan to detain her so they might linger in conversation. "Are you acquainted with my employer, Mrs. Wessly?" he asked reluctantly delivering her the package.

"Yes indeed," she responded rummaging in her purse for some coins. "I'm glad to see that she has had some good fortune in securing help . . . poor dear was smothered under with work, but help is so hard to obtain now that so many of our young men are in *His Majesty's Service*. Christopher held his breath hoping she wouldn't be so curious as to inquire why he was not in uniform. Every day questions are sometimes too arduous to explain, and how could he begin to relate the series of happenings which carried him to London. "How much please?" she asked, and her voice brought Christopher back from his musing.

"One shilling, sixpence, ma'am."

She placed the money on the counter then started to leave.

"Should I mention to Mrs. Wessly that you were here?"

"Please do," she murmured and once more took up her steps.

"Beg pardon, ma'am, but whom shall I say was here?"

The young woman turned and viewed him over her shoulder, causing Christopher to understand his presumptuous behavior. He smiled and somehow beguiled her to do the same. "Just mention that Miss Fredrica Hobbs inquired of her health" was her cold insolicitous reply. She departed from the shop and Christopher watched her from the large shop widow. He felt he would meet her again . . . sometime soon.

The spring days grew longer and warmer, and although the days were more cheerful in climate, the lingering strains of the war grew worse. Emperor Wilhelm's army seemed to claim everything its thundering boots trod upon.

When Christopher was not musing about the lovely Fredrica Hobbs, he would be prospecting with the thought of enlisting in the army, for he understood fully well that his first duty was to a free nation; moreover, he was humiliated to be seen in the street without uniform. But regardless, in whatever direction his emotions beguiled him, there would always be an ever returning ghost to loom out of the past to remind him that he was a man without a memory . . . memory is identity and if memory be lost, how can one be the same man he was yesterday. Moreover, he possessed no passport or credentials to prove that he was truly the person whose name he claimed.

One afternoon, to his great delight, Miss Fredrica Hobbs came into the shop. "Ah! good afternoon, my dear Fredrica!" cried chubby Mrs. Wessly, her face all aglow with hospitality; she quickened her steps to greet the girl, and her black patent leather shoes pattered merrily over the cement floor. Meanwhile Christopher, at the rear of the shop, who was busily employed at one of the presses, ceased his work and watched the pair embrace and exchange greetings. "Naughty girl," Mrs. Wessly continued. "It's been weeks now since you ain't been in 'ere to see me. Naughty, naughty girl . . . and look at them black clouds in the sky, it's goin' to rine fer the occasion." Fredrica started to contrive an explanation, but the old woman was talking so fast that she couldn't find a breach for a word. "Now, Dearie, don't be giving me excuses. You're goin' to stay fer tea . . . already I've got a pot boiling."

With such warm persuasion, how could Fredrica possibly turn down the invitation. Moreover it would be only a vain gesture to decline, for by now, Mrs. Wessly had taken her side brim hat and parasol and tucked them beneath the counter for safe keeping. "Really Dearie," spoke Mrs. Wessly again, "what 'as kept you away fer so long, I've been fretin' fer you I 'ave."

In reply, Fredrica explained that it was her fitful bronchitis which kept her in bed for these past three weeks.

"Ah, then you are a naughty girl. I should turn you over me knee fer not sending after me. Now, why didn't you send me word. I'd 'ave been glad to nurse you back." She locked arms with Fredrica and they started toward the stairs. "Oh! Christy!" she wailed in her high cracked voice: "where are you boy?" Christopher appeared before them sponging his hands on a towel. "Miss 'Obbs and me is goin' up to me parlor fer a spot of tea," she said glancing down at the little gold watch pinned to her breast. "Ah, 'tis already past four . . . bolt the door and put up me *Out To Tea* sign. Then after you're washed up climb above stairs and join us lad. Miss 'Obbs is a lidy and I should want a bit of gentlemanly company to sit down with us. Now put a move on you lad."

Christopher replied with an emphatic 'Yes, ma'am', for no sooner was the command given when it was executed. Presently he went bounding up the steps, taking two or three in a stride.

There in the Victorian furnished parlor sat the threesome, sipping their tea and engaged in chatty conversation while a driving rain lashed at the building and tiny liquid fingers clawed the window panes. Mrs. Wessly squirmed in her chair and returned her second cup of tea to the polished mahogany table. Fredrica

Hobbs commented on the weather, but received no reply from her hostess on that subject. Mrs. Wessly's thoughts were taken up by another matter of more importance; although she was up in years, she believed that that was no cause for the spirit of romance to die in her. She hadn't called her employee away from his duties merely to have a cup of tea. Christopher Wensdy had exhausted her all too thoroughly with his subtle interrogations of Miss Hobbs.

Now that he was properly acquainted with the lady she thought, that from this moment forward she would leave the matter completely in his hands, and as soon as the opportunity presented itself, she would contrive some excuse to depart from them. At length, Mrs. Wessly thought of a paper consignment that had not arrived. She excused herself from the room telling them it was most important that she telephone for the shipment right then.

"Mrs. Wessly tells me you're an authoress, Miss Hobbs," said Christopher endeavoring to fill in the awful breach of silence which gaped between them. The only sound between them, save for the rattling of the tea cups, was the sound of the rain and thunder.

Frederica's round high forehead seemed to burn crimson; the thought of Christopher referring to her as an authoress somewhat embarrassed her. "Good heavens!" she sputtered. "Mrs. Wessly flatters me. I do write—yes. But I don't think one has a right to that honor until one has at least a little something in print, and I am sorry to admit that I cannot boast of such glory; although, I do hope to have the privilege of doing so in the near future."

"Oh, then you are waiting for the word from your publishers."

"No; not quite, Mr. Wensdy. My book is not yet near completion."

"Then you must promise me, that I shall be the first to read it. May I ask the title or plot?" He looked at her from a side glance and noticed the little flesh mole at the side of her neck and the spinning ringlets of golden hair falling beside it.

"It pleases me to find someone who has the patience to listen," she smiled. "And if you promise not to think me vain, I myself believe that it is an admirable story." Then she laughed as a mode to cloak her modest embarrassment. "How utterly foolish you must think me, Mr. Wensdy." She went on to say, "I suppose every author must think his or her work must be the best achievement of the moment, or how could they have the courage to continue."

"I don't think you at all foolish. Truly I don't," he said restoring her faith. "Please continue."

She folded her hands in her lap. "First I must tell you the title . . . I call it, *Three Brave Hearts*," and this she said with some amount of pride.

"At least it has a captivating title, Miss Hobbs, I'm sure it must be an excellent story."

She lowered her eyes. "The story concerns the brave hearts of: Shelley, Keats, and Lord Byron, their lives, their time, and their loves." She shifted her position and crossed her slim ankles. Then for some length of time she related the story to him and as she spoke in her calm pleasant voice strains of old poetry sounded in his head:

I saw pale kings and princes too,

Pale warriors, death-pale were they all;

They cried—"La Belle Dame sans Merci Hath thee in thrall!"

. . . In thrall . . . In thrall! . . . the shadow of Rue's beauty haunted his imagination. The marble clock on the mantle shelf rudely struck the twilight hour, and the ghost of Keats faded into the purple dusk of evening . . . "Goodness me!" Fredrica cried with a start. "I've completely forgotten the time. I'm really sorry, but I don't think I can stay to finish the story."

"Then perhaps another time," Christopher murmured in regret.

"Perhaps." Soon she was on her feet preparing to depart from the room.

"Miss Hobbs," he called after her and she paused midway between the open door. "Would you honor me by . . . by . . ." He hated himself for being so clumsy, but he soon plucked up courage and cried the words in a very awkward tone. "Miss Hobbs, may I take you to Convent Gardens this Friday?" At first she seemed to lose control of her voice; she thought of answering him a very polite "No", but suddenly had a change of mind and answered him in a light and colorless: "Yes."

3

More than a year had passed since the morning Christopher stepped into the little printing shop on Portugal Street; and in that breadth of time, from season to season, Christopher and Fredrica were confessing their love for each other. But in those black sick days of war, like so many young lovers, their love was only a fire of the moment and all too soon the time had motivated itself when Christopher learned, he too must steep himself in the conflict of the times.

One April morning while he busied himself with a few boards, a hammer, and some nails trying to patch a gaping hole in the side of the shop which was caused by *Gothas*, the boastful name the Germans called their huge bombing planes, Mrs. Wessly came running into the shop, breathless, excited and somewhat at a lost of speech. "Christopher, m'boy!" her voice sharp and excited, and in her hand she waved a newspaper. "'Ave you 'eard the news. Oh! 'ave you 'eard the news?" She ran across the shop to him, her voice droaning above the knockings of his hammer. "America is in the war!"

Christopher stiffened at the news; the muscles tightened in his back and his face was horribly pale. For the moment he seemed to be composed of solid stone. Now he must do something! Of many things there was doubt in his heart, but of one thing he was positive and that being he knew he was an American.

His long silence startled the woman at his side. "What's come over you, lad? she asked in a light breathless manner. "There's a strangeness about you that frightens me."

He looked at her, saying belligerently: "I'm going to join the fight, Mrs. Wessly. I must!"

"Of course, lad," she murmured to appease him, "but I don't see—"

He took her by the wrist and sharply cried: "You've got to help me Mrs. Wessly. You must!"

The woman was completely surprised by his actions. "Yes, Christy . . . You know I will. But what 'tis it that I must do?"

He ran his fingers through his hair nervously. "Remember when I tried to join some time past?"

"When the Gerries torpedoed Commander Kitchener's ship? yes, I do; but you ain't never told me what 'appened that changed your mind. Was it Miss 'Obbs?"

"No," he told her and for some reason he was suddenly angered. "No," he repeated. "They wouldn't have me."

"You ain't sick or somethin' is you Lad?"

"No."

"Then what?"

Christopher drank in a full breath of lungs and within time he spat forth the whole affair that had troubled him for so long. Because . . . Well, because, I haven't a birth certificate, or anything of the like to prove who I am. "That's what!" And with the conclusion of those words he struck his fist against the wall with such an angered blow that blood poured forth from his knuckles.

Mrs. Wessly rushed behind the counter and brought our her little first aid kit; she returned to his side, took his hand and began to bandage it. "Now, come lad, booster up. That seems like a crazy reason when we need boys so bad." She knotted the bandage about his hand," There it will be alright," she said, and once more resumed the conversation. "Tell me now, 'as 'Is Majesty's soldiers suddenly gone crazy?" She looks up into his face. "You ain't told me what I must do fer you, Chris?"

"I must have your permission to forge some kind of papers for myself. Oh, don't look at me that way. I know it's dishonest but what else can I do?"

The thought amazed her and she choked for some fresh breath. "I can't do that, Christopher. Scotland Yard would be upon me like a cat on a mouse. You know that."

"I suppose you're right," he said dejectedly; he turned his face to the wall. "It was a foolish idea from the start." Christopher picked up the hammer despondently saying in a light voice: "I better complete the patching. There's a lot of work for me to do in the shop today."

Mrs. Wessly left him alone for a while; she went upstairs to her living quarters. In some half hour or so she returned downstairs to the shop. She saw that Christopher had finished patching the wall and that he was now working feverishly at the printing press endeavoring to lose himself in work. "Stop the press, Christopher," she told him in a firm manner. "I want to talk to you." He obeyed her, and when he looked up again she was standing at his side. "You know, lad, I've taken a right good fancy to you," she began and touched her hand to his arm. "The good Lord knows that I couldn't think more of you than if you was my own. I've been up in me rooms walkin' about like crazy, trying to think of some way to 'elp you. and now, I think I know 'ow I can."

She smiled and patted the back of his hand, pleased at the smile on his face and the color coming back into his cheeks. "Chris, you ain't told me much about yourself, but I guess that's your business and you know right well that I ain't never asked. But there are two things I know and the first is that you are an American. That was easy to guess, any fool would 'ave knowed that when I brought in the news. You looked as white as a sheet, you did. Like I said, these things you ain't never mention to me, but you can't fool old Charlotte at everything. The second thing I know is that you ain't got no folks."

She had hardly mentioned the words when she noticed a quick change of expression flood into his face. "Now don't be climbin' on your 'igh 'orse; I mean no offense. Them things is your business. The first day I saw you, I seys to myself, seys I, this 'ere lad is a gent inspite of his raggy clothes, and I could see that you 'ad fine bringin' up. As I say it ain't my business nor anybody elses fer that matter, so what 'appened to you before you walked into my place is your own. And I guess you must of 'ad a rotten time because fer days afterwards you seemed pretty down in the mouth." She patted his hand again. "What's past is past . . . but to git down to the business. My plan ain't what the law would want it to be, but the Lord knows we got to deal in a bit of trickery to git along in this black world. Bless 'Im, I know 'E will forgive us."

She waved a piece of paper before him and Christopher watched on with curious eyes. "This 'ere piece of paper," she told him, "I found in me 'usband's things . . . It's a birth certificate. We can eradicate 'is name and date and put yours in its place. But we've got to be careful lad," she told him dropping her voice in the strictest of tones. "Else we will both be in trouble with the *Yard*."

At first Christopher could not find the words to express his appreciation; he threw his arms about her and kissed her cheek, repeating his gratitude many times until in order to subdue his joy, Mrs. Wessly applied the flat of her hand in a stiff affectionate slap to his tough backside, but she only succeeded in stinging her own hand.

Together they conspired on how to alter the paper and as they worked, Mrs. Wessly went on to explain that her husband, deceased, was of good aristocratic stock, and how his family shamefully disowned him when he married her, but this act made little difference in their married life. For from the day they married until the day he died they were happy.

When they removed *Wessly's* name and substituted *Christopher Wensdy* in its place, Mrs. Wessly cautioned him to great lengths that his name was now on a British certificate and that it might prove to be a ticklish situation if such a deed was called to account; and if he wanted to substantiate his right as an American citizen. She advised him that it would be more sagacious to enlist with the English, although she was aware of his strong desire to be in the uniform of his own country. Besides it really was of little importance which uniform he donned as long as he was fighting for the right cause.

After all, the only important part that really counted was that one does his bit . . . that was all that could be asked of any man.

Christopher enlisted as a mere recruit, but after many months of rigid training, it wasn't too long thereafter that he succeeded in pulling himself up by his own boot straps, so to speak, to the rank of lieutenant, but having foresight and a good education this was not too difficult for him to do.

Now once more Christopher returned to London, but this time on a brief pass. He paused outside of Mrs. Wessly's printing shop, squaring his shoulders and holding his head high, he stole into the shop plotting to take the old lady by surprise. However, it wasn't long before she spied him and soon he was in her embrace. She reproved him lovingly for not mentioning his coming. Christopher's first words were to inquire of Fredrica and he was troubled at not finding her home when he called there.

"'The poor dear," Mrs. Wessly explained to him: "She's been down with her bronchitis again and you know 'ow she suffers with that. Then staying in 'er room and writin' all day with 'ardly ever gittin' out fer a breath of air. She's been right sick. Oh, she's well now! I expect she is sittin' on one of the benches in St. James' Park. At least that's where I made her promise me she'd go. Now, I tell you what you do. Like a good lad you go over and fetch 'er and I'll beat it down to 'Enry's meat shop, and if the Lord's with me I'll find a good cut of meat, and fix up a 'ome cooked meat fit enough fer King George, 'imself to eat. Now 'urry lad this is a celebration! Close the door after you and don't forgit to 'ang me *Gone Out* sign . . ."

The little reunion at Mrs. Wessly's table was pleasant; as was promised, a splendid meal was served, such as those hard days of war would permit. But so swiftly had the time fled, that the sweethearts hardly had time to say all the important things which they had hoped and planned to say to each other.

Now only an hour's breath from train time, they were in each other's embrace, dancing on the crowded floor in a little café in Piccadilly. Fredrica followed Christopher's moments automatically, her left hand was pressed over his lieutenant bars on his shoulder;

her body was so close to his, as though she were boneless, and her blond head rested on his chest.

"Damn it," said Christopher. "Why don't they play a waltz?" and he sidetracked just in time to avoid colliding with a red-faced young captain who sped across the floor tipsy to the ends of his toes; reeling a girl to some disjointed rhythm. "Fritz would pick our last night together to try and blast Parliament off the map." He murmured the words under his breath in small belligerent tones.

Fredrica trembled and he tightened his grip about her slim waist. How glad she was that Christopher was there to hold her; she would try to forget the madness raging outside. The Germans were flying low like some hell-bat, performing to an audience of screaming whistles, wailing in tune with the clamorous voice of the anti-aircraft guns, which the search lights cut through the blackness like a deadly razor.

Suddenly she remembered the time. O, God! she thought. Christopher would be leaving her soon. She swallowed her tears; her heart was breaking. The lights came up a little brighter then, and some one said that it was all over outside—the Gerries were gone. Presently there was a change in the music, and the orchestra began to play, *Roses of Picardy.*

"I love you, love you," Fredrica whispered. "O, darling, I'm so frightened!" He bent over and kissed her on the cheek. "Please don't be, Fredrica; there's no need to be afraid." Again he kissed the side of her face and whispered in her ear: "When it's all over," he paused, "will you marry me, Fredrica, I love you, sweet?"

She answered him smiling, but he didn't understand what she was trying to say because the music came up louder, but at the end he could read her lips saying "yes, yes!" Somehow the dance floor didn't seem so crowded as before and they could move about with more ease. Fredrica was humming with the orchestra.

"What is that tune . . . is it new?"

"Yes," she said. "I have John McCormack's recording of it. I love it so, sometimes I think I'm going to wear out my gramophone. My landlady threatens to evict me if I play it one more time. O, you'd love the words, Chris . . . . Roses are shining in Picardy in the hush of the silvery dew . . . something about roses will die with the summer time—O! I can't remember it all.

"*Fredrica!*" He called her name in a light gentle voice; there was no need for him to say more—she understood. She nodded her head, all the color seemed to leave her face and Christopher could feel the breath going out of her.

They walked from the café to the railroad station; it would make the time seem longer that way. How over crowded the station seemed. Everywhere one turned, there was khaki to be seen, and how intimate were the scenes about them: parents weeping, married couples and lovers embracing, not concerning their actions with the public or really caring. Everyone was sputtering their farewells— perhaps for the last time. The faces of so many young men, boys in fact, were framed in the windows of the railroad carriages. Now, here they were, stiff and selfconcious on the platform. The brakeman screamed the final *all aboard*!

"Kiss me Fredrica! Then walk away and never turn back to look, Darling . . . This is au revoir!" She sobbed; her face close to his. Fredrica felt as if some angry hand with icy fingers was closing about her heart. The engine began to puff and give off steam. She squeezed Christopher with all her strength. "Do you know where you're to go, Chris?" She heard her own voice in her ears and thought how empty the words seemed. She felt disembodied, as though a ghost were using her lips to speak; she had no control; these were not the things she really wanted to say.

He kissed her again. "They don't tell us such things; the boys think we will be in France before the end of the month." He practically shouted the words to hide the tears and the pain in his voice . . . "You'll write, Darling?" he said, and kissed her once more on the lips.

"Everyday!" She trembled a little and her voice was high and strained as she tried to be heard above the brass band which had suddenly taken on life.

"Take care of that bronchitis. And don't forget to tell me how your book is coming along—I love you Fredrica. God knows I do!" "Yes, Darling, yes," and the burning tears were rolling down her cheeks. "Chris, if you go to Paris, send me a souvenir . . . a pair of earrings. I've always wanted a pair of earrings from Paris."

He released her from his embrace; her hand still in his, they held firm their grip until he hopped aboard the last carriage. Christopher took one final glance at Fredrica. Her face was tear stained and smiling; he waved goodbye and stepped into the car. It was crowded to capacity with soldiers, officers and enlisted men, and the boys were striking up a lively chorus of *It's a Long Way to Tipperary!*

4

Captain Hans Ellgate peeled off the tunic of his army uniform; he laid it carelessly over the arm of a chair, then walked across the floor, clad in his khaki trousers and undershirt. He sank down in an overstuffed chair enjoying the homelike comforts of Sarah Morrison's Paris apartment. Sarah slid the footstool beneath his feet, and then knelt down beside him; she unstrapped the leather puttees from his long legs, then she removed his shoes to massage his tired burning feet. Ellgate wiggled his toes and looked down at Sarah in a languid contented glance. He saw her hands and noticed that she wasn't wearing his engagement ring, but he brushed the matter from his mind assuming that perhaps nurses weren't permitted to wear such love amulets while on duty. He thought how prim and lovely she appeared in her white uniform. Sarah lifted herself onto the footstool; again he wiggled his toes, but this time sighing and grunting. "Ah! that's what a tired soldier needs," he said, "a beautiful nurse to massage his aching feet. Rub the top."

"Metatarsal bone or the instep?"

"All over . . . Ah! get the back, Sweet."

"That's the tendon of Achilles—"

"Oh! to hell with Achilles; he's a dead Greek. Anyway, I was for the Trojans." He winked at her plaguingly, "Get on with your duty *nurse.*"

"I always thought he was a Trojan."

"Who?"

"Achilles."

"Oh, I can't remember. Get the other foot, the foot is so important."

"You should read what Freud has to say about the male foot," Sarah said in a giggle.

"You nurses know too much. Anyway, I think Siggie Freud, is a little loco himself." He grinned: "Do you know what he has to say about the shoe?" The blood came into Sarah's face and within the moment she turned crimson. "Aha! I said you nurses know too much," and with that he laughed. "Have you anything to drink, now that I've put that good meal away?"

"So, now at last you praise me. I thought you'd never get around to it. It isn't easy to buy the food you want nowadays."

Ellgate dropped his hands to the arms of the chair. "Alright Love. Thank you for the meal you've cooked for me. It was superb! Now, what about that drink?"

"There might be a little cognac left in the bottle—do you want that?"

"Yes, anything."

Sarah pulled her legs from under her and stepped over to the console-cabinet. "Oh Hans," she wailed despairingly, "there's none left. Evidently you drank it all last night—will a glass of milk do?"

Ellgate lifted his hands in a melodramatic gesture. "Don't be silly." She came back to his chair where he was stretched out half sitting, half lying; he reached out his hand and suddenly caught hold of her, pulling Sarah down on top of him. He held her body along his and they lay facing each other in the chair. Everything seemed so still that Sarah could hear her pulse throbbing like mad. He kissed her on the lips holding her body fast to his. Sarah squirmed to climb back on her feet; she pushed her hand to his chest and she could feel his heart striking against it.

"Let me up Hans!" she cried, but her voice was light and faint. He tried to kiss her again, but this time she was on her feet trying to smooth the wrinkles out of her uniform.

Ellgate called her back and with some reluctancy she sat down on the footstool. She looked pale and for the moment he thought Sarah would order him from her apartment. Then in a careful sheepish voice he said: "Don't be angry, Sweet, but it's your own fault. You shouldn't look so damn attractive in that uniform."

She put her hand to her throat: "Hans, you make me feel indecent."

"How long is that uniform going to keep you away from me?" he asked, and there was a tight drawn line about his mouth.

Sarah looked at him, she feared their same old argument was going to begin anew: "As long as the war lasts," she said sardonically, but suddenly she changed her tempo, realizing that this was the time to use savoir-faire; who knows how little time they might have for each other in times such as these. "Oh, Darling!" she said in a voice that seemed pulsed with tears. "Let's not quarrel. This is my duty, just as you have yours. If you could see the mutilated bodies of the men that pour in from the front, you wouldn't ask me that. Why most of them are mere boys. Your heart would have bled with joy, if you could have witnessed the faces of the Belgiums when our Red Cross chapter arrived. I shudder to think of their fates, now that the Germans have taken over. The beasts even fired on our ambulances . . . I remember, just before we were forced to leave, they had started to shell our little hospital. Oh, Hans! I'm needed here—the men at the front need me."

". . . But that's still no reason to delay our marriage. I love you Sarah . . . how long is a man supposed to wait? I only have a day or more left. At any hour word may come for us to move front." He held his finger up: "Two nights in Paris, and we haven't been out together once—not once!" the ends of his words seemed to burn and curl up in anger. "Why can't we get married tonight?" He got out of his chair and went over to the window in his stocking feet. Ellgate looked down, below him slumbered a quiet dimly lit Parisian street. He could hear the muffled bells of *Notre Dame* and in the opaque distance, the *Eiffel Tower* loomed high against the murky sky.

Sarah looked at him; his back was turned toward her and she sensed his brooding mood. "Hans," she called to him lightly, "I've got to be on duty by eleven tonight and it's past ten now."

"There," he said without looking at her, "that's what I mean! Besides, that's not answering my question."

Sarah went over to the window beside him; he held her in his embrace and began to stroke her hair. "Oh, darling, you know I love you and would marry you in a minute, but not until this is all over with. *I can't—I will not* have you just for a little while . . . I don't want to borrow you for a day like you were a book, then have to hand you over to *Mr. Pershing* every time he snaps his fingers. Moreover, we both have our duty to perform." Sarah took his hand and beckoned to the sofa. "Let's sit down and talk before I leave," she told him. "There are so many things about home I want to ask you to tell." Sarah lowered her head and pondered a while. "God, it's been so long since I said that word, *home*. It's been years since I've spoken to a real American at all."

"Three years in October," he rejoined with precise sarcasm. He was pouting when he sat down beside her.

Sarah gave him a love slap and kissed the side of his face; he smiled showing a row of perfect white teeth. "How is Elaine and your father? He and I are pals you know."

"Elaine's alright . . . doesn't she write you?"

"Yes. You know what I mean, you can't say everything in a letter."

"Well, as for Pops, all I can get out of him is: '*Sarah is a sensible girl.*'" he mocked his father's voice and they both laugh.

"Did you have any success in tracing your friend—What's his name? You spoke so highly of him. I really did want to meet him that summer, but I just couldn't get away."

"Yes, I know," he scorned. "Your career."

"Hans!" Again they laughed but it wasn't what it should have been.

"No. I couldn't find anything about him. It seems so strange that one man could disappear so completely. I've asked the Prioress if she tried to solve his identity when she first found him."

"What did she say?"

"Yes, of course, but just as I, she had no luck. There were people who came to see him, but as you may assume they were not his." He raised his eyebrows: "You know he hasn't any memory of his early childhood."

"I've heard of an amnestic condition, but it's rather unusual to hear of it being prolonged such as his. I suppose he'll never recover himself after these many years . . . but still."

"Still you think there might be a chance of recovery?"

"Yes . . . sometimes. What did you say his name was?"

"Christopher Wensdy." Ellgate set his jaw: "Poor Wen . . . I wonder what's become of him? It would be great to see him again."

Sarah glanced down at her lapel watch. "Oh, Hans," she said excitedly. "Don't get angry, but I really must leave now." She got up from the sofa. "Walk with me to the door. When do you have to get back to camp?"

"Tomorrow sometime."

"Then why don't you sleep here tonight. You can get a good nights rest and get an early start, feeling fresh. I'll be back around five and I'll fix you a breakfast." Ellgate nodded his head and told her he would stay. Sarah threw her cape over her shoulders and paused to look at him once more; she touched the side of his face with the tips of her fingers. "Hans, I do love you!" Once more they embraced; he kissed her and closed his body against hers until she was back against the door. Sarah was crushed beneath his chest; pulling her face away she uttered: "Hans! Don't be that way. This war is making a beast of you! He kissed her again for reproving him. "Would you rather I slept the night at *Madame Celestine's*, there are plenty of ladies there who are willing!"

Sarah slapped his face with such a sting that the reflex carried sharp tears into his eyes; his face was burning red. "I'm sorry, Hans," she said with a touch of humiliation in her voice. "You made me do that. You seem tired and nervous. I suppose I can't blame you too much—this war is a strain on both our nerves. Forgive me again . . . Do you want me to give you something to make you sleep?"

"No, Dear," he said and kissed the palm of her hand. "It's I who am sorry; it was all my fault. I earned that slap. It was good of you to correct me . . . forgive me. I am a complete ass, but the fact is that I'm so damn in love with you that I can't sleep worrying over you."

Sarah stood on her toes and kissed the side of his face. They exchanged smiles and everything seemed alright between them. "Good night, Darling. I'll wake you in the morning," she said softly, and with that she left closing the door after her.

5

To the new recruits and officers, their first taste of actual warfare was fierce, but they were quick to comprehend that this was only a grim prelude before the trembling curtain would lift on what was real. Christopher's battalion was just a mile or so behind the front line; the multitude of work kept every man employed, hand and foot. Since long before sunrise the stretcher bearers were journeying to and from the front, evacuating the wounded. Communication lines were repaired and motorcyclists were grinding here and there with ominous dispatches, and always—always was to be heard the tattooing of machine guns, shrapnel bursting in the air, and the thunderous growl of the hand grenades.

It wasn't until long past ten o'clock that night when Christopher found time to read his letters from Fredrica and Mrs. Wessly. After reading them, he tucked the envelopes of paper inside his tunic and stretched out on the ground to sleep; using his knapsack for a pillow. Above him the blackness unfolded thick and heavy; there was no moon, but the night was thick with stars and the summer breeze laced throughout the poplars; their graceful boughs rustled in the cooling breeze. The night was beautiful.

For some brief hours there seemed to exist an informal truce between the men at the front; everything appeared so motionless that it was an uncanny feeling to behold the stillness. The men were moved, and trembled at the silence; wondering if each side had completely murdered the other and that out there now perhaps only the dead were dancing with the breeze in the phantom tranquility of the night.

Alas! but no—on the contrary, this was not so; a British rifle rang out! then another and another. Soon from end to end there seemed to be an agitated fusillade, and the bullets rocketed through the blackness, flashing silver and fiery gold like rain drops of hell, while the outraged host on the other side hurled back every charge. For three minutes the hurricane raged. Then suddenly a rocket had burst into the air and it hailed to the earth like small magnesium stars. Suddenly, for no apparent reason, it all died away; the men behind the lines cursed . . . it was a false alarm and perfect silence reigned once more. Again the men tried to rest; it seemed to be all over, at least for a while. Christopher curled up in a ball and tried to sleep. The dampness had begun to spread it's mist over the ground; he felt tired and cold. But the warmth of Fredrica was in his heart . . . Miss Fredrica Hobbs . . . An admirable story . . . Shelly . . . If you go to Paris . . . Emerald earrings . . . Emeralds . . . Chris I love you! . . . He was soon sound asleep.

In the grey mist of morning there was a rumor among the men of Christopher's battalion that orders had arrived from headquarters stating that the men were to be sent back and rerouted. At any event, this news brought about a feeling of joy; the men questioned each other, who knows, this might mean fresh food and clean uniforms; perhaps a pass for some adventure in Paris.

The days dragged by, and the incredible hours appeared to be much discussed, for they were a mere stone's throw from the city, but no passes were issued. Each day they drilled, and each day the generals complained that the men were not ready for actual battle. With each new day there came more training, and the men were taught to use their gas masks. Christopher did not seem to think his group unprepared, and he was quick to realize that all this extra training was for some special affair. There was talk among the officers that they would soon be moving up directly to the German front.

Finally the day arrived when the men were issued passes, and they were granted permission to journey to Paris. It seemed as though each man had made up his mind to get good and drunk; they comprehended to the fullest that it would be a long time before they would again witness such civility.

In the *Golden Toad Café*, Christopher threw a leg over the back of a chair; for *Madame's* café was over crowded to the rafters that night, and to draw the chair from the table seemed almost an impossibility; he sat down straddle fashion hooking his boots behind the fore legs of the chair.

"Ah! this table will do nicely," said Lt. Lorrie to Christopher, who was his boon companion and fellow at arms. "Besides," he added: "We'll have an excellent view of the stage. There will be no trouble, old man, in seeing the girls kick high tonight, eh?" He winked, and Christopher laughed loudly. The scene about them was revelry at it's grandest, light hearted and vivaciously animated. A waitress brought them a dusty bottle of vermouth, but it was beer that they wanted, and plenty of it. It appeared as if every man in that grand chamber of merriment was intoxicated to his capacity; before the night was over, six months pay would be squandered. The men danced and howled while the music beat around the café like whirlwind. With tired bloodshot eyes, they would seize a female companion with red cheeks and sit her astride their legs; they'd sing and stop, and sing again, only to stop once more and swill the claret wines and golden beer down their throats; each man unchained the brute within himself.

From time to time, on the wooden steps behind a large painted screen, the four feet of each couple kept tramping up and up until the trading would muffle out beneath the dim and gaiety of the café. A string of raw recruits lined from wall to wall against the black mahogany bar, downing their beer as though it were oxygen. The *can-can* that was being enacted on the stage was over, and the girls filed off the platform one by one to disappear behind the scarlet velvet curtain. It was some minutes before the next act, and the young men were growing impatient. They pounded their fists upon the bar and tables, clamoring in a chorus for *Madame Celestine's* appearance on the stage. Their hoarse drunken voices vibrated the floor and the timbers overhead. *But Madame* would not be hurried, and so they were obliged to wait. They decided to sing. And such songs they sang: K-K-Ka-Katy was massacred in adulterated French, and there were parodies of girls and of hymns; parodies of the Kaiser, and sheer unpolished nonsense for they knew that fun must be taken whenever possible. They tried to forget the war and themselves, but it seemed like a difficult thing to do, for whenever the wind blew westward, it carried with it the rolling thunder of *Big Bertha's* dark booming voice from the front, which was miles away.

By this time of the evening's enjoyment, Christopher was good and drunk; he lifted his head from the table and looked across to Lt. Lorrie, who's face wavered like a phantom behind the veil of tobacco smoke. Christopher lifted his tankard to his lips, but it was empty and he called for more beer. In time, it was brought to him by *Une petite brunette*. The lovely little French girl fell very nonchalantly into his lap and kissed his lips ardently; she put her face to his whiskered cheek and babbled something in French. Christopher was obliged to turn to Lt. Lorrie to untangle the words, and he did so with much ease and skill. Christopher laughed at the translation, but his tones came bitter and hollow. The girl wanted to know what his *Ma-Ma* would say if she knew he was so drunk and obscene. Christopher asked the girl if she was a virgin, for she looked it. Again Lt. Lorrie translated for him. With no false modesty the girl replied that only last week she was; she explained that she was of good peasant stock and that she was newly imported from the farm with her parent's consent, for they knew that *Madame Celestine* is really a good woman, and always goes to church on Sunday. Christopher learned that such things were not uncommon in France. The girl kissed him again, she had to leave and wait on more tables; her brown eyes stared at Christopher. She thought he was nice and did not want to leave, but she must . . . the boys were calling for more beer.

Suddenly the lights were dimmed and the noise settled down, dying away in the shadowy corners . . . *Madame Celestine* was on the stage. She was beautiful—undoubtedly the loveliest woman in Paris! A slick haired Frenchman struck up a melodious tune on the piano,

Madame began her song . . . *Je suis une femme el tu es un home* . . . Her voice was deep and soft. Most of the men could not understand what she was singing; but they were quiet and listened intently . . . *Viens prends moi a ton Coeur* . . . The lyrics touched them; the words had a magic that was warm and blood like and the music was sweet to listen to . . . *Le Dieu qui fait le monde, fait notres vies plus breve* . . . *Amour! Amour!* Her deep cut claret gown trailed the floor and she moved across the boards as a phantom in a dark dream. The jewels added luster to her dark silken hair, and the diamonds in her pink ears caught the light. The entire café was in darkness, except for the silver ribbon of light which illuminated Madame. She brought a little circular mirror from her breast and used it to throw a circle of light out to her audience; she glided across the stage singing while her mirror lit up the face of a man. As she sang her mirror moved from face to face; she thought how young and full of life the men were, a smile played upon her lips but her heart was weeping for the men . . . she felt she could weep for all men born and graduated into the blood and fiery tears of war. Madame continued her song thinking, tomorrow they will be dying on the battle fields.

The curtain came down and the men took up their merrymaking; the applause thundered strong for a great length of time. But it was of no use . . . Madame would not sing again tonight. Christopher turned about to continue his drinking. He had to drink for *Madame* reminded him too much of Rue, almost the same figure to say nothing of the dark eyes and hair. He looked for Lt. Lorrie but he was gone. Christopher laughed to himself in a manner that seemed almost sensual. No doubt he is in bed, he thought and laughed again and pondered whether or not he was the same person he used to be. Christopher drank his tankard dry and in his drunken stupor he grew aware that a waiter was whispering in his ear . . . it was a message from Lt. Lorrie; he and his female companion were above stairs drinking champagne with *Madame Celestine* in her living quarters, and begged for him to join them.

He staggered from the table almost too drunk to walk, but he tried to do so with some amount of grace, remembering that he was an officer. His footsteps rang sharply on the wooden steps and he was forced to cling to the banister for support; his head was spinning and he was laughing foolishly. He could not help but think of *Madame*, he understood that she was over forty and he was only twenty four. Christopher continued up the steps haunted by a thousand vague memories of the past. He paused a the head of the stairs and below him he heard the girls shout: *Vivre Les Americans! Vivre Les Estas-Unis!* He sharply turned away endeavoring to escape the intense bitter moment of melancholy. He heard them shout again: *Vivre Les Americains!* But how was he to know that below Hans Ellgate and his confederates were on a howling wild night of pleasure in ancient Paris! In Madame's Golden Toad Café.

6

On the Eastern front the October rain fell thick and cold. Finally after many weeks of waiting, the mail caught up with the men in the rat infested trenches. Just mere scraps of paper and bundles, but the men snatched them up as if they were gold. Christopher crouched on his haunches and threw his waterproof sheet over his head to keep the rain from beating down upon him. He used his rifle to help support the improvised roof by running the bayonet into the soggy earth; in this manner his hands were free to rip the cord and paper from the little package he received from home. Within the flat box was a pair of hand knitted socks from Fredrica and some homemade cookies sent by Mrs. Wessly. The cookies were hard and stale but he really didn't mind, for he was grateful that someone thought so much of him. Then, flat at the bottom of the box was a manuscript copy of Fredrica's book. He smiled and kissed the cover, how he would have liked to read it then and there, but of course, there was not time. He murmured the title orally and tucked it within his tunic for safe keeping, thinking that perhaps in his spare time he could read it in part. He read his letters but was a bit confused. Fredrica wrote of nothing but her love for him and ended by saying that she was fine and well; on the other hand Mrs. Wessly made a blunder by informing him that the poor girl had come down with another attack of bronchitis. He looked at the knitted socks in his hand, and a knot came into his throat. *"Dear Fredrica,"* he murmured.

Christopher would have liked to put on his new socks, for his feet were wet to his ankles, but he decided to wait until the rain was over. He pulled his rifle from the mud and drew the waterproof sheet around him. "Perhaps Lorrie might like some stale cookies," he said and nudged the crouching figure beside him who was also smothered beneath a waterproof sheet. He intruded on the fellow by poking his head under Lorrie's leaking shelter, then with a superficial air of grace he shoved the box of cookies beneath the lieutenants nose. "Would Monsieur Lorrie care for a stale crumpet with his tea?" He grinned plaguingly.

Lorrie, who was seized with laughter, glanced at the box clutched in Christopher's wet dirty hand. "To hell with such nonsense," he said, "and pull down my canvas—rain is dripping into my collar." He took a cookie; it was so hard that it almost broke his tooth. He spat it out and cursed with ease. "Save me a few for later on," he replied sardonically. "When I run out of cartridges, I'll hurl them over to *Fritz*."

"Look," said Christopher bringing out the manuscript. "Fredrica had sent me a copy of her book."

"Fredrica . . . ? So that's the lady you preach to me about. If she's as truly beautiful as you say, I'll warn you right now, that someday I will try to steal her away. Let me see her manuscript." He read: Three Brave Hearts. The title intrigues me. But here—take it back, its getting all wet. You seem a lucky dog, Wensdy . . . A box of cookies and a love story from a beautiful woman. Me? All I get is a short letter and a picture of my uncle. I must say ole man, a picture of my uncle I longed for dearly." Then playing the buffoon, he added: "I must pin it on the Kaiser's underpants when I meet him."

Suddenly their chatting was curtailed in the middle of a word. Above them in the grey wet sky were three German aeroplanes; Christopher and Lorrie threw off their waterproofs and sprawled face downward into the mud. A bomb came whistling toward the earth! Fortunately no one got hurt. Christopher lying on his belly, turned his face toward the sky attempting to see if more hell was falling his way. Just above them was a war machine and he could see the black Maltese cross painted on the wings; evidently the flying coffins were returning from a mission, taking advantage of the murky skies of the day. It appeared that they were recently out of bombs, for they discharged none after the first one exploded to the ground. However, this didn't prevent them from amusing themselves with the crawling men below and they began to open fire with their machine guns. An anti-aircraft lifted its nose toward the heavens and with a precise hit it brought one of the hell-bats to earth in flames; the occurrence scared it's two companions away.

"That'll teach them to play tag with us," retorted Lorrie as he watched the plane hit the ground and explode. He climbed to his feet and inquired: "Anybody hit?"

"No," answered one of the men. "So far alright."

"I think I'll make a check about," said Christopher turning to Lorrie. "Those bullets came pretty close."

"Alright, if you want to get wet; go ahead. But you better keep your head down if you don't want to be blown to kingdom come!"

The remainder of the day was quiet but this was only accredit to the rain which fell continuously in a slow monotonous drizzle. The men huddled about shivering beneath their waterproofs, cursing their luck and the weather. At length, in the late evening, the rain relented and the men eagerly wished for the next day's sun, hoping that it would dry their uniforms, for they were wet to the skin and perhaps the puddles of muddy water beneath their feet might sink into nothingness. It was after dark when Christopher made good use of Fredrica's gift; the warm socks felt good on his feet. He had just completed the task in time, for now, the enemy had once more taken up their arms and a shower of bullets came pumping from the opposite trenches—the battle was on! A machine gun rattled it's nose across the darkness, and soon every man had opened full fire on the enemy. Then, from the enemy's side, a deafening charge thundered crimson and white from the blackness across the way. It was a bomb! The men dove into a shell hole for protection. Soon this attack was followed by another and another; in an instant a dozen men were buried alive! Christopher glanced about him; the sight was horrible. The men about him, who seemed steeped in blood, were falling to the earth like stringless puppets. Soon a command was ringing in his ears; *Forward*! shouted the captain. A minute or so later they were over the top storming the enemy; using their bayonets to gorge out their eyes in hand to hand fighting! The men were savages. Finally they were in the German trenches.

"Don't shoot, Comrade!" the foe cringed and threw up his hands, and when he saw that his victor was taken in by his cunning plea, relaxing his guard, the invidious viper shot his sympathetic victim in the face with a tiny pistol which he had concealed in the palm of his hand.

The hand to hand battle seemed to rage on for an eternity, but then at length, the rat crawling trenches were theirs', and a few more yards of enemy territory belonged to the noble free men. Christopher fell to the ground! He put his hand to his chest so he could rest his beating heart, and his fingers met with something which was blunt, metallic and hot—a bullet was lodged in his tunic! But fortunately, Fredrica's manuscript, which he carried in his bosom, halted the fatal shell from reaching it's mark!

Dawn began to stretch it's pallid fingers above the dank mist of the Eastern horizon, looming like a specter out of a black grave. Christopher pushed open his tired eyes, unlocking his subconscious from a profound dream of Rue. The illusion of his dream was so genuine that even now, as he lay awake, still and startled with his eyes on the fading sky, a breath of her provocative perfume dared to linger in his nostrils. He was wrapped in it's sweet fragrance and he pondered for some time as to whether or not he was truly awake. He looked around him; he saw the sand bags built upon one another and the sharp barbwire looping over the ground. No, this was no dream, he thought.

He was awake and the perfume was actually in the air; he investigated. Rolling on his side, he realized suddenly that he had been sleeping with his head on a dead man's chest. Amazed and startled, he pulled his legs under him and crouched on his knees beside the corpse. One side of the man's face was horribly mutilated—the flesh of his left profile was completely blown away; the cheek, jaw-bone, and exposed white teeth lay beneath Christopher's fixed stare. A ghastly brown eye oozed from it's socket.

Christopher could not bear to look upon the sight of horror much longer and after much hesitating, turned the mutilated side to the mud. The other side of the corpse's face was whole and untouched. The features were sharp, but handsomely young in appearance . . . a mere boy of high German lineage. There, on his open and blood spattered tunic, lay a partly exposed letter. The light blue envelope was scented with perfume.

"So my fine friend," he said to the lifeless form before him. "It's your love letter which caused to dream of Rue . . . Rue with her magic and silken web. I didn't enjoy my dream, but I trust the dream in which you sleep is sweet. It must be, you paid the price for your iniquities on this earth. Sleep deep, my comrade; the battle is over for you and if we should meet in the beyond—please know that I meant no harm to you direct. If only your love had made her amorous note thick, as my beloved has done for me. I owe my life to her pen. She never dreamed that it would wall the bullet from my heart, and I reward her by dreaming of another—such is man in this world." He removed the contents from the letter and tucked it within the man's tunic. "I'll keep this envelope," he said, "and when it is all over, I'll write to her saying you fell like a brave warrior."

Christopher covered the man's face with his handkerchief, then pushed forward in the trench to search for Lt. Lorrie. He crawled on all fours, and at every second yard lay a dead man; the men hovered about trying to bind their wounds, others were moaning in pain; at every turn the wounded were patching the wounded. Their lemon yellow skin and bead like eyes were haunting to the imagination. A bit farther on, Christopher shrank back with a hissing intaking of breath, and in horror he stifled the scream in his throat. The nausea and mental pain could not exceed the agony of birth or death. Before him lay a fragment of a body, the limbs and lower half were blown away, and a crew of fat red-eyed rats were squealing and tearing at the intestines! With this another man, still alive, but with no arms was trying to beat a rat off of his naked chest.

"Shoot me!" the man cried. "I'm already gone beyond repair—*shoot please!*"

Christopher lifted his service revolver and shot the half crazed man between the eyes. The rats scattered.

7

Christopher stood bare headed in the cool silence of the morning; the breeze cooled his face, which was now thick and stubby with beard. He tried to think of Fredrica and struggled vainly to recall the music they had danced to that night so long ago, but it's waltzy and silky strains would not echo in his mind. He could imagine her voice speaking the lyrics . . . of the trembling roses in the silvery dew, and her saying how much she adored the melody. He regarded this as a good omen, for as long as he could imagine Fredrica speaking to him, he knew he was safe. Strange, he thought, he could remember her voice, but he couldn't picture her face. He took out her last letter and re-read it, although it was already a month old.

July, 1918

Dearest Christopher,

At long last I received your letter. I read it and re-read it. How I worry when a day goes past and I don't hear from you. Mrs. Wessly has to laugh at me for the way I trouble the postman so much. People would think that he and I are old friends, for we meet on the street and greet each other by our given names. He's a funny fat little man, and his name is Will. I even showed him a picture of you in uniform. I guess you think me silly.

O! Dear, how I wish the black war was over and you were back again. Mrs. Wessly was at my flat last night. I know that she has told you that I've been ill, (but you mustn't fret, I'm all well now), I scolded her a little for telling you. It's really nothing Dear, and I don't want you to worry me. Promise me you won't worry—please promise.

Together we sit and read the papers, and sometimes brood over the maps, of course, we really don't know where you are, and can only make guesses. But it makes me feel closer to put my finger on the map and say, you are here. I've sent you a parcel, and I imagine that you will receive it before you get this letter. It is only some socks I've knitted, but you must promise to put them on when your feet get wet.

O! Darling! I love you so: Take good care of yourself and don't get killed. It will be a grand day when you come home—May God send that day soon! Send me a letter whenever you can; I myself, will write you every day. You're in my every prayer and I ask the Holy Mother to care for you.

Always your love,
Fredrica

He returned the letter to his breast pocket and took up the periscope, peering over to the enemy's trenches. "Anything doing with them, lieutenant?" asked a corporal from the sanitary squad, who had been working his way along the trenches, sprinkling creosol and chloride of lime. "No, it seems quite over," Christopher answered. "I guess we peppered their pants good and proper last night." He looked through the periscope again.

"The grass is so high in front—I see nothing but the enemy's improvised parapet and the tip of *Minnie's* nose." "O, sir, 'er very name makes me tremble. It would take the Gerries to invent a hellish cannon such as 'er. I'd rather be blown to bits than 'ave the *Minenwerfer* bury me alive. I tell you she's a most unpleasant lady—the boys say she can spit two 'undred yards at a clip." The sanitary man wiped his forehead and started to move on, sprinkling the disinfectant.

Christopher called him back. "There's some work for you here," he said. "Where?" "Under your feet," Christopher replied with some amount of displeasure in his voice. "the ground is as soft as putty and smells putrid—I slept on the spot last night and it turned me sick." "Perhaps there's a dead one there, A Gerrie, I mean. 'E might a gotten trampled under the mud. Gimmie yer entrenching tool, sir, and I'll 'ave a look."

The man dug into the ground and presently a particle of clothing and a boot was unearthed; he labored a little more and the vile bundle of decayed flesh was on the surface. The stench was nauseating; the man flung fists full of lime on the body, and Christopher obliged him by dumping a half sack of the spot. They turned the thing on it's back; the man might have fallen the week before; his features were remarkably well preserved. He was a strapping fellow with clear cut features; his glassy blue-green eyes were turned toward his left temple, and his forehead was clearly marked where the fatal shot had gone through. His boots and trousers were in fairly good condition, indicating that he had not been long at the front. A dirty white handkerchief was tied about his neck, and he wore no shirt—he might have been cut down in the early summer. He also wore tattoos on his body; the German insignia was stamped below his heart, and above the naval, printed in an arc, were the letters: T-I-N-A.

"What'll we do wit 'im, lieutenant?" inquired the astonished corporal. For the moment Christopher was confused. "Wrap him in a waterproof, corporal, and place him in the largest shell hole you can find; then pack him over with mud and chloride lime."

After another mean battle, Christopher slumped to the ground and braced his back against the earthen pit which walled him from the enemy. For a time he watched the stretcher bearers as they journeyed to and fro throughout the trenches, endeavoring to evacuate the wounded. He wiped the sweat from his face; the horror of war had gripped him, heart and throat, making him feel that he could no longer endure the utter madness about him without breaking in mind and spirit.

The men about him looked like miners from the depths of the earth rather than soldiers. Christopher no longer felt young. He pulled his legs up and rested his head on his knees; soon he fell into a day dream of Fredrica. For a moment he escaped his reality, but his musing was not long spent; a dispatch man crouched by his side and shook him by the shoulder.

"Lt. Wensdy . . . telephone message from headquarters, Sir." The dispatcher pounded a metal peg into the side of the trench and endeavored to untangle the wire before handing the instrument over to Christopher. "Why bring the message to me Sergeant?" asked Christopher, reluctantly taking the telephone and fitting the receiver to his head. "Where's the captain?"

"The captain and seven others were buried alive—they are trying to dig them out now, sir." "Have you seen Lt. Lorrie, man?" "He's in the rear trench, wounded. That's why I came to you. I guess you're in command now." Christopher was thunderstruck. "Wounded! Badly?" "Dunno, sir." A contact was coming through the wire. "Hullo— hullo k27—Number 1 gun; Lt. Wensdy reporting," he chanted into the instrument nervously and waited in short breath for the electric response to charge through the wire. "Field headquarters . . . Major Cabot speaking . . . Give account of your sector, Lt. Wensdy, where's your captain?" "Captain Little and seven men were buried alive, my men are trying to dig them out, and Lt. Lorrie is wounded. How long will it be before reinforcements reach us, Major?"

Reinforcements will not reach you until another twelve hours . . . It is vital that you and your men hold your position . . . Beyond the enemy lines lies a small manufacturing town, so you can readily see the importance of your station. You may expect some help from a troupe of Americans who are working their way up to your sector. Their lives depend upon your destroying the enemy's gun—"

Suddenly the lines were dead. Christopher tried repeatedly to re-establish connections, but it was all in vain. "What's the trouble?"

inquired the wide eye dispatcher at Christopher's side. "Lines gone dead—Find Sergeant Rogers, I want a count of the men. Where did you say Lt. Lorrie was?" "Rear trench, Sir." Christopher nodded his head. "When you find Sergeant Rogers, send him to the rear, I'll be there."

"How goes it with you old fellow?" Christopher asked of Lt. Lorrie who lay on the ground; the left leg of his trousers was torn away and a bundle of crimson stained gauze was swaddled about his thigh. Lorrie tried to smile, but that only succeeded in revealing his agony to Christopher—the one thing he endeavored to conceal. "O, good old Billy, our corpsman binded me up. He claims that he gave me something to put me to sleep, but as you can readily see I'm hellishly awake. You know, I think *Fritz* got angry and threw back that cookie I hurled at him some time back." Christopher found that he could smile at that. "I understand the show is in your hands tonight," continued Lorrie; he saw the surprise creep into Christopher's eye. "O, yes, I know already; the news comes fast in these rat holes. What of the captain?"

"The men dug them out, but it was too late. All died of suffocation . . . not a bullet grazed their skins. It's hard to go that way—Can I do anything for you?" he inquired. "Thank you, no. I imagine the stretcher bearers will be along soon. What did the old man have to tell you?" "He didn't quite finish, the lines went dead, but I guess I know what to do, at least I have an idea what he wants." Christopher lifted his eyes to a crouching figure crawling their way. "O, here comes Roger." "Sergeant Rogers, reporting, sir." "Did you count the men, Sergeant?"

"Yes. We are only 57 able bodied men in number." Christopher frowned.

"See that able men move to the front trench, and have all the wounded carried as far in the rear as possible." He glanced at his watch: "See to it that the men get some rest Sergeant; it's 2245, no, I'll alert them around midnight. That's all for now, Rogers; I will join you later."

After the sergeant left, Lt. Lorrie took up the conversation once more. "What are your plans, Chris? Damn it! Wouldn't you know I'd get it just when I should be around to help you."

"I really don't know Lorrie, the old man says it's vital that we hold our position. I don't like our number, I am sure they out number us by far."

"What about reinforcements?"

"They won't reach us for another twelve hours."

"Didn't I hear something about Americans in the field?"

"Yes. I think they are north of us."

"Many?"

"I doubt it, perhaps thirty at the most."

Presently the stretcher-bearers came and carried Lorrie to the rear. Christopher retired to the front trench and tried to get some much needed rest; there he worked out a plan to overtake the enemy. At length, he turned over on his side and tried to sleep, but it was of no use, he couldn't. Christopher climbed to his feet and peered over to the enemy's parapet. All was still and quiet on the other side; apparently the enemy was asleep but he couldn't afford to speculate with the game of chance—perhaps some watchful eye was on the alert.

Approximately, there stretched a breadth of some thirty yards of *No-man's Land* between he and the enemy. Christopher stealthfully climbed over the top and then pulled up a keg of powder after him. He crawled on his stomach amid the tall grass; halfway near the center of the field he started the keg in a rolling motion and it rolled in a straight line, leaving a wide ribbon of powder in its wake. He set a long fuse to the powder then crawled back into his trench. His clothes were damp with perspiration. It was a long tense wait until the hour of attack; Christopher felt suddenly drunk with fatigue, he rested his forehead on his knees and fell suddenly asleep . . . He dreamed he was back in school again . . . Answer the question Master Wensdy . . . I can't . . . the question! . . . the question! . . . God save the ancient Mariner . . . With my crossbow I shot the Albatross . . . dead men . . . they stirred, they all uprose . . . the dead men gave a groan . . . beneath the lightning and the moon . . . I killed! . . . I killed! . . . Christopher awoke from his nightmare into the awful reality of living!

The hour was on hand. He alerted his men, stressing upon them the given plan of attack; then tense and sweating, the men watched nervously until the birth of the death moment. At 0200, Christopher ignited the long fuse; it glowed and sparked into being. In a matter of seconds the fuse reached the powder; the wet dewy grass caused it to puff and billow along the line in an ingenious smoke screen. "Foreward!" shouted Christopher.

Protected by the smoke screen, the men leaped over the top, their knapsacks brimmed full with hand grenades. Man after man aimed a grenade at the big gun, and in a fragment of time four columns of earth leaped simultaneously into the air. The enemy hadn't time to get their war machine into action; the *Minenwerfer* and the men about it were buried under a mountain of falling earth and debris. A round of artillery thundered out of the morning darkness, rocketing back and forth across the field like bits of fire. The enemy's machine gun blasted away, pumping the bullets remorsefully against the men, spitting forth a hurricane of red and silver explosions. Presently the shelling started again and a bomb hissed to the ground like a leaking valve, whistling its anticipation of sudden death! No longer did the smoke screen exist; Christopher and his men were cringing under the enemy's hellish barrage. men were falling like broken automatons; the human machines of either party had suddenly gone mad. A private had his head blown off and still he ran a full yard with blood gushing from his neck like a broken water main. Another had his skull blown open, he couldn't control his actions and fell to the earth firing his last shot. Still they pushed forward; directly before Christopher's eyes fell Sergeant Rogers, over his clasped hands bulged his intestines.

Out of the small number of fifty-seven men; twenty had met with vile and nauseating death. Christopher seized an abandoned machine gun and picked it up. He himself had suddenly turned mad! He stood above the enemy's trench and riveted their bodies with hot burning lead. So thunderstruck were the enemy, that they had not time to think before they were dead. Now the men had taken possession of the trench and were fighting in hand to hand battle. Then from out of nowhere appeared the small group of Americans, entering the battle with surprise and brilliant attack! With Christopher's men storming the entrapped enemy like demonic savages, augmented by the sudden rushing attack from the Americans, the enemy felt they were out numbered and surrendered.

8

After the battle; the repulsive, offensive mutilation which lay about the field and trenches was horribly disgusting to the eye; even as the men trampled over the blood stained earth, the rats, which the men had come to call *corpse rats* were stealing out of their holes to attend the feast of the dead. Christopher and his men gathered the German prisoners and hoarded them into a trench. There were hardly enough men to guard the captives, but he competed with the shortage by having the war prisoners lie flat on their backs while a half score of men stood above the enemy's former parapets. They trained their rifles on them, and each guard had explicit orders to shoot to kill any prisoner who moved with the slightest air of suspicion.

Christopher was making the rounds trying to console the wounded, when a Cockney recruit sought him out. "Lt. Wensdy," he said. His young face was lean and haggard; he tried to salute and at the same time hold fast to the improvised bandage on his right forearm. "I've an American sergeant with me, Sir—'e would like to speak with you." Christopher nodded to the recruit indicating that he would turn his attention to him in a short while. He was comforting the wounded man he crouched by; he lit he lit a cigarette and put it between the man's lips.

"Where is the American?" he said, climbing to his feet and glancing to the left of him. "I made 'im lie down just a ways over there, Sir, 'e 'as it pretty bad."

Christopher accompanied the recruit for a yard or so, and found the man lying on his back in the tall grass; he was bleeding profusely and life was nearly out of him. He crouched beside the American and propped his head on a knapsack.

"I want to report to somebody, Lieutenant," the American said in a faint voice. "I'm the only one left in charge now, and the men under me are a few inexperienced privates . . . I suppose you'll have to take them under your charge until they can be returned to the American Sector." "How many men did you have?" "We are 35, in number, not including our captain. I think we are only 16, now." "What happened to your captain?" "Captain Ellgate was shot down not more than nine yards north of us." Christopher's jaw fell to his chest; he could not believe his ears.

"*Captain Ellgate*, did you—" The American closed his eyes, and his head rolled to one side.

"It ain't no use, Lieutenant, 'e's a gonner." "No, he isn't, he's just fainted," replied Christopher. To reassure himself, he turned to the recruit and inquired what name did the American address his captain by. "It was somethin' like *Bellgate*, 'e said, Lieutenant." Christopher bit his lip; this time he realized that it was not his overwrought imagination that whispered his friend's name.

"See that this man gets some medical attention," he said lightly," and try to get some rest yourself." He then walked away dejectedly; his head and shoulder bowed. Presently he was approached by a dispatcher which he had sent ahead to gather information on the little manufacturing town some two miles in the distance. "The town is deserted," said the dispatch man." "It's practically level with the ground. I walked through the streets as bold as a spirit; I didn't see a human."

"Good work," Christopher answered, endeavoring to fuse some spirit in his tone, but his voice was flat and listless. "If the town is deserted, it will keep; we won't approach it until day light. Try to

get in touch with headquarters, and retaliate the word to the major."
They exchanged salutes and the dispatch man walked away.

Abstractedly, Christopher strayed toward the north field.
The news of Ellgate's death was such a devastating shock that he
wandered in a daze; his thoughts confused and fashioned in no set
pattern. He chewed his lip until it almost bled, a lump was in his
throat and he struggled to keep a tear from welling in his eye. Then
on the spur of the moment, he composed his mind and set out in
a determined passion to find Ellgate's body. For some forty-five
minutes he prowled among the dead, turning the corpses on their
backs and examining their features in the dark.

Then, at long length, he found him! Ellgate lay on the ground
with his head and shoulders braced against a small earthen mound.
He simply lay there, wide eye and staring; his uniform seemed neat,
without so much as a spatter of blood on it, and his crisp blond hair
seemed almost perfectly in place. Christopher touched his hand to
the body and it was still warm!

"*Ellgate!*" he cried in hoarse jubilation. "*Ellgate, you're alive!*" Hans
Ellgate's lips quivered; he spoke in a light trembly voice. "I—must
be dreaming . . . are y—"

"Yes, yes, Ellgate, it's your old friend Chris Wensdy." His voice
was trembling with joy. "How is it old man; I can't see where you're
hit?" Ellgate returned a faint little smile, and Christopher could see
the same old merriment burning feebly in his friend's eyes. "You
don't think I would get hit where an old cuss like you could see at
first glance, do you?" Christopher smiled, but it wasn't what it should
have been.

"You mustn't worry, old friend," Ellgate murmured, "It doesn't
hurt very badly, but since you must know . . . Somebody pumped a
straight row of bullets across my back."

"Can I do anything for you?" "Light me a cigarette; I can't seem
to move a muscle." Christopher placed a lit cigarette between his lips.
"I prayed that I might find you someday, Wen, but I never knew
it would be like this," he lifted his eyes toward Christopher's face,
"—are you pleased, that I prayed?" Christopher lowered his eyes,
and in embarrassed tones he said: "I'm not a chaplin, Ellgate . . .

I don't pray either, anymore. I don't even wear the uniform of my country."

"Don't try to explain, Wen," said Ellgate and there was consolation in his tone. "It's really not important, but I am glad that God has arranged it so we could see each other before I—" the muscles in Christopher's back tightened, and Ellgate caught the grief on his friend's face. "Don't feel pain for me old friend. I don't want you to. '*Give warning to this world, that I am fled from this vile world*', if I can remember *Mr. Shakespeare* correctly." He smiled, and tried to rest, for he could feel his strength was no longer in his limbs and breath. After much hesitation, he prompted himself to inquire of the life *here-after*; at first he thought if he were to ask his friend such a question, it might cause him pain to retrospect on the past, but with the look of concern in his eyes, he knew it would be alright.

"They did teach you, Wen, that there is another life after this . . . one of eternal bliss, or is it really fire and brimstone, as they say?"

"No," replied Christopher in a modest voice. "I believe not in such a place. *God* would not permit it. I think the fire and brimstone is merely a fear to dangle before us so that we may truly behave. Why should our *Maker* purge us with passions and permit us to sin, to say nothing of our delights and follies. What deeds we commit, are allowed by *His* permission. True, we are not so like *gods*, but then again in a fashion we are, because we can discern right from wrong, which is more than the beast of the forest can do. And thus, you see, we are to be punished, but I feel it is not the kind which is popular belief of man. *He* would not damn us with such an incredible fate. Moreover, *God* himself, at one time, was merely a man such as you and I . . . *He* knows all the gaping pits and that we are not so devine that we can escape them all. Face your *Creator* as you would face an old friend; *He* knows you and what you are. Together, you spent every moment of your life."

"You make death easy for me, Wen; you say you have deserted your God, but I'm sure you haven't forgotten him."

"I'm nothing but a fool," he said sharply. "What ever fate befalls me, I deserve."

"You were always a good friend. Do you remember when we met on the road before St. Thomas' . . . I was thinking, just before you came, of when we were boys. I had to laugh in spite of myself when I thought of Masky."

"One never forgets their childhood, Ellgate—I feel that somewhere in heaven, things are always young." Ellgate tried to speak then, but he coughed instead, and little river of blood oozed from the corner of his mouth.

"Give me your hand, Wen . . . I want to feel you near before— will you say a prayer for me like *father* used to do? I want to hear a prayer." Christopher took his hand and nodded; he felt so completely helpless crouching there beside him.

"*Promise—promise*," whispered Ellgate hoarsely, his eyes were wide, and panic shadowed his features. "*Promise me*," he reiterated, "that you will bury me, and not leave me out here for the rats to feed upon . . . and someday, when it's all over you will see that my body is returned home. I couldn't rest in this foreign soil; I believe it is haunted with the blood of noble warriors who spilt their blood here through all these thousands of years, that's why there is never peace here—those dead souls cannot slumber peacefully here for there is no tranquility in the ground. In my pocket is a letter, Wen . . . I want you to write to Sarah, and tell her about me. Tell her I loved her . . . I'm glad I knew you Wen."

Christopher could feel Ellgate's fingers loosening in his grip; he pulled the small chain and medal from his throat, he had always worn it since the day the Reverend Mother put it on him. Christopher wrapped the little silver chain about Ellgate's fingers and pressed the medal into his palm. He knelt beside him and prayed:

Judica me Deus et dicerne causam mean de gente non sancta: ab homine iniquo et doloso erue me. Emitte lucem tuam, et veritatem tuam: ipsa me deduxerunt in momtem sanctum, et in tabernacula tua. Et introibo ad altare Dei: ad Deum qui laetificat juventutem meam. Miseratur vestry omnipotens Deus, et dismissis peccatis vestris, perducat vos ad vitam aeternam . . . . Amen.

While Christopher crossed himself, he glanced on Ellgate's face, a faint smile played upon his lips. He was dead. Christopher carried

Ellgate's still warm body on his shoulders to the open field. he laid him on the ground and then, with his entrenching tool, he began to dig a grave beneath the mutilated arbor of a willow tree. As he excavated the earth, Christopher's body oozed with sweat and tears burned his eyes. When the grave was deep enough, he laid him in, and then with his tunic, he covered his face and shoulders. With pain and reluctance he heaped the earth upon his friend's body. At length, when he was through, he threw himself over the little mound and wept . . . he wept for many things of past and present.

The men marched in double file along the deserted and shell torn road. A Cockney recruit craned his neck, endeavoring to peer at the head of the ranks to secure a glimpse of Christopher.

"What's the matter with the lieutenant?" he asked of the man at his left, as they plodded along the road leading to the town.

"Blimey, friend, I really can't say; 'though I must admit that he's actin' sorely broken up 'bout something'. When 'e give us the orders to march, 'e sounded a bit down in the mouth. It gives me the willies to 'ear 'im that way. Somehow, it mide me feel sorry for the bloke, the lieutenant is a right nice chap, you kno', 'nd 'e is brive too. "Ell, what I thinks we all nees is a damn long stretch of kip (sleep)."

One of the Americans, marching behind the two men who were speaking, heard their conversation and interrupted. "I know what is wrong with your lieutenant," he said, and his tone was somber and confidential.

"'Ow would you know', my *Yankee* cousin?"

"I was out in the field," he replied modestly.

"Doing what?" another man chimed in. The American didn't answer, and turned his eyes from the Britisher's face, who was at least ten years the boy's senior. "O, I cetch," he growled in a dirty tone, and he nudged his companion in the ribs and laughed impurely, which was crude and uncalled for. "Go on with it," the Cockney said to the American. He swayed his head to the right of him. "This bloke's got a dirty mind and no sense.

"Well, by chance, I overheard your lieutenant talking to my captain—"

"I thought the Gerries 'ad let 'im have it, and 'e was dead."

"So did I. You can imagine my supprise when I heard the Captain's voice. I really didn't intend to eavesdrop," he admitted in all earnestness, "but, I was so surprised that I just stayed there and listened."

"Well, what 'appened?"

"Nothing really, that is, nothing that was any of my business. It seems as though your lieutenant and my captain were old friends."

"So what?"

". . . Well, it sounded strange to me, but I say the lieutenant knelt down and prayed. He prayed in latin just like he was a priest." At least this much turned a vein of curiosity in the man. "Are you sure, Yank?" "I saw it with my own eyes . . . I really didn't want to stay there, but I was afraid to move. Suppose I would have made a crackling noise in the brush? The lieutenant might have thought I was the enemy and shot without asking questions. I tell you, I was afraid to move."

"Lucky for 'im you wasn't the enemy."

"But, you say 'e prayed like 'e was a priest?"

"Yes."

"Stringe, I'll say."

"Then what 'appened?"

"After a while, I saw him pick up my dead captain's body, and carry it away. I suppose he must have buried him. I didn't stay after that—I saw my chance and got away."

"It all sounds stringe t'me."

"Well, I seys it ain't none of our busniness, what the lieutenant did. I'm sure 'e 'ad 'is reasons. I say we 'ad all better keep our mouth shut . . . first thing you kn' we'll git our arses in trouble."

"I guess you're right . . . The lieutenant is all right with me." He looked up the road: "'Ow far di they say that bloomin' town was?"

"Who cares?"

"'Ell, I wish the damn war was over!"

"So do I. Who doesn't wish that, 'cept maybe the Kaiser."

"O, to 'ell with the Kaiser. You know, they say 'is desk chair is mide like a saddle."

"I told you 'e was crazy—anyhow, what would you do if the war was really over?"

"'Ell! I'd show you what I'd; I would pop in bed with the first buxom wench I could find. You know, one of them kins we seen in them ancient paintin's in the Paris museums—the kind with a pair of 'ips that a man can git hold of."

One of the men in front of them turned about; a demeure expression was on his face and his voice was cloaked with false modesty. He said: Who'd think them nice Parisians would allow pitches of nekid wimen 'ang in their museums." His pun set the men about him roaring with laughter, but somehow it wasn't genuine. They were sick of their great discomfort and the vile talk. They were tired and homesick.

Christopher led his men into the town, which was nothing more than a heap of mutilated timber and mortar; a place of utter devastation and decay. It was like invading a city of the dead. All was quiet and the phantom silence lurched in the gaping black holes of the buildings. Suddenly from out of nowhere, a squad of the enemy's aeroplanes were droaning overhead. Christopher shouted the alarm to his men to seek shelter. Presently, the war machines were flying low and spitting their bullets to the ground. When Christopher turned around for a bried inspection, he saw a thin hazy film rising from the ground into the air.

"Gas attack!" bellowed the men in panic, and soon each man was fitting his mask to his face. As Christopher endeavored to herd his small band of men into shelter, he himself was trapped in the deadly grey-white mist. As his men turned about to view him, they caught a glimpse of his figure in the mist. He had just enough time to fit his gas mask to his face; he started to impart a dash for shelter, when a stray bullet cut him down. His men watched him fall, and in a moment he was completely hidden from view—smothered beneath the poisonous vapers.

PART FOUR

1

Perhaps he was only dreaming, or maybe he was going through a drowsy memory of what happened to him, but he awoke with a start; he felt the sharp hot ball of fire burn into his chest; he recalled shouting orders to his men, and then came that burst of hissing grey mist that was to swallow him in its deadly white cloak like an evil apparition. Christopher was fully awake now and a film of perspiration stood out on his lips and forehead. He awoke to find himself on a bed with clean sheets and his body in fresh linen. He didn't exactly know where he was but he knew that it was a place that gave him a feeling of peace, and the grime and dirt of the trenches was behind him. He closed his eyes and extended his arms outside of the fresh crackling sheets, there was a pain in his chest but he was actually too tired to feel it. Without a struggle he permitted himself to fall into the soft blackness of slumber, and slept for three perfect days in succession.

When he opened his eyes again he discovered a nurse standing by his side, and as the layers of sleep began to unfold themselves from his mind he breathed the name of Sarah Morrison; the memory of Ellgate haunted his tired thoughts. The nurse urged him to lay still, then prepared to change the dressing of his wound. Christopher inquired of her as to where he was, and though she was French, she informed him in perfect English that he was aboard a hospital ship bound from Boulogne to Portsmouth. He was astonished, for it seemed to Christopher that he had fallen on German soil but an hour before. Where and how did so much time elapse?

The nurse could read the questions in his dark blue eyes; she told him: "You were in delirious fever for more than a week, lieutenant. You were even asleep when they carried you aboard ship." She smiled, "Three whole days, in fact. You were a very tired man," she added putting the final strip of adhesive tape on his chest wound and closing his pajama coat. "Are you going to sleep again, lieutenant?" she teased."

"I've slept for three days?" he murmured astoundingly, "but that's impossible." He looked at the nurse and she merely smiled at him in return. ". . . Did you say we were sailing to Portsmouth?" he inquired, then questioned as to where they were at the moment.

"Where else but the English Channel," she answered quietly taking his pulse in her casual, professional manner.

"Then we're to be in England soon," he muttered voicing his thoughts orally; his muse turned to Fredrica and he began to imagine himself stealing up to her apartment, then as she would open the door, he'd kiss her surprised face and sweep her in his embrace. He would watch her eyes with that certain fixed look which always gave Fredrica a wonderful and singular appearance of purity, and before the startled, fascinating glow could die from her cheeks, he would present to her the little emerald earrings he purchased in Paris. The words of her letter came back to him . . . 'It will be a grand day when the black war is over, and you will come back to me' . . . His blood flowed joyously through his young veins. He turned to the nurse: "I had a manuscript in my belt," he said, "do you know where it is?"

"I don't know . . . I suppose it's with your things," she rejoined obligingly and started to rummage through the possessions in his knapsack. "Yes," she cried quickly, "I guess this is it."

He held out his hand: "May I have it, please?"

"Certainly. Is it a story of the war?" she asked, and cringed when she saw his fingers as they automatically sought the brown bullet hole in the dog-eared papers.

"It's just a story," he said modestly, then tightened his grip on the faded yellow pages.

The nurse gathered there was some strange relationship between her patient and the dog-eared papers he clutched so eagerly between his fingers, and being an experienced woman in the nursing profession, she also understood that he had no desire to discuss the matter with her. She changed the subject: "There's a friend of yours who has been inquiring after your health," she told him. "Do you feel strong enough for visitors?"

Christopher shot her a long sympathetic glance as though he thought her quite foolish: "Strong enough?" he echoed. "Of course I am. Where are my trousers, nurse? I want to get up." His eyes narrowed curiously, "Did you say a friend of mine has been asking for me? Do you mean Lt. Lorrie, is he aboard too?"

"I do," she murmured, "but you're not getting up. At least, not up on your own two feet. If you'd like to go up on the sun deck for a while, I'll get you a wheel chair."

"But nurse—"

"But you just stay in bed until I return, and if I see the lieutenant, I will tell him you are awake and can have visitors now." When the nurse was about to step out into the companionway, Christopher called out to her suddenly. She turned around in anticipation of his request, and waited for him to speak. He wanted to inquire of her if she knew anything of Sarah Morrison, hoping that she could give him some information as to where he could locate her. Who knows, he thought, they might have been acquainted. But then he had a change of mind and didn't wish to go into the awful business just now. He would wait—wait until the time was right. It wasn't going to be easy to break the news to Sarah, and he sensed a melancholy moment of grief as he thought of Ellgate in his shallow grave; that desolate burial mound under that mutilated tree with perhaps only the wind and cold rain to mourn him out there. He waved his hand to the nurse in a gesture of dismissal, and when she left he was glad to be alone with his thoughts. Suddenly he felt tired and weak again.

Christopher tried to rest, but too many faces and memories poked at his imagination; soon he drifted into a muse concerning Rue, it was always her face that haunted him the most. He closed his eyes to try and shut out her memory, but he only succeeded in picturing her more vividly, and for some reason he seemed to remember her crying, then smiling through her tears.

Presently the nurse returned, and caused some amount of racket with the wheel-chair she pushed before her. Christopher looked past her shoulder, and there stepping off the companion way was Lorrie, hobbling with a cane, he came toward Christopher and a haughty smile glowed on his face.

Later they settled on the sun deck. Lorrie made himself comfortable in a steamer chair and the nurse rolled Christopher beside him then left. The deck was quiet and uncrowded except for a pair of recruits who leaned on the rail to talk and smoke. A stout breeze blew off the churning green water and at times the sun would pour down burning hot then fade out into a faint weakfish flow; between its fittish coming and goings Christopher and Lorrie sat in the breeze engaged in light and informal talk.

"What perfect weather," remarked Christopher after a lapse in the conversation. He turned his face toward the wind and looked out over the water to the haze of dark purple which started to loom above the horizon. "That can't be England so soon," he said but before Lorrie could answer him he turned the conversation back to the weather. Later he asked: "Just what day is it?" his question came in a shrill voice conveying a somewhat facetious ring.

Within another hour the disembarking began and the men filed down the gangway into the grey cold morning, then according to special troops and categories they were assigned to different coaches on the train which was to speed them to Fort Arundel. Once more Christopher and Lorri were separated; Lorrie being capable of getting about fairly well was naturally assigned to the day coach for travel, but Christopher was still maintained with the hospital division for he was still weak from the loss of so much blood.

It wasn't until another eight days that they were to see each other again, when Lorrie sighted Christopher he was sitting dejectedly at a lonely corner table in the officer's club. His head was bowed while his eyes were fixed on a small pair of emerald earrings he held in his open palm. Lorrie hobbled over toward him; he held a drink in one hand and with the other he balanced himself on a walking cane. His friend was so deadly locked in thought that he didn't see Lorrie until he wrapped on the wooden table with the tip of his cane. He startled Christopher into looking up.

"Is this table reserved for thinkers?" smiled Lorrie, "or mightn't an old crony join you?" When Christopher stood up to greet him he pretended not to see the earrings he slipped into his pocket; the expression on his face seemed all too obvious that he hadn't received mail from Fredrica and was brooding about it. They sat down; Lorrie took a swallow of his drink then opened the conversation by making some comment concerning the sling which supported Christopher's arm. "Don't tell me the medics broke your arm while trying to patch up that scratch you call a wound?" he laughed in gest, but actually he was seriously aware of the grave wound for it almost claimed his friend's life.

"They tell me it's supposed to relieve the strain," he smiled quietly. "but you and I know it's only there to cause a dramatic effect. The same as that cane you're sporting, ole crip." He laughed and Lorrie joined him. "They had to find some reason for discharging me. I have to look lame when I depart from here this afternoon."

"Blast you!" bleated Lorrie forging some pretense of anger, "So you were going to leave this damn fort without so much as a pat on the back for me, or a thank you old friend, it was swell warring with you. Now is that showing gratitude of a war-buddy!" he said enjoying Christopher's harassed expression. Lorrie had known about Christopher's discharge approximately a fair twelve hours before he did and took the trouble of going to some length in order that they might share the mutual train compartment on their journey back to London.

"But honest, Lorrie," Christopher began to sputter forth his apologies, "I've inquired all over the camp for you, and this is really the first morning I've had to shift for myself," as he spoke he caught a flick of guilt in Lorrie's eye. Christopher gave him a sharp look and the rogue broke down in laughter. "Why you dirty scoundrel!" he cried. "I suppose you knew about it all along and you must be free to leave yourself, or you wouldn't be looking so jolly."

"A thousand pardons old man, a million apologies!" Lorrie continued making some attempt to quell his laughter, then in another moment his grinning features took on a bright glow of pride. "If you'll pardon my boasting old fellow, I don't mind informing you without any special qualms of modesty, that I'll be coming up for the Victorian Cross in the by and by."

A smile broke upon Christopher's face; he reached out and took his friend's hand. "Lorrie! how good for you. You must be the proudest man alive. Did you mention this to your uncle?"

"Hell no!" he bleated in a bright voice, "I'm keeping it as a surprise for the old boy. I'll not tell him a word about it until he reads it for himself in the *Times* . . . besides, I'd better not show any glory, or crow about it in any way, or he'll disinherit me in two shakes. The old humbug is damn funny at times, you know." He sighed abysmally: "But I must be nice to him. After all, he's my only living relative.

Whenever someone or other spoke of relatives, Christopher couldn't help feeling a little bereft as if something great and blood like had been taken from the dark cool depths of his soul. He assumed that it must be a good thing to have a blood affiliation with another human being regardless of all the objurgating he heard others speak of their connections by birth and marriage with their kith and kin. In any event, he felt that it was something one could cling to and feel a part of. He thought of Fredrica . . . there was someone he could give his life to; she could make him know that feeling of being a member in the family world. A feeling of warmth kindled itself in the small of his stomach rising up to his heart, burning his chest and climbing over his throat and cheeks until he sensed himself blushing for no apparent reason. That is, for no other reason except that there was Fredrica to go back to. He suddenly felt alive and fresh again . . . time was running too slowly for him now, and he felt he couldn't restrain himself until train time. He had to get started; to get back to London and know once more the life and warmth of Fredrica's lips; to feel her arms around him and the heat of her body against his when they were to embrace once more after the long and ugly war that parted them.

The conversation between he and Lorrie soon fell away. Christopher continued his reverie concerning Fredrica and Lorrie was absorbed in the time-table he pulled out of his pocket. Then after a time he finished his drink telling Christopher to meet him at the fort gate by 4:30 that evening. He limped away on his cane whistling, then passed through the doors of the club and made his way to the officer's quarters and finished his packing.

Christopher stood in the November wind talking to the sentinel on watch when the army hack rolled up to the gate and suddenly stopped. Lorrie pushed his head through the window and beckoned to Christopher to get in. The door opened; he tossed in his baggage then ducked into the hack; the gears grinded into place and they sped away to the depot.

Two days later they arrived in London. The train hadn't been fully emptied of its passengers when Christopher and Lorrie, standing on the platform retrieving their baggage, were suddenly startled! Within a matter of minutes Victoria Station was in an uproar with disturbances! There was a confusion and clamor of loud voices, heated and thrown into excitement! In the next moment news boys were hurrying pell mell amid the excited crowd shouting *Armistice*! *Armistice*! and the end of the war! Christopher and Lorrie flashed joyous, startled glances of relief and happiness to each other.

2

Girls ran up to Christopher and Lorrie, throwing their arms about their necks and kissing them ardently upon the lips in a wild moment of ecstasy to welcome the returning warriors. The station seemed littered with men in khaki, they tossed their caps into the air, jumping up and down and yelling happily. A Salvation Army Band boomed its way through the crowd and to the strains of its lively free music both civilian and soldier danced gaily with the other. Lorrie and Christopher pushed out of the crowded station into the street. A multitude of happy thundering voices roared with shouts and laughter and confetti rained from the crowded windows like snow. Then, from practically nowhere, appeared another Salvation band; its brassy strains were endeavoring to soar above the roar of the crowd, playing, "Keep the Home Fires Burning" in flying tempo! An old woman darted up to Lorrie's side and seizing his hands kissed them, proclaiming in a strident voice that he had saved the world, which of course, caused him to blush and feel quite foolish. Again some girls came up to them and they were kissed once more, which they consented to without the slightest objection. Then, when they had gone further up the crowded street, Christopher touched Lorrie's shoulder in order to gain his attention, for it was almost impossible to speak above the happy din. Lorrie bent over to hear what he had to say, and understood such words as: "It's goodbye for now. You're in the directory, aren't you? . . . I'll telephone." He felt Christopher grasp his hand tightly, then before he could say a word he saw Christopher walk away and get swallowed in the laughing crowd.

Christopher was tall and that gave Lorrie the advantage of keeping sight of his friend for awhile without losing him entirely in the crowd. He watched the back of his head and could see him every now and then tilt his chin in a laugh whenever a girl stopped him for a kiss, or someone delay him for a chat. Lorrie couldn't help feeling a slight twinge of melancholy and a sense of loneliness. Not so much for himself as much as for the quiet noble man he had acquired for a friend. "He's going to his girl . . . Fredrica, I believe he said her name was," murmured Lorrie to himself, "I hope all's well between them," he continued in a kind of dreadful calm. "Christ, he was so worried about her not writing him." Some girls came up to him and showered him with handfuls of confetti; they took him by the hands and pulled him deeper into the crowds, he went laughingly, but looked over his shoulder to catch a final glimpse of Christopher—but he was gone.

Number #136-B Gower Street, which at one time had been the place where Fredrica lived, was nothing but a vacant lot heaped up with destruction, charred timber and crumbling stone. The building had been bombed! Christopher gazed panickingly upon the utter ruins! His heart, that only a short time before was singing with high hopes, was now cloaked with worry, desperation and grief. He couldn't believe his eyes! Was this the address he had scribbled on so many envelopes which held the words of his heart! Was this the place he visioned so often in dreams, where he would steal up to the door and surprise the one he loved? There wasn't a door to be seen! He felt strangely cold and sick. If Fredrica had been killed under that horrible rubble that lay before him, then he had no desire to live either! The revelry of victory was still crying high in the street he stood in, but he could feel no cause for merrymaking now. He felt more like the crushed oppressor. Then suddenly a new hopeful thought fled over him. He remembered Mrs. Wessly and believed Fredrica might be there; in the next jubilant moment he went running down the street and the crowds of people who stood in his path proved only an impediment to his speed.

Christopher's wild run through the streets had caused him to sweat and he was robbed of breath when he finally reached Mrs. Wessly's printing shop. But once again he was faced with disappointment. Mrs. Wessly's property was completely abandoned and desolate of occupants or care. The buildings façade was all boarded up, and a no trespassing sign nailed across the door! Christopher couldn't comprehend its meaning; a profound current of dread and bewilderment began to engulf him; he felt suddenly weak and dizzy with the anticipation of something black and broodingly loathsome to come. Then as he stood there facing the barred dust laden door, with only his sick and odious thoughts, the words of Fredrica's letter came back to him thin and mockingly as if to carry more sorrow to his troubled heart: . . . *It will be a grand day when the black war is over, and you'll come back to me* . . . Blind burning tears sprang into his eyes as he tilted his head back to sing out in a clip bitter laugh! Then he chanced to turn around and sighted Mr. Peres standing in the open door of his aquarium shop. He bolted past the merry people standing on the sidewalk and sped across the street. Christopher startled the little man when he seized him by his frail shoulders and demanded of him in a rude and excited tone why Mrs. Wessly's shop was so boarded, and if he possessed any knowledge of Miss Hobbs, or where she might be staying?"

Christopher had forced the breath out of the man so that he stared at him foolishly. "Why . . . why good Gawd, Lieutenant!" he sputtered in a brittle tone. "Ain't . . . ain't you 'eard? Poor Miss Wess' was killed in an air-r'ide . . . Why I thought you knew, the man added when he read the startled awe and dismay smoldering in Christopher's dark blue eyes. "I thought you knew!" he repeated hoping that the words might prompt Christopher into giving him some sort of reply, for he simply stood there like a frozen statue. "I'm glad you are back," he continued. "I've been actin' like trustee over Miss Wess's plice . . . I'm suppose to let the solicitor know when you got back. Mista Chris!" he demanded in order to pull him out of his muse for he could see that Christopher hadn't been listening to a word he was telling him.

"What about Miss Hobbs?" he sharply asked the man. "Miss Hobbs, the blond haired lady that use to visit with Mrs. Wessly."

"I ain't seen Miss 'Obbs in the n'ighborhood for weeks, Sir. She just seem to disappear after poor Miss Wess' passed on."

The man's words fell over Christopher and burned into his heart with such pain and fire that he appeared deaf and blind to all else about him, and a cold dread numbness stole over his back and shoulders like a paralizing thing. Christopher realized that it was a foolish vain hope to believe for a minute that the man could tell him anything of Fredrica. Mr. Peres rattled on telling him something about a solicitor of some sort but Christopher couldn't trouble himself to listen. He felt that somewhere Fredrica was still alive and he had to find her.

A cab rolled up along the side of the curb and Lorrie stepped out. He had a vague forboding when Christopher left him in the crowd that something of this nature might occur, so he took it upon himself to follow him. "You forgot your baggage at the station," he told him as a matter of excuse for being there. "I had your address, so I thought I'd bring it out to you." Lorrie glanced over to the other side of the street and viewed the abandoned printing shop. There seemed no need for Christopher to explain anything, with a little elementary deduction he put matters together and came out with the correct answer. No Mrs. Wessly; no Fredrica . . . so that accounted for Christopher not receiving mail for so long. He beckoned Christopher to the cab, and he ducked in with a loose dejected movement, but feeling grateful that he had found a friendly face in his hour of despair. The little man followed after them, endeavoring to tell Christopher something before they drove away, but Lorrie put him off by giving the man a card explaining that he would be residing at the address on the card. He stepped into the cab and they drove away leaving the little man standing on the pavement.

It was the butler, Joseph who opened the door for them; his bent figure appeared sharp black and white against the Victorian richness and color of the polished hall behind him. Joseph's leathery face glowed then kindled into a bright grin when he saw Lorrie standing on the stone steps beneath the heavy eaves. He was so surprised to see his young master that he seemed rooted to the spot he stood on. He looked past Lorrie's shoulder taking in Christopher with one swift glance and then back to Lorrie. "Oh! God bless us, Mr. Lorrie! God bless us . . . you've come back safe. And on this of all days, now we can really know what the armistice means! Come in, Sir, come in!" He shouted his greetings in a thin cracked voice; he reached out with his white blue veined hands taking both young men by the arms and pulling them within the broad polished hall. By this time the butler's happy voice resounded throughout the entire house and its very occupants appeared from every which way to investigate the old servant's racket. It roused Uncle Thad from his noon-day nap; it brought the cook and maids from the pantry; it summoned Ann, the housekeeper from her duties in the morning room, and even the Cocker Spaniel crawled from under the sofa to yelp and bark its greetings to the returning warriors.

"Oh! my soldier-boy!" whimpered Anna. She appeared before them looking very kind and matronly in her black crep dress with her silver groomed hair so neatly in place and looking like Lorrie had always remembered her, as if she seemed always ready to go out for a walk. "Eric Lorrie! Eric! Eric!" she ran up to him and threw her arms about his neck, then reaching up on her toes she kissed his face. Anna was all flushed with happiness, and with some awkward little gesture she endeavored to hide the tears in her eyes. It was then that she had time to notice Christopher; he seemed so lonely and melancholy standing there, that without waiting for an introduction, she took his strong brown hands in her's and reached up to kiss him. A blood red warmth flooded his handsome face. "You're back!" sobbed Anna, "both of you. Thank God it's over with at last!"

The click of the old gentleman's heels were heard coming down the broad mahogany stairs. Everyone looked up toward him, and for the first time since the front bell sounded there was silence in the great hall. He stood on the bottom step and looked affectionately toward his nephew. The Cocker Spaniel dashed over to his heels and sniffed him. Lorrie stepped quietly over to his uncle and shook his out stretched hand, but a mere handshake wasn't quite enough to satisfy the old gentleman's affections, he stretched open his arms and clapped his nephew in his embrace patting him fondly on the back. He didn't speak or say anything—there was no need for words here, all was obvious in a fond mute understanding.

Later Lorrie pulled Christopher over to introduce him to his uncle. Uncle Thad was still paused on the bottom step, so that now with Christopher standing before him they met on an eye level. They shook hands and spoke a few words of greetings. The old gentleman possessed a strange flare for viewing all new acquaintances from all angles; he asked Christopher to turn first to the left, then right, and then completely around. He observed his strong neck and the round head with is clean cut features which rested there, the broad shoulders and the slim flanks and hips, and the long straight legs. Yes, he made up his mind. He liked him, finding something aristocratic in Christopher that pleased him. Although he was democratic to the letter, he had no use for people who didn't carry themselves like thoroughbreds; one had only to look around to observe that feature, even his servants were ladies and gentlemen. Then looking at Christopher square in the eye, he said: "Leave it to my nephew to discover fine people . . . he has a knack for it. I like your handshake, young man," he said smiling down on Christopher. "Strong fingers . . . that's a good sign in men. Welcome to my house." Thereafter he turned to his nephew and they fell into conversation which left Christopher outside the circle again; he felt strange at having had the old man observe him in such a way, but remembering Lorrie's warning before hand about his uncle's peculiar traits he brushed the matter from his mind and started to play with the little dog who yelped and whimpered at his heels begging for some attention.

Presently the old gentleman left his nephew's side and began giving orders to his servants: "Cook, I want you to prepare the finest dinner of your life. Anna you supervise the job so it will be certain to come out just right, and Joseph! Joseph! get me the keys to the wine cellar I want the finest wine we have on stock. It's to be a celebration for our fighting men here! And just a sample of zubrovka—or whatever its named, you know that Polish stuff—wait I'd better come with you and be sure."

"Have you ever tasted zubrovka?" asked Lorrie crouching beside Christopher who still played with the golden haired, long eared spaniel.

"No, not that I remember."

"No? Well, it'll enchant your pallet; It's hellishly delicious if you don't get soused on the first glass."

"I'm looking forward for a taste—What do you call her?" said Christopher in reference to the dog he was coaxing to sit up.

"Dee," he muttered. "She's a champion, the baby of the family."

Late one morning Lorrie stumbled lazily into the billiard room. Christopher leaned on the edge of the oblong green cloth-covered table propelling the tapering cue against the ivory balls. He was still in robe and slippers and his hair was greatly disheveled and uncombed. Lorrie bade him good morning then fell into a wooden round back chair propping his legs on top the circular card table. "Well old boy," he grinned. "I'm waiting to hear the good news. Joseph seemed all in a tizzie about the envelope he carried to you this morning. he said he was positive that it was *palace* stationery which bore a *coronet seal*. What's it all about?"

"What are you talking about?" he answered sullenly.

"Oh, come, don't be so damn modest . . . or should I say elusive," he laughed. "Joseph rarely makes mistake about such things. If he thought it was palace stationery, it must be. Coronet sealed letters don't run hither and thither in any old channel." He lifted his brows in an odd curious fashion: "Well, aren't you going to let me in on the matter, or don't you care to?"

Christopher dug rather doggedly into the pocket of the black robe he was wearing and brought forth the crumpled white envelope. He handed it over and Lorrie snatched it up gingerly. He unfolded the official paper: "Ahh!" he cried, his eyes literally danced over the printed page, and his voice jubilantly on fire, he read: "From the king's administrator and special minister to the affair of state, the most Reverend Lord Chancellor of the Great Seal of England—"

He stopped reading, "Man! do you realize what this means? You are to be knighted for valor, by His Royal Majesty King George The Fifth!" Lorrie continued to read on in silence, then looking up again he cried: "Damn your lack of enthusiasm! How can you stand there so calm? Oho! and I was boasting of my *Victorian*—" by this time Lorrie was throwing a fit of joy.

"I can't accept it," Christopher replied presently. Lorrie flashed him a wild uncertain look; he shrugged his shoulders saying: "I just can't," his tone carried a final ring, but it lacked everything it should have ordinary possessed.

"What!" he sprang to his feet. "Have you suddenly lost your wits? I've heard of modesty in my time but this—this is beyond belief. Here you are being recognized for merit and patriotic service, and you say you'll not accept. What an insult to the crown!" Then his voice dropped into a dry abysmal whisper, "*Why*? What are your reasons . . . ?"

Christopher sensed the old sick nausea rising in him once more; he felt the old storm beginning to rage, and he could imagine the skeletons of his past rattling their bones mockingly. He thought he should enlighten Lorrie of the circumstances which encompassed him. How bitter it was to recall the old haunting trouble again. He had no heart to bring it all back. Let the dead past bury the dead . . . And yet, he must offer some explanation. First he thought of some fable which might satisfy, but realized all too quickly that it would really be of no avail. There would be others to whom he must expound his refusal to, such as the officials of the British Crown, and possibly they might release the story to the press. He didn't want that. The situation loomed horribly before him. What was he to do? At length, he composed his mind. He would face the truth no matter how bitterly the consequences might prove. He faced Lorrie and told him as much that seemed *absolutely* necessary.

"You are in a hellish mess," Lorrie whispered after a long pause. "I'm sorry I pounced upon you with such venom. I had no idea."

Christopher clenched his hands together and brought them up to his forehead in a tight ball. "But what am I to do Lorrie? That's my big dilemma . . . what am I to do?" After a long hesitating pause of despair, his pale worried face looked up to Lorrie in a strange troubled frown. "I just can't do it Lorrie, I'm worried and scared. I could never hope to escape with such a low lying masquerade like that. Besides, won't they investigate my character and background first? Why I'm not even a citizen."

"No doubt they have already made investigations, or at least enough to satisfy them or I'm positive you wouldn't have received that letter if they were in anyway skeptical. I think the only real thing they investigate for is to find a criminal background. Really you shouldn't fear, your war record speaks highly of you."

"Are you trying to tell me I should accept?"

"Precisely what I mean! I think it would be the wisest thing to do under the circumstances, or you will be steeped in trouble up to the very neck. Possibly the first chafe against you is this business of not having a passport, how did you let such a thing get away from you?" Christopher flinched under the words, that part he didn't think necessary to explain about leaving his passport with Rue, and it left Lorrie in the shadows. "And there's this affair about Mrs. Wessly," he went on to say, "She forging those papers for you. To say nothing of all the legal entaglements, and the unheard of misdemeanors on the British statue books. And when they'll get through with you, how will you ever prove that you are an American citizen in the first place. The newspapers both here and abroad will have a field day at your expense. Not only will you be disgraced, but a laughing stock in both countries."

"But what a dirty life to live . . . What a rotten dirty lie!"

"You lived a lie this far; I fear that you'll just have to continue it. Who can say, possibly this is faith's way of compensating you for all the tricks she's played on you. But then, if you did come out with the whole story, they might take your war valor into consideration but I for one wouldn't advise it. No, I wouldn't take the risk." Then with a feeling of consideration for his friend he added: "Who knows, Chris, it might all end by you going to prison. I'd go through it if I were you—You've got to!"

"But what if I'm asked questions concerning my family background and education . . . what will I say then?"

"Just mention that your father was a gentlemen farmer; so many Englishmen are and do very well with that for a background . . . As for education, merely explain that you were privately taught. You know that classic learning for the very rich." Lorrie looked at Christopher, his face in the shaded light of the billiard table appeared strained with deep hollow patches of black upon his cheeks and eyes. It was hard to imagine what was going on there in his troubled mind. He just remained standing there in a quiet air; his utter silence left Lorrie bereft of words; he went over to the console then returned with two drinks and gave one to Christopher. He accepted it in an abstract manner and looked upon the frosted drink fiercely. He set the untouched drink down on the table before him, then in a quiet nervous air he looked at Lorrie. "Alright," he said, "I'll go through with this farce. I'll tell them any lie that pops into my brain . . . and if they should find me out—" he suddenly stopped speaking with an abrupt and disregarding air for everything. He simply didn't care anymore; he took up his glass and drained it dry with one final draught.

3

In the days that followed, Lorrie failed to see very much of Christopher, for he rose early in the mornings long before the household would stir out of bed, and didn't return to the house until the small hours of the following morning. Lorrie didn't question him about these mysterious coming and goings of his, but later he discovered the reason for Christopher's actions . . . he spent the majority of his time in walking the streets of London in hopes of finding some trace of Fredrica.

They were sitting in the library that afternoon when Lorrie chanced to lift his eyes to see Anna standing in the doorway. "Mr. Lorrie, there's a gentleman asking for Mr. Chris, shall I show him in?"

"I'm afraid that I don't fully comprehend you, Mr. Woods," reflected Christopher, his mind doting on the legal aspects of the situation. The man's visit began to trouble him.

The attorney lifted his brows in utter surprise. "Surely, Mr. Wendsy, you must be aware that the deceased Mrs. Wessly had endowed you with her worldly fortune, and I must say it is a tidy sum!"

Lorrie whistled. "I say, Chris this is a windfall!" Christopher remained silent, thunderstruck at the news. He turned a quick glance at Lorrie who now stood to the left of him. He wanted to make some comment on the matter, but his mouth felt too dry to speak. Mr. Jules Harold Woods continued to ramble on; Christopher rose to his feet, then slumped back into his chair. Things were happening too rapidly for him, he felt he was on a speeding train and couldn't get off.

"Now, to get down to the business of the legacy," said Mr. Woods; he picked up the document and above Christopher's constant interruptions, he read:

I, Charlotte Wessly having no living relatives, and being sound of mind, bequeath all my worldly goods to one Mr. Christopher Wensdy, which are including: My property and business on Portugal Street and all the furnishings therein contained, A manor house in Chelsea, seven (negotiable) Gold Bonds, at deposit in the Bank of the British Commonwealth: A total sum of 10,000 pounds sterling (cash) with the Bank of London—

Again Lorrie whistled; Christopher could only sit back and listen. He never once dreamed that poor Mrs. Wessly possessed so much, and to think she made him her heir. He could scarce believe it. "These papers require your signature, Mr. Wensdy." The solicitor handed Christopher the pen and he took it with a trembling hand. "This one first, transferring the property to your name . . . now these for the bank. Ah! thank you." The attorney rose to his feet; "Well, my man, as the French say: *nouveau riche* but understand that I connote no vulgarity with my words. I merely wish to congratulate you on your inheritance. Good day to you sir, Mr. Wendsy . . . Mr. Lorrie. Oh, by the way," he murmured putting on his grey derby, "are you not the Mr. Wensdy whom I see by the *Times* is to be knighted?"

The man's words startled Christopher; he had no idea his name had been mentioned in the press. He looked at Mr. Woods and managed to stammer a very non-intelligible, "Yes."

"No need to be modest about it, Sir," replied Mr. Woods who caught the flash of embarrassment on Christopher's face. "I'm certain that you deserved the reward. Permit me to offer my congratulations once more." They shook hands; he bade them good day, then departed.

Christopher and Lorrie sat in the rear seat of the long polished limousine which sped them through the lamp lit streets of London to St. James' Palace. This was the appointed night that they were to be honored by the king; a special ball had been prepared for the solomn occasion. For a length of time they rode in silence, awkward tense and stiff, each preoccupied with their own thoughts, both were attired in the height of fasion: formal dress, white tie, opera hat and cape; their feet, not long released from warrior's boots seemed pinched and strange in the newness of the patten leather fitness.

"I am still troubled at going through with this," Christopher murmured to Lorrie in subdued tones. "Suppose some one should find me out?" He could afford no risk at having the chauffer overhear his conversation, his voice was so low that Lorrie could hardly understand what he was saying, but he felt he couldn't be too confidential.

"Are we to go through that again!" said Lorrie snapping him off; he missed most of Christopher's words but the expression on his face seemed easy enough to read. "Besides," he added, "it's too late to think of that now."

"Couldn't you just announce that I suddenly dropped dead!"

"I'll soon have to, if you don't shut up . . . damn! don't you think I'm just as much on edge as you are? One doesn't get the opportunity to meet with the king every day."

"That's what I mean," said Christopher, "If only I didn't have to meet the king. The only kings I ever knew were in story books, and sometimes they were terrible. I suppose if I wasn't so damn worried about Fredrica I wouldn't be so scared," he said, "I tried to find her again today and turned London upside-down without any success."

"Why don't you put a man on the job?"

"What do you mean?"

"Scotland Yard; hire a detective from the *Yard*, and in no time your problem will be solved . . . It's merely the case of the missing person. Haven't you a picture of her?"

"At one time, yes. But I think I lost it somewhere in France."

"Well no matter, a good description will do just as well. I feel as though I could describe her, and Fredrica I've never seen." Lorrie slapped Christopher's knee, "At the moment we have something else confronting us!" The limousine turned into the palace gates; the magnificent structure of granite and marble seemed ablaze with a thousand lights. Christopher felt his heart leave his body.

4

Pale and handsome, Christopher knelt on one knee at the foot of the great monarch; he trembled with emotion, and his young heart was wildly beating; he could feel every eye upon him; he felt like a small boy and wished he had someone to cry his joy to. The great opulent chamber was thickly peopled with extravagantly dressed men and women, those of noble and medium birth. The splendid hall was luxuriously embellished from the polished marble floor to the great domed shaped ceiling from which hung gorgeous crystal and gilt chandeliers.

Before Christopher could fully comprehend as to what was ensuing forward, the king's jeweled sword was on his right shoulder and then on his left. The handsome and graceful king spoke: "I, King George the Fifth, Lord of Great Britain and Ireland, and Emperor of India, and the dominions over the seas, dub thee knight; bestowing on thee the most noble Order of the Garter; For valor and heroism beyond the call of duty in defense of the empire." Then the king dipped his hand into a silver jeweled chalice which contained holy oil, and using his thumb, he anointed Christopher's forehead. Presently a page stepped up to the king, trodding upon the scarlet carpet, and bearing on his out stretched hands a silken cushion where rested the beautiful gold and enameled *Collar and George*. The prelate placed the *Collar* over Christopher's head; it spanded over his breast from shoulder to shoulder, and upon his chest hung the pendant of St. George mounted on a pure white steed. The *Collar* depicted the saint poised on the rearing steed while George, the noble knight speared the scaley jaded dragon.

Within the edge of the disc were inscribed the words: *Honi soit qui mal y pense* (Evil be (it) to him who evil thinks). Once again the king tapped Christopher thrice with the flat of his sword, saying: "Rise Sir Christopher!" Then he kissed the newly appointed knight on either cheek with the words: *"Avencez soy Chevalier."*

What followed after that, Christopher could not remember, nor could he recall where the great flood of handshakes and congratulations started, but he felt happy and honored. His hand clasped with one nobleman after another and the hearty slaps on the back were numerous, in fact too numerous for his part; for after a time the slightest touch felt like a sting. Pleasant music, supplied by a string ensemble, filled the sumptuous ballroom; laughter, champagne and rare wines seemed to flow like a free and commonplace thing and a multitude of gay chattering voices were chirping in a happy jubilant din.

Christopher and Lorrie stood before the great buffet which was adorned with ancient and silver ornaments, where was contained rich and exotic foods. He was fumbling with the *Victorian Cross*, which was suspended on a ribbon of dual tone about his friend's throat; Christopher was admiring it with pleasure when he was affronted by a striking silver haired gentleman in his mid-fifties. "I realize, Sir Christopher," said the gentleman in a thick and noble accent, "that this is frightfully assumptious of me to approach you in this manner, but I fear that I do not act rash, this gala evening shall spin away without my earning your acquaintance. Permit me to introduce myself, I am Lord Dennsworth." They shook hands, and the Lord's grasp was firm and virile.

"A pleasure to make your acquaintance, Lord Dennsworth— may I introduce my colleague, Mr. Ericson Lorrie." He nodded and took Lorrie's hand. "A pleasure, Mr. Lorrie." He turned once again to Christopher, but addressing both, he said: "Do you hunt, Sir Christopher? I myself am an enthusiast on the sport. Perhaps you might visit my lodge in Devonshire sometime in the near future?"

"Perhaps, my lord," reflected Christopher; "But I fear my hunting days are done with."

"O! how stupid of me," sputtered Lord Dennsworth. "The sound of gun fire must be painful to your ears, you've had so much lately. Surely you must think me an ass for suggesting such a thing."

"On the contrary, no, Lord Dennsworth, I think it was an amiable suggestion, and it was rude of me to decline. Who knows, perhaps in the future my taste will change, and I will snatch up your offer without prudence or hesitation. Still, I'm certain that Mr. Lorrie will take you up—he's a great one on the sport."

"By all costs, Mr. Lorrie, you must accept; try to persuade Sir Christopher to accompany you." Lorrie smiled and nodded.

"You understand, we don't only hunt at my country place," continued the lord in gracious tones.

"I ask you to meet one more person . . . someone near and dear to me—my wife, Lady Dennsworth."

"Christopher smiled again, at first the unknown had troubled him. "Of course, my lord—where is the lady?"

"Well, she complained that the crowd made her feel faint. She was obliged to rest in the ante-chamber where the air is not so dense. Come right this way with me."

Christopher turned to his left. "Lorrie, would you care to join us?" A leer came into Lorrie's eyes, and by the smile he flashed Christopher he knew he had assumed the Lady Dennsworth would be old, fat, stuffy and tiresome.

"No, thank you, *Sir* Christopher," he said, emphasizing the Sir, "if you don't mind, I prefer to wait until you return." Lord Dennsworth ushered Christopher to the ante-chamber; a handsome room decorated in deep green and gold; the floor was of solid white marble, and mirrors with huge heavy gilt frames adorned the walls from the floor to the ceiling.

But, it was neither the walls, nor floors or mirrors which entranced Christopher, but rather the sight of the most perfect, the most lovely creature he had ever known! He couldn't believe his eyes. Was the lord's wife *his* Rue! He felt a weakness in his knees and the scent of her perfume awakened the dim wavering memories, good and bad, that he tried so hard to forget. He had never known her to look so beautiful, and on that cold winter night, only Rue would dare to dress so lightly; amid the brocades, satins and the furs of winter, Rue stood apart from the world like the promise of spring in the dead of winter. Compared to her, all others seemed put together with pins. Her silken dark hair was cut as pleased the fashion of the day; she was dressed in a dazzling white gown, dropped shoulder and superbly fashioned down to her extravagant hem line; a thin diamond necklace encompassed her lovely white throat, and her fingers were lavishly jeweled.

For a little while they spoke to each other like gracious strangers, then for some reason Lord Dennsworth was called away and they were left to themselves. "Well Sir Christopher," Rue murmured in her deep rich voice. "We appear to be persons of title and rank these days." There was a quickening pain of emotion when she looked into his eyes, those eyes that use to look at her so affectionately. Rue looked at him again knowing that he was the romance of her life, but for now she would play cool and unreceptive, for a while she would hold him at a distance.

"How true that is, my Lady Dennsworth," said Christopher joining her pretentious little game; he moved back a step as though she were a beautiful, but poisonous flower. He'd not let her tangle him in her web again, but if he would have been rash enough to release his emotions, he would have taken her in his arms and kissed her tender lips.

Rue moved nearer to him and touching his collar of rank, she took the pendant of St. George between her jeweled fingers. Rue parted her lips to smile; she smiled as though she and her other self were sharing some personal little secret. She thought she might have a bit of fun with him; somehow, he afforded her a certain amount of pleasure when she could cause him to be clumsy. She teased him, "How came you by this title, Sir Christopher?" Her heart bore the scar of his affections and she was certain to settle the score with him. She thought of the careless way he had deserted her, the memory of that was awful.

"Didn't you understand what was said to me in there, or were you taken up with your vain beauty? I earned it in defense of the empire—like a good soldier. But mightn't I inquire how you came by yours?"

"But it is so obvious . . . undoubtedly the champagne has dulled your wits, or perhaps you are merely drunk with your own accomplishments?"

"Neither. I take it that Lord Dennsworth's bank balance must double Paul Hastings' some tenfold."

His sharp words cut into her heart; her face seemed flushed and the memory of Paul's tragic death in a collapsed mine shaft fled across her memory, but she would not let herself be moved by either, she threw back her head and laughed mockingly. "You haven't answered my inquiry, Sir Christopher," she said regaining her poise. "I can't suddenly believe that you have become a British subject?"

"I don't give a damn what you believe," he told her lightly. The blood came into his cheeks, "I've been knighted, that should answer your doubts."

Suddenly Rue could no longer continue to waste time, soon her husband would return and there were so many things that had to be said. She was tired of her foolish little game and was sorry she had started it, for she only succeeded in angering him. She heaved a weary sigh: "Oh, Chris, I still love you!" She looked into his face. "We are so foolish to waste our precious lives. Don't be mean to me Chris, our love is all we have!" Her words moved him and the manner in which she spoke his name rekindled the old fire of desire, but his face showed no emotion; he stared her down, which seemed a hard thing for him to do seeing that her moist warm lips were so terribly close. Rue looked at the pendant suspended on his chest, and then back again into his eyes. "You would like to kill me, Chris, wouldn't you? Just as St. George has slain the dragon . . . Am I such a dragon, Chris?" Her eyes were moist with tears, she sobbed: "My only sin was to fall in love with you, is that so shameful?"

The little artery at his temple started to pulsate rapidly; he looked down at her, his heart wanted to melt. "Did you really love me, Rue?" he said huskily.

"If you aren't sure, Chris, ask your heart, your heart!" This time her lips were so near that he couldn't turn them away; he kissed her with an irresistible will which seemed not like his own. Rue couldn't help but smile inwardly at her triumph; she was certain she could win him back. But she was mistaken, his mind was still on Fredrica.

"No, Rue," he said. "We can not begin again—it would be of no use; moreover, the scandal might ruin us. As you have said, now we are both people of rank.

She put her fingers to his lips. "Please, darling don't say anything." Rue cried in a hoarse breathless voice. "Oh! you can't know how proud I was of you-there when you knelt before the king! I wanted to shout to the roof tops that you were mine . . . mine from the very beginning, and down to the very end. Why should we worry what anyone will say? We can go away—the south of Italy is beautiful at this time of the year . . . Just you and I together, and never will we have to worry about money. I've plenty of my own now."

He stiffened: "Is that all you care about money, Rue? Doesn't your name mean anything to you?"

"Yes, darling, I know all about the modesty of reputation. 'When I lose my good name, I lose that part of me which is immortal and all else becomes beastial'—but this is a speeding world, Chris. Life and happiness must be taken when it can before all will ebb away. It's just as the philosophers say, life is the gift of nature, but beautiful living is the gift of wisdom.

"No, Rue, it can't be that way!" He looked at her and saw the smoldering fire of bitterness kindle in the deep silence of her dark eyes. He felt that God placed woman on earth to tame man, but Rue came to excite him.

"And why can't it be?" lamented Rue. "Is there someone else?" He nodded.

"May I not ask who?" she relaxed the muscles in her body and looked at him scornfully. "No doubt she is some whimpering frail creature who clings to you like a wet mop. Or possibly she is some saintly virgin you discovered in the streets of London!"

"Rue, I won't have you speak that way about Fredrica—she's a lady."

"O! is that her name?" chirped Rue. "She sounds like a filly that I once claimed a purse on at Ascot. A lady you say? . . . and what am I?"

"Undoubtedly a lady also—your title tells me that."

Rue bit her lip and restrained herself from slapping his face, for a foolish little grin was playing on his lips. Then soon, there was a quick shift in the conversation; Lord Dennsworth was approaching them.

She lowered her voice to a whisper. "I live in Mayfair, Christopher—*No.#9 Mayfair*," she said hurriedly. "Lord Dennsworth goes to his hunting lodge every weekend, and I'm usually alone. I'll wait for you then," and with that she walked away feeling sure of herself; she looked over her shoulder and whispered: "You'll come Christopher . . . I know you'll come."

5

After seeing to the painful business of having Ellgate's body returned to the United States, Christopher spent some time in Paris hoping to find Sarah Morrison, but on the third day he learned that she had sailed for home more than a week before, a lonely broken hearted girl. Secretly he was rather pleased at not having to face her; to tell of Ellgate's death would not be easy; moreover, he thought, what avail would it do? Possibly he would only succeed in causing a partially healing wound to bleed afresh. He would write her a long letter.

When Christopher returned from the continent, an idea came to him, he thought of converting Mrs. Wessly's printing shop into a publishing house, with a little financing the scheme seemed greatly possible and he would start the business by putting Fredrica's manuscript in book form. He told Lorrie of the project. He thought the idea an excellent one and even suggested himself for a partnership in the enterprise. "The idea is grand, in fact perfect!" sang Lorrie as Christopher inserted the key into the lock, he opened the door and they entered.

As Christopher walked across the dust laden floor, he stepped on one of Mrs. Wessly's door cards; he stared down reading the little card, *Out To Tea*. He covered it with the sole of his shoe he was crossed with a feeling of melancholy, waiting any moment now to hear her voice call out to him. He walked behind the old wooden

counter. The old shop seemed alive with ghosts and memories . . .
Just say, Miss Fredrica Hobbs inquired of her health . . . He could
fancy the old lady stepping out of the shadows . . . A pair of tupins
to your name and no place to lie your 'ead . . . Bah! don't be lieing
to me lad! . . . All my worldly goods to . . . A shaft of warm sunlight
jetted through the boarded window, and somewhere from the dimly
lit glow, he heard Fredrica's silver laughter . . . Good heavens! Mrs.
Wessly flatters me . . . It will be a grand day when you'll come back
to me . . . . Don't get killed Darling! . . . A little pair of emerald
earrings, Chris . . . Ha! ha! . . . not real ones, of course . . . love
you! . . . love . . . you . . . you . . .

"The presses seem to be in good order," said Lorrie waving his
hand about and contemplating on the possibilities of the business;
his words broke rudely upon Christopher's thoughts. "With a few
more," he said, "we ought to be able to cope with the situation. I
don't think it will take too much money to finance us. Why, with
what you have, and some few thousand pounds of my own, will do
nicely, and whatever more is needed—why, dash it all, I can get from
Uncle Thad. I know he'll be pleased with the idea. Anyway, he's
always telling me to settle down." Lorrie propped one foot against
the counter, resting his elbow upon his knee, "What about the
manuscript, Chris, do you think we have a right to use it?"

"I really don't know," he rejoined," but I'm going to take the
chance anyway."

"No, Chris, you don't understand. I don't mean that. What I
am trying to say is, supposing she has submitted it to some other
publishing firm, and they are ready to set in print?"

Christopher gave out with a halfway laugh, his tone seemed
hard and indifferent. "Lorrie, the publishing houses were the very
first thing I had the man from Scotland Yard check. Surely, man,
if Fredrica had submitted her work to any of them I would have
learned her present whereabouts."

"Oh," whimpered Lorrie in dry defeat. "You must think me a
thoughtless ass. Then I gather she has never tried to get the thing
published?"

He shrugged his shoulders: "Evidently. My greatest hope is that Fredrica will see her book and come to the publishing house to discover why we printed it without her knowledge."

Lorrie whistled: "By golly! why hadn't I thought of that? Incidently," he asked, "have you any inclinations as to what we might call the firm? It's got to have some kind of name you know."

"How does the *Wessly Press* sound to you?"

"Alright. Yes, I can understand why you would call it that."

"Then you agree?"

"Unanimously. Hurrah! for the Wessly Press!" he cheered, shaking Christopher's hand. "Sir Christopher, the occasion warrents a drink!"

"Don't call me *that*, Lorrie. I can't bear to play this *royal fable*— at least not with you."

"Sorry old fellow, you know I was only clowning. Why I say the devil with it." He patted Christopher on the shoulder. "Let's get off to the club for a drink, and then down to business." He grinned: "Why I can see it all in my mind. In no time we'll be millionaires— Hurrah for capitalism in a democracy! And I say any man that thinks otherwise is either a complete ass or ready for the grave!"

Before a year had expired, the Wessly Press, officiated by Lorrie and Wensdy was an overwhelming success. By the end of the year Fredrica Hobbs' book, (Three Brave Hearts), had seen its fourth edition, but to Christopher's profound disappointment, the now famous Fredrica Hobbs was nowhere to be found. Still Christopher never abandoned his hopes for recovering her—the search continued. Also, in that same year, Christopher became a rich man, moreover he grew accustomed to his title, seeming to him now like an old and familiar thing. He would have forgotten the past also, but as long as there was Rue he could never forget; she was always there to remind him.

Eventually, Rue was to have her way with him, but one thing she could never accomplish was to make Christopher forget Fredrica entirely. But somehow this she didn't mind too much, although her jealousy of the woman she had never seen sometimes resulted in a quarrel. At times, if only to satisfy her vanity, she told herself that this Fredrica Hobbs was nothing but a ghost of Christopher's imagination, some one he invented to make her jealous. She thought that even this so called book of hers, was also his doings. There were times, when they were together, Rue would break into a cry asking him: "How could he be so cruel when she loved him so."

At the St. Clair, a small obscure hotel, where they met on weekends, a suite was reserved for Rue and Christopher under the name of Mr. And Mrs. C. Thomas.

Through the open bedroom window, Christopher could hear the bells of St. Paul's gonging somberly in the distance; he had been awake for a short time and drowsily, he watched the outline of the room and furniture slowly come into view. It was an hour before daylight and the coming dawn was stirring up a gentle breeze. It was very cooling to his body and it refreshed him. The spring night was moonless, black and very warm. Christopher looked at Rue who lay beside him with her head on his shoulder; she was sleeping lightly. Presently he kissed the side of her face and she opened her eyes. "Chris," she said with a start, "did I sleep long?"

"I really don't know," he answered huskily. "I haven't been awake for long either . . . I was just looking at you." He removed his arm from under her, then turned on his side resting his weight on his elbow. For a while he just lay looking at her then brushed her silken hair back from her temples. "It will be daylight soon," he said. "What time do you expect Dennsworth to return?"

"Oh, Monday; so soon," she murmured in a detached tone and looked up into his face. "He usually gets back sometime in the afternoon . . . anyway, if he does get home before I do, the servants will tell him I've gone to the Peter Whartons for the weekend."

"Is that where you're supposed to be?"

"No, but he doesn't question where I go, anyway, I don't care if he does—do you?"

"No. At least not now," he answered kissing her smooth white shoulder and the hollow at the base of her throat; he lifted his head, "But we must be careful Darling, it would do us no good to have people talk . . . We must be careful, not so much for my sake, but for yours. Gossip is vile, it can ruin anything."

"Gossip is only fatal when it is denied, Darling. Leave it alone and it will go as fast as it came." Then after a brief silence, she suddenly asked: "Chris, did you ever fly when you were in the service?"

"Yes, I've been up once; I enjoyed it immensely."

"What's it like?"

"Like nothing I can describe . . . there's something magical about it."

"One day we must drive to the airport. I want to fly with you, Chris."

"If you want; we'll go sometime."

"Yes, Darling I want to. Can't it be sometime soon. I never get to see you like I want—'cept on weekends."

"We'll see," he answered and kissed her again. The wind came blowing through the window more briskly now and it chilled their naked bodies.

"Are you cold, Rue! You're all goose flesh, shall I pull the coverlet up?"

"No, Chris I like the wind," she answered with a giggle, and curved her back outward burrowing a little deeper into the cradle of his stomach and thighs.

He put his arms around her, and curved about her. "You're funny", he said, "sometimes you won't admit to anything, not even when you're cold."

"But I'm not, Chris, really I'm not."

"Yes, that's what I said," and with that he laughed.

Suddenly she turned to face him, saying: "Oh, for heaven's sake, Chris, kiss me! Nothing like you has ever happened to me before. I love you."

He took her full in his embrace and kissed; she was flushed against him face to face. "I should have said that, Rue . . . no one like you has ever happened to me."

"I'm glad, Chris; I couldn't bear to think of you being mixed up with someone else."

"You are the only woman I have ever been mixed up with, and damn you! you know it."

"There must have been women in France? I've heard talk about the women of France."

"Have you now?" he murmured in a tease, but his tone seemed very indifferent.

"Yes, especially that Madame Celestine. I've heard talk of her." Then behaving very girlish she asked: "You never did visit her place, did you Chris?"

"I think that is my business. And if I did . . . would you mind so terribly much?"

"Did you?" she inquired again.

"You answer me," he said insistently.

"Well . . ." Rue hesitated. "Yes, I would. Tell me, is she really as beautiful as they say?"

"Yes."

"There! I knew you went there."

"I thought I told you, that was my business."

"Oh!" she cried sharply and began to pout and sulk.

"Listen," he told her firmly. "Don't be silly, it's almost morning, and I will have to leave soon. We won't see each other for the remainder of the week—there's a lot of work that has to be done at the publishing house."

"Yes, the publishing house," she murmured sarcastically. "I think you care more for it than you do me."

"I can't very well leave all the work for Lorrie to do; I've neglected the business shamefully these last few months."

"Lorrie!" she said sputtering his name forth contemptuously. "I don't like Lorrie . . . he looks at me funny. Besides, I think he hates me."

"Don't be absurd, Rue. Lorrie is one of the finest men I have ever met; moreover, he's my closest friend."

"You think more of him than Ellgate?"

"I can't say—anyhow, that was different. We grew up together, he and I were like brothers."

Then out of a clear sky she asked: "What about her?"

"What are you talking about?"

"You know . . . The one that wrote that book," her tone turned very mean, "That Miss Hobbs."

Christopher exhaled a long troubled sigh. "I thought we made a pact never to speak of her." He started to move closer to her but Rue grew angry and annoyed, freeing herself from his embrace she moved to the far side of the bed. Christopher understood that she had worked herself into one of her moods, so he got up and went over to the window. After a time, Rue crept over to his side. In the smoke blue light of dawn they seemed unreal to each other. Standing side by side, quiet and poised in the dark cool silence their bodies appeared like magnificent carvings hewn from the white Hellenic rock . . . Grecian figures from the living birth of culture.

Rue took up her dressing gown which had been thrown carelessly over a chair, and put it around her shoulders, cape fashion. "Forgive me, Chris," she said sheepishly, "I'm sorry Darling. I promise—never will we speak of her again."

She was trembling when he kissed her. "Is the wind too much for you?" he asked.

"No, why do you ask?"

"Then take this darn thing off," he said lightly and removed the robe from her shoulders. Her back was toward him; he put his arms around her tightly, and curving his head around her neck he kissed the side of her throat. For some while they remained at the window looking down at the shadowy court-yard and the blue-black silhouette of trees against the sky; their leaves trembled in the morning breeze.

"Chris, what are you musing about—you seem so quiet?"

He held her close against him; his arms around her with his fingers locked over her stomach. "Those trees below us," he said. "They remind me of a poem I used to know."

"Oh! which one . . . is it by Shelly?

"No. I am afraid I don't remember the title."

"Say it."

"I can only remember the last part . . . I think it's one of Herrick's poems." He corrected himself, "No it isn't; I remember—" and with that he laughed.

Rue put her hand to the side of his face and patted his cheek. "Why are you laughing?"

"Because it's so strange: *I Remember*, is the title of the thing— Thomas Hood wrote it:

> 'I remember, I remember,
> The fir trees dark and high:
> I use to think their slender tops
> Were close against the sky:
> It was a childish ignorance,
> But now 'tis little joy
> To know I'm farther off from heaven
> Than when I was a boy.'"

Suddenly Rue turned around, throwing her arms about his neck and weeping against him. "Oh, Chris!" she sobbed. "You're not thinking of—of the monastery. I couldn't bear to have you think of that place like that. It hurts me!"

"No, Rue, please. It was stupid of me to recite it. I had no intentions—don't cry, Rue it was just a poem I had to study once in school, that's all. You know I wouldn't purposely hurt you."

"Oh, Chris! I wish I had known you when you were a boy. Maybe things might have been different, she traced the line of his eyebrow. "Do you remember the first time we met at Elaine's house?"

"I think I do, and if I rightly recall, I was scarce graduated from boy's estate then."

"The first day I saw you, I was standing at the head of the stairs. I watched you for a long time, you were shaking hands with Hans' mother and talking with her. I remember when I walked away you looked up, but I was gone before you could see me. I think I made a noise or something—anyway, that's what caused you to look up, and I saw your face."

"I don't remember seeing you."

"Well, I do, and I knew then that I loved you . . . knowing that you were the only man for me. I guess I'll always love you, Chris!" Then suddenly for no apparent reason she started to weep again.

"Oh, Chris," she whimpered. "Why must we always remember the past? Sometimes I feel you must hate me for all the things I've done."

"No, Rue Darling, I don't. I couldn't." He kissed her tear moist cheek, and taking her up in his arms he carried her to the bed. For a while he looked down at her in pleasure. As ever, Rue appeared tender and beautiful with her silken dark hair spread out on the pillow. He dropped down beside her and wrapped her tenderly in his arms . . . When dawn filled the windows they were asleep.

6

Lorrie came briskly into Christopher's office. It was the first time he had been at work after an absence of many days, and this being so unlike him caused Lorrie to worry; he tried to smile cheerfully at Christopher, but his attempt was unsuccessful. To avoid staring at him, Lorrie turned a quick glance to the window, later he turned around moving his eyes over the carpet and up to the wall; the clock chimed 4:30—stepping over to the liquor console he poured two drinks of scotch and water. He came over and put a glass into Christopher's hand. "Well, here's to you and me, ole man," sang Lorrie; they clicked glasses. "I may be some eight hours premature," he said, "but let this be our private toast to the *New Year*."

Christopher put down his glass, Lorrie's bright spirits seemed too obvious to over look. "You must think me rotten, Lorrie," he muttered clumsily, "and I can't very much blame you. At all cost, I should offer some excuse for my behavior, but—" he thrust his hands into his pockets and made an about face to the window. "I don't know what's wrong with me, Lorrie," he bleated. "I haven't a damn thing to say for myself."

"I don't want any excuses, Chris, not from you," rejoined Lorrie in a friendly voice; he sensed Christopher's troubled self. "But I do say, you might warn a fellow when you're going to pull these disappearing acts. I was troubled about you. God knows you might have been lying in some morgue. One more day and I would have been prompted to turn your name in to the missing persons." Then quite forgetting himself he asked in a sharp voice: "Where in thunder have you been?" And he immediately regretted asking the question, but the words fell from his lips without control; he possessed a vague suspicion as to what kept Christopher away from home and office. Lorrie endeavored to smooth over the matter by urging Christopher to continue the toast they had begun.

"Well, here's to 1920 and the *new decade!*" he cried and with that they took up their glasses and drank. Lorrie put a hand on Christopher's shoulder: "Look here, Chris," he muttered in a voice that seemed fraternal and warm. "I'm expecting you home tonight. I've planned a grand celebration to welcome in the new year—And what's more, I have a surprise for you."

"I'm sorry, Lorrie, but I don't think I can be there tonight. I'm going out right after supper."

"Oh," he murmured disappointedly. "May I ask why?"

Christopher shrugged his shoulders. "I really can't say."

His vagueness angered Lorrie, he understood that Christopher wasn't himself, but that seemed like a poor reason to be rude, and he swapped him off for something that had been preying on his mind. His temper got the better of him: "Look Wensdy, there's something on my mind and I feel I should tell you about it." Christopher knitted his brows, and his expression unhinged Lorrie, somewhat. "Well . . ." he hesitated for a moment. "Well, it's about what they're saying—hell! Chris, this isn't easy for me to say, but there's a bit of dirty talk going on about you and this Lady Dennsworth. It's vile stuff to hear, and I got into quite an argument over it with some men at the club. If this talk goes on it will ruin you."

"What business is it of theirs what I do?" he cried angrily. "Let them talk if it makes them happy to do so."

By this time they had created such a racket that it aroused the two secretaries in the outer office; amazed and curious, they opened the door and sheepishly stuck in their heads. "It's really nothing to be alarmed about, Miss Bipps," crooned Lorrie in a blith, innocent tone as he supported the limp vomiting creature over his arm. "Nothing at all," he repeated. "Merely Sir Christopher and I celebrating the new year, you know." He waved his hand in dismissal, "you may leave." The door closed and the lock clicked with a ridiculous caution; the wondering women were paused on the other side of it mumbling to each other in quiet tones. Lorrie couldn't help but laugh. "When you're quite through your business, Sir Christopher, I will help you to the lavatory," he said still full of laughter. He looked down on him, "Ah! all through? Good man!"

Christopher straightened up and staggered to a chair. In the meanwhile, Lorrie secured a cold wet towel from the lavatory, and applied it to Christopher's face. "I repeat: I'm sorry," said Lorrie. "How do you feel?"

"Alright, damn you!" snarled Christopher but his tones weren't bitter.

"*Tut tut*," thwarted Lorrie, applying the wetness to the back of his neck, "such gratitude." Then in a more solicitous tone said: "In all respects you deserved this, and what's more you brought it all on yourself. Chris, no sore feelings between us, eh?"

Christopher looked up in a devilish halfway smile and they shook hands.

"Good man!" cried Lorrie; he sat on the edge of the desk and lit a cigarette. "Perhaps friends should administer a fairly sound thrashing to each other every now and again, it gets so much out of the system without the clumsy use of words," he laughed. "Possibly that's why some men beat their wives, who knows?"

"What frivolous philosophical tripe!" bleated Christopher, but somehow he couldn't help laughing. "I don't say such a theory is good, mind you, but anyway I must confess that I do feel better." He stretched out his hand, "Give me a cigarette, please."

Lorrie looked at him and grinned, "I hope this doesn't brew the storm again," he said, "but I insist upon knowing why aren't you coming to the celebration tonight?"

"Believe me, Lorrie, I don't know. I guess I don't feel like it."

"That seems like a lame excuse—is it because you have an appointment with Rue tonight?"

"Are we to begin again?"

"Don't be such a hot head . . . I was merely asking." He dropped his voice and toyed with one of the pens on the desk, "A fellow does like to have his best friend present when he announces his engagement."

"Engagement?" the words moved him. "You mean Wanda Richard and you? Oh, sometimes I can really play the perfect ass. What an ungrateful dog you must think me." He extended his hand in congratulations: "The best of everything, Lorrie, I know you deserve it."

"We had planned to surprise you at midnight." He shrugged his shoulders, "Well, if you really can't come."

"I won't promise anything certain," said Christopher; something benevolent tried to loom in his voice, but it seemed as though his heart and spirit had abandoned him and he was sounding empty words. "But I am going to try and be there . . . and please don't think I'm going to see Rue tonight. Anyway she's giving some extravagant party tonight. God knows that if I don't wish to attend your party, I certainly have no desire to be at her's—I understand her place will be stuffed with nobility. It's just—well, it's only that I felt like being alone tonight, and that's the truth."

"What! alone on the New Year? You must be in a state."

"Yes, it is true, I am upset." He crushed his cigarette into the silver ashtray on the desk. "Lorrie, don't you think I am aware of the gossip concerning Rue and me?"

Lorrie flinched. "Now, you make me feel like an ass. Does this Lady Dennsworth mean so much to you that you can't bear to give her up?"

"I don't know," he said lightly, "I don't know."

"Hell, man, you certainly are notorious for *not knowing*."

"You don't understand, Lorrie—I knew Rue long before she became the Lady Dennsworth, even long before I set eyes on Fredrica . . . It seems as though Rue was always a part of my life."

"—And so what difference does that make?"

"I'm afraid you don't know Rue. She takes hold of a man . . . she's not the sort that can be brushed aside like other woman. I tell you she's in my system and I can't get her out." He looked at his fingers and cracked his knuckles, as some escape for his nerves. "I don't know," he said, "Rue seems to have some magic spell over me—she's poison, and then again she's my very life's breath."

After a long silence, Lorrie said: "You leave me in a fine state of suspension . . . After telling me this, I don't know what kind of advice to give you. Damn! I'm confused myself. O, hang it all, at least for the present—tonight is the New Year. I can't have you going about brooding, at least not alone. No one should be alone on the New Year—Ole Lyng Syne is sad enough without adding solitude to the pain. I guess that's why we seek the crowds to smoother our melancholia beneath the din of fire works and shouts." Lorrie slapped Christopher on the shoulder and cried: "To hell with the melancholia of life—let's have a drink!"

7

New Year's Eve in the Strand, and amid the gaiety of excitement and laughing voices, Christopher paused and looked up at the lighted theatre marquee; he read what was there but could scarce believe his eyes!—A—REVIVAL!—STARING—ABIGAIL TRENT—IN—A—NEW WOMAN—He remained there on the fog shrouded side walk for a length of time reflecting on the past. It seemed to him that in the dim recesses of his mind that he had known from somewhere—sometime, the very letters which now gleamed before his eyes. But how thin was the ribbon which tied the past with the present. His infant memory flashed no relationship with the young man in evening dress who stood musing in the misty fog . . . *John Fransworth* was a lost specter—a mere rattling skeleton storming at the door of time and memory. The door was closed; locked forever, and the name on the marquee reflected *not* the name of his mother, but the recollections of a girl in the path of his boyhood; a friendly little town, a benevolent Reverend Mother, some friends, and the old clock tower of St. Thomas' that happily gonged away the hours of the long ago past.

Soon his musing was intruded upon by an old lady harking her sale of flowers: "Violets, sir? her voice seemed cracked with age. "Violets, Sir? A gent can't go back stage without violets for the lidies."

Christopher had no idea of going backstage to see Abigail, but now that the thought had been suggested, he found it a good one... and why not? After all they were old friends. He selected a large bunch of violets and paid the old woman double their worth. Then he sought Abigail's compartment, he went down the wanly lit alley until he reached the stage entrance. He saw other men waiting about with flowers and boxes of candy tucked under their arms, and Christopher couldn't help smiling to himself and muttering: "*Stagedoor Johnies*", perhaps they thought he too was one of their comrades in the fold. In time he discovered himself knocking on a thinly paneled door with a brightly painted silver star on it; he waited for a response with some hesitance, intermingled with intruding embarrassment. Presently a maid answered his knocks and he understood in a moment that she also was an American, and he thought her accent pleasant to listen to. The woman requested his card and he explained that he had neglected to carry any with him that evening: "Just say that an old friend from Fairlee would like to see her," he told the maid, "I'm sure she'll understand.

The woman left, and through the partly opened door, he heard her deliver the message, and Abigail's cry of joy. Before long he was shaking hands with her and between smiles and tears, each was endeavoring to express their happiness for this joyous reunion . . . for reunions with old friends are the golden moments of our lives. "Chris, you've brought me violets—how sweet." She took them from his hand and placed them into some water.

His little token of friendship caused him some amount of awkwardness, and he flushed a bright pink at the smallness of his gift. The room was filled with extravagant bouquets of red, yellow and white roses. "Yes," he said sheepishly, "violets for the primadonna."

"Someone should always bring violets to the primadonna," she said touching his arm and kissing the side of his face. "They let an actress know that she is a woman and a human being, not some creature fashioned out of words off of ghastly white paper. It's always roses for the actress, which is an empty and expensive token presented only for pomp and effect—But when we receive violets, Chris, that's when we know we are really being admired. It's the exhaulted color of heaven that gives them their magic." She smiled, "Thank you, Chris. What makes them precious to me is that they are from an old friend."

Christopher sat back and looked at her; Abigail had matured into a truly lovely woman. She was dressed in a swirling green gown and a delicate sheer white chiffon scarf was wrapped about her shoulders. "I realize I'm detaining you from some great appointment," he said, "but don't put me out just now—"

"Detaining me? Yes." she laughed. "But put you out? No! There's entirely too many things we must talk about, and for number one, what are you doing in London? This is the last place on earth I had ever hoped to discover you."

"My business is here," he replied modestly. He saw Abigail's brows rise questioningly as if to ask, a business man no less! "And what's your work?" "I'm in the publishing business, you know. Possibly you may have read some of our books? . . . But no more about me—Tell me about yourself. You said you were going to become famous, and you have."

"It was my dream and I have made it come true. At least I'm happy Chris, but sometimes I think it's more work than fame."

After a pause he inquired: "Do you still keep up with the people at home?"

"I use to get a letter now and then from Charly."

"Charly Lock! Grand old Charly . . . what's he doing?"

"When last I heard he was in the automobile business, and I suspect he's making a fortune. Someone told me he married Ruth Celine—you remember her, don't you?"

He laughed: I should hope I do. She always played the Moonlight Sonata whenever she got angry." Then without so much joy in his voice he asked concerningly: ". . . And the Reverend Mother, is she still at St. Ann's?"

"I suppose so. She wrote me a lovely letter after my aunt died. I remember that after you left she seemed quite worried about you, Chris. You should have written her no matter where you disappeared to. Mrs. Tergauer told me that she was almost ill when she learned that you left the seminary."

Christopher had asked a question and the answers were beginning to trouble and humiliate him. He toyed nervously with the little emerald earrings he carried in his pocket, he thought of giving them to Abigail as a token of remembrance but somehow he couldn't bring himself to part with them. "After I left," he stammered, "was there much talk about me?"

"No," she answered but she was not the sort to say even if there was. "No, not that I remember. Of course, you know Fairlee, they have nothing better to do and talk is their favorite sport. They thought it scandalous that I planned to go on the stage. But I'll make them change their tune when I appear there this summer!" She squared her shoulders finding some satisfaction in her words.

"You plan to go home soon?"

"Yes, right after the Southampton tour. I'm so terribly glad you decided to come tonight—We leave for Hampshire in the morning. It would have been dreadful to miss you. I'm glad to go though, I think I'll be grateful for a change of scenery and what is another one of my joys is that we are reviving another one of Paula Fransworth's plays there." The maid appeared in the room then, urging her young mistress about the time. "I'm afraid I must dash, Chris. I'm so sorry!" Christopher rose to his feet. "Would you like to join me?" she asked. "It's only a New Year's party for the cast, but I must be there."

He shook her hand warmly. "No thank you, Abby. I appreciate your offer but I think I might be out of place among all those theatre people."

"I'm sorry you won't come, but perhaps it's just as well. We do get rather stuffy and we will be chattering show talk all evening."

"Will I get a chance to see you before you leave?"

"I think not. Heavens knows what ungodly hour the director has set for departure. But give me your address—I'll write you."

"Just write me in care of the Wessly Press, London—it will reach me."

"Wessly Press, London," she murmured repeatively. "Yes, that seems easy to remember. I really must rush now."

"I'll walk you to your car."

"Please."

Christopher walked with Abigail to the side entrance of the theatre where her chauffer awaited her. They said their final goodbyes, and in parting he kissed her on the cheek bading her to take care of herself. After his farewell to Abigail, he walked the streets of London for a great length of time. The night had turned fairly warm and the streets were crowded with New Year revelers. He strolled listlessly along smoking a cigarette; the folds of his opera cape were thrown over his shoulders, so as he walked its white silk lining caught the light. Occasionally he could see a couple in evening dress walk past the blurred street lamps which dripped with mist and fog. Then as he walked further on, the lights became fewer and the streets seemed darker and narrow. When he had realized how far he had walked, it surprised him and he turned about searching for a cab to take him home. A lively breeze began to sweep down the narrow street carrying with it the faint roar of happy voices from Piccadilly, and in the dark black breath of night, the great tower of Big Ben was chiming the New Year hour in deep muffled gongs. His heart was struck with melancholy. Then at that moment, a woman's voice called out to him from the dark shadows of the gloom fog. "Come home with me my fine fellow, I know a place where we can escape this wretched fog . . ."

Christopher was thunderstruck! The voice was too familiar to be true; he immediately approached the woman and forced her beneath the sickly glow of the street lamp. He saw her face. *"Fredrica!"* he gasped.

"Let me go!" she cried in a faint voice, endeavoring to free her wrist from his grip. "I'm not your Fredrica," she said denying her identity and turning her face from the light. "Let me go!" she cried again in torment. The poor woman seemed wretched, harassed and humiliated. She seemed to have fallen and degraded beyond the limits of shame that mere words could not describe the dishonor she felt, she longed to run and flee into the protecting blackness of the fog; her very breath seemed to leave her body and she began to tremble. How could she make the mistake and not recognize Christopher . . . but how was the poor woman to know? She had lived all this time believing that he was dead! Killed on the battle field. Oh! she thought to herself, how could she not recognize him! This above all was the last thing she would want to happen. The pain was bitter humiliation. She could no longer bear it. Fredrica fainted.

Christopher held her limp body in his arms. There in the yellow glow of the street lamp he saw her face and kissed it. How emaciated she had become, but her face was still lovely—retaining most of its virgin beauty. At last he had found Fredrica! But why had she come to this, he asked himself. He hailed a cab and took her to his home in Chelsea.

8

"But why have you brought me here?" Fredrica asked in the dawn light of the New Year; she sat up in bed and her eyes took in the richly furnished surroundings. How different this seemed compared to the horrible little hut she called home.

Christopher had recently had the great house renovated, but never set foot in it until this night. Fredrica appeared dreadfully pale and he hoped that the doctor wouldn't be much longer in arriving. Christopher took her hand in his, he felt that if he held it a bit too firm her soft frail fingers might break in his grasp. "This is your house Fredrica," he told her sitting down on the edge of the bed. "I want you to have it."

Fredrica turned her face to the wall and sobbed: "Oh! Chris, I'm too ashamed to face you . . . how can I explain?"

"Explain nothing, Fredrica, Darling. The past is gone and if you regret you'll only create a brooding monster for yourself that will sooner or later devour you. My great joy is that I have found you—let nothing mar that."

She threw her arms about his neck and wept: "Chirs, you're too good to me. You can't know how I suffered when I read you were listed among the dead . . . a part of me died that day!"

Christopher stiffened under her words. "Listed among the dead?" he echoed. "Fredrica, when did you read that—where?"

"In the Times . . . Oh! months before the war ended. I didn't care if I lived or died after that. But the awful part was that I didn't receive a letter from you in weeks, when I read you were—I believed it. It was the same day poor Mrs. Wessly got killed."

"You poor darling."

"I still continued to write after that, but it was of no use . . . something went out of me. What I had written the publishers turned down. They only wanted something pertaining to the war. Chris, I wanted to die! How could I write about the thing that had taken you away from me. The mere thought of the war made me sick." Tears were flowing down her delicate cheeks, and once more she started to weep bitterly. "Besides," she whimpered," I had but a meger subsistence and I had used all the little money I had writing the Brave Hearts."

"But that's what I want to tell you Fredrica, your book is published. It turned out to be a tremendous success!"

Her face broadened into a wan smile but it was soon spent; her humiliation was as a knife in a wounded heart, and she was weeping again. "You must not think I'm not good Chris. I'm not a bad women, really I'm not! You must believe me I did—I did try to find honorable work I—" She could say nothing more after that, her voice seemed choked with tears and the words remained frozen in her throat. Fredrica's lovely features were twisted in pain; the poor frightened girl had known shame and now she had reached the point of hysteria. Between her sobbing and attacks of strangling coughs, Christopher turned half crazy with worry.

"Please Darling," he begged. "Let's speak no more about it." He found it a bitter pain to see a noble woman such as she reduced to this mean existence. "I love you, that's the only thing that matters. To have you near means everything to me." He tried to kiss and console her.

She turned her face away. "Please, Chris don't try to kiss me— you mustn't! I'm sick—sick bad! I don't want you to get it too." She began to cough and between her choking she managed to tell him." It would be an awful trick if you were to get sick too. I love you too much to hurt you."

He held her near him, "I don't care, Fredrica. Whatever the pain is, I want to share it. I want to take care of you. I want to show you to the world, to walk with you down Picadilly and the Strand, to take you on my arm and let them know that you're my lady. A man wants a woman he can be proud of . . . without you I am a thing of nothingness." He kissed her hands: "Why before long you'll be well and we'll forget that we were ever apart."

"I'll never be well again, Chris."

"Don't say that!" He looked into her eyes, "You know what I am going to do? The first thing in the morning, I'll make some arrangement for leaving London. It's too damp and cold for you here—How would you like to go to Capri? Yes, that's where I'll take you and you will get well there. We'll swim in the blue Mediterranean and brown our bodies under the warm Italian sun—Darling, say you'll get well for me!"

"I'll try, Chris," she answered with a smile but her voice was dreadfully weak and the color drained from her face.

"Don't frighten me, Fredrica. you seem so still. Fight! Darling." He stirred from her side and opened the windows wide. She was struggling for breath. "Why doesn't the doctor get here?" he said desperately.

"He'll come, Chris," she patted her hand on the bed. "Come sit down beside me, I want to hear more of Capri."

Christopher returned to her side and began to stroke her golden head. "We will get ourselves a little cottage somewhere along the beach . . . Remember you once told me of Byron's little cottage near the Hellespont? We could even visit there. In the evenings we can stand on the shore and watch the burning sun sink into the sea . . . Then when the spring comes we can stroll on the sands beneath the starlit black of the warm night. We'll live apart from the world Fredrica and never worry about tomorrow."

"I don't want to think of tomorrow, Chris. It's ugly."

"Nothing will be ugly when we're together."

He tightened his fingers about her hand and after a time asked: "You haven't said anything about your book, aren't you interested?

"Terribly so, but I was afraid to ask for fear I might trouble you. Is it really as you say, a great success?"

"Beyond a particle of misgiving. It has made you rich and I've saved every penny the book has earned for you. I can't understand why you haven't discovered its publication long before this."

"—But who published it, Chris?"

"Why don't you understand, Darling, we did. But I haven't told you . . . My partner and I converted Mrs. Wessly's printing shop. We named it the WesslyPress. Why, I haven't even told you of Lorrie—you'll like Lorrie. At any rate, he's thoroughly acquainted with you."

"With me—how?"

"You were all I ever talked about at the front. Wait until I tell him I've found you again." He dug into his pocket and placed something smooth and round into the palm of her hand, "Do you remember asking for these?"

"Chris! My little earrings and so green!"

"As green as the sea, my darling."

"They look so—are they real?"

"Real! Small but real—" The door bell rang then, and the tingling sound was followed by a pounding fist on the glass. "It's the doctor," he told her, "I'll go down and let him in."

It was with laden heart that Christopher learned the doctor's distressing report. Fredrica was in the determinate phase of tuberculosis! There seemed little or nothing anyone could do to prolong her young life. After a time the physician departed, his only prescription being a little medicine to help relieve her cough. He impressed on Christopher that she must have happiness for as long as her short life was to endure; he concluded by promising that he would stop in from time to time to see how his patient progressed. Christopher's spirits plunged to the lowest depths. Why had God so arranged it for him to find Fredrica only to lose her to the grave? He found the price far greater than his sins, and for the moment he discovered some satisfaction in having deserted his God. Why should this evil fall on his shoulders? He wondered whether God could still the torments of the world, but refused to, or desired to quench them and could not. Tormented and dejected, he wrestled with the problem for some length of time, and finally decided never to burden Fredrica with the dreadful knowledge he possessed. Instead he would strive to fill every hour of her ebbing life with happiness, to love her and live every moment to its fullest.

The flame flares brilliantly before it dies . . . As the days sped past something of the old Fredrica seemed to revive. She wanted to live and meet people, for after all she was a successful author, and then too, there was her public. The famed Fredrica Hobbs had been veiled too long beneath the dusk of obscurity. At first Christopher frowned upon the thought, it wouldn't be very sagacious to have Fredrica squander her remaining days so foolishly, but yet, she didn't know the end was so near; moreover Christopher would rather die than tell her . . . and of what merit would it be if she knew? He must remain silent and permit her to live her days as she willed. The important thing was that they were together. Let the end glitter extravagant and carefree; let grandure play the stage! He alone would bear the pain, Fredrica must be kept happy at all cost.

The great house in Chelsea was thrown open for gaiety! Almost every night the house was ablaze with party lights from attic to cellar, and shining merrily until the small hours of the morning. Most everybody who was anyone of importance came to pay homage to the famed and lovely Miss Hobbs. Her home was a *must* on every social calendar . . . luxury and superb entertainment was the nightly theme. At one particular gathering, Christopher was startled to hear the butler announce the arrival of Lord and Lady Dennsworth! He had been conversing with Lorrie and his fiancée, Wanda Richard, when the name assailed his ears. Lorrie and Christopher exchanged glances, they appeared to be astonishly transfixed. Christopher turned and looked over his shoulder in time to see Rue glide gracefully across the floor. Her silver evening mantle and magnificent attire would have put a queen to shame. Fredrica went up to greet them; she curtsied to Rue, and then to his lordship. Christopher watched the proceedings, wondering what choice bit of polite cruelty might be dripping from Rue's painted mouth. Her smile was all gloss and enamel. They spoke for a long while. Christopher assumed that all must have been running smoothly; moreover, Lord Dennsworth was standing by them. Rue knew how to be charming when she had to. Fredrica lifted her shining head and her voice danced on silver threads of laughter. Christopher smiled in spite of himself . . . Rue could also be witty.

The little string orchestra took up the music and played a lively waltz. Christopher started toward the billiard room for something to drink. He thought the "Prelude to Light" to be good; there was a mocking frailty in the music and no depth to the melody. When would Rue bring up the trembling curtain? Presently, the party reached the point where sociality shivered its rigid margin and the chatter and champagne flowed freely. The evening grew lax and the music spun high and lively. Its rhythm pushed through the chilled frosty panes of the closed French doors onto the starlit garden terrace where Christopher stood in the brisk March night. Then he heard the terrace door open and soon close rather menacingly. Christopher turned to look around and in the semi-dark he recognized the immaculate silver head of Lord Dennsworth, his diamond studded shirt front seemed to glow and move nearer to him. "So there you are," he told Christopher in a belligerently bitter manner, "It's time we should have a show-down!"

Christopher squared his shoulder and prepared himself to face the man, there was no doubt in his mind as to what the man seemed to be referring to. He had been expecting the moment for sometime now and wondered why it hadn't occurred sooner, but why here of all places? Dennsworth's face was dark with rage.

"I would have never set foot in this house, if I thought for a moment I'd find you of all people here!" Lord Dennsworth went on to say. "But I'm not a man to run away from trouble. I waited for you to step out here so I can speak my mind. When I first met you, sir, I assumed that you were a gentleman, but now from the slanderous gossip I overhear at my club and barber shop, I've sound reasons to change my mind. If I were a younger man I'd strike you down! I give you warning Mr. Wensdy, if this matter between you and my wife continues, I'll not be responsible for what I might do! Do you understand?"

"There is nothing between me and the person you speak of," replied Christopher modestly, "But if you will feel justified in striking me go right ahead. I'll not lift a hand against you."

"Nothing between you! Why you dirty young pup, don't lie to me. Do you mean to imply that it is I who am lying?"

"I mean what I have said," stormed Christopher. "There is nothing between your wife and me. I admit that I'm guilty of what you say, but whatever has been is over with. I promise you I'll never see your wife again. Take my word as a gentleman for it."

"Your word is as good as a breath against the wind. I want more proof than that. Do you believe I think she'll keep away from you? Oh, I've seen her flirt with other men, but it really meant nothing. But when she looks at you the clock stops ticking. I want your word that you'll drive her away by some deed of yours so she will never look at you again."

"I've give you all the proof I can. My word is my bond. Take it or throw it away. I can't do anymore." Then Christopher looked up at him sharply, "Have you discussed this matter with your wife?"

Suddenly Dennsworth grew pale and he looked much older than he actually was. "My wife?" he sputtered. "I haven't spoken a word to my wife for fear she might leave me at the drop of a hat. You have youth and can easily bear the loss of one woman or another. Why you can't be more than twenty-five at the most. But I, my young friend, am an old man in his sixties. I can never hope to win another woman as attractive as my young wife. She's all I have in the world and I think if it wasn't for my title and money, I wouldn't have kept her this long. That's why you've got to promise me that you'll give her up. I can't fight your good looks and youth. And if you don't, I'll . . . I'll . . ." His voice broke and his old eyes were moist with tears.

Christopher sharply turned around and looked out into the shadowdy garden. He couldn't bear to look upon the old gentleman any longer; he was ashamed and humiliated beyond measure. He sensed pangs of loneliness for the man. He clenched his fists in torment. "I've given you my word, sir. I can do no more except keep my promise."

For a long while there was a bitter silence between them, then Christopher felt Lord Dennsworth's hand fall upon his shoulder for a moment and after that he slowly turned away and walked doggedly into the ballroom. Christopher heard the French door open then quietly close, and as if in deliberate mockery the small string orchestra was playing some old and favorite melody concerning youth and age. It wasn't too long afterwards that Rue ventured out onto the terrace to discover Christopher alone with his thoughts.

"Good evening, Sir Christopher," she greeted him in a cold stiff voice. "This isn't the proper weather for outdoor sitting is it?"

"Rue! What the devil are you doing out here?" He looked at her bare shoulders, his mind was taken up with health these days. "For God's sakes woman!" he cried. "You're half naked—you'll catch your death out here in that dress."

"How thoughtful of *Mr. Thomas* to fret for *Mrs. Thomas*," she sneered and gave forth with a small bitter laugh. "You worry for my health but care nothing for my heart."

"I'm afraid Mr. and Mrs. Thomas are dead as far as I'm concerned, Rue." He snapped her off: "Anyhow, how did you get invited here?"

"You forget Dennsworth's prestige, my Christopher. Besides, how could I possibly stay away from these delightful parties Miss Hobbs gives. It's all one reads about on the social page these days. Naturally I was curious . . . I had to come. Especially when it's Miss Hobbs, that keeps Mr. Thomas away from me." Rue pulled her delicately sheer stole about her shoulders murmuring: "I too must write a book someday . . . as soon as the time presents itself. But first I must have a chat with Miss Hobbs, I am so unlearned in that field and wish to get some first hand pointers on the matter." She looked at Christopher from the corner of her dark flashing eyes. "I wonder what makes her so interesting?" she muttered in a light menacing voice.

Christopher was struck with alarm wondering and feared what might result if Rue should excite Fredrica's frail health. "Rue! I want you to leave her alone. Do you understand?"

"My! Christopher, how venomous are your tones. Are you so enamored of your new paramour that you forbid anyone to speak with her?"

"Rue."

"Well it's true," she said in a light taunting way, but suddenly she turned upon him in anger, she was tired of playing cat and mouse. "What does this little pitiful frail creature possess that she turns you away from me!" she demanded. "This can't be love . . . or is it a mere physical infatuation? I saw her in there clinging to you like wet laundry."

Christopher flashed Rue a stern glance; he hoped she wasn't going to create a scene. "Hell, how troublesome can women get?" he muttered boyishly under his breath and turned his back on her.

Flaring up again she snatched his arm; he turned around to view her. "I'm not going to stand by and let you throw yourself away on this little nothing," she said. "I'm not the sort to play a spectator's part."

"You can't," he answered raspingly. "Only gods and angels can be spectators. You, like everyone else, must play some part. No matter how pure or vile your lines may be, you must still play it . . . as for me I'm tired of the whole rotten play."

"Then you're tired of me you mean—I am no longer useful now that you have the great Miss Hobbs!"

He didn't answer her; he thought it best not to, one word would only lead to another. The fog began to settle about them now, and it was beginning to get quite cold for Rue to remain outdoors much longer; moreover, her anger seemed to be climbing.

"Don't exhaust my patience, Chris," she said in a final way. "Miss Hobbs is playing the grand lady, right now, and I can't seem to get a chance to speak with her, but as soon as I am able to, I intend to have this matter out with her."

"Don't be irrational, Rue. You forget that you're married to Dennsworth and really have no claims on me. Fredrica would think you completely absurd. She'd never believe a word you'd have to say. Anyway," he continued endeavoring to play her out, "I've already told Fredrica about you."

"You're lying, I know you are!"

Again there came no reply from his lips. He was thinking of his promise to Lord Dennsworth and after a while he said: "Let's have it understood, Rue. I love Fredrica."

A joyous smile broke upon Rue's lips and she almost laughed in his face; her beautifully painted mouth seemed twisted and mockingly cruel. "I know you better than you do yourself, Christopher. You don't love her. You only think you do. I know you; there's some kind of sympathy you feel for her. I guess there is something of the saintly virgin that you seem to find in her, but believe me she's not. Women can't lie to women, they know each other too well." Again she smiled. "I always thought you were a little boy, and now I know. It's just simply that you have found a new toy to play with." Then she began to laugh high and openly: "Yes, I'll leave you both alone," she murmured lightly. "You will soon grow tired of her . . . Why should I worry."

Her laughter continued and her sudden behavior troubled Christopher. It was hard to believe that Rue would keep her word. It seemed so unlike her, especially where Fredrica was concerned. He wondered what diabolical scheme might be taking form in that beautiful head of hers. Suddenly Lorrie burst forth onto the terrace. His face was pale, almost ash white. Lorrie's entire conternance reflected the alarm of some grave message. He gave a quick nod to Rue, then turned to deliver his message to Christopher that Fredrica had collapsed on the ball room floor. "I carried her to her room," he said with a kind of dread calm. "Don't worry, I've already sent for the doctor but you better get up to her, she seems pretty low!"

For the moment Christopher appeared stunned, seeming unable to stir from the spot. Then he moved stiffly, almost like a sick man; in the next instant he departed. He sped through the French doors and out of sight. Once more Lorrie and Rue exchanged glances. "Why don't you leave him alone," he stated bitterly.

"Dear, what a vile creature I seem to have become," Rue murmured lightly, and with an unconcerned shrug of her shoulders she said: "People are always asking me to leave someone alone." Then she walked away as though she had been thoroughly alone on that fog and wind swept terrace. "When will the spring come? . . ." Rue murmured in a detached voice as she shuddered in the foggy cold, and turned her steps toward the house and music. "Winter is so ugly . . ."

Then once again came those awful days of confinement for Fredrica, and Christopher knew in his heart that it was to be the end of her. She remained in bed for some four or five weeks, then by the turn of the spring she passed into death, quietly and without pain. Her passing caused quite a stir, for all of London seemed to turn out for her funeral. When she was finally laid to rest, it was not done so without due and abundant shedding of tears from both public and close friends. Christopher didn't attend her burial for he was too broken up with grief, and it was to be quite a while before he seemed himself again. Until his interlude with grief was to fade away he took up lodgings with Lorrie, who once more proved himself the much needed friend.

In May Lorrie wedded Wanda Richard. It was the only social gathering that Christopher attended since Fredrica's death, and this he attended mainly because he was Lorrie's best man at the ceremony. He saw the honeymooners depart and greeted them when they returned. Christopher watched spring blossom into summer, and summer fade into fall; he read of Lord and Lady Dennsworth's mid-summer journey to the continent, and read once again of their return. But all these things were happenings in a world he seemed removed from. All spring and summer he busied himself with work and nothing more. He didn't join the laughing crowd of theatre goers which he was once a part of, nor did he care for the company of others. He found himself a suitable bachelor apartment in Grosvenor Square, and adopted Dee, Lorrie's Cocker Spaniel, who in reality was his only companion through the long spring and summer.

Then in September came that very singular morning that was to alter Christopher's life. A day that was to make a new man of him, and to clear the doubt and confusion in his mind. He awoke that early fall morning feeling fresh and clean as though destiny had pre-warned him of the good news which lay in store for him that day, for when he arrived at his office he discovered among his business mail a letter from Abigail Trent. He did not think too much of the blue envelope which lay before him, that is, no more than it was a friendly letter from a distant place. At length, when he completed the sorting out of his mail he turned his attentions toward Abigail's correspondence.

The last of August

Dear Chris,

So much has occurred since I have written you last that it makes my head swim to think of it. I am positively reeling with good news! I trust you won't think me a busy-body who has gone and stuck her nose in where it wasn't wanted, but I have taken all kinds of liberties with your private life, that I feel like a nervy old spinster who has nothing better to do than meddle in other people's affairs. (Believe me that is not so! I'm too busy to breathe these days.) I hope you won't mind. On second thought you had better not mind because I've delayed my tour on account of you. But it was worth it! So far you must undoubtedly think: Abby's gone mad! But to get down to the point that I'm so clumsily endeavoring to get over to you.

On the 28th., of this month, I opened in Charleston S.C. with another one of Paula Fransworth's plays. (Of course, so far that means exactly nothing to you.) After the final curtain of the second' night's performance, an elderly couple came back stage to talk with me, and before they departed they invited me to have dinner at their home the following night. In my haste to tell you this much, I have run ahead of my story. The couple that journeyed back stage to talk and be so kind to me were a Mr. and Mrs. Henry Fransworth, the brother of the famed John! Imagine my delight at being a guest of the family I have worshipped since childhood. I was elated!

The following night I had dinner at the great mansion, and in the course of the evening, when we later retired to the library, the family albums were naturally drawn out for exhibit. (This is the point where I simply had to delay my tour and play sleuth.) Within the album were countless pictures of a small boy who so profoundly resembled you, that I couldn't believe my eyes!

I stared at the picture for such a length of time that I was beginning to arouse suspicion. In a matter of moments, I had gathered in my lap at least a dozen pictures of this particular boy. But still I kept mum about the matter, for I had to be sure. Absolutely sure before I shot off my mouth (as the vulgar speak). In time I inquired of Mrs. Henry Fransworth if she possessed a magnifying lens? I had to examine the boy's features more closely (the cat was out of the bag). Then I was forced to tell them of my suspicions, and within five minutes I succeeded in putting the entire household in an uproar! Even the old butler was called in to listen to my story when I related in a tense breath that I was positive I knew the boy in the pictures, and that he was well and alive! Chris! I can't restrain my pen any longer. You are John Fransworth Jr.!

Well, certainly if I had one story to tell the Fransworths, the Fransworths on the other hand had a more interesting one to relate to me. I can still see your Uncle Henry's eyes as I set the following down to you. The picture of his face will always shine in my memory, for it was not his eyes I watched so keenly but yours, and it was then that I saw the strong family resemblance between you and he. First he told me of the fire. Oh, I've forgotten, you know no remembrance of that awful night. My heart goes out to you, and it was mean of heaven to usurp your memory in such a manner. Poor boy! Bu it was no wonder your memory fled, mine would too if I had witnessed your experience! As far as

I can construct in words, this is what your uncle related to me:

Your parents were enroute to spend their Christmas vacation here with your grandmother in Charleston, but before they were to have their break in the season, they were obliged to give one or two extra performances, and it seems in that winter they had taken you with them on the road. (Incidently, their final play together happens to be the very one I am doing now. 'A Drawingroom Scandal', so you can see how unexpected-I too have brought back to him some amount of pain, but I assume if it wasn't for this particular play, he might not have come back stage to see me. So you see everything does happen for the best! I realize that my constant side-tracking must be annoying to you, but in a respect, it is necessary if I'm to make myself explanatory to you.

The theatre of your parents final performance was a very large and old one constructed entirely of timber. It appears that the wardrobe mistress must have been an untidy and careless woman because through her negligence she allowed a pile of rag-like costumes to multiply through the years, and the results were that they gave birth to flame. What the newspaper clippings refer to as spontaneous combustion. The old theatre went up in smoke and flames like so much tinder, and your parents were trapped in a burning dressing room! How you escaped from the holocaust, is yet an unsolved mystery, but it is believed that your father possibly pushed you through the grating of a transom window. At least, that is your uncle's conception of the incident. I can only hope that as you read this, something of that terrible experience might possibly wend its way back to you. I pray for that much.

Now still you must wonder how I know the other parts . . . Well that too is due to my role as a busybody. I immediately dispatched a fast letter to Mrs. Tergauer in Fairlee for I knew of your summers there as a boy. In turn, Mrs. Tergauer turned the letter over to the Reverend Mother Eugenia of St. Ann's. This is the part I fear you might frown upon because I know that long ago you made your break with Fairlee and the people therein, and God knows how Fairlee can gossip, and I fear that I have succeeded in placing your name back on their gossiping lips. Although Mrs. Tergauer means well, she's incline to let the wrong things slip out of her mouth at the right time. But the devil with it all, I say, and can only feel grateful (if for once) at their idle chatter; for it was through their talk that I learned some things about you which are now proving a blessing in helping you to come into your own.

I believe the affair is settled now. I have had at least two good and stiff correspondings with the Reverend Mother. From the information I (rather we; for the Fransworths are deeply concerned) have gathered through her letters and their newspaper clippings, the pieces of your unknown life have been welded together. The rest is up to you now because I still haven't informed the Fransworths of your where abouts. I feel if you want to rejoin your family, you yourself must make the final arrangements. I have only told them that you are alive, not that I can restore you to them. But Chris, they want you back! That much I am sure of. Again I say the choice is up to you. Either you can write me of your decision, or take matters in your own hand and resuscitate the past with your people. I have meddled enough. So for now, it is goodbye, Chris, until our next correspondence. I can only say that I have been proud in knowing you, and hope that our friendship will continue to endure whether you be Christopher Wensdy or John Fransworth. But I believe God wants you to be nothing more than your true self, because I feel He has always put me in your path if it was only to tell you who you truly are; for all my life I have babbled about the magnificent Fransworths, and now you are one of them. The world's so small!

Thanks again for listing to my girlhood dreams, for after all they are coming true, and to both our advantages. Forgive me, if you think I am wrong, and if we should not write or see each other again, I will feel grateful if you will sometimes look through the years and remember my friendship. May God keep you,

Sincerely . . .
Abby

Christopher could no longer see the written words before him; joyous tears sprang into his eyes and he was blinded with happiness. He could not remain seated, for so exuberant was he that he strode from one end of the room to the other. He glanced at the letter. Could he dare hope to believe what it said? Abigail wasn't the kind to mislead one. Of course, every word was true! But if he could only *remember! remember* but the past was still dark in his mind. Once again he referred to the letter. What were the words Abigail wrote? . . . *You yourself must make the final arrangements . . . the choice is up to you* . . . Then he would decide for himself. In a matter of moments he composed his mind; he knew what he wanted to do!

Lorrie came in just then, he didn't appear as calm as usual, although he wasn't exactly what could be termed excited. Nevertheless, Christopher could tell that he had something on his mind. "Have you seen the *Times*?" he said falling into a chair and spreading the paper open on top the desk. Christopher was too occupied with his own thoughts, therefore he missed what Lorrie said and was obliged to ask him for a reiteration. "The morning paper," said Lorrie. "Lord Dennsworth committed suicide at his club last night!" He continued to read on about the incident of how Dennsworth lingered in the refreshment lounge until after midnight; he had been drinking heavily and when the lounge was finally deserted he put a bullet through his head with a small Colt pistol. Lorrie concluded:

"He is survived by his only heir, the Lady Dennsworth, who is the soul recipient of his estate which is valued by some six or seven million pounds!" Lorrie whistled in amazement. "In other words," he murmured, "no one need trot over to the Bank of London for withdrawals, Lady Dennsworth can take care of them admirably well!"

Christopher murmured some sympathetic comment concerning the man's death, but his spirits had soared too high that morning for him to shed grief for any distant acquaintance. "It's too bad about poor Dennsworth," he told Lorrie and forgot it. He couldn't think of other people's troubles this morning. Not even Rue's; although he could see little or no trouble in store for her. She inherited his money, that's all she wanted all along—*Money*. Was that trouble? Then at that moment an idea flashed in his head. He would give up everything and go back to America, look up his family then perhaps do the thing he wanted to do all along. He turned to Lorrie and informed him of his plans and astounded him. "Lorrie, I'm signing my half of the publishing firm over to you!"

His face lengthened perplexedly. "What the deuce! What has come over you? I thought you looked a little green about the mouth when I came in, but I assumed that was due to the changing of the season. Look here, do you feel well? Christopher dug into his pocket and came up with Abigail's letter. He handed it to Lorrie demanding that he read it. When he was through reading he looked up into Christopher's face and observed that it was flushed with excitement. "Chris!" he caught him by the arm and squeezed it tightly. "Chris, old fellow. How Good. How very good for you!" Lorrie looked at him blandly, "It makes a difference now," he murmured, "doesn't it? But look here, what's this damn nonsense about giving up your share of the firm? Just because something good has happened to you, that's no reason you should throw a fortune in my path."

"No, Lorrie, you don't understand. I want to give up this life I know and start out fresh and new. I have enough cash to see me through. That's all I want; I'm leaving the rest behind. You see everything seems different now, and I think that if I go back to America and the people I know, I might find myself! Already I feel like a new man. It was never that way before. In the past I felt as though I had a shadow over me. Now I seem to have the strength to throw that shadow over. Can't you understand? I want to be myself and do the things I want to do. It was never that way before . . . I listened to the advice of others, now I want to listen to myself."

"I see that there is no sense in disputing with you," Lorrie told in a quiet tone," and heavens knows I have no wish to defer you from your true self any longer. I can only give you my hand on the matter and wish you good luck. But this affair about giving up your share of the firm is out of the question. I'll not hear of it! Just leave things as they are, Chris, and if however and whenever you decide to take it into your head to come back or sell out to another partner, your share will be here for you to do with as you wish."

They shook hands.

"Thank you Lorrie. I felt you'd understand."

"No, on the contrary, thank you for a pleasant friendship. I hope this isn't the end of it?"

"Never."

"Then right now I'll not detain you any longer. I gather they're many things you want to attend to."

"Yes. You know, packing, passport and the like . . . See you down at the house tonight. We'll have a good long talk, eh?"

"Righto . . . run along and good luck, Chris!"

Twilight had not yet fully descended, and but even so soon the evening sky had darkened into black night and a thin veil of piping fog began to shroud the streets when Christopher stepped out of his cab and up the broad steps to Rue's door. He paused ringing the bell. There were two reasons in his mind why he wanted to see Rue; the first being that he wanted to do the decent thing by telling her goodbye and part like friends; and other because he remembered that she possessed his old passport and he wanted to retrieve it in order to save time. He pulled the bell cord. Presently the butler admitted him and when he walked from the entry into the wide hall, he saw Rue descending the curved and polished marble stairway. She was clothed in a deep scarlet dressing gown and her dark hair was swept high on her beautiful round head. Christopher couldn't help remembering a similar moment when she glided down the staircase to meet him. He recalled, thinking of her as a Roman Goddess then, but that was long ago, she was robed in blue then and so much had happened since.

Rue stretched out her jeweled hand to him. He closed his hand on hers and she pulled him toward the drawing room. "Chris, Darling how good of you to visit me in my widowhood." She looked up smilingly at him, "And just when I thought the evening would be so dull. Let me ring for refreshments and we can have a long talk. Just like old times, eh? Chris, Darling!"

"No, Rue, don't trouble. I'm not going to stay long anyway." He saw her eyes narrow when she looked at him, and he realized that it wasn't going to be so easy to break away as he hoped. As for her array of jewels and choice of color he could tell that Lord Dennsworth was now only a shadow in her memory, and Rue had disembarked upon new plans. "I was wondering if you'd mind returning my old passport to me," he told her."

"What . . . You're planning a trip?" Then a joyous smile broke upon her painted lips, "Oh! I can't blame you," she cried. "I was also planning a voyage. I want to get away, I'm tired of Europe." She threw up her arms excitedly, "Oh! Chris, let's travel together. We'll live the old days over again! And this time happy and carefree and never worry about money. There's no need to now. We're both so rich! Wait!" she cried, "I'll get our old passports." In the next moment she fled from the room and when she returned, she carried a large square jewel case in her hands. The object in itself must have cost a fortune for it was fashioned in a rare black wood and inlaid with gold. Rue placed the case upon a marble top table, then proceeded to touch a concealed spring at the base of the precious box, and when she did a secret drawer snapped into being. Within the velvet lined drawer were both their passports, resting side by side. Rue took them out and handed them to Christopher. She was talking so fast that he could scarce get a word into the conversation. He took his passport and put it in his breast pocket, then returned the other to her.

"What does this mean!" Rue rasped tensely.

"That I am going back to where I started—home."

"You can't mean that horrible little town, nor the gloom of that awful monastery!"

"Possibly," he answered her in a calm tone, for he made up his mind that Rue was never to know his plans again. "My plans and my life are my own. I'm free, I can do what I want."

"You're joking," she said, and tried to force a laugh. "Oh, you can't be in earnest. You couldn't go and leave me behind. Not after all we planned?"

"I haven't planned anything. I merely asked for my passport. It was you who jumped to conclusions. The reason why I came was to tell you good bye." He saw the hurt creep into Rue's eyes. "I'm sorry, Rue if you thought—"

"Goodbye!" she sobbed. "There can be no goodbyes for us. We might have parted from time to time, but there was never a goodbye between us. Can't you understand, Chris? We're both free now! There's no Hastings nor Lord Dennsworth, or Fredrica between us now."

"No, nothing save a little friendship. Let's keep that much. In the past we've had our differences, but it's all over between us now. Let's look to the future; it lays before us golden and untouched. In the past there was always too much Hastings—too much Dennsworth. I can't say who was to blame. In a way we were both at fault. But your fault being that you loved money and not enough for love itself . . . And mine because I was weak." He lowered his eyes, "I've learned my lesson. I can only hope that you have learned yours . . . Someone will come along in the future that you will really love. When that day comes, love for the sake of loving. That's the only way you can find happiness . . . I give you my blessing on that."

"Then you have never loved me?" the words seemed to freeze in her throat. She could no longer act and felt the cold bitter pangs of reality. She started to weep. "Oh, Chris! It's you who are cruel not I. Is there no way to show you I really love you. I have not been really bad to you or anyone, but merely a woman as God has made me. Is that such a sin? I have loved you like I have loved nothing else, but